Humphrey Hawksle[...]
[...]espondent who spec[...]
[...]rom Sri Lanka in 1[...] while covering the Tamil
[...]ar and opened the BBC's first television bureau in
[...]hina in 1994. He moved to London with his wife
[...]nd son in 1997, from where he has covered conflict
[...] Kosovo, Iraq and Timor.

'The second thriller from the author of *Ceremony
of Innocence*, draws on his experience as a BBC
correspondent to produce a novel of considerable power'                                    *The Times*

'Hawksley's world is too close to the real world
for comfort. It is also sufficiently ambiguous to
make it real. And that's why *Absolute Measures*
is such a page-turning read'
                          *Far Eastern Economic Review*

Praise for Humphrey Hawksley's first novel,
*Ceremony of Innocence*:

'Provocative and topical' *Daily Telegraph*

'An exciting thriller'
                    Phillip Knightley, *Mail on Sunday*

'A gripping story, told with great imagination
but also with knowledge and authority that one
rarely sees in such thrillers'
                          Jon Swain, *Sunday Times*

'Much convincing detail' *Express on Sunday*

*Also by Humphrey Hawksley*

Ceremony of Innocence

# Absolute Measures

## Humphrey Hawksley

HEADLINE
FEATURE

First published in 1999
by HEADLINE BOOK PUBLISHING

First published in paperback in 2000
by HEADLINE BOOK PUBLISHING

A HEADLINE FEATURE Paperback

10 9 8 7 6 5 4 3 2 1

ISBN 0 7472 5907 0

Typeset by Palimpsest Book Production Limited,
Polmont, Stirlingshire
Printed and bound in Great Britain by
Mackays of Chatham plc, Chatham, Kent

HEADLINE BOOK PUBLISHING
A division of the Hodder Headline Group
338 Euston Road
London NW1 3BH

www.headline.co.uk
www.hodderheadline.com

For Charlotte and Sebastian

# Acknowledgements

Part of this story was drawn from the life of a young fighter I met years ago in one of those seemingly insoluble guerrilla wars. He was educated, intelligent and courteous. His father had been a senior civil servant, yet by nineteen, with everything going for him, he was convinced there was no alternative but to kill for his cause. I remained fascinated why he had become what he had.

Firstly, I would like to thank Neelan Tiruchelvam, a tireless human rights campaigner and my first guide within this horrible world. Neelan was murdered in Sri Lanka by a suicide bomber on July 29th, 1999.

Many others who helped with this book prefer to remain nameless because of their work.

I can, though, thank Dr Magnus Rainstorp of the Department of Political Violence and Terrorism at St Andrews University; Dr Malcom Dando and his colleagues at the Department of Peace Studies at Bradford University; BBC colleagues Mark Tyrrell and Anandhi Arakulanamum; Edmund Macmahon Turner at Moorfields Eye Hospital; Ranald Macdonald of Her Majesty's Customs and Excise; Dr Gyula Lux and Gyorgy Biro of the Hungarian Customs Service; Patrick Holt for his mechanical ingenuity; money laudering expert Bob Cooper; Rudi Saavedray in Zamboanga; Bill Massey; David Grossman and Liz Jensen for their work on the book and, certainly not least, my wife, Jonie Lai.

# Chapter One

Timothy Pack left Jennifer in his house in Queensborough Terrace, lying face down on the bed. Outside there was a clear winter sky with a new, thin crescent moon, hanging over London. It was bitingly cold, colder than he had thought or he would have brought a scarf.

There was a hazardous attraction about Jennifer of both wildness and committment. She was not the type to disentangle after casual sex with a kiss on the cheek, and he had never meant to sleep with her, certainly not so soon before his posting, because, right now, he couldn't afford that complication.

When Stephen Walmsley called out of the blue, Jennifer didn't try to hide her irritation. She lit a cigarette and lazily let the ash grow until he fetched an ashtray.

'Only be about an hour,' he said breezily, getting dressed, and topping up her glass of champagne.

'Lunch 'em, bed 'em, leave 'em,' she said, sarcastically.

'I'll dine 'em as well, if they hang around.' He kissed her on the lips and she raised her head just enough to show she wasn't rejecting him.

Out on the street, Tim pulled up his jacket collar and looked across the road where two prostitutes paced back and forth around the corner, keeping warm.

1

'Hey blondie,' one of them cat-called, and Tim walked the other way, down towards the park to find a taxi.

Stephen Walmsley was his ticket out of England, and until Tim was safely ensconced in a foreign country, he would trot along every time Walmsley beckoned. The alternative was too grim to contemplate: the English winter, the tube and family weekends where he would be nagged about not having a wife.

At Walmsley's club, overcoats were hung up in rows on a wood-panel wall and Tim put his jacket among them. It was a building of faded glory in Pall Mall, a place for settled people, older people who knew their roles in life, and Tim felt awkward, at least a generation too young to be at ease with the portraits, history and low voices. Walmsley was in the library pouring himself a coffee at a table by the door. 'Didn't interrupt anything, did I?'

'Not at all,' lied Tim.

Walmsley waved his hand over the table, indicating that Tim, too, should help himself, then he walked as far away from the other guests as he could to a pair of corner chairs near the fireplace.

When Tim sat down, Walmsley put an envelope on the table. 'Betrayed, captured and being held just outside of Khartoum.' He let his statement hang, leaving time for Tim to absorb it. 'We know the house. We know the room. We want you to go in there to check it out. Guide the men in, as it were.' Walmsley was in his early fifties, twenty years older than Tim, yet his piercing eyes were both youthful and commanding. 'Don't open it now,' he said. 'No documents are allowed in the main club rooms.'

Tim picked up the envelope and turned it over. 'Who is it?'

'You don't need to know. This operation is known to the head of SIS, the director of 22 SAS, 38 Group Air Transport, the Prime Minister, some Americans, me and you. People will be watching because it's your first with us, first since that unilateral bit of action you did in the Balkans.' Walmsley paused allowing Tim to put his own past in context. 'So I know you won't let us down.

'We're using a Hercules,' he continued. 'There will be an SIS person from the embassy at the lobby bar in the Hilton Hotel in Khartoum from 19:30 to 21:30 on Saturday. You don't know what they look like. But they will know you. Once they see you there, they will signal that the Hercules can proceed. If there is anything wrong at all, don't go to the Hilton.'

'And then?'

'There's no flight until the early hours. Ask the hotel manager to arrange a trip to some archaeological sites the next day. Get back to Khartoum in the evening and then get the hell out of the place.'

Walmsley tapped the envelope. 'Your name's Raison, archaeologist. Your great-grandfather was an official in al-Kadarou, the town you're checking out. These are briefing notes and some stuff on archaeology in the Sudan. Commit it to memory and don't take the file with you.'

Walmsley fell silent as a waiter came out from a door on the other side of the fireplace, making his way to the other end of the room. 'I always find things are safer when there's no safety net. Try not to involve us. Think of being totally alone.'

When Tim got home the bed was still a mess and Jennifer had left a note on the fridge with her phone number on it.

Darkness swirled around the airport and stinging sand whipped Pack's face. Outside the terminal building, figures in ice-white robes moved around like people from a madhouse.

There was nothing on the streets of Khartoum except packs of dogs running across rubbish in the gutter, nothing to show it had not been evacuated because of some terrible plague. The hotel entrance was concealed in the dirty whitewashed walls of a corner building. A guard slept in a chair outside the hotel. The stairs of green and grey stone were chipped, and faded photographs taken by the Ministry of Tourism hung from the walls welcoming Tim to pyramids and river cruises as if he was on a holiday package tour.

In his room, Tim flung open the high glass windows onto the terrace, dogs ran and howled below and the bulb of a street light flickered and then went dead. A gust of wind blew sand down the street and there was nothing else around.

No sound. No movement. No people. No life. He had an urge to ring Jennifer but there were no phones.

Pack booked his four-wheel drive for the next day to take him to the sites of Naqa, Musawwarat and the pyramids at Meroe. He told the hotel manager, Theo, that he wanted a day to settle in, so Theo sold him a Khartoum and Omdurman city tour in a 1969 Hillman taxi at five dollars an hour.

'Once you've seen the Mahdi's tomb, the Khalifa's house and the Omdurman Fort, that's about it,' said Theo, pushing old brochures across the desk towards him.

'Anything worth buying? Carpets, that sort of thing?' asked Tim.

'Swords. They have excellent swords here.' Theo held open the door to let Tim out. 'But this isn't Egypt, you know. Nasty place, really.'

Three special-forces engineers had been in just two days earlier, posing as Australian archaeologists staying at the Acropole, like Tim. They took a four-wheel drive out

4

towards Naqa and measured the California Bearing Ratio which determined the hardness of the desert surface. It came out at seven along a 2,500 foot stretch just three miles north of the town of al-Kadarou and they left infra-red signal lights at either end of the strip to guide in the aircraft.

Abdul, Tim's taxi driver, drove through filthy traffic over the Blue Nile bridge. Everything was covered in a yellow-brown dust. Bus passengers peered through glassless windows, standing in the doorways, hanging on to rusted metal outside.

'Swords,' said Abdul, whose eyes were on Tim in the rear-view mirror. He pulled up in the narrow streets of Omdurman Souk and guided Tim around the rubbish pushed up against walls in sandstorms.

The shop smelt of leather and animals; silver coffee pots and camel whips bound with gold, red and green wire hung from the ceiling. The wooden counter was strewn with leather and canvas scraps. An Arab craftsman worked with a knife and hammer on a bright-orange, half-made camel saddle in the middle of the counter.

A teenage boy squatted on a stool behind and polished the black sheath of a sword with shells sewn onto its sides and straps hanging from it to attach to the warrior's saddle.

'From the Red Sea,' said Abdul, and the owner of the shop nodded. In Arabic the owner told the boy to stand up and introduced him as his son, Yasin Omer, drawing the customer into his shop and his family. Yasin handed Tim the sheath. His father broke off his work on the saddle to bring down another sword from a higher shelf. It was in a brown, dusty sheath with a tassel caked in the muck of the villages. The handle was wrapped with silver leaf and he drew the weapon out to show Tim the Arabic writing inscribed on the steel.

He spoke to Abdul, who translated. 'This is an old Sudanese poem . . .'

'From where?' said Tim. Yasin produced a cup of sweet tea in a glass for him.

'He's a Mahas. From the north,' answered Abdul. 'You can tell by his skin colour. The sword is from his village.'

Tim absorbed the stench of animals and spices and he enjoyed the safety of what he was doing; with a taxi driver, buying a souvenir in the Omdurman Souk. The success or failure of an espionage operation was as narrow as the blade of the sword in front of him. Tim liked where he was because he could justify it and because he wanted the sword. He would take it home and hang it on the wall of his house in Queensborough Terrace.

'When you meet the enemy and there's no way to win,' Abdul read from the inscription, 'it is better to die than to run away.'

There was a stirring of blankets in the corner and Tim thought a dog was waking up behind him. But as he turned, he saw curious child-like eyes peer out in a frame of blackness and dusky colours.

Samira appeared as she always did when a tourist was getting interested and about to buy. She moved around the shop, sometimes to his left, sometimes to his right. Tim couldn't work out whether to see her as a child or a woman. Her breasts were beginning to form. She wore a school uniform of green and white, but her eyes and facial expressions were mature and wilful and something about her youth, innocence and playfulness amid the rankness of her environment captivated Tim, just as Samira's father intended, so that from the moment he spotted her, the swords were as good as sold.

'The swords will be cleaned very well,' Abdul was saying. 'What is your address?'

'The Acropole Hotel.'

'Your home address.' Yasin spoke for the first time. 'I will write it on the bag in case it gets lost on the plane.'

'The boy will make you a special canvas bag to check it onto the Lufthansa flight,' said Abdul.

In the late afternoon he found another taxi outside the Meridian Hotel. Soon, they were back crossing the White Nile Bridge which Abdul had told him was built by the British, then past the modern buildings of the Koran University and the Parliament on the right.

On this return journey, Tim felt he was getting familiar with the city now. They went straight through Omdurman this time, heading north along the sealed road to Meroe. The driver was dressed Western style in slacks and an open-neck shirt. His car was a Toyota, not a Hillman, but the back seat was equally torn, sunken and uncomfortable, the windows immovable, one jammed with sand, the other by a broken handle.

As soon as they left Omdurman the desert scrub stretched before them in a heat haze. Women in orange and white stood in clusters waiting for buses. Construction sites, with no one working on them, sprang up at the side of the road. These were the villas built on money from the Persian Gulf. Some were finished in compounds with high walls and air-conditioning units sticking out of the windows. Most were unfinished and empty, the sign of no planning and loan money which had run out or never really existed.

Tim had gone over the maps with Walmsley and he knew that if he passed a regular military check-point he was at Kogallat and had gone too far. The rescue squad had to get in and out without touching a check-point. The Nile to his left was hidden by farmland. The railway was on the right, with goats wandering between the tracks, and it stretched away into the scrubland, disappearing into desert and eventually ending up through war zones and broken track in Port Sudan on the Red Sea.

After almost half an hour of silence, the driver said suddenly in English. 'Why are you going to al-Kadarou?'

'My great-grandfather used to be the district commissioner there,' said Tim straight away. 'I want to take some photographs for the family.'

The driver didn't react. He lit a cigarette, slowing, steering with one hand and cupping the other against the wind for the flame to catch. When he put the lighter away, Tim caught his eyes in the mirror.

Tim noted the landmarks given to him. The radar beacon to his left, in a wired-off compound with a red light flashing on the top. Half a mile further on was a junkyard of old electrical transformers from a substation and pylons, stark and ugly, stretching across the desert towards Omdurman.

'Al-Kadarou,' announced the taxi driver.

Tim got him to stop two hundred yards from the villa, which he recognised from the satellite photographs. There were rows of new villas, but this one was distinctive because it was finished and lived in, with bright red flowers trailing over the wall and fairy lights strewn around conifers which towered over the garden.

Two white-painted water tanks stood against the front wall, which was whitewashed. The metal gate was locked and as Tim walked down the alleyway at its side, he noticed another wooden gate, also locked, at the end, which hadn't been picked up by the satellite.

There was a radio playing just inside the gate and soft voices. Cigarette smoke drifted up.

Standing back from the wall, Tim could make out the sloping roof of the guard house. A second compound butted onto the back, but this was empty and a gate hung open, unlocked. After that, there was nothing except fields and dirt tracks all the way down to the river.

The only window across which blinds were drawn was on the northern corner of the house. There were two chairs outside on the balcony, with the pages of a magazine flapping on one. A glass of water was on the floor beside it. This was the room that the hostage was being held in.

No-one else was in the alleyway.

Tim dropped the map he was holding, then knelt down and took out two commercial car-tracking devices, each disguised as a small mobile telephone. They sent out an intermittent homing signal which was picked up by a special computer normally fitted in police cars and helicopters. Not perfect, but an acceptable risk to bring through customs.

Tim pushed one tracker into the sand by the wall, burying it about an inch deep. He put the second ten yards further along. Each had an independent algorithm or special code. The signal would be activated by the SAS units as they came in, giving them the confirmation that they were attacking the right target.

The taxi driver was having coffee at the restaurant next to the villa. Blue metal tables were on the street outside. Water urns, stacked up high, formed a boundary between the café and the alleyway and cases of empty soft-drink bottles made up the counter between the shop and the house.

Tim opened the back door of the taxi, prompting the driver to jump up and hurriedly call for the bill. He was about to get in when he saw that the boy coming out from the back of the shop was Yasin. Tim leant on the roof of the car, watching as the driver paid. Then Yasin recognised Tim, at first surprised, then waving and talking to the driver about him, pointing. Must have been telling him about the swords.

Tim closed the door and walked over to them. Yasin shook

his hand enthusiastically, clasping it with both of his: 'This is where I live. My mother owns this tea house,' he said in schoolboy English. 'Do you want some coffee? On the house?'

Yasin's enthusiasm was overwhelming and Tim couldn't help smiling. 'I have to get back.'

'The driver says your great-grandfather was the commissioner at al-Kadarou. You should meet our Mayor. He is a very nice man. I will take your photo together.'

Afterwards, Tim would stand by what he did next; would do it again in the same situation. He was damned by coincidence, because he would never know what happened and he should have just got in the car and let Yasin take his chances with the Special Forces. Instead he said, 'It's really lucky I bumped into you, because I need to buy more swords and to have them by six tomorrow morning.'

Yasin looked unhappy and bewildered, 'But it takes hours to prepare them to a high standard.'

'I know. But it really is important. Perhaps your sister, anyone else in the family could work overnight in Omdurman for me. I'll pay double.'

Yasin whistled through his teeth, while putting the driver's grubby notes into his pocket. 'I'll have to ask.' He shouted out for his father, picked up the driver's coffee cup and wiped the table. Yasin's father eyed Tim suspiciously as he emerged, Yasin explaining the proposal, trying to sell it.

'The old man doesn't want to do it,' said the driver. 'He's not sure if he's got four more swords.'

'Why do you need them so early?' asked Yasin, switching to English. Now Samira was running towards them. Yasin spoke to her abruptly and gave her the cup and the towel to take in.

'I have to leave for Meroe. And from there I'm going straight to the airport.'

Tim took out a packet of panatellas and offered one to the old man and one to Yasin. The old man didn't respond, so Tim took another out and gave three to Yasin and said: 'It's what gentlemen smoke when they don't like cigarettes.'

Yasin took them and passed them under his nose, smelling the tobacco through the cellophane. His father was shaking his head, and his son translated more of what Tim said, tapping the old man's arm to convince him, but the father was adamant. 'I'll meet you at the airport with them,' said Yasin, as if that was in recognition for the cigars. He shrugged. 'My father won't let me go.'

Tim could do no more. He told himself that for months afterwards.

He found a seat in the foyer bar and ordered a Hilton Dream fruit cocktail. He didn't study the other guests.

Instead, he bought postcards and wrote them to his mother, to his brother in Suffolk, to his sister in London and to Jennifer Chandler, whose home address he didn't know, so he addressed it to the bank in Copthall Avenue. He laid a copy of *Time* magazine which he had bought at Heathrow on the table, just as Walmsley had told him to.

Charlie Mills, first secretary, SIS agent, a diplomat specialising in the world's hell holes, recognised Tim from the photographs sent over, finished his soft drink and called for the bill. Tim's magazine gave Mills a final confirmation and he left for the embassy where he signalled the go-ahead. For what, though, he had no idea.

At the Akrotiri Royal Air Force Base in southern Cyprus, a Mark 1 Hercules received take-off clearance and taxied onto the 8,000-foot runway. It was a few minutes before 19:30. Permission had been given for an overweight take-off. Fully laden with fuel for the ten-hour return journey, the

11

empty Hercules was 142,000 pounds. But her total weight was now 160,000 pounds. She carried four extra crew, two aircraft ground engineers and two mobile air movements staff, together with sixteen men from the Special Air Service and three Toyota pick-up vehicles, already muddied and chipped to blend in with the Khartoum traffic.

The pilot didn't bring up the nose until she had covered more than five thousand feet of the runway. As soon as she was airborne he spoke one two-syllable word – RABBIT – on the agreed high frequency band 5897.

The soldiers inside sat back in their red nylon paratroop seats for the long, uncomfortable journey. They lined up on either side of the three pick-up vehicles with the Toyota logo prominently displayed on the back. Before boarding for the last leg of this journey, they had checked their personal equipment, the MP5 Heckler and Koch submachine gun, two Remington 870 pump-action shotguns to blast their way into rooms, an SSG 3000 0.308 sniper rifle to take out a dangerous single enemy, CS gas stun grenades, light aluminium assault ladders coated with rubber to dampen the noise of leaning them against the building, explosives and their own personal sidearms, mainly the 9mm Browning High Power, SIG-Sauer and Glock 18 semi-automatic pistols.

For the first hour the aircraft had a clear run in international airspace. But still the pilot kept to the dangerously low-level altitude of just 250 feet to escape all radar. Only the Israeli government had been told of the aircraft's routing, which was why, instead of flying almost due south, the pilot veered slightly to the east to avoid Cairo and the sensitive areas around the Suez Canal.

The Hercules was a solitary, lumbering, vulnerable aircraft. It travelled at only 250 knots. Its only stealth was its low altitude. Its daring lay in the bravery of the men who flew her. They were alone, in radio silence, with a weapon of war which for many was so outdated that it was laughable. The ground temperature was 19 degrees Celsius. There was no wind and no slopes in the terrain they were heading for.

One hour before landing, twelve of the men slipped white Sudanese robes over their light-weight Kevlar body armour.

Two got into each of the three cabs of the Toyota vehicles. The other six climbed into the backs, securing themselves against the impact of landing. The two mobile air movement staff unlashed all but three of the chains securing the vehicles.

The daytime build-up of humidity and cloud over the Nile had cleared by midnight. With the river as his landmark and the desert lit up by starlight, the pilot studied the landscape, which appeared before him in shimmering but clear green through the night-vision goggles. He began the approach with the Global Positioning System, but soon spotted the infra-red beacons laid by the special forces engineers.

One minute before landing, the engines of the three Toyotas started up. The back door was fully open, the ramp closed. On touchdown, the pilot immediately brought the nosewheel down, threw all four engines into maximum reverse thrust and braked. The Hercules was enveloped in sand thrown up by the airflow from the propellers. A roar from the engines shattered the night quietness.

As the aircraft slowed, the movements staff undid the remaining chains that held the vehicles. Five seconds after stopping the ramp was on the ground. Ten seconds later all three vehicles were off the aircraft and speeding across the desert to join the paved road south to al-Kadarou.

Four men stayed with the aircraft and set up two fields of fire with heavy machine guns and anti-tank weapons.

The vehicles came off the desert onto the sealed road, south of the check-point at Kogallat and entered al-Kadarou from the north. It was 01:30. Tracking signals in the lead vehicle's computer confirmed their destination. The traffic was thin, but the road was not completely deserted so that groups of men riding towards Omdurman in three Toyotas were not an unusual sight that would arouse suspicion. They drove slowly through the town.

Yasin was sweeping the floor of the tea house, just behind the crates of Pepsi when he saw a vehicle stop across the road, with the men just sitting there. Two other vehicles came down right next to the house, a place cars hardly ever went. And never two at once. He heard the engines fade and then stop. Yasin ran upstairs to the roof to get a better look and by then the men were acting like nothing he had seen before. They ran silently towards the gate at the back of the compound. One moved forward and pressed something against the metal gate. Two carried a steel ladder. Three others fired fat-barrelled guns into the air. There was a soft bang and suddenly the whole compound was filled with thick black smoke, spreading along and rising up, so he couldn't see the men any more.

He heard a shout through the smoke, then it went quiet. Yasin called out for his father, who was already awake and coming up to the roof in his nightclothes. Yasin told him they had guns, and as soon as he saw the smoke, his father ran down downstairs, picked up his old rifle from the cupboard in his bedroom, loaded it and ran out past the Pepsi crates and even out beyond the water urns so that he was in the street facing the villa. Others were stopping like passers-by at a traffic accident. Yasin heard his mother from the bedroom calling for his father to come back.

Everything happened in seconds, but for Yasin each movement was slow and vivid. As the smoke thinned the attackers threw a dead body over the balcony.

The two vehicles beyond the alley started up. They

stopped between Yasin's house and the villa, next to the blown-down gate, and now Yasin could see the machine guns of the men as they came out of the villa. On some, their turbans or *emas* had come off, and Yasin was sure that they had the light hair of Europeans, although it was dark and there was still smoke around.

One of them was led along by two men. He was definitely a European, and not a soldier, with glasses and a beard, his face white and smudged. He wore blue jeans, a white shirt, and there was the blank look of shock on his face.

They jumped into the back. Two vehicles moved off. The engine of the third vehicle started across the street. The headlights went on. Yasin looked across to the villa, where he could now see the broken windows and the bodies of more guards on the ground near the gate. Smoke rose up from small burnt patches of grass.

Yasin saw his father step out in the path of the vehicles, defending the home and the town, shaking with anger, raising the rifle to fire.

This time there was a shout in Arabic, but bad Arabic, the student Arabic of a European who might have come to his father's shop. Before the shout had finished, his father was falling. Yasin thought he heard the crack of a weapon, but as the years passed he wasn't sure if he even knew then what the sound would have been like. The rifle fell from his father's hands and he buckled, not like in the movies when people are thrown backwards with force, but like a man who had suddenly lost all strength and energy.

Yasin did recognise the sound of the gun going off when it hit the ground because it was an old weapon which his great-grandfather had used in the time of the British. He heard the scream of his mother as she stumbled into the open, her arms flailing, and this time Yasin saw the man with the gun, in the passenger seat of the vehicle across the road which was turning to head north, its headlamps lighting up his father, who was writhing from side to side, his legs twitching in the dry dirt.

The man fired and his mother stopped just like that, standing perfectly still for a moment until she fell over and he saw blotches of blood seeping through her clothes.

Yasin burst through the door from the roof and ran downstairs. Samira was coming from their bedroom, just ten feet from the Pepsi crates and about to run outside, straight after her mother.

He threw himself at her, bringing them both down onto the concrete floor. He held her head tight in his arms and lay on top of her to protect her. He breathed heavily and felt her breathing as well.

He heard the vehicles drive off north, and felt the sweep of the headlights as they turned past the shop. He heard people shouting and through the legs of the tables and underneath the crates of drinks, he saw people gathering around his parents, saying that his mother was dead, but that his father was still alive.

Tim set off for the archaeological sites at dawn. Khartoum was not a city which woke early. Nor was it crowded like other African and Asian city nightmares. It was dirty and broken down and nothing had been invested in its roads and infrastructure since the British left in 1956. It was like the Toyota four-wheel drive with its air-conditioning unit ripped out and windows so caked with grit that they had jammed, the right back window permanently open.

Nervous young soldiers were on duty outside the villa which had been attacked during the night. Fear showed in their eyes and in the way their hands slid erratically up and down their weapons and around the trigger guard. Tim's guide, Ahmed, showed documents at the road block outside of Yasin's house, with the permit to visit the archaeological sites and the document to allow Tim to carry a camera.

Ahmed told them Tim was an archaeological student from England, and he pressed a packet of cigarettes into the soldiers' hands.

'Road block,' said Tim, stating the obvious and wishing at least to acknowledge an abnormality in the situation.

'Routine,' said Ahmed, lighting a cigarette.

'The Meroitic era lasted for about 700 years from 350 BC to AD 350. This was one of the very important eras in the history of the Sudan,' Ahmed recited as they walked away from the four-wheel drive towards the Roman-style kiosk which marked the entrance to the settlement of Naqa.

The ruins rose starkly from the drab yellowness of the desert. Ahmed hunched himself up and cupped his hand to light a cigarette. 'You should do your PhD on this site,' he said. 'It is more interesting than anything you will find in Egypt.'

'It's been written about a lot,' said Tim, gently touching the sandstone carvings. 'Pliny, Diodorus and Strabo, the Greek geographer, all mention the Kingdom of Meroe.'

'And Herodotus wrote about the Sun Temple at Meroe,' said Ahmed, more enthused now with his subject. 'The lion and Amun temples were built by King Natakamani and Queen Amanitore at the beginning of the Christian era. You notice how the faces of these subjects show every culture, Arab, Christian and African.'

Ahmed dropped his cigarette into the sand. 'What sort of archaeology are you interested in,' he suddenly asked.

'Oh,' said Tim. 'I've been in Canada where all you get is the old flints from the Indian tribes. Nothing like this.' He took a photograph of the kiosk and then asked Ahmed to take one of him with the city of Naga and desert as the backdrop.

\* \* \*

Mills sent a FLASH message to London, copied it SINGER so it went to SIS and to POWDER BOX, because Tim Pack was a British citizen so MI5 had to be informed. The message from Khartoum simply told Stephen Walmsley that Tim Pack had been seen in the Hilton Hotel, writing postcards. In Cyprus the hostage, Jack Jensen had been given a clean bill of health and was now flying to Britain, together with the men who had rescued him. There had been no diplomatic response from the Sudanese government, although one was expected. The shooting in al-Kadarou was unfortunate, but given that they did not leave a trail of wrecked vehicles and British casualties, it could be seen as a minor hitch in an otherwise successful mission. Walmsley closed the file and placed it in his out-tray. In a few hours' time, Tim Pack would call in from Frankfurt while changing planes for London.

Ahmed and the driver squinted against the sun as the four-wheel drive headed north along an unmarked desert track towards Musawwarat el-Sufra, the next stop on the itinerary.

'This is one of the most intriguing sites,' Ahmed explained, although his concentration seemed to be more on the desert ahead than on his recitation. 'But it remains the focus of much discussion among scholars as to its function.'

There were numerous tracks, criss-crossing each other. Ahmed adjusted his headgear and talked to the driver in Arabic. Tim picked up that Ahmed thought they had taken the wrong track at a fork about five hundred yards behind them. The driver stopped the vehicle and began to reverse, then appeared to get bored and, putting it onto low ratio four-wheel drive, he swung round to cut straight across the sand to the other track.

In front of them, two men were herding goats towards

a settlement with children scampering by their side. Trees rose out of the sand in clumps and desert nomads peered against the sun into a cloudless sky, holding their rags around them as if a sandstorm was about to sweep through the desert.

The rear wheels of the vehicle began to spin and the driver twisted the steering wheel violently back and forth, revving the engine, trying to get through the sand.

He opened the door, engine still on, and jumped down. Tim and Ahmed got out on the other side. The wheels had dug themselves into soft sand. The driver, back in his seat, tried to reverse, but each spin of the wheel carved a deep hole in the sand. Children broke away from the goat herd and came to gawk.

Ahmed and Tim tried to push the vehicle, while the driver powered the engine, shoulders against the back, heads down, sand spewing in their faces, breaking sweat, dry mouths and the roar of the engine, so close and desperate that neither heard the helicopter until it was low and landing, sand flying up around them like a storm.

Then the sound of the Wessex helicopter, with black smoke spewing from the huge exhaust just under the fuselage door, became overwhelming. Sand flew everywhere and the children fled back to the goat herd, curled up and lay face-down in the sand as the aircraft came in to land.

The noise made any words indecipherable. Armed troops jumped out of the doorway. They grabbed Tim by each arm and dragged him onto the Wessex. It took off in a swirl of sand, cutting visibility to zero, until the helicopter rose above it, its nose twisting to the south, gaining height, and heading back to Khartoum.

General Ahmed Ali Uttman, director of the Sudanese National

Security Council, ordered Tim handcuffed and brought into the air-conditioned and windowless office in the basement of the prison.

'The President wants you executed this evening,' he began, snapping open a can of Fanta orange juice and pushing it across the table towards his prisoner. Tim took it with both hands and drank thirstily. 'But frankly I want you the hell out of my country alive. My government does not need the international condemnation that your death would bring.'

'I'm a student archaeologist,' said Pack, putting the can on the table, welcoming the cool dryness of the air-conditioning.

'It doesn't matter,' said Uttman. He spoke in fluent and clipped English.

'Yes it does.'

Uttman shook his head. 'In fact, if you are an archaeologist, I feel sorry for you because you don't have people in Britain who can help you.'

'I came here to investigate the possibility of doing a PhD on the decline of the Meroitic . . .'

'It isn't an issue, Mr Raison,' Uttman interrupted. 'I'm not even interested to know what an archaeologist was doing outside the villa in al-Kadarou a few hours before it was targeted for attack by British special forces last night.'

'My great-grandfather used to be district commissioner there.'

Uttman held up his hand. 'You're not hearing me, Mr Raison. I said I don't care. The President is angry. He needs to show his strength by executing you. He has the advantage of being a Third World dictator, so he usually gets what he wants.'

Uttman swept his hand around the room to take in the wider images of the prison they were in. 'Most of your fellow inmates here are neither innocent nor guilty. There is no such thing with dictatorships. They are simply enemies of the regime.'

*If things go wrong*, Walmsley had said, *try not to involve us. Too much to lose.* Tim Pack stared straight at Uttman and rested his hands, cuffed together, on the table.

'If you work for the special forces or the SIS,' Uttman was saying, 'tell me whom you report to. I will call them and we will try to work something out because we do each other favours. We have a little less than twenty-four hours.'

'And if I am a mere archaeologist?'

'I don't value your chances.'

Tim's jailer took his clothes, then beat him and left him on the concrete floor of a cell. There was no blanket, no latrine, just heat, mosquitoes and cockroaches scuttling across the floor. The cell was in the basement with light coming in through a window wide enough for three bars. After sunset it was dark and cold. Tim tried to warm himself by moving around, but the food had got to him and he vomited and felt so weak that he lay on the floor shivering.

He spent the night amid the stench of his own vomit, shit and urine. The whole prison smelt of decay, rotten food and disease. Tim listened to the racking coughs of other inmates. He tried to haul himself up to look out through the bars, breaking his fingernails on the wall, but it was too dark outside. Music played from across the compound where the guards were.

In the morning they locked him in shackles hanging off the wall. Then they fed him, but he couldn't keep it down. When the jailer pulled him up, his chains clanked on the concrete, disturbing flies in the corner of the cell so they broke out and buzzed around him. Tim stumbled outside, the sun blinding him, and he was made to sit down on a chipped concrete bench. He watched as they threw buckets of water into his cell, the filth swilling around, then they pushed him back inside while it settled and dried.

Just past midday, when heat seemed to blast straight through the roof of the prison, they unlocked the doors and dragged Tim into the courtyard again. His legs buckled and they had to hold him up. He shut his eyes against the glare of the sun and they sat him in a chair. They gave him water in a tin cup and let him drink it without hitting him.

Slowly, he got used to the light and saw Uttman standing in front of him, sweat patches under the arms of his tunic. Charlie Mills was with him, tie undone, jacket slung over his shoulders, taking off his dark glasses when Tim was opening his eyes: 'Your fucking animals do this, did they?' said Mills to the general, in English, loud enough for Tim to hear, pointing at the bruises round his eyes.

Uttman didn't answer. Instead he barked a command in Arabic and Yasin was brought forward, to stand in between Uttman and Mills. Tim's sight wavered and blurred, but he saw Yasin's eyes hard on him.

'Raison,' shouted Mills. 'This is an identity parade. Your taxi driver is a petty criminal so we objected to his taking part. If the kid doesn't recognise you, then you're off the hook.'

Yasin glanced up at Mills, then to Uttman, then to Tim again. He shook his head and spoke in Arabic.

'He says the guy at al-Kadarou was much taller,' said Mills.

Uttman turned to leave: 'Get him onto a plane, before the President finds out what I've done,' he said to Mills, putting his hand on Yasin's shoulder, propelling him out of the prison yard, Yasin glancing round, a last look at Tim, knowing who he was, telling Tim that in his expression, but defiant, to the general, to Tim and only Yasin knowing why he had done it.

# Chapter Two

## Zamboanga – Southern Philippines

December – Five years later

Zamboanga was built as if on the edge of the world, a hot, impatient frontier town, its filthy harbour and slums marking the beginning of the Sulu Archipelago. The archipelago stretched south towards Malaysia and Indonesia, a scatter of miserably poor and untamed islands such as Sulu and Jolo, where people still died to defy the sovereignty of the Philippine flag. They were violent. Proud. Brooding with resentment.

Yasin Omer sat in a rattan armchair on the verandah, his legs curled under him, reading and watching.

Abu Musa, the stepfather who had given him a new home after the death of his parents, paced the lawn outside his mansion as the guest was shown in. Musa, a stocky man in his early sixties, had hated Rudy Osmeña for thirty years and he wasn't looking forward to this meeting, although he greeted Osmeña with a broad grin and a stretched-out hand.

'I'm living with the most beautiful young woman and the most solemn young man,' said Musa, looking across the swimming pool towards Yasin.

Osmeña didn't offer his hand in return; but Musa hadn't expected it. The banker looked uneasy standing by the swimming pool, thin and tall with swept-back grey hair, solemn against Musa's joviality, awkward in his barong shirt, black trousers and polished shoes against Musa's shorts and T-shirt.

'Hello, Mr Osmeña, it's very nice to see you,' said Samira in English, her voice heavy with the British sarcasm she was learning at school. She had just got out of the pool, showing off her dark, statuesque African features. Her height set her apart from the shorter Filipina physique, and she let Osmeña gawk as she sashayed over to him, leaving a trail of dripping water on the swimming pool tiles and not even bothering with a towel. She was detached, aware of her sexuality and confident. The water glistened off her, running down her back, shoulders and legs.

'My father has told me so much about you.' She held out her wet hand formally and as soon as Osmeña had taken it, she withdrew it, skipping off and plunging back into the pool again.

Osmeña coughed and put his snakeskin briefcase on a garden chair. 'Where did you say they come from, the Sudan?'

'They're twins.' Musa waved at Yasin. Osmeña waved, embarrassed, but Yasin ignored the banker.

'I adopted them five years ago after their parents were killed,' said Musa. 'It's something we rich Muslims do: pluck bright people out of the slums, educate them and hope the next generation won't be as repressed by you Christians as we are.'

'You talk as if we control the world,' said Osmeña lightly.

'You do, or you wouldn't be here now.' Musa picked up the cigar which he had left burning in an ash-tray. He dabbed sweat off his face with a handkerchief and took a chair at a table in the shade away from the pool, indicating that Osmeña should sit opposite.

Musa watched Samira lap the pool, two lengths freestyle, one length breaststroke, turning over for backstroke, then finally just floating on her back and looking at the bright clear tropical sky and the colours of the rhododendron trees around the garden.

'The peso could devalue by another thirty per cent before it settles,' said Osmeña, taking a sip from a glass of fruit juice. 'And thirty per cent would be a total devaluation of fifty-five per cent. Then take the devaluation with the stock market drop of fifteen to twenty per cent.'

Figures and bankers bored Musa. 'Tell me something I don't know,' he interrupted, yawning and letting smoke drift out of his mouth. 'So there's an economic crisis and you've been sent to protect the bonuses of your Manhattan bosses and cancel my loans.'

There was an arkward silence, as though Osmeña were offended by the directness of his host. He looked around the compound, avoiding Musa's stare. The house was on the edge of the city, down an unpaved road. The walls were draped with bougainvillaea. Guards with M16 automatic weapons were on duty outside the gate.

In the air-conditioned guard house, sixteen television monitors covered all parts of the property, keeping watch: two Pajero jeeps, a Land Rover and a Mercedes 230 E class saloon in the driveway; the verandah, decorated with sea-shell lampshades and embroidered straw mats; the satellite dish on the roof where Musa kept in touch with the global financial markets; and the aerial for the radio to contact the archipelago, where old friends from the independence movement still refused to make peace with the government.

Musa had built other houses for his staff on the edges of

his land – rows of one-storey huts for the single maids and gardeners, a bigger house for Nelly who ran the household and one for Jesse who had fought with Musa in the war of the seventies, stayed with him ever since, and ran the property.

'Some of this will have to go,' said Osmeña. 'We're not after anything you have outside of the Philippines, Abu. You have my guarantee that we won't try to touch them.'

Samira climbed out of the water and laid out a towel to sunbathe on the grass. A net splashed gently on the pool as Jesse cleared away leaves and insects and Yasin looked up at him from his reading. 'Tell me when we're going to get more coconuts,' he shouted across the garden.

Jesse smiled, lifting the dripping net from the pool. He raised a hand, but didn't say anything.

Musa didn't answer Osmeña directly. Instead he pushed himself up, balanced on the garden chair and eventually stood up. 'Shit,' he said, rubbing his leg and grimacing at the pain which was always there. 'Shrapnel. One of your grenades,' he said bluntly. He walked around the pool and when he passed Samira, she looked up at him with a hesitant smile. Musa winked at her as if he didn't have a care in the world.

Then he barked at Osmeña, 'The trouble with you Christians is that you're such pessimists.'

'Don't start, Abu,' retorted Osmeña. 'Unless we sort things out . . .'

'You can sort them out by letting them blow over.' Musa stopped at the corner of the pool, closer to Osmeña. 'Do you know how many people you'll throw out of work if you close me down?'

Osmeña put his elbows on the table: 'Tell me what to do then. I have to go back with some crumbs to throw to the vultures in New York.'

'Tell them to get fucked.' Musa hunched over his cigar trying to light it again, but the breeze blew out the flame.

'Not a solution. You know that.'

'You and they sold me the debt. Tell them to ride through it. Reschedule. Wait for the economic cycle to pick up.'

'And if it doesn't?'

'The fundamentals are sound.'

'Yours maybe. But it's more than that, Abu. There's no money in this country. Only debt.'

'And whose fault is that?'

Osmeña picked up a packet of matches from the table and as the breeze dropped he managed to light a cigarette. He exhaled proudly. 'You are a powerful man in this town, Abu.'

'Damn right I am.'

'That's why I need your help, so we can get through this together.'

'My factories are doing what I always said they would do. Your New York bankers are running shit-scared and going back on their promises.'

'But the contract says . . .'

'Don't get contractual with me.'

'. . . if you don't have collateral, we can call in the loans. Your businesses are worth a tenth of the price they were valued at.'

'My businesses. Your valuation. You talk to Manila and New York right now and tell them to stick to their side of the deal.'

'I can't.'

Musa held up his hand. 'If you do that, I guarantee your investment will remain good. As a last resort I can shift funds back here from the Middle East. But rescheduling the banks out there will need time.'

'New York thinks the next few days are crucial.'

'New York doesn't know shit. My repayments are on schedule. If you call in that loan now, my businesses will close down. Those people thrown out of work will take to the streets. The first place they will loot and burn is your bank . . .'

'Is that a threat?'

'It's a fact.' Musa banged the table with such fury that Osmeña's glass flew off the table and smashed, juice splattering among the shards of glass, then running down to the edge and falling off it in heavy drips. Both men ignored it. 'Zamboanga will burn,' said Musa.

'You mean you'll incite your Muslim cannon fodder,' shouted Osmeña, his lower lip quivering.

'Muslim my ass. Young people, out of work, poor, jittery, with no hope. They riot. Muslim or Christian, it doesn't matter. It's what young people do. Look at Indonesia. Look at Thailand. Look at black America. Look at Manila, for God's sake!'

'You can stop it.'

'Why should I?'

'They respect you.'

Musa sat down, moving the chair away from the dripping juice. 'Why should I stop them burning your bank when you're the cause of the problem, just so you can get an extra ten per cent on your bonus this year?'

'Even my job's not safe, Abu,' said Osmeña softly, leaning forward and putting his hand on Musa's shoulder.

Musa shook it off. He picked up his cigar and held it away from his mouth between two fingers, concentrating on lighting it and turning his back to the breeze so the flame would hold.

'On the morning they take to the streets,' said Musa once the tobacco was lit, 'they will be young, looting thugs. In the evening, as debris is being cleared, they will be

Muslim heroes, warriors against Christian discrimination. The Imams will preach that in the mosques. The Moro commanders will shout it in their training camps. The young men will flock towards the only things they understand: their race, their religion and their culture. They will attack. And they will die, but not before many of you die as well.'

'You *are* threatening us.'

'I don't have the power to create what I have just described. But you have the power to prevent it.'

'Abu, I don't,' said Osmeña wearily.

'Then stay away from it. Don't be the man who lights the match.' Musa shifted uneasily in his chair. 'That bit of shrapnel from 1974,' he grunted. 'Every step I take reminds me why we don't want another war.'

'This is different, Abu.'

'It's not,' said Musa. 'People will wreck without knowing what they want. They keep looking for things to destroy because it's easier than creating them.'

'The markets can't withstand . . .'

'Don't give me markets. How much is it going to cost your precious bank if every loan in this city defaults?'

Osmeña hesitated as if he was actually trying to calculate an answer.

'Go back and do your figures, Rudy. Go back and tell New York that what they're suggesting is economic garbage.'

Osmeña stood up and picked up his cigarettes from the table. 'Don't fight us.'

'You deserve to be fought,' Musa snapped. 'Arrogant shits that you are.'

Yasin watched as Osmeña walked alone to his car, unescorted by Musa who stayed drumming his fingers on the table until he had left. Yasin stepped down from the verandah and walked over. 'He *will* cancel your loan,' he said.

Musa let out a huge roar of a laugh. 'What the hell is your basis for saying that?'

Yasin put both hands on the table but remained standing. He had been only thirteen when his parents were shot dead in front of him, and he had learned to control emotions such as sadness and fear.

'Because he has to,' he said. 'If he doesn't he will lose his job, just like everyone you were describing.'

Musa kept his smile, but his tone became more serious. 'Then what should he do?'

'He can't do anything and you can't do anything.'

'How do you know?'

'Because I read, and because we talk about it at school all the time. It's how wars start.'

Musa raised his eyebrows in surprise. 'What exactly do you talk about at school?'

'You know,' Yasin was impatient, looking around the garden for something more interesting to occupy him than an invasion into his life at school.

'You talk about how there are no solutions,' pressed Musa.

'We talk about what you were saying to that man; that we are controlled by the Christians. They have the banks and the armies. We have nothing except what they give us.'

'Who's "we"?'

'Anyone who's not part of that group, who doesn't live in the West. You know, like the boys at school: Muslims, Tamils, Tibetans, Sikhs – all of them.'

'Is that right or wrong?'

'It's wrong. It's that system which killed my parents.'

'Don't talk like that,' said Musa quickly.

'My parents were killed by British troops outside my house. How else should I talk?'

# Chapter Three

January

The heat had a soft edge to it, hanging with humidity. Yasin impatiently flicked at flies as he and Samira squeezed across the road through the motor-scooters and jeepneys. It was the last day before Samira went back to school in England, and he wanted her to enjoy it.

February, next month, was their birthday when they would both turn nineteen and Yasin had promised to celebrate in advance by buying her a drink at the Lantaka Hotel where the rich of Zamboanga went with their Mercedes and guns. From the bar you could look straight out to the sea and watch the trading boats coming in from Jolo, Sulu and Sabah.

But Samira didn't want to go there straight away. She pulled Yasin through the shops and teased him into helping her choose which clothes she should buy for the new term.

The upper sky was clear as glass, throwing down a haze which hovered over the fields and stretched away towards the mountains. You could see far beyond the buildings to a tropical landscape which looked so peaceful against the drone of the city around them.

They had coffee near the Rizal monument, the tranquil city square, and felt cushioned from the clogged streets. They listened to the cries of the street traders and the impatience of the traffic which seemed to come from another world.

Young people sat at blue-painted metal tables and a guitarist played outside. They overheard conversations about the currency crisis. But when Yasin began to talk about it, Samira slapped her hand over his mouth. 'Please, don't be a bore,' she groaned in the posh accent she was picking up at school.

She glanced across the road and waved at a motorcyclist coming towards them, but fast, weaving in traffic, not planning to stop. He waved back and Samira tossed back her head, laughing.

'Who's that?' said Yasin.

'Just a friend,' she said. She peered at him, teasingly, over her coffee cup.

'A boyfriend?'

'Sort of.'

Yasin looked away, and Samira got up, finishing her cappuccino while standing and brushing the back of her hand across her lips to get rid of the froth.

Yasin stood up, too. 'You mean you've . . .'

Samira grabbed his arm with both hands and began marching him along the street with her. 'It's more fun than talking about international debt,' she said, laughing. 'Come on – buy me a lovely birthday present.'

They left Metro Plaza, down the escalator, Samira ahead and Yasin behind her with two huge carrier bags. They walked across the foyer to the street, and Yasin kept the automatic door open for her. The heat came down like a wall from outside and people hung around the doorway to be cooled by blasts of air-conditioning from the building. Scooters and three-wheeler taxis were parked four or five deep on the road, picking up shoppers, pushing the boulevard into a single lane and causing traffic to pile up.

School children passed by, walking into the road paired off with handkerchiefs over their faces to protect them from the filth. A cigarette vendor, a sweat scarf wrapped around his head, weaved through the people, snapping his wooden box shut and open so the noise would attract attention. Music, clashing and different, came from different stores: a Verdi opera from a tourist antique shop, American rap music from a sports boutique, and singing from a church where the doors had been flung open for mass and worshippers spilled outside onto the street. Far away from another part of the city, the lunchtime call to prayer sounded from an unseen mosque.

Yasin told Samira to wait in the coolness of the doorway. He pushed past her onto the pavement, trying to catch the eye of a taxi driver.

Suddenly, Samira was flung against him and she crumpled to the ground like a broken leaf. He felt glass spraying down onto him, cutting him around the face, plaster hitting him on the shoulder. A blast of hot air burst out of the building, then leaping wild flames, a wave of heat, scorching, so different from the heat of the weather. He tried to get to Samira, but debris was falling all around him, and burning paper swirling, falling from higher up. Glass, metal and concrete kept hitting him, but he didn't feel any pain.

The roar of the explosion came later, as if so much had happened before it, as if only now he saw, heard, smelt the bomb. People bumped him, violently, running away, anywhere, to escape danger. They tripped and fell, and their bodies were trampled upon, as if they were nothing. He saw Samira again, down on the ground, trodden and kicked, crying out, angry, yelling because no one seemed to be hearing her.

Yasin threw himself onto the ground next to her. She was twisted up and breathing heavily. He used his arms and body to protect her, feeling the blows of feet crashing against them. Shooting. Screaming. The smell of burning everywhere. People running through the smoke with their clothes in flames. Samira was choking. Her feet were curled up as if making her smaller would make her safer. A boot tripped over Yasin and pain shot through his shoulder.

'Just wait,' he reassured. 'No one will hurt you.'

Samira heard her twin brother comfort her in Arabic. He always did that when he was frightened for her.

She stopped shouting and buried her head in her own arms, her face squashed down so much that she couldn't speak. She squeezed Yasin's hand to let him know she was hearing him. She felt Yasin's strength. She heard the sirens of police cars and fire engines. The stampede was thinning and Samira found herself thinking of another place. Images rushed before her of the Sudan, of al-Kadarou, on the day their parents had been killed. Yasin held her down, just like then: she lay there, hearing Yasin's breathing and sirens in the distance.

Samira lay with the room darkened to keep out the harsh sunlight and the heat. Yasin sat by her resting his hand next to her head on the pillow and she could feel its warmth.

A doctor injected her with a tranquillizer and gave her painkillers. He dressed her arm where the skin had been torn off the elbow and treated the cuts on her face. Samira heard him say that he would get in a nurse for the night. She lay with her eyes closed, listening to the sounds around her, hurting, getting impatient.

'Please, everyone just leave us,' she said angrily. 'Get out. I want to be alone with my brother.'

She listened, irritated, turning her head wildly because she didn't know if they were gone or not. She would only know if they made a noise.

When she opened her eyes it was just like having them closed, darkness, flickering of colour, greys and flashes of white; but no shapes, no focus, nothing of what was in the room around her.

She didn't want anyone else to know, just in case she was in shock, imagining it. Perhaps when she went to sleep and woke up again, she would be able to see. Parts of her body were numb, too. She knew there was pain there, but it was unspecific, somewhere down her right leg where they had trampled on her. The pain in her head was far worse, screaming down across her eyes in violent throbs which made her seize up.

'Have they gone?' she asked Yasin.

'Yes.'

'I can't see. I can't bloody well see.' Anger. Fear. English idioms from her new culture.

'Nothing? Nothing at all?' Yasin sat on the edge of the bed, gentle. In control. Yasin was fearless. Her twin. Her blood.

'Some light. That's all.' Samira's eyes were wide open and facing straight towards him. They were sad, deep brown and full of dread. He helped her sit up, then guided her hand to a glass of water and helped her drink. She couldn't co-ordinate properly and the water dribbled down her chin.

Yasin dabbed it with a tissue and they tried again. Samira took two more sips. 'Put it down,' she said. She burst into tears and tried to reach out for Yasin, but she didn't know exactly where he was and her hands hit his chest and his cheek. Gently, he put them around his neck. He embraced her and let her bury her face in his shoulder.

'We have to tell Musa,' he whispered after a while.

'Why? Why me? I'm not part of their war.' Samira held her brother even tighter. 'We don't even belong here.'

Yasin stayed with her. When she dozed off for a few

minutes and woke again, there was no visual distinction between light and dark, perhaps even between consciousness and dreams. Samira hardly knew when she was awake and when asleep. In the blackness, the dream which flashed back and forth was of fire, of being trampled, and then of her home and the beauty of the Nile and the desert.

'Do they know?' she said.

'They must.'

'If the doctor doesn't, tell Musa not to pay him.' She laughed at her little joke. Her own defiance.


Musa sat alone, staring out across his garden, not caring that the cigar in his hand had burned away to dead ash.

'She's resting,' said Yasin softly, pulling out a chair and sitting down.

'I don't know whether she should recover here or get back to school and the safety of England as soon as possible,' said Musa, shielding his eyes from the morning sun.

'She's hurting. She can't go for a few days.'

'No,' said Musa. 'But I'm not sure this is the right place for you any more. For either of you.'

Musa's mobile phone rang. He flipped it open and listened. 'The cease-fire's been in place now for God knows how many years,' he snapped. 'You know who did it as well as I.' Pause. Impatient. Listening. 'My daughter is sick. I'll talk later.' He shut the phone.

'Who was that?' said Yasin.

'Hassan Hatimil. I fought with him in the war of the seventies. In fact we share shrapnel from the same grenade.' Musa tapped his leg. 'I got it here. His was in the shoulder. I gave up the war and he runs what's left of our armed movement.'

'Is he going to kill the people who did it?'

Musa gave a dry, resentful laugh. 'He's got problems.

The bomb was planted by a Christian militia, but they're blaming it on us.'

'I don't understand.'

'It's far easier for people to hate a Muslim terrorist than an American banker, so they set off a bomb and blame the Muslims. There'll be a poster of Hassan up soon describing him as the mastermind of the bomb attack. After that, anybody who riots because of the economic crisis will be accused of supporting terrorism.'

'How do you know that?'

Musa fell quiet for a moment. 'I've been through it before. So many times. One bomb we can control, but if they're determined to create a backlash, they will.'

'We don't want to control it. We have to kill the people who did it.'

'They're nothing. Just uneducated peasants.'

'We'll kill whoever ordered it then.'

'You'll never get them . . .'

'Have you tried?' interrupted Yasin.

Instead of answering, Musa picked up his cigar and spent some moments re-lighting it, ignoring Yasin until it was lit and he was exhaling smoke: 'Yes,' he answered. 'And that's what's so frustrating. If I didn't understand the causes of war, they would be easier to fight.'

# Chapter Four

Musa heaved on the sides of the chair and pushed himself to his feet, reaching for his stick. 'Samira is sleeping. Come,' he said to Yasin. 'I want to show you something.'

Musa took him to a shanty town on a tiny spit of land barely a mile from the Lantaka Hotel where Yasin and Samira had been going for a drink. The shacks were on the other side of a creek, some perched on the rocky shore-line, but most on stilts built into the sea-bed, with boats and canoes moored underneath them, banging back and forth with the swell.

A wide, broken-down footbridge stretched across a creek of filthy water and an old man was paddling in a canoe against the current. A girl, her hair tied back in a bun, wearing a cap of military camouflage, paddled in the opposite direction towards the sea. She looked up at Musa and Yasin on the bridge and waved.

Plastic bags, cans and boxes piled up around the stilts under the huts. There was a stench of decay and rotting vegetables. The roofs of the huts were different hues of corrugated iron. Beyond them were mountains on one side and sea to the other where the current was taking the boats towards the Sulu Archipelago.

Musa steered Yasin towards a mosque which was little

more than a shed of splintering wood. Next to it stood a basketball court, its walls streaked with graffiti in English: 'Yankee imperialist go home.' Bricks and rubble from unfinished building work lay around the square. A girl carrying a child on her back gaped at them.

'I wanted you to see how your Muslim brothers live,' said Musa.

'They're not my brothers.' Yasin kicked an empty drinks can. 'And I've seen it in the Sudan.'

'Fellow Muslims, then.'

'I don't believe in God.' He walked ahead separating himself from Musa, who stayed quiet.

Adults watched from a distance in clusters, but the children were bold enough to scamper around their feet, looking unsure of who Yasin and Musa were and what they were doing in their slum. As a Mahas River Arab of the Nile, Yasin was taller than most Filipinos, but his skin was dusky and brown, not as dark as the African-Americans they were used to.

Yasin stopped and squatted. He picked up a stone and drew lines in the dry ground. 'What's the point of bringing me here?' he said. Musa walked slowly towards him and put his hand on his shoulder. Yasin didn't react. 'To show you that there are no men here.'

Yasin became curious. He glanced around him and then up at Musa, not speaking, but his look demanding an answer.

'They left last night after the bombing,' said Musa. He tried to bend his knees to be on the same level as Yasin, but the shrapnel hurt his leg too much. 'Stand up, for God's sake, so we can talk,' he said, gently pulling on Yasin's shirt. 'We need to talk.'

Musa held Yasin's elbow and walked him over towards a cluster of huts. The first ones were built on land which gave way to the sea and the other homes were on stilts with the water brooding and swaying underneath. The stench of rotting rubbish got worse as they moved further into the village. Long canoe boats carried people between the stilts to their homes. Children's faces peered in clumps out of glassless windows. They walked on, ducking under washing draped across their path and cockroaches scuttling around their feet and up the sides of the huts.

Damp, draining heat sucked up humidity from the water, making the bamboo drip with moisture. Mosquitoes hovered in the air.

Yasin saw they were being watched. At first people smiled, then as word got around that Musa was there, they became more furtive, watching him from their houses, a determined, limping figure, whose wars had given him the authority to go wherever he wanted in places like this. The old people who watched had known his face for forty years. He was one of them, but also their leader.

'Where have the young men gone then?' said Yasin, looking behind him at children staring at them in their rags, barefooted, their skin ruined by sores.

Musa wiped the sweat from his face. 'Where do you think?'

'To fight.'

'To run. To fight. There's no difference.' Musa turned left along the rickety planks of the walkway. Sea splashed onto rocks underneath. He opened the door of a hut, pushing through a curtain which hung over it. Light streamed in narrow pin-prick rays through gaps in the wood, showing them a woman in a hammock with a baby lying on her. When she saw Musa, she fumbled to her feet and scurried out of the door, leaving the hammock swinging and the room empty.

'Help me,' said Musa. It was even hotter inside and sweat

streamed down his body. He leant down and pulled up a plank. Yasin helped him move it to one side. They shifted two more planks before Yasin saw that underneath was not the sea as in other huts, but a steel chest. They lifted off the lid.

'I can't see properly,' said Musa. 'Is anything in there?

'It's empty. Some plastic bags at the bottom.'

'Pull them out,' said Musa.

The bags were heavy-duty plastic, with grease around the edges. Musa examined them affectionately like an old book. 'This is where we kept weapons in case war started again,' he said. 'Every time there's violence I come here to check the weapons are in place. Now they've taken them. Hassan must have given the order.'

'To do what?' said Yasin. He stared through the broken planks at the sea.

Musa shook his head. 'God knows. To fight. To make a show of defiance. To get killed.'

'To kill the bombers?' Sometimes Yasin showed the brilliance of a genius twice his age. Sometimes the simplicity of a child.

'Kill the bombers,' repeated Musa. 'These people have been fighting for generations and they've got nothing. Just filth.'

Yasin looked up from the floor. 'Don't you think I haven't seen places like this before?'

'What do you think of it, then?' said Musa. He wiped the sweat off his face with a scarf. 'That's why I brought you with me. To find out what you thought.'

'It stinks.'

'It reminds you of the Sudan.'

'Yes.'

'So help people move away from it. Help them end it.'

A breeze streamed into the hut from the sea and for a

moment cooled them both. Yasin stared through the planks to the sea below.

'Like I said, we talk about it at school,' said Yasin.

'Talk about what exactly?'

'Tanks, aircraft, warships, satellites, the nuclear bomb, oil and banks. Is that why you sent me there?' said Yasin, becoming impatient.

'To India and not with Samira, you mean? Yes. I wanted to you to mix with other children of wealthy families, but not in England or America. You needed to confront the issues of race, culture, religion, poverty, issues which have fuelled just about every battle I have ever fought.'

'You're very clever, then,' said Yasin.

'Sit and let me talk to you. You've been with me since you were thirteen. You had just saved the life of a complete stranger, the British man who bought your swords and gave you cigars. Yet your parents had been killed by British soldiers. Sit with me in this horrible place so we can try to understand it.'

But Yasin didn't. He leant against a wall, dislodging filthy water which fell on him. 'I don't want to talk,' he said, looking away from Musa, out to sea.

'Sit down, damn you,' Musa roared at him, his voice carrying far beyond the hut, making children scurry away. Yasin turned back, his face angry, but surprised. Before he could respond, Musa spoke again. 'Sit down, you arrogant little shit, and listen to someone who knows more about life than you do.'

Sulking and adolescent, Yasin sat cross-legged on the floor with the plastic bags beside him.

Musa let him settle, then continued, not looking at Yasin, but staring through the gaps in the bamboo towards the light. 'I was a father once. A husband. I had a son. And I almost had a daughter. I married late because at the beginning of the war I was fighting all the time. It was a love marriage. She was twenty-eight. I was thirty-six. The cease-fire had been in place for about a month and for the first time in my life I could plan and have something to look forward to. My son had just turned three and was sleeping. Our daughter was due in about a month. It was the happiest time I can remember in my whole life. I wasn't rich, but we had a roof over our head. It was early evening, just before dark, and I was lighting the kerosene lamps for the evening. I heard gun-fire. But it seemed far away and even after the cease-fire, there was a lot of firing at night. It takes time for fighting men to stop.

'I went inside and changed Rene.' Musa's eyes were transfixed somewhere beyond the sunlight coming through the bamboo wall. Then he looked straight at Yasin. His eyes were grey and wavering. 'The light, the lamp I lit, attracted the men to our house. I was unarmed and suddenly they were inside. Drunk. Laughing at us. Laughing at family life. They pulled me to one side of the room and held me there. They knew who I was, they . . .'

A woman came through the door, old and walking unsteadily and Musa stopped talking. She sat next to him and took his hand. The door stayed open, letting in more breeze, drying the sweat on their faces. Other people stood outside the door.

'Who's "they"?' said Yasin quietly.

'He means the marines,' said the woman.

'They made me watch,' said Musa, letting the woman hold his hand, still looking at Yasin. 'They shot Rene. I know the man who shot him. I'll tell you about him one day. Then they cut open the belly of my wife. A different man did that and that's how I know I nearly had a daughter, because they tore her out of the womb and held her in front of my eyes.'

Musa cried, although there were no tears, just irregular breathing and trembling, and he never took his eyes off Yasin. 'My wife. Her last seconds alive were the worst of any human being. Her child ripped from her. Her husband unable to protect her. Herself in absolute grief and pain. Her eyes looking straight at me with all those emotions, but she showed nothing of fear, although she knew she was going to die, and she was still generous enough to show love for me. One day, Yasin, I hope you will see the same love for you in a woman's eyes.'

'Name?' whispered Yasin. 'What was her name?'

'Eva. She was a Christian. That's why they hated us. They cut her throat and threw her onto the floor. Then they dragged me away.'

More people came into the hut, silently as if taking their seats in the middle of a film. The children sniffled, wiping their running noses and scratching sores. Only women and children. No men, just as Musa had said.

'Go on, Abu,' said the old woman sitting by him. 'You must finish the story.'

'They marched me off,' Musa said. 'There were five of them. But we didn't get far because Hassan ambushed them. In those days, we watched each other's houses. After they raided, we would wait in the jungle and ambush them when they came back to loot. Hassan killed four. Did I tell you there were five? And the fifth had a grenade, which he was throwing when Hassan shot him. We all got hit by the shrapnel. Hassan in the shoulder. The marine and me in the legs. He was the one who cut Eva's belly.'

Musa tore a loose piece of bamboo off the chair and twisted it in his fingers. 'That horrible smell of battle hung around and the three of us lay bleeding on the ground. I was the least hurt. Hassan's shoulder was shattered. He had an arterial wound, so I stemmed the flow of blood.

45

No one came. I talked to him for hours, keeping him awake, finding him water, giving him cigarettes, talking to him so he wouldn't lose consciousness and die. We forgot about the marine, until suddenly he asked for water.'

He threw the bamboo onto the floor. 'I gave it to him and said, "Why did you kill my family?" Do you remember how you felt, Yasin, as your mother and father were dying? It wasn't anger, was it? That comes later to stop us going mad.

'"Some of you killed my friend last night," the marine told me. "But not me. I didn't kill him," I said to him. He wanted more water. Hassan had hit him in the stomach and you get thirsty when you die from a gut wound. He was much younger than me. Maybe twenty, maybe eighteen, nineteen, like you. Suddenly, I felt like a father to him. He had such a pathetic, stupid face. I gave him water again. I had to rest his head in my arms so he could swallow it. And I waited with him, giving him water and holding him, while he died.'

'You did it to comfort him, didn't you, Abu?' said the old woman under her breath. The children started talking to each other, creating a murmur around them. The old woman clapped her hands and they fell quiet.

Musa nodded. He got up, putting his hand on Yasin's shoulder. 'Let's go,' he said. Yasin stood up and dropped the plastic bags back into the chest.

'We are in a long, horrible battle, Yasin,' said Musa. 'Go to school. Get your exams. Get to a good university. Because if ever you use a weapon in anger, just once, you will be like me. You will lose.'

The nurse discovered Samira's blindness while Yasin and Musa were out.

When the doctor spoke to Samira, she was startled. Her

eyes blinked and she propped herself up on her arm, as if to get a better look. But she could see nothing and tiny streaks of blood criss-crossed the whites of her eyes.

'I think I've gone blind,' she said finally into the darkness. The nurse opened a window and Samira reacted to the sound. 'Who's there?' she said, frightened. 'Who's in the room.'

She stretched out her hands, moving them back and forth, then lashing out in frustration. The nurse calmed her until Yasin and Musa got back.

In the hospital, the first tests determined that tiny splinters of glass might have got into her eyes. There were small cuts on her forehead and cheeks and bruises on the back her head where she had fallen.

In the early evening they gave her a scan which found that her optical nerve was intact. After that, they removed a dressing over a wound at the back of her head and attached electrodes at the rear of her skull over the primary visual cortex. The response was positive. Vision was passing through the optical nerve to the brain, but it was bland and distorted because her eyes had been torn up by glass.

The specialist wiped his glasses on a cloth. 'We must all wait,' he told Musa. 'She should stay in hospital with complete rest, while we see what we can do.'

Before he flew back to school, Yasin moved Samira's photographs to her room in the hospital.

'They'll be here, by your bed, so you can see them as soon as you get better.'

'Take them out of the frame for a moment,' asked Samira. 'I want to feel them.' She ran her hand down the photographic paper. 'Which one is this?'

'It's you, me and father in his shop,' whispered Yasin. She made a tear in the left-hand corner.

'And this?'

'I'm steering the boat . . .' Samira made two tears.

'This one?'

'Mother and father outside the tea house.'

'Where they died,' said Samira, tearing the top of the photograph three times.

'What's this?'

'When we were children. Before any of this happened.'

Samira put them in a pile on her bedside table. 'Leave them there,' she said. 'I will feel them every day. Every hour of every day and draw their pictures in my mind.'

'I'll miss you,' said Yasin, helping her up in the bed so he could hug her.

'Me too,' said Samira. 'Me too.' She gulped to stop herself from crying. He ran his fingers down her face, careful not to hurt her. She reached up and felt his forehead, his nose, his lips and chin, imagining the strong black features of her twin brother.

'I'm fine,' she joked. 'Waited on hand and foot in a hospital room. You. You be careful. Don't think about this, too much. Find a girlfriend instead.'

Samira tried to laugh, but instead she coughed and burst into tears.

# Chapter Five

## *Dehra Doon, India*

February

Late at night, they celebrated Yasin's nineteenth birthday. Because of his late entry into the school, Yasin was older than his contemporaries and Ablimet Nor, two years younger and the house prefect, hosted the party in his study. Nor was a bookish boy, modest, with long, straggly hair which kept just within school rules. He pulled a bottle of Johnny Walker Red Label from a padlocked cupboard underneath his bed and insisted on playing Paganini violin concertos on his CD because he said it helped him draw better cartoons.

Nor sat at the armchair of his desk. Others lay on cushions on the floor or sprawled on the bed. Gurjit Singh, a six-foot Sikh who bowled for the house with Yasin, stood by the window to have a cigarette, filling the room with cold Himalayan air.

Yasin tilted his chair back against the door and listened out for the footsteps of patrolling masters.

The conversation began when Venkat, who batted for the school, suggested that his home state of Tamil Nadu should field its own national cricket team to compete in world tournaments.

'Well, if you took on the Punjab, where I live, we would have cricketers from both India and Pakistan,' said Gurjit, turning towards the night air to exhale his cigarette smoke. 'Because the British cut us in half and put Punjab in both bloody countries.'

'Then you might lose,' retorted Venkat, who was sitting cross-legged on the bed. 'You would spend the whole time trying to kill your own side.'

'If we had Chinese in our team, I would certainly shoot them,' said Thondup, a Tibetan who had lived all his life in exile in India. He was lying virtually prone across the bed, dressed as he was most evenings, symbolically in the saffron of the Tibetan Buddhist priests.

'You wouldn't shoot me, surely?' said Nor good-naturedly, his feet up and doodling with one hand on a pad on his desk. 'I'm Chinese.'

Thondup pushed himself up onto his elbow. 'Don't blaspheme, Abby. You're no more Chinese than I am.'

'My passport says I am.'

'You're from Xinjiang. The Uigur people live under the Communist Party yoke just like the Tibetans.'

'All right then,' said Yasin, dropping his chair forward so that all four feet were on the ground. 'Should the Sri Lankan Tamils be allowed to play in Venkat's Tamil Nadu team? I need to know how to place my bets.'

Venkat laughed. 'Now that's a tough one. I'd have to look at the quality of their cricket.'

'But you know that already,' said Gurjit.

'True.' Venkat sat up in the pose of a thinker. He still had his prefect's uniform on from getting the younger pupils to bed on dormitory duty. He undid his tie, smoothed it out, folded it and put it on the bed in front of him. 'They would wreck our chances of winning, but I would have to include one or two for the purposes of cultural unity.'

'So the cricket is not paramount,' said Ablimet. He put down his pencil and looked at his doodling which had emerged as a sketch of his room and his friends, each having a distinctive feature, with Gurjit's turban sketched in silhouette by the window the most prominent.

'My money would go elsewhere then, where it feels safer,' said Yasin.

'I would happily take on a pan-Tamil team,' said Gurjit. 'As long as suicide-bombing bowlers were banned from the game.'

They all laughed except for Venkat. 'That's not funny, Gurjit.'

Gurjit began stubbing his cigarette out on the windowsill. 'Oh. And why is that?'

'The Black Tiger bombers are an integral part of our battlefield struggle. They must not be laughed at. The struggle is continuing.'

'Integral part of our battlefield struggle. What rubbish are you reciting?' said Gurjit. 'Your struggle is continuing, Venkat, because you don't want to finish it.'

Gurjit made sure the cigarette was completely extinguished, then he squeezed the remains in his finger to shake off loose ash and slipped the butt into the top pocket of his shirt so that none of the school staff would find it in the morning. He carried out the ritual slowly.

'Why should we stop fighting until we have our homeland?'

'Because what you end up with won't be worth having.'

Ablimet Nor tore his sketch off the pad and started on another one. The room was quiet, dominated by Paganini. Venkat poured more whisky into his glass and Thondup's. He offered some to Yasin, but Yasin put his hand over his glass. Ablimet shook his head, concentrating on his new sketch.

51

Gurjit moved away from the window. 'My father fought a war in the Punjab for God knows how many years,' he said. 'And he still has no idea who won the bloody thing.'

'What did he do?' asked Thondup.

'He blew up buses and killed Hindus.'

The Tibetan glanced at Venkat to acknowledge his support. 'That is what I am urging our people to do against the Chinese. We have to show the government they can't just take our land and not suffer for it.'

'So why don't you?' said Yasin.

'The Dalai Lama is a man of non-violence. He forbids it.'

'I thought all Buddhists were men of non-violence,' said Ablimet. 'Not just the Dalai Lama.' He was using crayons now and concentrating on Thondup's saffron. 'And I agree with Gurjit. What good does it do just to blow up a bus?'

'What does your father think, then?' asked Yasin

'He's a businessman. He doesn't care much about politics,' said Nor.

'But your independence movement is getting stronger,' pressed Thondup. 'Why isn't he involved.'

'Father says it's better to keep your head down and make money.' Nor took a cigarette from Gurjit's pack and lit it.

'My father wanted to create Khalistan,' said Gurjit.

'What does that mean?' asked Yasin.

'Land of the pure.'

'What's the name for Xinjiang, then?' Yasin asked Ablimet.

'East Turkestan,' said Ablimet. 'But don't ask me what it means.'

'My cricket team would be the Eelam Eleven,' joked Venkat. 'The ancient Tamil kingdom of Eelam with its capital in Jaffna. What about yours, Yasin?'

Yasin put his empty whisky glass on the floor. 'The bomb that wounded my sister. It went off in a shopping mall. We were just walking past.'

He took time to look around at everyone in the room with probing eyes.

'And?' prompted Gurjit.

'I don't know what the bombers were trying to achieve.' He stared at Venkat, without a hint on his dark North African face of where his thoughts were heading. He didn't mention Samira's blindness or the other victims he remembered, charred and screaming.

But Thondup answered. 'There has to be sacrifice. In Tibet . . .'

'You've never been there,' interrupted Ablimet pointedly, but appearing distracted by colouring in Thondup's eyes on his sketch.

'Personal experience should not be allowed to dictate policy,' said Venkat.

'Rubbish,' said Gurjit. 'My father killed dozens of people out of petty revenge. All in the name of Sikhism.'

'He gave up,' said Venkat sharply. 'That's why Punjab is still part of India. He didn't see it through.'

'Cool it,' laughed Ablimet. 'None of us really have a clue. Every holiday, I go back to Xinjiang and see the Chinese army in our cities and towns. Every holiday some Xinjiang separatist group or another wants me to join them. Every holiday I remind myself that we would never be able to take them on and win.'

Venkat turned to Yasin: 'So are you saying, Yasin, that just because you were there, you think the bombing was wrong?'

'Right or wrong doesn't concern me. What did they achieve? That's what I want to know.'

'Freedom takes sacrifice,' said Thondup.

Yasin shook his head: 'The people killed in that bombing were totally innocent of any crime . . .'

'Sometimes it's necessary . . .' interrupted Venkat.

Yasin put his hand up to make his point: 'Why not kill a whole city then, or a whole country?'

'Don't be stupid,' said Venkat, draining his glass.

'People get used to bus and shopping mall bombs. They have factored it into their lives.'

'I take it you don't want to be a bus bomber when you leave school then,' said Ablimet. He tore off the sketch and handed it to Thondup.

Yasin drained his whisky, shook his head. 'I want to be a millionaire,' he said. He took out a panatella from the top pocket of his shirt. 'But I have a feeling it won't work out like that.'

'You're a Muslim,' said Gurjit. 'Why?'

'Am I a Muslim?' said Yasin. 'I'm an agnostic. I don't even know that there is a god.'

'An Islamist, then?' ventured Venkat.

'And what about the suffering in the rest of the world?' said Thondup.

'I think money is a better weapon to end it than bombs.' Yasin lit the small cigar.

'That is a worthy goal,' said Gurjit Singh.

'I want to be a great artist,' said Ablimet. He held up his latest sketch. It showed a bowler, with dynamite strapped around his body, running towards the wicket. 'To Venkat with my best regards.' He dropped the sketch onto the bed.

Venkat held the sketch in front of him, and Thondup moved across to look at it. It took a few seconds for them both to take it in. Venkat glanced up at Ablimet. Anger flared in his face. He crumpled the paper into a ball and hurled it towards the window.

'Owzat,' said Gurjit, catching it.

'How could you?' Venkat said to Ablimet.

'I'm an artist.'

'So many Tamils have died fighting for freedom. It's not something for cartoons and jokes,' said Venkat angrily.

'I can draw what I want.'

Ablimet poured more whisky into his glass and was about to drink it when Venkat knocked the glass out of his hand. It smashed on the floor. Venkat threw himself at Ablimet, hauled him off the chair and grabbed him by the neck.

'No,' said Yasin, moving quickly. He wrenched Venkat's arms behind him, pulling them high up his back, then hit Venkat in the face, catching him on the edge of the nose, making it bleed.

'Yasin!' said Gurjit, moving towards him.

Yasin pushed Venkat away and turned to Gurjit: 'You don't attack friends.'

Gurjit stopped and helped Venkat to his feet, giving him a handkerchief for the blood. Ablimet picked himself up, catching his breath and Yasin returned to his chair, tilting it back against the door.

'Ablimet is right. Your little bombs and killings will never work,' said Yasin, as if there had never been a break in the discussion. 'They start wars which go on for ever, like in Sri Lanka and the Balkans. Civilians die. Families are left in poverty and arms salesmen become rich. Governments are used to these things.'

'You are saying something to us,' said Thondup.

'What will your bus bomb do except get more Tibetans arrested?'

'But we must not give in . . .'

'Crap,' said Yasin sharply. 'Either you give in and make money like Ablimet's father. Or you attack the enemy with something so powerful that they will never ever think of exploiting you again.'

'Tell us how you would do it then.'

'I wouldn't. I have no country to hate,' said Yasin. He

walked over to the window to dispose of the cigar, putting his hand on Venkat's shoulder as he passed. Gurjit moved aside and as Yasin was stubbing it out on the windowsill, Gurjit whispered. 'Why is there so much war and hatred in you?' He exhaled a cloud of smoke from his own cigarette which got swept up in the night breeze and disappeared out of the window. 'Why?' He repeated.

As Yasin was dropping his cigar stub into Gurjit's shirt pocket, there was a knock on the door, one rap, and it opened straight away, pushing Yasin's chair with it. The housemaster came in to the smell of smoke and the more pungent one of freshly spilt whisky from Ablimet's glass.

'Well, at least we don't have any bloody women in here,' muttered Gurjit, buttoning down the flap over his shirt pocket.

'I'm looking for Yasin Omer,' said the housemaster. He shone a torch in Yasin's face and then around the room, stopping for a moment on each of the boys.

'I will deal with this later,' he said, waving his hand back and forth in an exaggerated movement to clear the air. 'But for now, Omer, there is an urgent telephone call for you. From the Philippines.'

With no coat to protect him from the night mountain chill, Yasin ran across the courtyard to the boys' phone in the other building. As soon as the housemaster transferred the line, he recognised Samira's breathing.

'I'm sorry,' he said quickly. 'Happy birthday. I should have called, but . . .'

'Stop,' she snapped. 'I don't care about our birthdays.'

'You mean you can see again.'

'No,' she said. 'I am the same. But Musa is in a terrible state. They've taken everything.'

'What do you mean – everything?'

'Our house. The cars. The money.'

'They've repossessed them, you mean?'

'Call it what you like. But he's gone crazy. He's fighting . . .'

'Who?'

'Yasin.' Then, '*Hirba*'. She spoke in Arabic now. *Chameleon*. His nickname from the streets of the Sudan, from when they were children. '*Hirba*, I think you had better come home.'

# Chapter Six

*Beijing, China*

February

Whatever else happened on his last day in China, Tim Pack planned to ride hard and fast along the river bank, concentrating only on the horse, the mud and the ice.

On his way to the stables, he let the Cherokee jeep kick up the dry, cold dust from the dirt track, its wheels breaking ice on the puddles and leaving a trail of filthy water draining down towards the banks of the frozen river.

He accelerated as the road stretched out straight in front, lined with elegant evergreens. Pot-holes threw the vehicle around, bouncing it to one side and then the other. But he didn't slow; instead he pushed the Cherokee on, the wheel held loosely in his hands, letting the suspension and the steering do the work, trusting the machine. The window was down. Chilled and exhilarated by wind and grit, he put the CD on loud.

He needed the music and blasts of cold air to clear his head. Slowly, with each twist of the road, last night's argument with Jennifer drained away. By the time he saw the stables in the distance across the fruit fields, he wished it had never happened, that he had never flared up at her. The rows were more frequent now that Tim was leaving China and he hated them: the screaming, the slamming of doors, the long silences, the love-making which had become a pain-killer and not a cure.

A farmer with a herd of goats walked hunched up by the river as if he had come from another age. Pack guided the vehicle into a particularly deep, but unavoidable, pot-hole which was his marker to change down gear and turn right onto a narrower track. A board, with faded paint and nailed onto a tree, directed him towards the Beijing International Equestrian Centre. It had been set up during China's boom of the nineties and now lay neglected, the plaster damp and the window frames rotting.

He slowed just inside the gate and pulled up next to a pit in the ground once destined to be a swimming pool. Pack's horse was saddled up, waiting for him, sweat glistening on her neck and flanks, clouds of hot breath swirling from her nostrils. Pack put on his riding boots, then mounted, testing the stirrups, holding the reins in, to let her know he was there, while she skipped on the concrete, getting ready to adjust to the new weight.

'Are you riding tomorrow?' asked the handler.

Pack shook his head. 'My flight's at eleven. The whole morning will be a bloody mess.'

He shifted his weight forward and nudged the mare with his heels. She took off into a canter, her shoes loud on the concrete, moving fast past the handler and turning right outside the gate, twisting from side to side, steering through the barren, winter trees, and then galloping on open sand down towards the river.

He let the horse go, like opening the throttle on the motorcycle, not caring how fast or how far, because he did not want to go back. Pack's eyes watered. His cheeks were chilled to numb. The horse's spittle flew back in the wind and caught him in the face.

Then he glanced back quickly and the handler was galloping up behind him, gesticulating. Pack steadied himself on the saddle with his right hand, while turning to understand the message, pulling up the mare, until she slowed and he wiped the moisture from his eyes.

'A man in a Lexus saloon,' said the handler. 'Says he has to talk to you urgently.'

The door of the Lexus was open. Stephen Walmsley, head of station for Britain's Secret Intelligence Service in China, was leaning against the roof, dressed in a black cashmere overcoat, buttoned up, and the collar pulled round to reinforce the protection of the scarf he already had on. He wore sheepskin gloves and held a VHS video cassette in his right hand, loose, not in a cardboard cover.

'You weren't at home last night and your mobile is turned off,' Walmsley began. Deep lines scored his face, a thin face on a thin body, probing eyes against the dullness of the landscape. At fifty-four, only a few streaks of grey had broken through. He always dressed immaculately, regardless of his environment.

Pack got off the mare but didn't answer. Walmsley stayed where he was, his look of irritation implying that it was Pack's fault entirely that he was made to come out to such an inhospitable place.

'If you were with Jennifer Chandler, I hope you told her it was for the last time.'

'None of your business,' said Pack, trying to smile.

'Everything's my business,' said Walmsley. One of the mare's back legs flew up in a kick and Pack stopped walking towards Walmsley, keeping a distance, in case she bucked and twisted so much that his boss became flecked with horse spittle and stable shit.

'I found this on the back seat of my car after the Finnish National Day reception last night,' said Walmsley, holding the tape up. 'I need you to look at it with me. It's not very nice.'

The mare stamped, restless at being brought in so early. Pack passed the reins to the handler.

'What's on it?' He unbuckled his riding hat and took it off.

'Torture. And confession,' replied Walmsley.

Tim took the cassette. It was Chinese-made and the black plastic cover was scratched, even chipped in one place. It must have been recorded on and wiped a dozen times. 'I'm leaving tomorrow, so what exactly is the point of my getting involved now?'

'The only point you need to know, Tim, is that I do not come out to places like this without a point.'

'Who left it for you?' said Pack.

'Not sure.' Walmsley slipped in behind the wheel of the Lexus and loosened his scarf and coat collar. 'That's the trouble with this bloody business. You never know anything until it's too late.'

'To the embassy?' asked Pack.

Walmsley shook his head and started the engine: 'China World Hotel. I've booked room 2113 at the end of the corridor on the Horizon Floor in the name of Patrick James. I'm calling in at the Embassy, and I'll meet you there.'

On the twentieth floor of the China World Hotel was the Executive Club. Its lounge had walls and cityscape views of Beijing, and free drinks and snacks. Guests checked in there at a small reception desk. Next to it was a spiral staircase which led up to the twenty-first floor.

Tim Pack passed a security guard, who wished him good morning, then came to room 2113 at the end of the corridor, as Walmsley had said, and pressed the bell.

The door was opened immediately, but not by Walmsley. The man was tall, about forty-five with a slight paunch and a neatly trimmed moustache. His hair was dark, going grey at the temples, and he let Tim in at first with a look of complete blankness which, as he closed the door, turned into a mocking smile.

Tim looked around, expecting to see Walmsley at the writing desk or by the window. But he wasn't there.

'I'm from the Embassy,' said the man anticipating Tim's question. 'I've been instructed to entertain you here for a few hours.'

It wasn't a subtle statement. He was derisive about the way he said 'entertain'.

'Which embassy?' Tim replied, not looking at the man, but checking his position, between the bed and the television set, blocking Tim's way to the door.

'Yours. The British. We work for . . .'

Tim obeyed his instincts. He needed surprise and he took his opportunity.

He hit the man in the face, before he could finish his sentence, putting his knuckles between the nose and the right eye and twisting it as it connected so it rotated like a missile smacking into the skull. The man was flung back, his head smashed into the corner of the television cabinet. Tim hit him again in the solar plexus and twice more in the face. He slid down to the floor, blood streaming from his nose.

Tim pulled him up by his lapels: 'Which embassy?'

'Fuck you.' It was barely a whisper and the English accent had gone.

Tim put his hand into the inside jacket pocket, looking for identity documents. Then he heard the distinctive click of a door lock. He rolled away as the bathroom door opened. Two shots from a silenced pistol shattered the television screen.

The gunman hesitated, half in view, moving his weapon around the room. Tim hurled himself against the door, flinging the man off balance, splintering the wood at the hinges, then sprang back and round so that he could see his enemy.

The man was picking himself up, gun still in hand. Tim kicked him hard in the groin. As the man buckled Tim brought his knee up and struck him in the chin, then kicked him again as he was falling back. His head cracked on the bathroom tiles. The gun fell from his hand.

'Who are you?' shouted Tim. But his assailant was unconscious, his body twisted up between the bath and the door. Tim went through his pockets. There was nothing. Back to the first man. Nothing again.

He unscrewed the silencer from the pistol. It was a Swiss-made SIG-Sauer 9mm semi-automatic with a twenty-round magazine, two rounds spent. It was the weapon he had used when he was with the special forces.

Quickly, he checked the room. The grey-brown winter smog outside. The bowl of fruit, untouched on the writing desk with a signed note from the manager. Glass from the television screen splintered on the carpet. Two unconscious thugs, slumped against the walls.

This was why he fought so much with Jennifer and why he was beginning to hate his job. They argued because Tim couldn't tell her about days like this.

She didn't know about the man he had shot on the river bank in Bosnia. She didn't even know he had been in the army and that he had done the right thing that day in Zenica, where flak jackets were meant to be off and the Serb guns out of range.

Tim had killed in cold blood an Iranian mercenary, who had shot a young British aid worker for the hell of it, for the *Jihad*, for something to do during a lull in the war. Jennifer didn't know how Tim had tackled him to the ground, had him a prisoner, helpless, surprised that suddenly he was beaten, asking to surrender, laughing with fear like some people do.

He shot him through the ANS, the automatic nervous system in the lower brain, the brain stem which controls heartbeat and breathing, so that his muscles would relax straight away, in case he had a bomb or was pulling the pin from a grenade.

The commander of 22 SAS regiment understood. Tim was congratulated for quick thinking. But everyone also knew that Captain Pack would have to go. So they gave him an easy passage out through Options for Change as the armed forces streamlined in the mid-nineties and found him a job offer from the National Investigation Unit of Her Majesty's Customs. Now he was in China, working for the customs and for SIS, under the pretence of being the assistant manager for an airline.

The first colleague he told laughed sympathetically. After that Tim kept quiet about his new job.

He wondered how Jennifer would react. He couldn't tell her because of the rules. Couldn't tell her about the agent he ran from Xinjiang whose nerves were so broken that they gave him away and he was arrested and shot; about his secret meetings with Walmsley as if they were Cold War spies; about his weekly tasks of drops, codes, signals and tradecraft when Jennifer thought he was merely rearranging passenger manifests.

Tim slipped the familiar pistol into his jacket pocket and the silencer into the inside top pocket.

He left the room, hanging a 'Do Not Disturb' sign on the door handle. He turned towards the lifts, but slipped into the emergency exit door twenty yards along. As he was running down the stairs, his phone rang. 'There's been a mix-up with the rooms,' said Walmsley.

Tim slowed, catching his breath. 'Bloody right there has.'

'They've given me room 2013 instead . . .'

'Forget it,' snapped Tim. 'Meet me at my house.'

The hotel lobby and the Cherokee might be being watched. He headed down an extra level to the basement. Old furniture was stacked up, half blocking the stairs. The 'Exit' sign above the door was broken. A smell of chlorine and stale water seeped in from the health club.

Tim wrapped his hand around the pistol inside his pocket. He pressed himself flat against the wall, making less of a target, and pushed open the door. It led outside to the back of the hotel, where a waiter, his bow tie askew and white shirt untucked, was pacing up and down, smoking next to piles of garbage. Roaring extractor fans blew out hot, stinking air from the kitchens. Tim slipped out and walked quickly past the waiter, while a rat ran across the snow on the path.


East Palace Villas was one of the first private compounds built in China. The little terraced houses looked like those on a first-time-buyers' estate anywhere in suburban England. It was designed for the Japanese, most of whom had moved out long ago to more luxurious accommodation, and was now ideal for people like Tim Pack, with no family, but a need for high security.

Tim opened the door to his town house and edged in through piles of removal boxes. He had left the pictures on the walls: an Impressionist nude, blue-tinted with stretch marks over her abdomen and an unusually bushy mound of pubic hair; a canal in Shanghai; a peasant woman carrying a basket of eggs to market. The removal company would see to them, together with his books which lined the walls of the small sitting and dining room and the landing space upstairs. The maid would handle the fish-tank.

Tim poured himself iced water from the fridge, watching Walmsley pull up outside in the Lexus and tramp angrily through the slush to the back of the house.

Walmsley was Tim's boss during the China posting, where SIS and HM Customs worked together in efforts against international drug trafficking and organised crime. Tim was an undeclared undercover agent, reporting to Walmsley, not the ambassador, who had not even been told of his existence. No one in the Embassy, apart from Walmsley, knew Tim's real job.

'What the hell are you playing at?' demanded Walmsley as Tim opened the door.

'Who was in that hotel room?' countered Tim.

'The reception allocated me another room as I was collecting the key. So I . . .'

'I don't buy it, Stephen,' Pack interrupted: 'Two thugs were in there. Said they were from the Embassy and planned to hold me there. One of them tried to shoot me with this.' Tim brought the 9mm from his jacket pocket.

Walmsley was taking off his coat. He looked at the weapon without making any effort to take it. 'Which embassy? Did they say?'

'I assumed ours. Then I detected an eastern European accent.' Pack slipped the weapon back in his pocket and walked through the cluttered living room. 'They weren't well trained. I left them both in a mess.'

Walmsley was silent for a while as he hung his coat and scarf on a hook by the door. 'Could be totally unconnected,' he said, following Tim into the room. 'Did they call you by name?'

'No.'

'Beijing's getting as bad as Moscow for violent crime,' Walmsley said, trying to defuse Tim's temper. 'Let's assume they were expecting someone else.'

'Don't fuck with me, Stephen.'

'I'm not,' snapped Walmsley. 'I didn't set you up for a hit, if that's what you're asking.' He handed Tim the video cassette. 'You didn't kill them, did you?' he asked more softly.

'They'll meekly check out of the hotel and keep their mouths shut, I imagine.'

'Good.'

Pack stepped his way through to the kitchen to fetch two Cokes from the fridge. He gave one to Walmsley, slipped the cassette into the player and turned on the television with the remote control.

'I watched a few minutes of this in the Embassy and thought you'd better see it,' said Walmsley. He lifted a chair off the top of a box and sat down. Pack perched on the edge of the sofa. The screen flickered in black and white. The first camera was above the door in a prison cell.

# Chapter Seven

The video picture was static, wide-framed black and white, and hadn't taken into account the havoc the lamp on the prison table played with the exposure. At times the prisoner was in silhouette, but the picture was clearly of a person, a boy, for he was no more than that, alone, believing he was not being watched.

In his cell, he prayed and read from the Koran which they had left there for him. The lens zoomed in shakily onto it. He fell asleep, breathing heavily with exhaustion. Tim recognised the tell-tale marks of bruising on his head, and on his wrists and ankles where he had been shackled.

The picture went black and then came to life again outside in a yard which seemed to be lit only with a light on top of the hand-held camera. The boy was being pulled across a courtyard, his feet dragging in the snow.

The lens in the interrogation room was set on a wider angle and the light was such that Tim Pack could recognise the changing facial expressions. A camera operator zoomed in and out and followed the prisoner when he was moved around the room.

There was no glass in the windows, just iron bars. Shackles and leg irons were fixed to the wall and ice hung around the windows and the corners on the ceiling where cold air came through gaps in the brickwork. A metal tub stood in one corner which Tim guessed was filled with sewage.

He wondered about the Chinese obsession for filming the atrocities they committed. He had seen so many interrogation videos pilfered or bought from corrupt officials: footage of prisoners crammed into trains in the dead of night to travel for days across China to labour camps; even men shot by firing squad, the blood spouting from their heads as they collapsed on godforsaken wasteland near a military compound.

'The officer is Colonel Yang Yong-guo,' said Walmsley, stepping round a packing case, walking up to the television screen and tapping it. 'He's a well-known sadist in Tibet.

'His victim is more of a mystery. We only get to identify him when he's asked his name. Ablimet Nor. He's obviously young, a Uigur, and a suspected separatist. A bomber.'

Colonel Yang wore a shabby green tunic and denim jeans. He sat at a table lit by a single desk lamp, the only illumination in the room. Ablimet stumbled. A rifle hit his back and he slumped onto the floor. A soldier kicked him in the face.

The colonel walked over to where Ablimet was lying, put his toe cap on his chin and pushed it up prompting Ablimet to roll over and look straight up at him. Blood seeped from a wound in his right eye. His hair was matted and pulled back, showing his confused, boyish looks. There was no freedom-fighter's defiance in the face, just pain and bewilderment.

'Your father has been arrested for subversion against the Motherland. Under Chinese law, he will face the death penalty.' The colonel spoke in Mandarin, which both Tim and Walmsley understood.

Two soldiers pulled Ablimet up and sat him in a chair in the middle of the room. He shivered. The colonel lit a cigarette. 'So will you,' he said, taking time to draw heavily and exhale the smoke. 'You have been planning to attack China with bombs.'

Ablimet shook his head.

'You have been calling for the dismemberment of the Motherland,' insisted the colonel, his voice louder.

'No,' said Ablimet.

'You have learned how to construct bombs.'

Ablimet's head dropped and he slumped in the chair.

'No?' said the Colonel. 'Is that what you are saying; that you are innocent of these charges?'

The soldiers lifted Ablimet up and carried him to the tub of sewage. A spotlight came on so the camera could see where they were taking him.

Tim knew what this was like because he had been there before, in the Sudan, when the stench of human waste clogs the back of your throat, making you retch and choke. He had felt the shackles so tight his feet went numb, bruises so painful that he couldn't sleep for days.

Once he had mumbled about it in his sleep after he and Jennifer had been to a war movie. When she told him, he laughed it off. But now, watching the boy's torture being played out in front of him, he was living through it again, fighting off memories.

They pushed the boy's head into the filth, holding him down by his neck and pinning back his arms so they didn't flail, throwing up sewage, as he struggled to breathe.

Tim turned away. He didn't want Walmsley to notice his discomfort. 'How old is he?' he asked.

'Sixteen or seventeen,' said Walmsley. 'He was arrested at an expensive private school in India at a place called Dehra Doon in the foothills of the Himalayas. The children of the rich go there: Sikhs, Tamils, Muslims, Hindus, Tibetans, and some Chinese. Now it seems they're suspected of being the seeds of the new generation of terrorism. By the Chinese and Indians, at least. This one comes from Xinjiang. He's a Uigur Muslim.'

'You're saying he was picked up from school and deported to China?'

'Something like that.'

'Sounds far-fetched,' said Tim, keeping one eye on the screen but facing Walmsley.

'Most things in our trade are far-fetched.' Walmsley turned his attention back to the video.

The soldiers waited for Ablimet Nor to lose his strength, pulled him out of the tub and threw ice-cold water over his face. That would sting, Tim thought. The cold would seep through his wet hair into his skull.

They shackled the boy to the wall, his arms strung up above him as if he was being crucified. A damp sack was pulled over his head. They opened the door to the cell so that a draught blew in, cutting through the sack and making him cry out and shiver. They played the Chinese national anthem, turning the volume louder and louder, so he would be able to hear nothing else.

Tim knew what that was like, too. When he had thought he was screaming so loud that he would go mad, they suddenly turned off the music and he realised that his scream had only been a howling around his head.

Tim picked up the remote and paused the tape. He walked to the screen to look more closely at the boy's soft, round face. His strength was sapped. He had no reserves left to keep him going.

'If they kill him, I don't want to see it,' said Tim quietly, turning away.

'Don't know if they do. I didn't get this far,' said Walmsley. His eyes were fixed on the screen.

The colonel was at his seat. 'Ablimet Nor, you are a Uigur Chinese national, who is campaigning to set up a separate state known as East Turkestan. You plan to do this by terrorizing the cities of the autonomous region of Xinjiang. You have attended training camps in India. You have consorted with terrorists from Tibet, Sri Lanka, Myanmar, Kashmir and the Punjab.'

The screen flickered, went to black while snow speckled across it and another picture appeared of the colonel sitting at his desk. 'You told us he was a dragon who changes colour.'

It could have been a day, even a week later. Ablimet was filthy now with his own vomit and waste. His body was covered in burns, welts and bruises and he was lying on a wooden board, his ankles and wrists strapped at each corner so he couldn't move, but with a hole in the middle to allow for his excretions to fall into a bucket underneath. He looked up at the colonel in his freshly pressed green uniform. His eyes were bruised, oozing pus.

'Your father was executed this morning,' said the colonel. 'I've got the fax here.' The colonel waved it over his face. 'Seven of them were shot. Their bodies have already been cremated.'

'Why?' croaked Ablimet, his voice a whisper.

'He was a terrorist, like you.'

They tore off his trousers and pants and splayed open his legs, so that the shackles cut into the skin of his ankles. They used an electric baton with a flashing crackling light, first on the inside thigh and then another shock on his testicles which made him convulse, tearing at the irons which held him.

'No,' protested Tim. Walmsley glanced at him.

Ablimet Nor slumped, losing consciousness. They pulled at the shackles, hoisting him off the board and letting him hang there.

'What exactly are we looking for here?' said Tim, his right hand holding the television remote as he rewound the tape.

'There's been a break-in at a biological weapons plant in Xinjiang,' said Walmsley.

Tim stopped the picture and stepped back from the television. 'The Chinese are telling you that?'

'In a roundabout way. Yes. It's just outside a horrible little town called Bachu. We don't make an issue of it because we don't want another Iraq fiasco.'

'I've seen the Bachu file,' said Tim, pointedly.

Walmsley walked forward and tapped the shaky, stilled picture on the screen: 'They think he might have something to do with it.'

'He's just a boy.'

'At sixteen or seventeen, they can be dangerous. We need to know if he said anything about bombs, war, insurgencies and the aspirations they create.'

There were two sections, each less than a minute, when Ablimet might have said something of interest. The first was when his head was lifted up from the bath of sewage. It was more a cry for help, for a return to familiar surroundings. He spluttered, retching at the filth around his throat and the stench. He spoke in Turkik, one of the languages of Xinjiang, saying the word school three times, repeated it in English and kept saying the words *Bian Shi Lung* in Chinese.

'We hear the colonel saying quite clearly the words meaning *the dragon which changes colour*,' said Tim.

'Which the colonel perceives as being the identity of a bomber.'

'*Bian Shi Lung* also means gangster. It's a sort of folklore character like Robin Hood.' Pack turned away from the screen to look at Walmsley. 'Is this really why the Chinese want us to see this?'

'That's the first question any of us ask when we get a piece of intelligence,' said Walmsley. 'Our job is to find out whether what we're fed today is complete crap or not.'

# Chapter Eight

S tephen Walmsley left him with the tape, and Tim made himself coffee, instant because the percolator had been packed. He lit a panatella and watched the whole tape through again, this time not stopping it, but letting it run as if it were a movie.

He needed to look at it without the emotional upheaval of his first viewing, where each time Ablimet screamed he re-lived his own torture in a ghost house in the Sudan. He drew on the cigar, opened the window to bring in a flow of cold, clarifying air and watched the story of Ablimet Nor as a technician, listening to tell-tale sounds and watching for flashes on the screen which might be a clue to where he was and why.

He identified a clear question from Colonel Yang, who asked Ablimet about his friends at the school.

'They weren't friends. I just listened,' Ablimet answered in Chinese.

'Listened to what?'

The camera was directly on Ablimet's face. A metal rod struck him from behind and Ablimet cried out and slumped forward. Yang repeated the question. Ablimet began speaking and the rod hit him again, this time with the colonel leaning forward, his shoulder obscuring Ablimet's lower face from the camera.

At the end, the camera ran in silence on the figure lying on the board. Colonel Yang and the other troops left the room. The frame shook and the video ended.

If Ablimet had said anything of use at all, it would have been then. Yang would have heard him, but the crucial information might never be sifted out in London. Not even the lip-readers would be able to get it.

Tim stopped working when his maid arrived and started clearing up in the kitchen. Fifteen minutes later, when the removal men streamed through the house, Tim ejected the cassette, put it in a bag with his towel and swimming trunks and walked across the compound to the pool.

Pack dived in, feeling the chill and moved quickly to warm up his circulation. It wasn't even ten o'clock yet, but the morning's events rushed through his mind like the water surging around him.

Walmsley might have been right about the men at the China World Hotel. He got the wrong room and they got the wrong target. But as Tim swam, counting lengths, he became less and less happy with the explanation, and then, when he ran out of theories, the row with Jennifer came back to nag him.

He had listened to a trail of Jennifer's efforts on the answer machine when he had got home last night. She had wanted to talk about London, about her moving back shortly after him, the idea of her moving into his house in Queensborough Terrace. 'Call me when you get back . . . whatever time it is,' she had asked. Persistent. New York. Aggressive.

Instead he had lit a large dark-leafed corona from the Cuban selection which he only kept at home, poured himself a Hine XO brandy and put on Benjamin Britten's *War Requiem*. He had found the violence and chaos of the music strangely soothing. When the phone rang he let the answer machine handle it. He was still with the Hine and his own thoughts when Jennifer pounded on the garden door, and he let her in.

The row flared up when she used the word *sacrifice*, as if to be happy with each other they first had to create unhappiness. 'What did you think I was?' she yelled at him. 'One of your casual fucks?'

For nearly five years now, Jennifer had represented a structure. She was of his culture and tribe, of his class and intelligence. She would have been the match thrown up for him by a computer dating agency. He knew her moods, her social graces, her private thoughts. He had explored and mapped her body to pleasure and exhaustion.

Unable to talk about the future, Tim did the next best thing and took her fighting up to the bedroom. Him silent. She berating him. Him restraining her just by the wrists and thumbs with skills learned in the job she would never know about. She lashed out at him, furious at his calm, at the brandy and cigars on his breath. Until he brought them to where they both wanted to be, in the bedroom, spending the night together, undisturbed, so they could argue and make love as they wished, like difficult lovers anywhere in a normal world.

Only the packing cases told them the calm was temporary.

After half an hour, Tim turned onto his back and swam a length using just his legs as propulsion. Clumps of snow lay on the glass roof above with the sun streaming down onto the water and hitting him in the face.

When he reached the end of the pool, he looked up and saw Walmsley standing over him, holding out a towel.

'The kid died,' said Walmsley.

'How do you know?' Tim heaved himself out of the pool, towelled his hair, then wrapped the towel around his shoulders.

'I bought someone breakfast in the Kempinski Hotel.'

'And the father was shot, too?'

'Not so sure about that. I talked to Delhi station again, and the Americans. Ablimet Nor *was* snatched from a private school in India.'

'Who by?'

'The Chinese police were allowed in so that India could keep her own hands nice and clean.'

'Jesus,' said Tim. He picked up a second towel and headed for the changing room.

Walmsley followed him in, closed the door and locked it. 'The Indians got wind of a dangerous clique of minorities: Sikhs, Tamils, Kashmiris, Tibetans, just like Colonel Yang said. Ablimet Nor – which is his real name – was a Uigur, and they claim he was fighting for independence in Xinjiang and all that. They took him to the border in a military truck, under Indian escort, and interrogated him in the police post on the Mana Pass.'

'They let Chinese troops operate on Indian soil?'

'That's what I said.' Walmsley leant up against the lockers. Tim stripped off his swimming trunks. 'What about the father?' he asked, stepping into the shower.

'Don't know. He is – or was – a wealthy Kashgar business-man. His execution could have been bullshit.'

Tim turned on the hot tap and steam floated up from the shower cubicle. The noise of the water pounding the tiles meant Walmsley had to move forward to catch Tim's questions: 'Do we know why they've given us this video?'

'There must be a connection between Ablimet Nor and the biological weapons facility at Bachu.'

'I don't see it.'

'My breakfast guest said that fifty kilograms of anthrax spores have been stolen from the plant.'

'Why are they telling us?' The changing room went quiet as Tim turned off the water.

'He asked my help in finding it. Apparently, the scientists there had successfully milled the spores to the optimum size of about three microns, specially made to stay in the lungs if inhaled. Any bigger and they would get caught in nose hairs and the throat. Any smaller and you would just breathe them out with the rest of the shit in the atmosphere. In other words, it's been stolen ready to use.'

Tim reached for his towel and stepped out, dripping: 'Do they think this stuff will be used in China?'

'They're running scared because it could be released easily by anyone, at any time. The challenge facing any bio-terrorist is the ability to transport and deliver the bacteria or virus. In this case the Chinese have done most of the job for them. The stuff has been freeze-dried and maybe polymer coated or micro-encapsulated to the extent that it may not be affected by ultra-violet sunlight or violent dispersion.'

'In contravention of every international agreement.'

'Yes, Tim, but China is a strategic ally, and that's a a job for the politicians. Our job is to find it or it will kill millions. When – or if – it becomes known that this stuff came from a Chinese facility, the consequences and humiliation for them would be unmanageable.'

'They want us to get the guys who took it. So they ask nicely by leaving a video cassette on the back seat of your car?'

'That's the way they do things, Tim. They will never officially admit there's a problem.'

In the foyer of the sports club, a cleaner was washing the inside of the windows with a dirty cloth. A waitress watched a television music video behind the reception counter.

'I'll have another look through,' said Tim. 'See you at my farewell party tonight?'

Walmsley smiled humourlessly. 'As deputy trade commissioner at the British Embassy it is my duty to attend a function in honour of the country manager for a British airline.'

Walmsley began to walk towards the car park, then turned. 'Will you still be seeing Jennifer back in London?' he asked softly.

'Why?'

'Will you continue it?' He pressed.

'She's asked to be posted back too.'

'She's not one of us, Tim. She'd never get the clearance.'

'So you've said before.'

Walmsley buttoned his coat and pulled on his gloves. 'If you are desperately in love with her and can't live without her, then you must marry her and leave the Service.'

'I'm not *with* the Service. As from tomorrow, I am back with Her Majesty's Customs and Excise.'

Walmsley ignored the comment. 'If you simply enjoy her company and her body, then ditch her. You have a promising career in front of you and there are many other women with similar attributes whom we would clear.'

'Clear for what?' Tim was annoyed and abrupt.

'To be your wife and the mother of your children, of course.'

# Chapter Nine

Jennifer Chandler addressed the envelope first, then briskly ran a pen through the company logo on the letterhead, hand-wrote in her home address and began the letter: 'Dear Mom, I plan to be posted back to London soon . . .'

She stopped there, uncertain whether she should say why she was moving. She looked out from her twenty-fifth-floor office suite in the China World Tower and reckoned the haze of pollution strung across the whole city a good enough reason to get out.

Just before all the big changes in her life, Jennifer had written to her mother and posted the letter, even if they had been living in the same house. Each had begun with a prediction: 'Dear Mom, I plan to graduate with honours this week . . . I plan to lose my virginity this year . . . I plan to become an international banker . . . I plan to get arrested today . . . I plan to have lunch tomorrow with the man I will marry . . .'

Not that she was superstitious, but the letters to her mother, neatly addressed to the New York apartment on the Upper East Side, were Jennifer's own determination of her destiny. If she sent them sparingly enough, her predictions always happened.

Amy, her secretary, rang through just as she was about

to begin the second sentence. 'Miss Chandler, Mr Beaton wants a word with you.'

Jennifer never understood how Henry Beaton had worked his way into such a well-paid job and ended up as her line manager in Beijing. Jennifer was twice, if not three times, as smart as him. He was forty-three, overweight, red-faced, and his clothes carried a permanent lingering smell of pipe tobacco and drink. The only initiative she had ever witnessed from him were lumbering attempts to seduce her, and once at the first Christmas party, to paw her breasts with one hand, while holding the tobacco down in his pipe with the other.

It wasn't so much the clumsy leching which made her dislike him as his persistent attempts to discredit Tim. Tim was uncultured and unreliable. The airline wanted to get rid of him. He wasn't a steady hand. Until one evening, when Henry was going on and on, Jennifer said. 'Henry, shut the fuck up.'

'No need to get . . .' Henry began with a stammer.

Jennifer interrupted. 'Henry, I'm never going to fuck you, OK? Firstly because I fuck Tim Pack. Secondly, because you couldn't handle the pace, and thirdly I don't fuck men less intelligent than I am.'

After that, Henry became a model boss and even a good friend. He asked Jennifer round for family lunches, usually when Tim was travelling, and Jennifer volunteered to act as hostess at bank dinners when his wife was away in England.

'Do you have time to handle some stuff from London?' said Henry, coming into the office as soon as Amy had alerted Jennifer.

'What sort of stuff?' said Jennifer pushing the letter to her mother under a pile of paper on her desk. She wanted to be out of the building within half an hour and across to the hotel for Tim's farewell party.

'Your line of expertise. I've opened a new file for it called EXRP1Q'01 because the request originated in London. A lot of money has moved from a couple of dodgy bank accounts in Europe out to our direction.'

'They want something tonight?' Jennifer swung her chair round to face the computer screen and called up the file. Beaton stood on the other side of her desk, better suited than Jennifer to the wood panelling and landscape portraits of Scottish moorland which the bank saw as its heritage.

'If you can shed any light on it off the top of your head, I'm sure they would like to know.'

As Asia Regional Compliance Officer with special responsibility for money laundering, Jennifer was responsible for protecting the bank's reputation by ensuring it wasn't used to wash dirty money from organised crime, terrorism or drug trafficking.

She changed Beaton's file name to fit into her own index and looked at her watch. 'I need to get out of here in the next half hour to go to Tim's party.'

'Cathy and I wondered if you wanted to come over tomorrow night.' Beaton smiled clumsily. 'You know, to cheer you up.'

Jennifer only half heard him because the e-mail from London was now on the screen. She speed-read it while scrolling through. 'Interesting,' she said more to herself than Beaton.

'We thought a boring family supper might do the trick,' Beaton continued, laughing nervously.

'No thanks.' Jennifer quickly typed an e-mail.

'Oh?'

'I'll work on this.' She pressed a button to send a message of acknowledgement then pushed her chair back. 'I think I can shed some light on it, Henry, and then you'll get a big feather in your cap.'

'What do you think it is?'

Jennifer clipped the plastic dust cover over her keyboard, stacked the papers on the desk and stood up. 'I'll tell you when I'm sure about it. Now, unless you want to see me half-naked you had better leave my office while I change.'

With Beaton gone, Jennifer slipped out of her working suit and put on a soft black silk dress hanging on the door of her en-suite bathroom. To face the freezing weather outside she put on a pair of black tights, designed to show off her exceptionally long legs, and slipped on a pair of black shoes she had brought in with her. She quickly checked herself in the mirror, proud of her physique, especially as she was just six months short of her thirtieth birthday.

Jennifer didn't mind getting old. She saw it as another challenge to be enjoyed by her formidable intellect. But she didn't plan to do it without having children, and she naggingly reminded herself of the unseen ticking of her biological clock. The ovaries were the only human organs, male or female, which packed up halfway through life, and there was nothing she could do about it. There was no way Jennifer planned to end up with millions of dollars in the bank, in a twenty-fifth floor office block, and with nephews, nieces and godchildren as her surrogate sons and daughters.

She planned to marry no one except Tim Pack and she hoped that once they had settled in London the rows would stop. However much emotion there was, however flawed the dream and however unpredictable were the events, Jennifer always liked to have a plan.

She was putting on the same dress she had worn the first time she had a drink with Tim five years earlier. She wanted to let him know she remembered, that it still meant a lot to her. It was her way of saying sorry for last night. Sorry for getting tense because of her work, the move, the uncertainty.

She undid her hair, let it fall, ran her hand through it, then shook her head to keep it loose and casual. She left her briefcase in the office, and just took a white woollen shawl and her overcoat and scarf.

Beaton was going out of the main door as she left. He held the lift for her. 'You're looking fantastic,' he said, pressing the lobby button.

'I know. I'm wasted in Beijing.' She looked at him through hair which had fallen over her face. 'I'm serious about my transfer, Henry. I want out by the end of the month.'

'I'm talking to London,' Beaton said hesitantly.

'Because, if the bank doesn't send me back, I'm quitting.'

The lift was juddering to halt. 'I had never imagined you as a quality-of-life-person,' said Beaton with a smile.

'And I would never have imagined you as a nice, sensitive guy either,' Jennifer retorted. She kissed him on the cheek.

She could have gone through an inside mall from the office block to the hotel. But she wanted the cold, so she walked briskly past the tourist shops and round the car park to the front door. Just as she was going in, she spotted Tim getting out of his Cherokee jeep across the other side of the courtyard. He had to lock each door, leaning over the front seats to get the ones at the back.

He looked around as if he was expecting to see someone, but not her. He wasn't looking towards the entrance. He cupped his hand to light a panatella. That was typical Tim, to walk in with a panatella in his hand. He checked himself in the wing mirror of the jeep and he was about set off for the hotel, when a man appeared behind him as if from nowhere.

Jennifer recognised him immediately as their friend, Jack Jensen, but Tim was edgy, turning suddenly, dropping the cigar, looking as if he was ready to fight. He moved like lightning in a way Jennifer had seen a couple of times before, when he was tense, and his mind not on what they were talking about.

'Tim.'

The cigar dropped to the ground, forgotten. Pack spun round quickly, his body language aggressive, his arms moving instinctively to fight.

Jack Jensen withdrew his hand and stepped back. 'Tim. A word. Only a moment. Please,' Jensen's voice was whispering and hesitant. Tim caught sight of him, the beard and the spectacles, lit up strangely by the hotel lights and a flashing neon sign from across the road.

'Jesus, Jack, what are you doing?'

'The guys who write the rules don't work the patch,' said Jensen. He smiled, but it was a smile of apology more than anything else. 'Don't worry. I'm not coming to your party.'

Jensen's hand was back on Tim's arm, guiding him away from the car, across the driveway and round the back of the hotel where huge air-conditioning ducts rose out of the ground. When he felt they were far enough away Jensen stopped and turned round. 'This will only take a minute.'

'Were you following me?' asked Tim.

'I knew you were coming here.'

Jensen, the scientist Tim helped rescue in the Sudan, had now been posted to Beijing. Like Tim, he was an undeclared officer operating outside of the American embassy with the cover of working for a pharmaceutical company.

Jensen had told Tim he owed him his life, and Tim and Jennifer became close to Jensen, his wife Pamela and their two children, Davey and Amanda. But Pamela had been cleared and knew her husband's job. Of the four of them, only Jennifer didn't know.

Jensen's voice was close to a whisper. He spoke only

inches from Tim's face. He was nervous, stroking his beard and adjusting his spectacles like the bookish East Coast American he always claimed to be.

'I'm meeting a contact tonight.' Jensen looked at his watch. 'Nine o'clock. I'd like you to be watching.'

'It's my farewell party, Jack.'

'It's a drop. He's passing me something. Down by the clothes market in San Li Tun. Sit in the Cherokee. Watch. Cover my back. I have a bad feeling about it.'

Tim pulled a cigar from his packet and offered it to Jensen who shook his head. 'For later, then,' said Tim, slipping it into Jensen's top pocket. He pulled one out for himself. 'God, Jack, you're a very dangerous man.' Tim concentrated on lighting the small cigar. Jensen was silent, running his fingers through his beard and watching Tim. Once the tobacco was a grey, smouldering ash, Tim took the lighter away, drew deeply, lifted his head and exhaled. 'I suppose it's one of your nasties.'

Jensen nodded. 'It's what I failed to get in the Sudan.'

'You think your man might change his mind again?'

'No. He's solid.' Jensen smiled. 'But I was burnt once on this in the Sudan and you saved my skin.'

This was the second time in a day Tim had been hauled back to the stinking heat and violence of the Sudan. His path had first crossed with Jensen's in the arid desert town outside of Khartoum. Jensen got out. Tim ended up in a Khartoum jail. The warm pungent cigar smoke curled from Tim's mouth, mixing with the cold polluted air of the city. 'What exactly are you expecting?' he said.

Jensen turned to face him. Even the darkness couldn't conceal his excitement: 'I think the Chinese have perfected a new type of anthrax, chemically coating the spores in three-micron measurements so they can be mixed with pesticides and used from the hoppers of crop-duster planes.'

'Anthrax? From where?'

'The Russians. They developed it in the eighties at the Stepnagorsk facility in what's now Kazakhstan. If it works it's four times more powerful than the traditional stuff.'

A gust of wind tore around the edge of the building taking the wind-chill factor far below zero. Both men pulled their scarves up over their faces.

'They want to have it just like they've got the nuclear bomb,' continued Jensen. 'It's a deterrent. If everyone has it, everyone's safe. So four or five years ago, when the Chinese signed a big conventional weapons deal with Russia – submarines, jet fighters, frigates and all that stuff – they insisted on getting anthrax and a handful of scientists to go with it.'

'You've got someone bringing you a sample?'

'Yes. But it's been two nights and he didn't show.'

'Yesterday?'

'And the day before.'

'Same place.'

'Different.'

'Tell me more,' said Tim, because he knew Jensen wanted to, because he understood the craving to speak, the need to be debriefed.

'He's a Russian, actually worked at Sverdlovsk east of Moscow. He was seconded to Stepnagorsk in the early nineties and then sent here, to a place called Bachu in Xinjiang the main bio-weapons facility. Six months ago, when he was on leave, he made contact with our embassy in Moscow and said he was disgusted with what he was doing. Said they were using prisoners as human guinea pigs. I guess he wanted to defect.'

'What did you tell him?'

'Bring us the evidence. Just a sample, a phial would be enough.'

Tim wasn't going to talk about Ablimet Nor and the missing anthrax because it seemed Jensen didn't know about it. He thrust his hands deep into his pockets: 'You're expecting the samples tonight?'

'Yes. If he delivers, we can stop them dead in their tracks. It's one programme, you see. Complete exchange of samples and information. If China has it, Iran has it. If Iran has it, Syria has it. One has it, the others have it. That's the deal. The strategic alliance for the twenty-first century. America and Western Europe against the rest of the world.'

Through the fog and the dark, they spotted a hotel guard turning the corner towards them. Video cameras would be recording the meeting of two foreigners, wrapped up against the cold in their overcoats. They had both spoken so their faces and particularly their mouths were hidden from the camera, so no lip-reader could decipher what they were saying.

'I'll be there before nine,' Tim said. He let Jensen go first, watching him blur away into the night and become indistinct from the other dark figures on the street.

# Chapter Ten

Tim was already late for his own party. He looked around the lobby to see if Jennifer was waiting and took off his overcoat.

He wore a bright yellow open-neck shirt, no tie, but a blue and yellow silk chequered scarf hanging loose around his neck and a dark blue blazer. He sprinted up, taking two stairs at a time, to the mezzanine floor and handed his coat to the waitress.

They cheered as he came in. He waved to everyone, grasping the hand of the manager of Finnair because he was the closest to the entrance, moving quickly on through Qantas, Thai, Air France, Virgin Pacific, and Lufthansa, hearing the pop of a champagne cork in the far corner over by the buffet, apologising for being late, explaining that he had not had his London name-card printed yet, discussing living near Heathrow, professing sadness at leaving China, moving with the momentum of the party, until Jennifer Chandler stepped right in front of him and kissed him full on the lips.

Then she stood back, ruffled his hair like a schoolboy and held his hand as if they were a politician and his wife on the campaign trail.

'We think it's so much better to be in central London,' she said to the diminutive manager of Thai Airways. 'Far easier to commute against the traffic. And with me in the City, we have to get a compromise between east and west, don't you think?'

As she stopped speaking, her eyes moved across the group of people clustering around them to end up with the manager from United Airlines, who had begun to speak to her.

'We did that when we were posted to London,' he said. 'But we cheated by choosing Hammersmith. It's so close to the river and the motorways.'

'In Bangkok, with the traffic, you have no choice but to be near our airport,' added the Thai manager.

Suddenly, Walmsley was there: 'I understand the bank wants you to stay out in Asia,' he whispered confidentially, touching Jennifer's hand. 'Your skills at tracking down dirty money are needed here more than in London.'

Before she could answer, he had moved on, with a slight humble smile, easing his way round to Tim, whose elbow he grasped and, with an apology, steered him away to a quieter corner of the room. Jennifer kept talking about London, bobbing up and down to watch Tim over people's heads.

'I need to see you later this evening,' Walmsley said quickly. 'Where will you be?'

'Tomorrow,' said Tim. 'Give me a break.' For a moment he thought of telling Walmsley about Jensen. But it was too complicated with too many people around, and Tim was uneasy that Jensen didn't know about the missing anthrax. Walmsley had said the Americans knew, but if they did, Jack Jensen, their biological weapons expert, was out of the loop.

'Call me when you get clear of here,' said Walmsley, ignoring his plea and melting away towards the door, shaking hands as he went, a smile on his face all the time.

Tim waited for the guests to thin. He made a speech. He endured congratulations. Whether they were for a wedding to Jennifer or a promotion with the airline, he didn't care. Both were imaginary.

Jennifer brushed her hand down his back. 'I've booked just the two of us into the Louisiana in the Hilton,' she whispered in his ear. Tim lifted a piece of sushi between his fingers from the buffet and put it in her mouth. He took one for himself. 'Something's come up with the move,' he said. 'Can I meet you at your place, later?'

Jennifer bristled. 'It's our last night.'

'Why? We've got years together in London.' He smiled and squeezed her hand, but it didn't do any good. She stepped away from him, rearranging the comb in her hair. 'No, Tim. Of all nights, not tonight.' Her voice was raised.

In forty minutes, Jensen would be in the markets of San Li Tun. But the meeting would be over in minutes. And Jennifer was about to be as Jennifer often was, forceful. 'Give me an hour,' he said with a huge smile.

Tim opened the passenger door of the Cherokee jeep and took the 9mm SIG-sauer and silencer out from under the seat where he had hidden it. Better to use this than the one registered through Walmsley. He slipped the silencer into his overcoat inside pocket and the pistol into his right-hand pocket. He had put on a pair of thin leather driving gloves which would let him use the weapon if he had to without leaving fingerprints. Then he walked out of the hotel compound, keeping to darkened areas, until he reached the main road.

He couldn't take the Cherokee with its traceable number plates and didn't want a saloon taxi, where his white face would be clearly visible through the windows. He needed a taxi-van with a sliding door which he could keep just open for escape and where he could sit at the back unseen by anyone except the driver.

The engine stalled when the van pulled up and the inside smelt of old carpets. The seat was damp. Tim could hardly see out of the filthy windows and traffic swerved to avoid them, as the vehicle started with a leap, the driver letting out the clutch and accelerating without looking around him. Horns blared. The van hit a pot-hole, jolting Tim out of his seat.

'San Li Tun,' he shouted.

'Where in San Li Tun?' replied the driver in Chinese. Tim crouched on the floor balancing himself by holding onto the door handle. It was fifteen minutes before the meeting with Jensen. The van had no heater and Tim rubbed his hands to keep warm. Icy air gushed in through the driver's open window.

'I'll show you,' said Tim. The driver swung round to the left, cutting through a stream of cyclists, and manoeuvring down narrow side-streets until he came out in a flood of gas and kerosene lanterns hanging from colourful stalls.

They reached San Li Tun five minutes before the rendez-vous and parked in a space outside the Tropical Café, engine running, but lights off. Through the café window, Tim saw a guitarist on a stool in the corner of the room. Young men threw dice on the bar. It was too early for the bar to be full. That might come later. Then again, it might be too cold.

The Tropical Café was the first along the strip. Behind Tim was the junction. The clothes market was on the opposite side of the road. Pack pressed money into the driver's hand. 'We'll wait here, OK? It might be some time.'

'If you want a woman, I know a better place,' said the driver. 'Much warmer.'

'Waiting for a friend,' said Tim.

He pulled the sliding door open an inch to give him a

clear view of the markets across the road. What was he looking for? Jensen, sure. He would recognise his gait from this distance. A young Chinese scientist. A man alone. Not in a group. Not relaxed like most in the street. Not on an evening out. Not unwinding. A man tense and with the hint of a mission about him.

The driver looked at him in the rear-view mirror. But it was too dark in the back to get a clear picture of his passenger, which was how Pack wanted it. Then, across the street, Tim recognised Jensen, walking down from the Capital Club building and stopping at a stall where thick colourful sweaters hung from racks. He moved in among the clothes, then turned himself around so he was facing the street, but obscured from view by the clothes.

Jensen's man would be looking for him at the stall. They would have been precise about the place, so the pass could be made quickly, without a meeting, without recognition. The stall-keeper engaged Jensen in conversation, taking sweaters off the hooks and holding them out in front of him. Jensen talked to her, but his eyes were looking everywhere along the street as if he was meeting someone at a train station.

Tim gently slid open the door of the van.

'How long will you be?' asked the driver.

'Just looking,' whispered Tim. 'Maybe a few minutes.'

The stall-keeper was tugging at Jensen's elbow to get his attention. Tim stepped out of the van and then he saw the man, not Jensen's contact, but a European man just like those he had beaten up in the hotel that morning. The neatly trimmed moustache again. The early middle age. The torso in the first decay from muscle to fat. The retired military man, for hire, but never of the calibre to get a top job, never able to shed the stamp of his identity, to cast off the army parade-ground gait.

He held a coat over his right arm and moved towards Jensen. Tim ran diagonally across the road. But his speed, the suddenness of movement, alerted the attacker. Pack dodged a cyclist. Then he tripped on the back wheel of another one and stumbled forward, slipping on the ice, his hands forward to break his fall.

The man swung round towards Pack. Tim crashed to the ground, his hands grazing on the ice. He rolled twice and came up with the 9mm out of his pocket. The gunman fired, smashing the headlight of an oncoming car. Tim got up and ran forward, a crouching, weaving, ducking target.

'Jack, hit the ground,' he yelled.

Jensen didn't hear. The attacker spun round, and Tim fired, pistol held in both hands. He shot to kill, to hit the brain between the eyes so that the body relaxes straight away and gunman's trigger is neutralized. The first round hit the head, a bit to the right, but effective enough. Then two more towards the area of the heart.

The gunman fell, his legs silently folding under him, his coat dropping to the pavement. The gun clattered onto the road.

Tim kept moving. He grabbed Jensen by the arm and pulled him off the street into an alley. They ran, their lungs rasping in the wretched air of Beijing. Deeper and deeper they went, looking behind them, no reason to their direction except to confuse.

Only when they were sure they weren't being followed, that the gunman had been acting alone, did they stop, pacing up and down to control their breathing. Jensen spoke first, squinting in the dim light. 'Tim? he said, panting.

Tim nodded. He bent over, resting his hands on his knees. 'Just keeping watch like you asked me to.'

'Who the hell was he?'

'You tell me. It was you he was trying to shoot.'

'That's twice I owe you,' said Jensen. He bent over with his hands on his hips, drawing in air.

'Happened to be passing,' said Tim with a smile.

'He wasn't Chinese?'

'Caucasian.'

They were in a good spot. The alley widened into a tiny sitting-out area with rubbish bins, seats and a streetlamp which threw light out onto the pathway but kept the place they were in dark enough to conceal them. They could see both ends of the alleyway. One, from where they came, faded, blurred and indistinct, the other more lively with dancing shadows of kerosene lamps and the distant noise of car horns and music.

'I think your man has gone,' he said. 'Got frightened.'

'No,' Jensen responded, too quickly, too ready to defend his contact. 'He's in trouble.'

'Did your people hear of any trouble at the facility?' asked Tim, referring to the CIA operation at the American embassy, the people whom Walmsley had said he talked to.

Jensen shook his head. 'He was going to take so little that no one would know it was missing.'

Tim felt awkward, not knowing where to go from here. He lit a cigar. For a few minutes it was safe, but the police would be there soon. 'I lost an agent once,' he said. 'His nerves were shot. He couldn't take a drag of a cigarette without coughing. He had to hold his beer glass in two hands to stop it shaking and spilling. It was terrible. He had sores on his arms which he scratched all the time he talked.

'"Give it up," I said to him. "Find me someone else and hand over the mantle. Go back to your wife and family."

'But he wouldn't.' Tim walked back and forth in tight little circles. Jensen was perched on the back of a park bench.

'Have you ever been in a situation like that? I shouldn't have let him drink. Shouldn't have let him meet me in the bar.'

Jensen was shaking his head: 'It's not like that Tim,' he said. 'Not at all.' Tim kept telling the story, uncertain about the impulse which made him start, so quickly after killing a man, so privately to Jensen, because he had never told it before to anyone except Walmsley.

'They shot him the next morning.' He threw the panatella to the ground, walked another circle and on his way back, trod on it. 'You know where they did it?'

'Out by the race track, like the rest of them,' said Jensen.

Tim shook his head: 'Right over there.' He pointed towards the flag of a military barracks, visible above the apartment blocks around them. 'Must have picked him up on his way from the bar, taken him there and shot him.'

'I'm sorry,' said Jensen, lowering his head, both perplexed and uneasy.

'We all lose an agent, Jack,' said Tim sympathetically.

Jensen stood up and moved to stop Tim's pacing: 'I've got to go to New York tomorrow. There's a meeting about the Chinese anthrax programme. If he's alive he can get out, too and contact me there.'

'You taking Pamela and the kids?'

He shook his head. 'I'll be back in a couple of days. Pamela goes volcanic if ever I try to disrupt their schooling.'

The darkness and uncertain light from the smog and flickering streetlamps could not hide Jensen's nervousness. But Tim had to ask him. Couldn't let his friend leave the country without testing Walmsley's story. 'How dangerous is fifty kilos of anthrax in the wrong hands?'

Jensen took off his spectacles which were steaming up in the freezing night temperature. They heard the first siren and police whistle. Tim looked at his watch. It was only ten minutes since the shooting.

'We'd better move on,' said Tim. But Jensen blocked his way, his spectacles off, his eyes red with the cold. 'Does Walmsley know you're here?'

'No. Didn't have time to tell him.'

He put his hand on Tim's shoulder, drawing him closer, so he could whisper, speaking quickly like a scientist addressing an audience which would understand him. 'You want to know about anthrax. Fifty kilograms. You've got to understand how they're making this stuff, Tim. Like beer. Fermenting it in vats.'

'How dangerous, Jack?'

'A downwind reach of twenty kilometres. In a town of half a million people two hundred thousand people could be dead. Twice that number would be incapacitated.'

Tim led the way towards the end of the alleyway, away from the commotion behind them. The street was only yards away. Fruit and flower stalls were lit up, alive with colours. Shops were open on the other side of the road: a hairdresser's, a video store, a couple of bars and a delicatessen.

Two police cars were parked across the road near the Zhou Long Hotel. An ambulance turned into the street from which they had fled. Police were extending their cordon, moving traffic barriers down the street towards them, patrolling in groups of four along the stalls talking to people, asking questions.

Jensen and Pack weren't out of place: two foreigners in a part of Beijing which was mushrooming with little bars. Tim looked back down the alley for a place to dispose of the 9mm SIG-Sauer.

'I'm going to Tianjin to catch a plane out of China from there,' said Jensen. He shook Tim's hand. 'Tell Jennifer to keep an eye on the family,' he said.

Tim let Jensen walk away first, then slipped back into the

alleyway, wiped the 9mm and the silencer and buried them both deep inside a rubbish bin. He walked, zigzagging from alleyway to alleyway, knowing where he was heading, but not wanting to get there yet.

Lights, blurred by the mist, lit up parts of the alley. A rat scuttled across yards ahead of him. He could hear television sets from the apartment blocks and the horns of cars on the other side of the building. He looked around, but there were no fleeting shadows behind him, changing lights, or the scuffling sounds of boots stepping into hidden doorways. Tim had a good sense for when someone was on his tail, and he knew it wasn't now.

He walked quickly out onto the Third Ring Road. Whoever they were, they'd lost the first round, he thought. Not least because they had one man dead.

# Chapter Eleven

Stephen Walmsley let himself into the side door of the British embassy with his own key. It was a colonial building set back from Guanghua Road amid the wide streets of the diplomatic quarter. He climbed the stairs to the first floor and turned left by the commercial section with his own door and name on the outside as deputy trade commissioner.

Walking on past the photocopying machine in a corridor alcove, he came to the more secure offices of the two defence attachés. To the right, he punched in the security lock code numbers of another door which clicked and he entered an ante-chamber. He waited for the door to close and then opened the last door with a different set of secret numbers.

The small conference room had no windows, just a table in the middle which could seat fourteen people at a meeting. Cartoons decorated the walls, ridiculing Mao Tse-tung.

This room, known as the Wendy House, was where Walmsley could talk on secure lines away from Chinese – or any other – surveillance. He dialled a number in London, waited for the reply and listened to the voice at the other end before speaking. 'Adam, any clues yet?' he asked straightaway.

'Stolen British passports. Kevin Deacon and Clive Simpson,' came the reply. 'We're investigating a freelance Russian or Czech outfit. Pack left them in pretty bad shape.'

'Anything more on Ablimet Nor?'

'I'm getting the list of his closest school friends over to you now. We know where all of them are, except for two. Venkataraman, the son of a wealthy Tamil businessman. Lives in Madras. Family left northern Sri Lanka in the early seventies. And Yasin Omer. He's got a complicated history, adopted son of a Philippine millionaire, and he's disappeared. No one knows where the hell he is.'

'Yasin Omer,' repeated Walmsley. 'Where have I heard that name before?'

'Hold on, Stephen.' There was the silence and twittering of a scrambled satellite telephone line. 'We're getting stuff in from very close to you.' Silence again. 'It looks like someone has shot either Deacon or Simpson – or whoever they are – somewhere in Beijing.'

Tim hailed a taxi to the Hilton Hotel and went straight to the washroom on the ground floor. He splashed water on his face and it ran off grey, from the pollution and the grit of the alleyways. He used the liquid soap to wash his face.

His eyes were bloodshot and his hands shook as the tension drained out of him. He dampened his hair and swept it back. Tim Pack looked all right, considering he had just killed one man and saved the life of another. He pulled his shirt down, tucking it into his trousers, and used the lightly scented aftershave supplied by the hotel to take the stench of sweat and garbage off his shirt.

Right now he wanted one thing. To be with Jennifer in the Louisiana Grill, just as she had arranged. They wouldn't attack him here, and not with Jennifer, an American banker, as witness.

He took the white curving marble staircase up to the first floor and walked straight past the racks of wine in the entrance, the waitress at the lectern with the booking chart and into the middle of the restaurant.

Jennifer's face lit up as Tim waved and moved between the tables towards her. She got up, flung her arms around his neck and kissed him on the lips: 'I thought you weren't coming,' she said, dropping her right hand and rubbing his back.

'Got tied up,' whispered Tim, squeezing her free hand.

'I ordered Krug.' She disentangled herself from him and sat down. The waitress pulled out a chair for Tim, unfolded his napkin with a flick of her wrist and laid it on his lap. 'I filled your glass, when I saw you at the door,' said Jennifer, lifting her glass and stretching across the table to clink it with his.

'Cheers,' Tim responded. Jennifer brushed loose hair from her face so that her deep brown eyes could look straight at him. 'I couldn't tell you at the party,' she said. 'But I'm sorry.'

The champagne tasted great. It hit the spot like a cold beer or the right brandy. He noticed a singer at a piano in a corner, yet when he walked into the restaurant the music had just been a cacophony of sound, indistinct from the restaurant chatter, the sirens, the slamming of car doors and the roar of the hand-dryer in the washroom. He watched her for a moment, relaxing in the chair. 'Sorry for what?' he said.

'Last night.' She stretched her hand across the table so their fingertips touched and played with each other. 'I was silly. I was being pushy.'

Tim laughed, careful to keep it breezy. 'If you weren't pushy, I probably wouldn't be here now,' he said accurately. 'And right now, this is where I want to be.'

'You know it's our anniversary.'

'For what?'

'You told me you didn't want to do lunch with anyone, but I persuaded you differently.'

*   *   *

103

Tim checked the date on his watch and Jennifer was right. Six weeks after Christmas, five years earlier, Pack had toured the City of London institutions in his official role as an airline executive off to China. His last stop was the offices of Jennifer's bank in Copthall Avenue where he had been kept waiting for twenty minutes among the portraits of the founders and the same Scottish landscapes as in her office in Beijing.

Then Jennifer Chandler appeared, dressed in a black suit, black tights covering exceptionally long legs, black shoes, carrying a black briefcase slung over her left shoulder with a long strap. She had sharp, grey-green eyes and blonde hair tied back in a bun. But she had loosened it by the time she reached Tim Pack, so that as she thrust out her hand to greet him, her hair was tumbling out and she was shaking her head to spread it evenly across her shoulders.

'Jennifer Chandler,' she said, not quite smiling, in an accent which he later came to associate with American East Coast money and education. Her lips moved in a gesture which Tim couldn't quite place as if the whole process of going through the foyer and picking up Tim was part of a rush towards another destination not yet determined. 'I was asked to show you around because you're going to China or something . . .'

Tim was now on his feet. 'Yes,' he said.

She brushed his hand more than shook it: 'But actually there's nothing to see in there,' she continued, tossing her head back towards the double doors through which she had just passed. 'It's boring as hell.' She unzipped her briefcase and dropped in her hair pin. 'And I hate introducing people around just for nothing. Lots of stupid small talk.'

She lifted her head up and looked Tim straight in the eyes, this time with a quick, but genuine smile: 'So I thought we would go for a drink and I'll tell you anything you want to know.'

'Anything?'

She had the door held open for him to walk through first. 'Sure. Why not? I hate secrets.'

It was just after three thirty and for the City the streets were empty, not yet filled with commuters heading home. Jennifer shifted the briefcase to her other shoulder and made sure Tim was walking on her outside, as gentlemen are meant to. 'Do you speak Chinese, then?' she asked, her voice raised because of the extra noise.

'Some Mandarin, and I also studied Turkik because I'm interested in Central Asia.'

'You must be awfully clever.' She steered him to the left down an alley next to a church and then into a bar.

'I thought this would be suitable. It's called the Tao.'

'And you?' said Tim.

'Me what?'

'Do you speak Chinese?'

'Worst luck,' she said, putting her case heavily on a bar stool and fumbling through the contents to bring out a packet of cigarettes and a lighter. 'Eight thousand characters as well.'

Tim caught the eye of a waitress who was polishing the top of the chrome bar. She talked in a Balkan language to another girl with two rings in her nose, three in each ear and bracelets running noisily down each wrist.

'I spent two years in Taiwan,' Jennifer was saying. 'And a year in Nanjing all the time thinking that China would be the great economic miracle. Get taken on by the bank and on my first day, they say, "China expert, are you?" – you know, in that pompous manner the English have sometimes. "We have very little exposure out there," he says. "Our area of concentration is really the Middle East."'

Jennifer offered Tim a cigarette and he shook his head. She took one out of the packet for herself. 'You know why I came to England?' she said, pushing the lighter to high flame and lighting up. 'Because they're trying to ban smoking in my country. And I hate that in a government.'

The waitress hovered. 'What did he want me to do?' continued Jennifer, switching the conversation straight back. 'So I said to him: "Why the fuck did you take me on then?" And that shut him up.'

Jennifer tilted her head skywards and blew out a cloud of smoke. 'I always find that a well-placed "fuck" in a sentence with an element of surprise saves hours of useless argument.'

The waitress pushed a menu towards Tim. 'What do you want to drink?' he asked.

'Well, Mr Pack, for you who released me so early in the afternoon, I thought we should have champagne. Krug.'

His afternoon drink with Jennifer had been on a Thursday. The next Tuesday evening, after eleven, she telephoned him while he was in his sitting room watching the police move in on a gang of black pimps and white hookers on the opposite side of the street. The window was closed and he was listening to old Marlene Dietrich songs, so the scuffling and flashing police lights below played out like a silent movie.

'Jesus,' she began, 'for a bloody airline executive you're impossible to get hold of.'

'Oh hi,' he said. 'How are you?'

'I got this through Directory Inquiries and you don't know how many T. Packs there are in W2.'

A police car drove away. Tim heard the siren. Another drew up, with men tumbling out the back. Three blacks were splayed up against the wall, being searched. Tim recognised some of the prostitutes who hung around within a cordon set up by the police. Pedestrians crossed to Tim's side of the street to stop and gawk.

'I gave you my card,' said Tim.

'Have you ever tried getting hold of yourself with your own card?' persisted Jennifer. 'They put you through, lines clicking all the time, then some bloody robot on voice-mail. Sounds like you're away on Mars.'

The cards, the cover, the visits to the City, to British Aerospace, United Oil and Gas, GEC, Unilever and the other British multinationals involved in China had all been set up by Stephen Walmsley, the man he was just getting to know as his mentor, his confidant, his controller.

'Is it something urgent?' said Tim, reluctant to explain.

'Nothing, except I've got you projection for air travel expansion over the next two decades, not only from us, but also from our competitors.'

'Thank you,' said Tim.

'And as a special bonus, I've got the projections of industry infrastructure projects for the whole of Greater China and the wild countries of Central Asia. They're meant to be secret, except I hate secrets so I'm giving them to you . . .'

'That's great.'

'. . . over lunch on Thursday. Can't do tomorrow. Take me to Kensington Place. I love that restaurant.'

He was at the table, watching her arrive through the wall of window which was being lashed by hailstones as well as rain. Even by English standards darkness had descended early on London that day. Headlights shone past them down Kensington Church Street and the floor of the restaurant was glistening with the water dripping from raincoats and umbrellas.

Apart from her black coat and the briefcase with the secret papers, Jennifer had dressed down for Notting Hill Gate, in a loose-fitting red blouse with a white silk scarf tucked into her neckline, regular Armani jeans and trainers. Her hair was loose and streaked with rain.

When they left the restaurant after two bottles of champagne, rain was pelting down and Tim managed to get a taxi which they both bundled into.

He said: 'Where do you need to go?' looking her straight in the eye and challenging her to name a destination. She confidently returned his gaze. 'I need to go to bed with you,' she replied, loud enough for the taxi driver to hear.

They took off their coats in the hall and by the time they had reached the sitting room, he was kissing Jennifer savagely, and she responded by clawing her fingernails down the back of his head. Depressed by the winter, buoyed by the champagne and lured by unpredictability, Tim led her up to his bedroom which stretched over the whole of the second floor, with windows east and west, rain and darkness on the skylight, huge plants wrapping their leaves up the walls and onto the ceiling, fresh flowers, and light, tropical rattan furniture.

Jennifer was result-orientated: she knew her pleasures and how to achieve them. It wasn't leisurely, it wasn't slow, and she allowed him just enough control to ensure she got what she wanted. When she was at her most intense, Tim wondered why out of all the men in London, she had chosen him in particular. His satisfaction came not so much from the pleasure she gave him, which was brief and purposeful, but from the respite between her orgasms when he realised that for a few minutes at least he would not be called upon to deliver.

When she asked for a rest and lit a cigarette, he fetched a chilled bottle of champagne from the small fridge by the bathroom, a signal to himself as much as to her that Jennifer Chandler would be welcome to stay the night.

Then Stephen Walmsley called and told him to come straight to his club that night and, in the morning, to the Sudan.

# Chapter Twelve

'You're right,' Tim said, looking across at Jennifer at the table in the Louisiana. 'It's been five tumultuous and wonderful years.' Howls of laughter came from a table of young European diplomats, who had chosen the restaurant for a birthday party.

'It's just that I'm worried about losing you,' Jennifer was saying. The waitress slipped two menus onto the place mats and filled their glasses with iced water. Tim took a bread roll from the basket, squeezed it in his hand, letting the crumbs drop onto the side-plate. It was warm and fresh, and he ate it without butter.

Jennifer took the champagne out of the ice-bucket and poured it into Tim's empty glass, catching drips of water from the bottom of the bottle in a napkin. Bubbles shot to the top of the glass and spilled over. 'I was taking refuge in easy nesting solutions, moving house together and all that.'

'Like couples having babies to stay together,' said Tim.

Jennifer nodded enthusiastically that he had understood. She put the bottle back in the bucket and they clinked glasses again. 'I knew when you first bought me lunch, fucked me, then stood me up for the night, that we'd have an exciting life.' She spoke confidently, not caring if anyone else heard. 'Didn't mean to get us in a tangle about mortgages.'

She bit her lip. 'Sorry,' she said, with a quick smile.

Getting up, she walked around the table and brushed her lips against his ear. 'I don't have any panties on,' she whispered. She took Tim's hand and led it down to below the small of the back so he could feel through her dress that she was telling the truth.

One of the diplomats weaved his way towards their table. He was a tall, gangly man involved in trade at the German embassy, whom both Tim and Jennifer knew from the cocktail party circuit. 'Won't stay a second,' he said loudly even before he was at the table, then kissing Jennifer on both cheeks. Tim stood up as well.

'It would be a crime to disturb any couple drinking champagne on their last night together in Beijing . . .'

'If you piss off now, I'll buy you lunch in London,' said Jennifer, laughing.

'Just I wondered if either of you guys had heard about the shooting around San Li Tun?'

The German was swaying, holding the stub of a cigar in his hand. Tim shook his head: 'Saw heavy traffic. Nothing else.'

'Seems a guy got out of a taxi, ran across the road, shot a guy at point-blank range and ran off.'

'Must be the bloody drugs Mafia again,' said Tim. 'Glad I'm getting out of this place.'

The cigar hand came up in the air, pointing at Tim: 'The thing is the dead guy is white. They reckon he was German or Russian.'

'How exciting,' murmured Jennifer dryly. 'Tim and I will let you know if anything crosses our desks.'

'Love you, baby,' said the German, stepping back to leave.

Jennifer drained her glass of champagne, then sat down and opened the menu: 'Can't stand the bloody rumours going round this town all the time. We'll find out tomorrow it was a gay Mongolian blood feud or something.'

'No smoke without fire,' said Tim blandly.

Jennifer looked up from the menu. 'That reminds me. Stephen Walmsley called here just before you arrived.'

'When exactly?'

'Ten minutes ago,' said Jennifer. 'He wanted you to call him straight back and I didn't hide the fact that I was very pissed off.'

'Did you tell him we were here?'

'He rang here. I spoke to him, didn't I?'

'Of course.' But Tim hadn't told Walmsley about the dinner in the Louisiana. That's why he had come, to somewhere he thought was safe, away from Walmsley and his world.

'He's a complete creep. I don't know why you spend so much time with the guy.'

'I need him to secure the extra slots in the Shanghai routes.'

'But he's just the deputy. Why don't you use the ambassador?'

'He's too busy. Walmsley's very good on the detail. Thorough. The Chinese like him.'

'I can't see why,' she murmured. 'He told me the bank wouldn't let me go back to London with you. What the hell business is it of his?'

'He's like that. He's nosy.'

'Has he got a wife or anything? I never see her.'

'His wife died of cancer. He doesn't mention the children much. They're grown up.'

Tim took her hand again. 'He might track me down here, so why don't we go to a place a little less public? Or the next thing we're going to see is Walmsley turning up.' Tim pushed back his chair and stood up.

'But we've just . . .' she began, feeling the strength of his pull. He slipped money under a fork and led her through the restaurant towards the stairs to the lobby.

111

'Walmsley's quite capable of walking in here and wrecking our evening.' Tim held Jennifer's coat for her to put on.

'Where, then?'

But Tim didn't answer and Jennifer buttoned up her coat without speaking, taking time adjusting her scarf. Tim watched her thought process, drawing in the unpredictable and unwelcome and then turning it around, so that she was still in charge. It was one of her assets. It was what he liked about her.

'My car's outside,' she said.

'With a driver?'

'Yes.'

'Get rid of him,' said Tim. His tone was too abrupt. She turned sharply to look at him.

'Sure,' she said, shrugging her shoulders.

They walked down the stairs, Jennifer hooked two fingers around his.

'Sorry.' Tim smiled quickly. 'It's been a busy day.' They were moving between the armchairs in the lobby, Tim leading, keeping in front.

Outside on the forecourt, he held back while Jennifer let the driver go, got in and adjusted the seat of the Audi and the mirror to suit her. Tim told her to go to his house in East Palace Villas.

At the gate, he asked if any visitors had called for him that evening. None had, said the guard. The torch beam from a patrolling guard caught Jennifer on the face. She slowed the car for a hump in the road. Two childen's bicycles had been left lying on the kerb. Melting snowmen stood in gardens.

'Stay here for a second,' said Tim, as Jennifer stopped the car at the front of his house.

'I thought you were going to seduce me on the packing cases.' She kissed him.

'They're in the warehouse.'

He heard the footsteps of the security guard fifty yards away near the tennis court. No lights were on in the house. The curtains were open, revealing its emptiness. The packers had cleared just about everything, except for Tim's luggage, which should have been locked in the wardrobe in the bedroom

'So let me come with you.'

'It's safer this way.'

'What do you mean safer?'

'Five minutes. We'll get some sushi and go back to your place.'

He didn't give her time to answer. He got out and walked across the garden past the sliding glass door which looked into the barrenness of an unlived-in building. He jumped down from the raised ground onto a pathway leading round to the back of the house and the main door.

Keeping the lights off, working with lamps from the street, he went upstairs. His travelling clothes hung in the wardrobe. His laptop was on his desk. He spun the combination lock to his suitcase, opened it, then found the button for the hidden compartment. The video cassette of the torture which Walmsley had given him was where he had hidden it. He quickly took his clothes from the wardrobe and packed them.

He looked around the bedroom to ensure he had everything important with him. It had been his home for nearly five years, but he felt nothing now except a desire to get out and leave the compound.

The packers had left behind a riding whip, which had fallen behind the bed. The darkness of the room gave him a clear view outside. Jennifer was silhouetted by a street light, tapping her hands impatiently on the steering wheel. She had kept the engine running for the heater. A Japanese television channel was playing loudly from a house across the road.

Tim hitched his laptop onto his shoulder, picked up his suitcase and briefcase, and began going downstairs.

Then he stopped halfway down, wishing he had kept the 9mm with him. Stephen Walmsley was at the bottom, pointing a pistol directly at him.

'Leave your bags where they are.' Walmsley made him stand against the living-room wall, hands flat and legs apart while he frisked him.

'Jack Jensen is dead,' he said, as he expertly checked down Pack's legs. 'Shot around San Li Tun and the word is that you killed him.'

Tim remained absolutely still. He didn't answer.

'Word is you took a US dollar seven-figure sum.' Walmsley's hands ran around Pack's, under his armpits and down the small of his back. 'That you used a SIG-Sauer 9mm and shot him right in the middle of the street in San Li Tun.' Walmsley stepped back. 'Turn round and sit on the stairs.'

Tim obeyed.

'Did you kill him?'

Despite the streaks of light from the streetlamps, Tim was able to look straight at him. 'He's not dead.'

'When I checked it out there was no Jensen in the morgue, but the corpse of an overweight, rather clumsy killer called Kevin Deacon. Do you know him?'

Tim shook his head.

'Didn't think you did,' continued Walmsley. 'That's what I said. That the whole story was absolute crap and I wanted to know who was spreading it.'

Walmsley chuckled and lowered the pistol.

'You think you're being funny,' snapped Tim.

'Checking your training.'

'That's not your job . . .'

'Calm down, for God's sake. Deacon was a Russian on a stolen British passport. He was one of the men you messed up in the hotel room this morning. My contacts from the morgue said his testicles were mightily bruised by your kick in the groin.'

Tim stood up. 'It's been an interesting day,' he said dryly.

Walmsley turned round to look out of the window. 'Is that Jennifer in the car?'

'We're staying at her place tonight.'

'Tell her you'll meet her there later.'

'Me tell her? *You* fucking tell her!'

'Stop pissing about, Tim.'

'Then tell me what the hell all this is about.'

Walmsley's voice was raised. 'It's about a weapon which can kill millions of people in one shot. And I put the gun on you to satisfy myself that your nerves were still good enough for you to go out and find it.'

Jennifer had the driver's window slightly open to let out the smoke from her newly lit cigarette. The garden lamp went dim and suddenly bright again as power fluctuated through the compound. She had let the seat recline so she was leaning back, letting the smoke curl up in the warmth of the car, and playing Mozart on the Audi's CD system.

She didn't see Tim until he knocked on the window. 'I'll meet you at your place later. All right?' he said softly. 'I've got a few things to finish off here.'

Jennifer lowered the window and dropped the barely smoked cigarette onto the snow at Tim's feet. The ash sizzled and went out. She straightened the seat and put her hand on the lock to get out of the car.

'No, that is *not* all right,' she said testily.

Tim shuffled uneasily. 'There's a few things I'd forgotten to do.' She pushed open the door, forcing him to step back.

'Only take half an hour or so,' he tried.

'Or you've got someone in there, and you're planning to fuck her on the packing cases.' She slammed the door. He tried to take her hand, but she shook him off, pushing him away. She jumped up onto the raised ground, went through a gap in the hedge and into the garden. Tim was behind her, sliding around on the icy ground, trying to catch up.

Suddenly she stopped dead in her tracks. With no curtains, even in the dim light, Walmsley was clearly visible in the house. Jennifer stood frozen right in front of the living-room window like a garden snowman. Tim caught her and she turned to him.

But it wasn't just the sight of Walmsley that made her seek protection, her hands clinging to Tim's coat. The noise in the garden must have alerted Walmsley, and Jennifer saw the silhouetted outline of his pistol moving round to cover the place where she stood.

Tim took her by the elbow and led her back towards the car. He wanted to get her to the other side of the hedge, out of view.

'Like I said, I'll be half an hour or so.'

'Was that Walmsley?' Jennifer asked.

Tim nodded. 'I told you he'd find us somewhere.'

She looked at him through strands of hair which had fallen over her face, her breath coming out in a cloud and her shoulders slumped. 'I'll go,' she said softly.

'There are things . . .' Tim began, but stopped not sure how to complete the sentence.

'That are too complicated, right?' She brushed his hand, glanced back at the house and left.

'Your weapon is visible from outside,' said Tim, when he got back in.

'Only when people run into areas they shouldn't,' replied

Walmsley, looking out the window at the tail lights of the Audi turning round in the car park area.

'You don't care that she saw you?'

'No.'

A wheel spun on ice before gripping and the car moved away, leaving the compound quiet, except for the boots of the security guard crunching on the snow.

Walmsley took a map out of his top pocket, unfolded it and laid it on the floor in front of him. He pointed to an area in far western China and tapped the map with his index finger. 'How much do you remember of the Bachu file?' he asked.

'It was when I first got to Beijing. Part of my induction.'

'So you know we've suspected that Bachu is the main Chinese biological and chemical warfare facility. It's here, on the western edges of the Taklimakan desert, near the border with Kyrgystan.

'Satellite photographs have shown incinerator stacks and buildings which could be large cold storage facilities. There is double and sometimes triple wire fencing, together with watch-towers. It is guarded by an elite unit attached to the second artillery regiment which handles China's long-range missile programme. There are routine visits by military convoys which could be used for transporting munitions and missile warheads to and from the site.'

Tim crouched down, looking at the map.

'The man you killed in San Li Tun must have been paid to kill Jack Jensen,' continued Walmsley. 'What we need to know is, Why? You completely flouted every regulation in the book, by undertaking an armed operation on foreign soil without permission. But we're grateful that you saved Jack's life.'

Tim said nothing, not even indicating that he accepted Walmsley's version of events.

'About six months ago a bio-molecular scientist called Sergei Nalyotov made contact with the Americans in Moscow. He had been seconded to Bachu from the Stepnakorsk bio-weapons facility in Kazakhstan, developing a new strain of anthrax, more deadly than anything else around. His main employers were at the Institute of Microbiology and Virology in Sverdlovsk, five hundred miles east of Moscow.

'He had helped the Chinese design the aerosol dissemination test room at Bachu based on the chamber at Sverdlovsk. It was a steel cube fifty feet on each side, where animals were tethered to the floor while poison was released from ceiling vents. But in the past year he said the Chinese had brought in prisoners from nearby labour camps to test his new strain of anthrax. He was made to watch them die.'

Walmsley let that sink in. The images of the video tape were still fresh in both their minds, so that both the concept and Nalyotov's next step was believable. 'On his next home leave, he got in touch with the Americans and offered secrets in exchange for asylum. They asked Jack for advice, and he said great, but insisted that Nalyotov deliver evidence, even just a phial, either to Moscow or to Jensen himself in Beijing.'

'Jack was meant to meet Nalytov tonight and he didn't turn up?' said Tim.

'Correct,' said Walmsley. 'Instead he got a Russian thug. Apparently, Jack had also wanted Nalyotov to stay at Bachu and be his man there until it got too risky. After that he could have anything he wanted.'

'Nalyotov agreed?'

'He did. But he must have changed his mind.' He took a photocopied sheet of paper out of his pocket and unfolded it. 'The Chinese gave me this.' He looked at Tim and smiled.

'They *want* us to believe them. Apparently, it's a letter

118

from Nalyotov to his bosses at Sverdlovsk – a straight request for a transfer home, for personal reasons.'

'He gave up the idea of America, then?'

'Must have done. He didn't want to stay a day longer. Sverdlovsk must have told him he could leave once he had let in the raiders. Which he did. Showed them a warehouse of milled freeze-dried anthrax and watched them load fifty kilograms onto a truck. Then as they were leaving, they shot him dead.'

Walmsley was silent for a moment, seeming to study scuff marks on the white walls caused by the packers.

'Are these the guys who were in the hotel room?' said Tim.

'Must be the same operation. But the ones here aren't as good.'

Walmsley moved towards the window. 'When you watched the tape, did you hear anything like "Yasin"?'

The sound had been scratchy for much of the time, and the colonel had yelled and beaten Ablimet Nor while he was speaking. 'Not that struck me,' Tim answered, carefully. 'Is that what we're looking for? What is it anyway – a name?'

'Yes – of someone the Chinese think they're looking for. Yasin Omer, two years older than Ablimet Nor, from the same school in Dehra Doon in India. When Nor was dragged away, Omer was in the Philippines for family reasons. Apparently, he originally comes from the Sudan, became an orphan and was adopted by a Philippine Muslim millionaire who's run into trouble with the currency crisis. Omer left the school, went to the Philippines, and now he's vanished off the face of the earth.'

Walmsley sat down at the bottom of the stairs, brushing his hands backwards and forwards across the parquet floor. 'Nothing at all on the tape? You're sure?' he asked again.

Then he straightened up. 'Three-micron spores, freeze-dried, micro-encapsulated to withstand the dissemination of an explosion. Whoever stole it is in possession of the most deadly private weapon, anywhere in the world.'

'But I don't get the automatic connection to Yasin Omer?' said Tim.

'Apparently a group of people were arrested, including a Tibetan, a Tamil and a Sikh. If Nor, for some reason, is tied up in it, then Omer is the only one of the group who isn't accounted for.'

'I know a Yasin Omer,' said Tim very softly. 'He was the boy who saved my life in the Sudan.'

# Chapter Thirteen

## Zamboanga, Southern Philippines

February

From the small airport at Zamboanga, Yasin caught a taxi straight to the hospital where Samira was. He was tired and dirty from his long, disjointed journey from the Himalayas. Some hospital staff recognised him, but looked away, as people do when things are difficult. They were wary of Yasin, with his dark Sudanese skin and exhausted, bloodshot eyes.

He took the lift up to Samira's room on the seventh floor. A young doctor with thick spectacles and a crucifix around his neck got in, fiddling with a stethoscope. He recognised Yasin. 'I'm so, so sorry,' he said, just as the lift came to a halt on the third floor.

Yasin wasn't sure he understood. 'Sorry about what?'

The doctor smiled sympathetically, holding the lift door open for a moment. 'It should never have happened. I am a Christian: I will pray for you all.'

He walked away and Yasin hurriedly pressed the button for Samira's floor. The lift seemed to take an age. Each movement, the doors, the automatic voice announcement, the whining of the electric motor, the shuddering of the cables, stretched out intolerably.

The doors stayed closed while the automatic voice told him he was on the seventh floor. He slammed the open button and squeezed through the gap as soon the doors opened wide enough, running along the corridor, his bag banging against his legs.

He counted the doors of the private rooms. Samira's was the tenth on the left, looking out towards the east. Most doors were open and he glimpsed the patients inside, the flickering television screens, the trolleys of food and medicines, the flowers and the families clustered around the beds. He dodged children playing in the corridor. He felt sunlight stream through, throwing up dust particles and hitting his face door by door as he passed.

Samira's room was open, with a food trolley just outside. Yasin grasped the edge of the door to balance himself as he stopped and turned to look inside. He brought his free hand up to shield his eyes from the sun. The television was on, but the room was empty, except for a nurse perched on the end of the freshly made bed, her attention caught by an early-morning television game show.

'Where's Samira?' said Yasin, catching his breath.

The nurse jumped, startled. 'Who are you?' she answered.

'Yasin Omer. Her brother.'

She broke into a broad grin. 'She said you were on your way.' She got up and turned off the television. 'She moved upstairs this morning. Mr Osmeña said she should go somewhere safer. Tenth floor.'

'Rudy Osmeña?'

'He's her new guardian.'

On the tenth floor, two guards from the Philippine marines were standing outside Samira's door. They stepped in front of Yasin, their automatic rifles raised, as he tried to pass.

'I'm her brother,' said Yasin softly, stopping inches from them. The marines didn't move. Their eyes were as hard as ice.

'It's Yasin, my brother,' he heard Samira call from inside the room.

'Let him through,' came a command from inside. The marines stepped back and Yasin pushed the door fully open.

A marine captain stood just inside the door. Samira sat on a chair by the window. The sun danced on her hair, which she had left loose, and on the white cotton of her nightdress. As she heard Yasin's footsteps, she turned, stretching out her hand. She moved her arm up and down trying to find Yasin's own hand by herself. It looked odd, though, like a robotic arm not quite in control of itself.

Her face shone with excitement. Her mouth, smiling, was open with expectation, but against the blankness in her eyes, it seemed completely empty, as if Samira was a sad clown, not yet aware of her own misfortune.

Yasin took Samira's hand, gripping it. He embraced her and she stood up, unsteadily, needing his support. She hung her arms around him, squeezing him hard. They ignored the soldier by the bed and spoke in their own language so he wouldn't understand.

'Your old room was empty. I thought you were dead,' said Yasin.

'They moved me because of Dad,' whispered Samira, ending the embrace but keeping hold of Yasin's hand. She sat down and Yasin crouched next to her.

'What do you mean – because of Musa?' he asked.

Samira spoke sharply to the marine captain in English. 'Leave us alone, please. At least stand outside the door while I'm with my brother.'

Once he was gone, she said. 'You should never have gone back to school. It was stupid.'

'What's he doing here?'

'That's why I called you,' continued Samira. 'Rudy Osmeña came round to our house in the morning three days ago and Dad had a big row with him. Osmeña said they would have to repossess the house and all Dad's things because the bank was withdrawing the loan.'

'But Musa was making the interest repayments.'

'Apparently they were special loans. The bank could end them at any time if they didn't think his businesses were worth enough. So Dad started shouting at him and Osmeña stormed out. Then in the afternoon, an army general came round, saying that Dad was responsible for the bombing . . .'

'In the mall?'

Samira touched the edges of her eyes. 'The one that did this, yes. Dad threatened them with a gun. He even fired shots at them. That night he barricaded himself into the compound. He put the Pajero up against the gate so no one could get in and set up a machine gun up the roof. He told everyone, Nelly, Delia and the rest of the staff, to leave. That's what Nelly told me. She said he had gone mad.'

'I'm not so sure,' said Yasin softly.

'He spent the night there all by himself. In the morning, that was two days ago, they over-ran the place,' whispered Samira. Her eyes moved over towards the door and the marine captain. She lifted a hand to point, but got the direction slightly wrong. 'Nelly says there was lots of shooting, but Dad escaped. She doesn't know where Jesse is. Our home . . .' she stumbled with her words, '. . . our home has gone.'

'Again,' added Yasin, looking out of the window, trying to rid himself of human feeling.

A marine unit, with sandbags, a road block and an armoured

personnel carrier, stood on a hill overlooking Musa's compound. Yasin skirted round it along hidden jungle paths he knew well, where he had collected coconuts with Jesse and played with Samira when they were younger.

He was as used to the jungle in the Philippines as he had been used to the Nile. He reached the compound without being spotted, finding a way in which Jesse had showed him, the hidden gate in the wall the gardener used when he didn't want Musa to see him.

There were no troops inside and, once there, the silence struck Yasin more than anything else. Then a door banged shut in the wind, making a dog scamper across the courtyard.

Every time there was a sound, like broken glass dropping from a window frame, the quietness exploded making him tense. He walked through the debris as though he were the only person alive, infallible, the last survivor.

A large set of double doors which sealed off the family compound from the outside world had been blown open with explosives. The Pajero jeep was smashed against the wall of the house and fire had blackened the paintwork.

French windows hung open on Musa's verandahs and first-floor balconies, just like Yasin had seen in the villa next to his house the day his parents died. The whitewashed walls were pockmarked with gunfire and in several places they were completely punctured where rocket-propelled grenades had gone right through into a wardrobe or a washing machine.

The first bulbs of the dry season were beginning to flower. Yasin stepped over sweetcorn, rice and onions which had spilt out of storage sheds. When he went inside the house, there was a sudden change from daylight to darkness; mattresses and boards had been put up in a futile attempt to blockade the windows. He stopped and let his eyes adjust, then went on, treading on clothes strewn on the floor, tiny foam-rubber balls cut open from a mattress, photographs scattered from their albums. The rings of hand-grenades and spent cartridges of automatic weapons littered the stairs, showing the path taken by the attacking soldiers on their way to Musa's communication equipment and machine gun on the roof.

Yasin wondered how many men Musa had killed.

Shadows passed rhythmically across the courtyard: brightness, shadow; daylight, darkness; normal life, as the washing blew backwards and forwards on the line outside, flapping and swaying, criss-crossing between the window and the sunlight like washing did in millions of households across the world.

But not like this.

Upstairs, inside Jesse's house, he found decomposing bodies just left there. Jesse's wife had been shot in the forehead, a tiny bloodied hole, and her skull blown apart at the back where the bullet had made its exit. Yasin had to step over her to see the children she had been protecting, two grandsons, a daughter, bundled up and holding each other, an arm around a shoulder, a head buried in a chest, legs curled up, as if it could protect them against the high velocity bullets which had killed them.

He touched Nina, Jesse's daughter. When he tried to move her, flies flew off her wounds. He remembered that she had been pregnant. Then, a stench suddenly hit him, making him retch and let go of her. Her belly had been slashed open.

Yasin stepped back, holding the wall to steady himself, breathing deeply. Jesse's little grandson lay at his feet, his head a mass of brown dried blood with flies all over it, the small ear half-hidden, but torn. They had done it and left them, just like they had killed Musa's family a generation ago. Nothing had changed.

*　　*　　*

Yasin edged himself out and went back into the courtyard, where he had a clear view of the marine guards on the high ground. He glanced up through the broken gate at them, not caring if they saw him, because he had done nothing wrong and they had.

He walked over to the tractor. The key was missing from the ignition, so he opened the tool box behind the seat, took out a screwdriver, and joined the two ignition points above the starter motor, just as Jesse had taught him. The engine burst into life, its sudden roar cutting through the quiet of the farm and he climbed up, put the tractor into reverse and backed it up so that the bucket on the front faced into the courtyard. Then with the fury pent up inside him he brought the bucket down, tilting its cutting edge so that it went through the soil made soft from the rain the night before. He scooped it up and tipped the clods on top of the piles of sweetcorn and onions.

Yasin worked furiously, wrenching the controls in their sockets and letting the sweat pour down him, soaking his shirt and gathering in his eyes so he could hardly see. He fixed his concentration on the ground and the tractor and refused to look at his surroundings, at the hills and landscape which Musa loved so much, the broken and burnt houses in the compound, the children's swing and a bicycle which stood untouched by the mayhem.

He measured the area he would need for the grave. They would have wanted to be buried together, side by side, touching each other, as they had lived and as they had been killed.

When it was right, he stopped and heard the sound of another vehicle from the army checkpoint. An armoured personnel carrier was heading down towards him, the machine gun manned, a voice shouting towards him through a tannoy, the vehicle trundling very slowly, as if it wanted to give Yasin time to get away.

Yasin ignored it. He climbed upstairs, knowing now what he would see and smell. He brought the bodies down, not caring about the blood on him, not caring about the flies all over him. One by one he carried the two adults and the children to the grass outside the house and found white sheets in the cupboards in the bedrooms. Quietly, he washed each body, hearing the splash of water from the yard tap and the growling of the military vehicle getting closer, moving slowly because the young soldiers didn't know who he was or why he was there.

He spread out the sheets and wrapped each body in one, then laid them in the grave, Jesse's wife and daughter in the middle and a child on either side, their heads pointing almost due west towards Mecca, just as Jesse would have wanted.

He didn't say a prayer because he didn't believe in a god. Instead he stood silently above them, his arms clasped and his head down, so he didn't see a marine sergeant appear at the gate, his M16 automatic rifle levelled at Yasin's chest.

When Yasin looked up, neither man said a word. Yasin saw the waver of uncertainty in the sergeant's eyes and knew there was none in his own. He felt more in control than ever before.

The sergeant stepped back a couple of paces. His gaze flickered to the open grave, took in the sheeted corpses, and darted back to Yasin.

Yasin climbed back onto the tractor. The engine was idling, and he put it into gear, turning the tractor so that it was in a better position to scoop the soil back up and return it to the grave. The sergeant was on the radio asking for orders.

Yasin worked methodically, not hurrying. His hands

drove the bucket, his feet worked the pedals, his eyes moved between the troops outside the compound and the bodies, whose white cloths were vanishing under the dark soil of the farmyard.

Yasin couldn't hear the armoured vehicle, the tractor was so loud, and he watched the marines coming towards him as if they were on a silent video. He didn't hear the helicopter either and only noticed it as a quick, leaping shadow which passed over him, blocking out the light for a moment, making dust fly up from the yard and blowing the vegetables about. Trees rocked backwards and forwards like in a typhoon. The helicopter made him more angry than the marines.

The helicopter was an act of violence. The noise, the power, the intimidation was a deliberate act of hostility against the burial. It violated the sanctity of death.

Then it was gone, and in a lull between different sounds, of tractor, helicopter and wind, he heard the sergeant's voice through a tannoy, shouting, in Tagalog, the Philippines' national language, then in the Muslim dialect, Tausug, and finally in English: 'Why don't you go? Just leave.'

But the grave wasn't yet finished. Patches of white sheet were still visible, and more than half the soil had to be replaced. Nor had Yasin paid his respects. He would say a few words from the Koran, just as he would have said a few words from the Bible if Jesse's family had been Christian. He didn't care about the god, only the people.

'Leave,' pressed the sergeant. 'Leave now, or we will have to come in and arrest you.'

Yasin climbed down from the tractor. He left the engine idling, and the sun coming down in the late afternoon hit him like a torch. He lifted his arm to shield his eyes. He could smell the undergrowth of the jungle just like he had learnt the desert smells of the Sudan. Everything was still, yet everything moved, like grains of sand in the wind which you couldn't see or the rustling of jungle leaves in thick, static undergrowth. A blue tropical haze stretched beyond the armoured personnel carrier and, far away, evening storm clouds rolled out from the hills towards the sea.

A mosquito jabbed his forearm and Yasin squashed it. Yasin didn't weigh up his other responsibilities; looking after Samira, finding Musa, going back to school, distancing himself from the riots and the bombing. He felt sad, strong and angry, just as he had on the day his parents had been buried. He had been frightened then and no good had come of it. This time he wasn't afraid.

Yasin had no idea what he was going to do once the burial was finished. He only knew that he was going to ignore the sergeant's command.

'Do you have a copy of the Koran?' he asked.

The sergeant's uniform was torn on the right shoulder and stains of sweat showed down his front. 'I am a Catholic,' he mumbled.

'A Bible, then?' said Yasin, walking closer towards him and feeling the first heavy drop of rain on his shirt. He was cooled by a breeze, the wind getting up before the storm.

'Don't come any further.' The sergeant tightened his grip on the weapon.

A voice from the tannoy. 'What does he want?'

'The Koran.' The sergeant into his radio.

'I want to say a prayer for the dead,' said Yasin.

The heavy machine gun on the armoured personnel carrier moved around to cover him. Then the tannoy. 'Put your arms on your head.'

Yasin let his hands hang. 'I cannot go anywhere until I have finished the burial.'

The sergeant held the gun on him. He was experienced with the use of weapons and, like Yasin, he didn't appear frightened, just unsure of his orders. 'He wants to finish the burial,' he shouted, his head twisting slightly to send his voice back over his shoulder.

Crickets started up in the trees, the sound like a surge of water rushing through the compound. The sergeant was on higher ground than Yasin, halfway up the slope to the high wall, and the armoured personnel carrier was above that, on the other side of the compound wall, up a hill, visible from where he was standing.

'Yasin Omer, you are under arrest.' The tannoy again. He couldn't see the man giving the orders. A gust of wind swept past them, stopping as quickly as it had begun, and the rain fell more heavily. Glass, dislodged by the wind, crashed onto the roof of the verandah, shattering into small pieces.

Yasin stepped back, still facing the sergeant, feeling his way towards the tractor. Only a few yards away was a wall of jungle. The light was going quickly. The first kerosene and oil lamps were being lit in the villages.

'I am going to finish my work,' shouted Yasin, walking steadily sideways now like a crab, one eye on the tractor, the other on the sergeant.

'Then we will open fire.' The voice on the tannoy. The sergeant was too far away and the light too dim for Yasin to see his expression, to see the tension of the finger inside the trigger guard. But he saw flashes from the machine gun on the armoured personnel carrier, and the ground torn up around him. Bullets cut into the soil and sent up clods of damp earth.

Yasin stopped. The firing scared him. He raised his hands and put them on his head and shifted round so that he faced his attackers. 'Why can't I finish?' he screamed.

On the hill, there was a flash and an explosion, so loud and unexpected that the sergeant turned automatically towards it, his weapon raised. Flames engulfed the armoured personnel carrier. In the distance, men ran towards the house, crouching and weaving until they came to the jungle. Then the sergeant's shoulder was torn off and, as a second round was fired from behind Yasin, he was hit in the side of his head.

Someone threw Yasin to the ground, pushed his face down into the soil. He heard people running past him, but no one shouting in the bedlam, except in the distance where the marines were.

'Keep down, stay quiet,' whispered a voice. A hand was lifted from his neck. Yasin could see the body of the sergeant. Water poured down his face: he hadn't realised the heaviness of the rain. He listened to the crack of gunfire and in those few seconds felt relieved that the decision to finish the burial was out of his hands.

More glass fell from Musa's house and shattered. Two men ran past him, set up a machine gun and began firing. There was another loud explosion and flames from the Philippine marine position again.

'Get Up. Move backwards. Follow me.' A voice. A command.

Yasin stumbled to his feet. The sergeant's body was being mutilated by gunfire. 'Why?' he gasped to the man who had talked to him. A boy. But he wasn't interested. He ran down a slope towards the main house.

Round the back, by the swimming pool, Yasin saw Jesse, directing the assault by his men and preparing for a withdrawal. The gardener's face was as he had never seen it before. It wasn't that the smile and mischief were gone, for he had lost his family and had come to retrieve their bodies. Nor that his concentration was on commanding a battle. Yasin saw a face like a dark cold cave filled with nothing, a place where no one would want to go.

'Jesse,' Yasin began.

'Follow Edgar,' said Jesse.

'I have to get back to Samira,' he objected.

'Forget Samira.'

Edgar held his arm and guided him towards the wall of jungle beyond the compound. 'You can't go back.' Edgar was a thin man, younger than Yasin, his body wretched with sores and scars up his arm, the military jacket hopelessly too big for him.

'Why not?' said Yasin. 'I've done nothing wrong.'

'None of us have.' Edgar was walking quickly, his breathing was heavy. The rain made the path slippery and Yasin noticed then that he was wearing rubber thongs. They stopped at the compound wall. There was a gaping hole where the guerrillas had blown their way through.

'They were about to kill you,' said Edgar.

They walked and ran through the jungle, for more than an hour, keeping to paths and going through villages where eyes peered out of huts and sometimes children ran out with food for them. After an hour, Edgar was relieved by another boy. They could see the searchlights of helicopters, but the jungle was too impenetrable for them to break their cover.

When they reached the coast, they stopped in a cove, waiting just inside the undergrowth until Jesse caught up with them. The rain was relentless. Four boats came round the headland, long canoes with hewn tree branches and trunks lashed across to stabilise them from the choppy waters of the strait.

There were about twenty people with Yasin. They ran down the beach and men held the boats, swaying backwards and forwards with the waves, their heads turned away from the driving rain and splashing water.

They pushed off one by one, the helmsman standing up, controlling the tiller with the inside of his thighs and his hands. He stayed like that for the whole journey, watching for a rogue swell which could turn them over or a wave which would break off the stabilisers from the hull.

When the rain eased, Yasin could hear the engines but he couldn't see the boats. Water crashed over them all the time. The night was one of roars of water and engines, of cutting wind and coldness.

At dawn they pulled into a tiny island, no more than a ring of sand and a clump of bushes in the middle. They hid the boats, ate, listened for helicopters, waited until dark and put to sea again. Early the next morning, before light, they pulled the boats onto the beaches of Jolo.

Musa was waiting for him in the hills, dressed in military fatigues and with a pistol strapped to his side.

# Chapter Fourteen

*Karakoram Highway, Pakistan – China Border*

Sadek Khan looked at his watch as the customs officer signalled for him to come forward, and a truck from Pakistan roared past throwing clouds of dust against his windscreen.

Khan had been waiting for almost four hours. Vehicles lined both sides of the road at either side of the customs post between Pakistan and China. If his company had not paid a regular bribe Khan would have had to wait for more than a day and even then he would never have got through without paying someone.

Even now, they would call him in for a search which was bound to cost him more. But he would pay because he needed to get home to Rawalpindi on Thursday night in time for prayers and the holiday on Friday.

Khan was a Pakistani who drove for a Chinese trucking company in Kashgar. For more than twenty years during the summer he had brought its trucks back and forth across the border. His wife had said he could only take the job if he promised to come home once a week and only five times had he failed her. On three occasions, the Karakoram Highway had been blocked by snow and twice his truck had broken down.

But today was crisp, warm and clear, and the vehicles had just been serviced.

Khan pulled into the lay-by opposite a customs shed. He heard a sharp rapping on the doors at the back and in his wing mirror saw a customs officer standing impatiently with a clipboard.

Khan had never asked what was on board his vehicles. When he drove one into the depots at Rawalpindi or Kashgar another was waiting for him to drive out. The owner of his company was a powerful man with high-level contacts in Pakistan and China, so he did not expect any serious trouble. Only the constant paying out of money.

He kept a manifest in an envelope above the windscreen on top of his sunshade and, as he jumped down from the driver's seat, he unfolded it, glancing at the inventory.

'What's in here?' said the customs officer. His name was Shahid and he was young enough to be Khan's son. He couldn't have been at the post for more than a few months.

'General goods,' answered Khan, showing the young official his papers. If Shahid became too difficult, Khan would ask for Malik, the most senior man at the border post, who had been there almost as long as Khan had been driving through it.

He swung open the door and pulled himself up into the back. Sacks were stacked up to the front. In the middle were piles of hardwood and bamboo and to the back, where Khan was, it was more cluttered. Ten television sets in Panasonic boxes were piled up, with other electronic equipment behind. There were two Honda generators on the left and several cases of Johnny Walker Red Label whisky. Cartons of cigarettes and rolls of silk and other material had been squashed in as best they fitted.

'It's illegal to take alcohol into Pakistan,' said Shahid.

Khan helped him up. Shahid steadied himself by holding onto a leather strap hanging from the ceiling of the vehicle.

'Take it,' said Khan, understanding that they were playing out the first round of the negotiations. Shahid clambered forward and looked at the hardwood.

Khan put his hand into a back inside pocket he had sewn into his trousers and delicately separated one US$100 note from the wad he kept in there. It was slightly over the going price, but it would ensure a quick deal and preferential treatment when he met Shahid again.

Shahid brushed his finger down the hardwood, then brought it up to his nose to smell it. 'Is this illegal timber?' he asked.

'No,' said Khan, moving forward to join the customs officer.

'What is in these sacks?'

'Food, I suppose. It's on the manifest.' Khan unfolded the paper again, but the light was so dim inside and the writing so illegible, he couldn't make out what had been written down. 'Is there anything specific you are looking for?' he added, making it clear he thought that negotiations should begin now without wasting any more time.

Shahid took out a knife and made a small incision in the sack closest to him. Grains of corn fell out. He caught some in his hand and tasted them.

'See, it is food,' said Khan quickly, glad he had been proved right.

Shahid pulled the sack down and pushed others to one side until he was at the bottom of the pile, right up against the back of the driver's cab. He inserted the knife again, but had to cut through several layers until a fine orange-grey powder trickled out. He damped his index finger with saliva, dabbed the powder onto it, smelled it and then tasted some on the tip of his tongue.

'What's this? Heroin?' he asked, as Khan was moving to get closer to him.

Khan laughed. 'Pakistan exports heroin to China. Not the other way round.'

Shahid was on his radio asking for assistance. 'What is it then?'

Keen to please, Khan smelt and tasted the powder himself. 'Maybe it's a spice or something,' he giggled nervously.

'This has no smell,' retorted Shahid.

The truck shook and two more men climbed up. One was Malik, who slapped Khan on the back like an old friend. Khan moved back to let them through and while they were smelling and tasting the powder, Khan separated four more US$100 notes from his wad. Malik would not get into a truck for less than US$300 and only then for old friends.

Once Khan was through the border post, he pulled up to tape over the cuts Shahid had made in the sacks. He arrived home in Rawalpindi shortly before midnight on Thursday, just as he had promised his wife.

On Sunday evening, the night before he was to drive back to Kashgar, Khan developed a fever. In the morning he was short of breath and had difficulty climbing into the back of the truck. By lunchtime his fever was raging and he was vomiting blood.

Khan's wife took him to hospital in Islamabad, where, after nearly two days, his illness was diagnosed as being caused by anthrax. He died in a sealed isolation unit, under observation by the most expert scientists from Pakistan's own biological warfare programme. The doctors used several vaccines, but Khan, his body covered in welts, didn't respond.

The anthrax which killed the driver Sadek Khan at the China–Pakistan border was spirited away from the depot in Rawalpindi. The leads went cold.

# Chapter Fifteen

## *Beijing, China*

Tim Pack arrived at Jennifer's apartment well after midnight and she didn't ask about Walmsley or the gun. She poured him a brandy and ran him a bath. Neither said anything of substance. They talked blandly.

Sex on their last night together in Beijing was perfunctory and dutiful. Both held back their emotions and went through with it because it was easier than finding an excuse not to. Tim was restless, sometimes holding her, sometimes pushing her away. She heard him mumbling in his sleep, but had no idea what about. When he woke up, he lay on his back staring straight up at the ceiling, his hands behind his head.

She brought him coffee like a hotel waitress and he smiled at her, not speaking,

Normally, Jennifer would have forced an explanation. But the sight of Walmsley's gun reminded her she didn't even know the man she loved, if indeed she still did love him. She was like an awestruck child who had made a huge discovery. The presence of a gun, fear, violence and death, were such absolutes that even someone with her tenacity was powerless against them. She was taken over by a calm which she had never before experienced;

someone or something was in total control, by virtue of raw power.

Jennifer saw Tim off at the airport, as she said she would. 'See you soon,' he said, kissing her on the lips. She whispered. 'I hope so.'

On the way to the office, she felt empty and took the lift in a daze. She had allowed for the usual emotions of separation and she had factored them into her working day. But the secrecy, mixed with love, with fright, with betrayal, was unexpected. If she didn't have Tim she didn't know what she had. But if she did have him, she didn't know who she had.

'I'm taking no calls,' she told Amy as she walked to her desk without taking her coat off. 'Cancel my meetings for the day.'

'Even the meeting with . . .'

Jennifer didn't let her finish. 'All of them,' she snapped and closed the door behind her. She slipped off her coat and threw it onto the couch. A pile of Amy's telephone messages was in the centre of her desk. She moved them to one side and lit a cigarette.

Amy knocked softly a few minutes later and pushed the door open, carrying a cup of coffee. She was hesitant. The cup rattled on the saucer as she put it on the corner of the desk.

'Sorry,' said Jennifer. 'Didn't mean to be a monster.'

Amy fetched an ash-tray from the drinks cabinet: 'The meeting with Mr Beaton is at three o'clock. Do you want me to . . .'

'What meeting?'

'I think it's about your transfer to London, but he didn't say.'

Jennifer smiled. She got up and took Amy's hand in both of hers: 'Thank you, Amy. Yes, keep the meeting.'

With Amy gone, there was only one job Jennifer wanted to do before seeing Henry Beaton in the afternoon. She took the dust cover off her keyboard and opened the high security file which Beaton had named EXRP1Q'01.

With her own algorithmic password she set up a scramble on her ISDN line, which simultaneously linked her to the bank's massive global database, and specialised data in London, New York and Tokyo.

She drew down the blinds to rest her eyes from the outside glare and lit a second cigarette from the butt of the first.

The file began with registration documents of the Carlson Navigation Company in Cyprus with the Ministry of Commerce and Industry in Cyprus. Two other companies, Conrad Ltd and Salome Ltd, were listed as shareholders with a thousand shares divided between them worth a Cypriot pound each.

A letter from the Mediterranean International Bank based in Nicosia authenticated the arrangement, which allowed the company to register ships under the flag of the Republic of Cyprus. The company received its funding from external sources and it was considered a *non-resident* business. The registration certificate, written in Greek, was numbered 4272F.

Jennifer quickly scrolled down through the documents. She had seen dozens like them from all over the world, and anything registered in Panama, Liberia or Cyprus automatically made her suspicious.

Most of them turned out to be legitimate businesses exploiting loopholes in tax laws. But not this one: the names of the company directors for Carlson Navigation had given her colleagues in London reason for concern.

Two of the addresses were in England: one in Surrey on the outskirts of London and another in south London. The third was a post office box in Mombasa, Kenya. The nationalities of the directors were listed as Indian, but Jennifer guessed from the names themselves – Subramaniam, Sivanayagam, and Asirwatham – that they were Sri Lankan Tamils, or at least from the southern state of Tamil Nadu.

London had sent her the file because she had been involved in tracking the funds of the Tamil fighters. What had begun as a naïve and disorganised rebel movement had become one of the most organised and wealthy guerrilla operations anywhere in the world.

Two years earlier, Jennifer had traced a payment of US$252,000 from bank accounts held by Tamil guerrillas to the account of a South African arms dealer in Singapore. A shipment of small arms and anti-tank weapons was tracked to a rusting old freighter just leaving Burmese waters. When it was intercepted by the Indian navy in international waters, they found two hundred half-pound blocks of TNT explosive, a hundred plastic detonating caps, 35,000 rounds of 7.62 ammunition, 92 machine guns, shoulder-held anti-tank weapons, 400 automatic rockets and 300,000 automatic rifle bullets. The guerrillas had skilfully forged the signature of the Defence Secretary of Thailand on a fake *end user* certificate, the document needed before any weapon can legally be exported, showing that it is being purchased by a legitimate government.

Jennifer was thanked personally and in confidence by the chairman of the bank for her role in the operation.

The transactions before her now were far more complex. They had become more cautious since then, and this was something else. Whatever lay at the centre of the web was designed to remain hidden. The bank had become suspicious after ten million US dollars were transferred from an account in London to accounts held by the Tamil guerrillas. Jennifer found that within a week, the money left the Tamils to make a path through a well-trodden tier of private banks often used for money laundering in Asia, Europe and the Middle East. Then most of it disappeared into Eastern Europe and Central Asia, areas with which Jennifer was not so familiar and where some banks still used paper documents more than on-line computers.

By mid-afternoon, her head buzzing with ideas and the room clogged with cigarette smoke, she switched tack to examining the Tamil operation to bring in funds. Tamil communities overseas were a major source, together with legitimate businesses such as shipping companies, import–export firms, restaurants, hotels and fuel stations. Jennifer separated them off into sections and began calling up their accounts one by one.

It was a tedious job and she kept stopping to walk around the room. She opened the window to let in cold air and allow the smoke to escape. Every time she sat back down, she became more convinced that the ten million dollar transfer was unconnected with anything she was looking at. It was a one-off and out of pattern, which made it even more difficult to handle. The key was in Cyprus. Jennifer called up her e-mail address book and found the name of David Antoniades who she hoped still worked for the Central Bank of Cyprus.

She had met him a couple of years earlier in Brussels at a conference of the Banking Federation of the European Union. They ended up at a drunken seafood dinner, when he used all his Mediterranean charm to try to seduce her, and she loved it. It was an evening when nothing happened, but when they saw each other the next day she felt guilty that it almost had and regretful that it hadn't.

'Long time no e-mail,' she typed. 'Sending you attached document and looking for help.'

Henry Beaton walked in just after three o'clock.

'Ah, Jennifer,' he began in his British way, infuriating her, as if he didn't even expect to find her in her own office. 'I'm so glad you're smoking like a chimney. It means I can have a pipe while we talk.'

He sat down on the sofa, moving her coat which she had thrown there that morning. Jennifer smiled at him, then saved her files and waited until the computer was running with screen saver before she moved away from her desk to join him in the comfortable chairs.

'Find anything?' asked Beaton. He pulled tobacco out of a tin and poked it into the bowl of the pipe. 'I told London you were locked away with the file.'

'Something's gone missing up in Central Asia.' She pressed the intercom. 'Amy, can we have some coffee in here. Henry, for you?'

Beaton shook his head. 'You go ahead.'

'It's not an area I'm too familiar with.'

She had to wait while Beaton struggled to light the tobacco. He turned the flame up, dancing it around the top of the pipe, until there was sufficient smoke to draw it through his mouth. Then he settled back, like a man conscious of a great achievement.

'Well, if you don't know it, no one does.' He paused, brushing his lapels clear of tobacco and ash. 'Listen, Jen, I've got bad news for you. Or at least I think it's bad news. It's about your transfer.'

For the past five hours, Jennifer had forgotten about everything except money-laundering. And that was how she had planned it, so that Tim, Walmsley, the gun and the upheaval in her personal life would not spread like a virus through everything she did.

'Like what?' she said.

'Well, I don't know how to put it except to say, they're not going to let you go back.'

'Back to London?'

'Yes.'

'Why the hell not?'

'They say you're too valuable out here.' He waved his hand and pipe towards the computer terminal. 'Doing things like this.'

'But I can do that from anywhere in the world.'

'I know,' said Beaton.

Amy knocked on the door and came in with a tray, a pot of coffee and two cups. She put it down on the coffee table. 'An extra cup in case you change your mind, Mr Beaton,' she said cheerfully. She fetched fresh ash-trays, then left.

'You bastard,' accused Jennifer, ending the silence brought on by Amy's visit.

'Hold on, Jen, that's a bit strong.'

'You tell me otherwise.' Jennifer stood up so that she was looking down at him. 'The way I read it is that you want me here, so that the Beijing office gets the credit for the sort of stuff I've been doing this morning and you get a feather in your cap . . .'

'Jen, calm down . . .'

Jennifer didn't. 'And if I go, they won't replace me so you will lose the establishment of a senior member of staff. They will build up Shanghai instead and maybe – maybe, Henry – they'll make you report to a China country manager in Shanghai. And for you that would be the end of the road.'

Beaton was on his feet now, pointing a finger at Jennifer. 'You are so wrong.'

'Then tell me, Henry. Tell me otherwise.' She turned towards the window because suddenly she felt like bursting into tears and hated herself for it. She didn't need this today. If there were problems with the transfer and Henry had any intelligence, he would have waited to tell her.

But Henry wasn't that bright. He had been hired in Hong

Kong by the bank as a local man and had slowly crawled up the ladder to run a small office in Beijing. The decisions were made elsewhere and Henry was a few years from redundancy.

He sat down again and brought an envelope out of his jacket pocket. 'This is the message from me to London when you first asked to go. I'll read it to you.' He took out the memo, left his pipe in the ash-tray and fumbled in another pocket for his glasses.

'"Jennifer Chandler has requested an early end to her contract in Beijing to return to London for personal reasons. Although she was posted to China for her language abilities and local expertise, she has, in the past year, been more and more involved in her role as regional compliance officer. This is a job which could be done with equal efficiency from London. Indeed, the bank's policy is one of localization and we now have an adequate pool of excellent Chinese employees to call upon.

'"I see no reason to keep Jennifer here. She has proved herself to be a highly intelligent, reliable and loyal member of staff who should remain a valuable human resources asset to the bank for many years to come."'

Beaton handed the paper to Jennifer. 'That's it,' he said.

She took it and read it in complete silence. 'What happened then?' she said quietly.

Henry picked up his pipe and hunched over it, lighting up again. 'Officially, I don't know,' he said when he had finished. 'Unofficially, I heard the government wanted you to stay out here.'

'Which government?'

'Ours. Or at least mine.'

'What business is it of theirs?'

'Could be something to do with money-laundering. But really, Jen, I don't know.'

'But I'm an American citizen. The British government can't tell me what to do.'

'You work for a British bank.'

'I'm quitting.'

Henry nodded. He poured himself some coffee and drank it, black, without sugar and tepid. 'I told them that last night, after our conversation in the lift.'

'Who's them?'

'Personnel.'

'And?'

'They said if you broke your contract, which has another thirteen months to run, they had instructions to sue you.'

'They would what?'

'They would take you to court and sue you for substantial sums which could render you bankrupt and ensure you never got another job in mainstream international banking again.'

'Could they do that?'

'They would tie you down in legal fees and ruin you. Yes.'

'What did you tell them?'

'That I was appalled. They said it was an instruction which came right from the top. I was meant to handle the situation without using the threat of court action.'

'But you've used it.'

'Not as a threat, Jen, but as information. I am trusting you as a friend to respect the confidence.'

'Then you're stupid, Henry.'

'I do wish you would stop telling me I'm stupid.'

Jennifer flopped down onto the sofa next to Beaton and flung her head back, staring through the smoke out of the window. 'Sorry,' she said. She took his hand and squeezed it. 'I believe you, I suppose.'

'I'm not very good on the emotional side of life,' said

Beaton. 'But if your thing with Tim is strong enough, it'll bear a year of separation.'

Jennifer remembered Stephen Walmsley's one contemptuous remark to her at Tim's farewell party: *I understand the bank wants you to stay out in Asia.*

'Walmsley hasn't discussed this with you, has he?' she asked softly.

'Absolutely not. It's you, me and London. Why?'

'Then how did he know? He told me at Tim's party last night.'

Beaton shrugged. 'If it was the government. He's trade counsellor. He might know, I suppose.'

Jennifer was on her feet. She turned off the computer and locked the files under a secure password, took her coat from the back of the sofa and put it on.

'Where are you going?' said Henry.

'To see Stephen Walmsley.'

Beaton stood up, too. 'If I were you, Jen, stay and work a few more hours.'

'No. If he's going to screw up my life, I want to know why.'

'What I was saying, and you didn't get this from me . . .' Beaton paused irritatingly to concentrate on re-lighting his pipe '. . . is that the best place to catch him would be the China Club after eleven.'

Jennifer drove fast down Jiang Guo Men Wei, where the traffic was thin, and through Tiananmen Square. Once in Xirongxuan Hutong, she recognised the red lanterns of the China Club shining through the night-time fog, turned through the gate and parked under a tree which grew diagonally out of the concrete courtyard.

The club was a series of courtyards, rooms and corridors with lanterns hanging from the eaves and candles flickering in weather-proof glass boxes. Staff carried chairs and tables back and forth to rearrange the club for the next day's bookings as the last guests were finishing their dinners in private rooms.

Jennifer found Walmsley to the right of the first courtyard in the Long Bar seated in a leather chair by the entrance. She slowed herself to try to identify who he was with, an overweight man in a dark three-piece suit who was resting a brandy balloon on his stomach, had a cigar burning in an ash-tray on a table by his side and was talking to Walmsley who listened without expression.

As soon as she opened the door, he stopped, as he recognised her.

'Miss Chandler,' said Walmsley. 'I wasn't aware you were a member here.' Walmsley got to his feet. His jacket hung on the back of his chair and he was wearing a striped shirt and red braces.

'I'm sure the club has many members you are not aware of,' retorted Jennifer. 'Can I have a private word with you?'

Walmsley glanced at his watch. 'My God, it's getting close to midnight.' He looked at the other man, ignoring Jennifer's question. 'I do apologise, Jim, for keeping you from your beauty sleep.'

'It's been a pleasure,' said Jim. He was American. He pushed himself to his feet using the arms of the chair and once he had found his balance picked up the cigar from the ash-tray and put it in his mouth.

'Miss Chandler is one of the most talented young bankers in Beijing,' Walmsley continued. 'And the most beautiful.'

Jim shook Jennifer's hand. 'As a matter of fact, we were just talking about you,' he said.

His handshake was wet and limp. She threw back her

head, then tilted it towards him with a flashing smile. 'Oh yes. What aspect of me?'

'Your transfer to London,' said Jim.

'What the fuck has that to do with you?' It was the moment to swear.

'Jim Crabbe is from New York. He's your senior vice-president for special projects,' said Walmsley pointedly. 'I'm surprised you don't know him.'

Jennifer gulped. She began to blush and tried to conceal it. 'Henry Beaton didn't mention any visitors coming to town.'

Crabbe handed her a card. The bank's logo was embossed across the top, his title and name as Walmsley said: 'Oh, I take an overview, Miss Chandler. Henry is involved in the nuts and bolts. I'm in Asia to see how we're going to ride through the financial crisis. The sign of a good bank is how it manipulates the bust times. Any idiot can handle the booms.'

'Is that why you knew about my transfer?' Jennifer looked straight at Walmsley, her defiance on hold, her voice soft, her manner that of a cocky student in the company of her peers.

'I do apologise,' said Walmsley. 'I was terribly indiscreet at Tim's party. Didn't let you hear it through the right channels.'

'And you saw Tim after that, didn't you? At his house?'

Walmsley beckoned a waiter who was polishing a lamp stand near the bar. 'If we're going to talk about this properly, I think we should have one for the road. Jim?'

'For sure,' said Crabbe, settling back into his seat again. 'I'll get them to close the bar so we're not disturbed.'

Jennifer asked for iced water and, as the two men sat in their leather armchairs, she was left with a hard-back chair which she had to draw up between them as if she was being interviewed.

'I'll tell you candidly, Jennifer,' began Crabbe. 'Can I call you Jennifer?'

Jennifer nodded. 'Sure.'

'The currency and economic crisis out here is hitting everyone real bad. We need good people to handle it and we don't have many in this part of the world.'

'Send them in from New York.'

'That's the thing, you see. We would have to put them on special packages, expensive hotels. They don't have your kind of local knowledge.' He smiled and sipped his new brandy. 'And the bottom line is that you are bought and paid for. Saving money is the word of God nowadays.'

'I want to go back to London to get married,' she said, looking sideways at Walmsley.

'There's no problem with that,' said Crabbe. 'But you have to come back again.'

'And separate from my husband?'

'I could count how many days I've been at home in the last few months on one hand.'

Jennifer pulled Crabbe's card out of her wallet again and looked at it. 'You're based in New York?'

'That's right.'

'I'm a London hire and I report to London. It's a British bank.'

Walmsley coughed and intervened: 'I'm afraid that's where I got involved, Miss Chandler,' he said. 'You see, Her Majesty's Government is keen that British investment, which carries many of the bank's loans, continues to flourish . . .'

'That's Henry Beaton's job.'

Walmsley shook his head. 'Apparently not.' He turned towards Crabbe. 'Jim.'

'Much of the reorganisation . . .' began Crabbe.

Jennifer interrupted. 'I don't care, Mr Crabbe. If you block my transfer, I'm quitting.'

'Of course, Jennifer,' said Crabbe. 'Because you come from a privileged family with money. You have that option if you are prepared to face the consequences.'

Crabbe stopped talking. The waiter fiddled behind the bar at the back of the room. Lights were turned off in rooms outside and guests left for the night. Crabbe flipped open the catches of his briefcase and pulled out a folder. He spent an irritatingly long time reading it and rearranging papers.

Finally, he said, 'Henry said you would threaten to resign. The thing is we can't let you go. You're bound to us by contract for another thirteen months.'

'You're going to sue me.'

'Yes, Jennifer, we will.'

'Why?'

'That's the decision of the board.'

'Then sue me. I'll go to New York and fight you . . .'

Walmsley put up his hand. 'Hold it, Miss Chandler. We mustn't let things move too quickly.' He was on his feet, standing behind Jennifer, resting his hands gently on her shoulders. 'When you came in, Jim and I were discussing how to help you out of this problem. No one wants a fight.'

By now, Crabbe had separated half a dozen black and white photographs from the file and began passing them over to Jennifer. She took them and felt like a boxer being given a series of knockout blows in the first round. She was stumbling, out-manoeuvred, and it was only a matter of time before she fell.

'These were taken ten or eleven years ago, when you were, what, eighteen or nineteen?' said Crabbe. The prints had been blown up and the pictures shot through a long telephoto lens. In several of them, Jennifer's face had been marked by a dark, inked circle as if by a felt-tipped pen.

'I was under surveillance?' whispered Jennifer.

'We all are from time to time, I'm sure,' said Walmsley.

In the first picture, she stood at the front of a line of demonstrators, her hair tied back with a red headband. She held part of a banner with others which said 'Freedom and Justice for South Africa.' She wore a red summer tanktop and a pair of denim shorts, cut off and torn high above the knees.

'What are you on about? The ANC runs the bloody government in South Africa now.'

Crabbe passed her a second photograph. It was after the demonstration, well back from the police line. A black arrow pointed to Jennifer, who was standing on a grassy hill in Central Park with two other people. One was the local African National Congress representative in New York, the other, a European involved in raising funds for the ANC.

'You remember him?' said Crabbe.

Jennifer nodded. A third photograph was through the window of a coffee shop on the corner of Columbus and 72nd street, with just Jennifer and the European.

'His name was Vlad,' she said.

'And you had a brief affair with him.'

'Is that your next bloody photograph?'

The next picture was a photocopied record of US$150,000 being credited to her student bank account. Crabbe handed over another picture documenting the transfer of money to an account in Dhaka, Bangladesh.

'When you filed your tax return that year, you said the money was a donation to a Bangladeshi aid agency,' said Crabbe.

'Yes,' said Jennifer. 'I thought the ANC would raise suspicions. That's why I sent it to Bangladesh.'

'Vlad was – he's dead now – a Serb, raising money for the Yugoslav war,' said Walmsley. 'He used you as a cipher. He told you the money would go from Bangladesh to the ANC in South Africa.'

Jennifer nodded. Crabbe tossed another photograph onto her lap: 'It didn't,' he said. 'It went to Singapore and what you have on the right of the picture there is an end user's certificate. It went to buy arms to lay siege to Sarajevo, against the terms of a UN embargo in place at the time.' He showed her the last photograph: 'And this one for luck.'

Again it had been taken with a long lens, through a window with lace curtains drawn across it. There was no arrow or circle, because Jennifer was the only woman in the room. A bathroom door was open and half the bed was in shot, the sheets crumpled and the covers half falling on the floor. Jennifer was dressed in only her panties, her breasts clearly visible. She was smoking and gesticulating with her left hand. Vlad was lying completely naked on the bed.

'You shit.'

'Thing is, the tax issue is a federal offence. The arms money, well, you were an innocent party there.'

'It's nearly ten years ago.'

'A crime is a crime, Miss Chandler. There's no ten-year rule, and you're not off the hook.'

'Jim and I were working out the best way to clear up the problem,' said Walmsley.

Jennifer was swept with a mixture of fury and helplessness. 'You're saying if I go to London you'll sue me, and if I go to New York you'll have me arrested.'

Crabbe and Walmsley said nothing.

'That's blackmail.'

'Yes it is,' replied Walmsley. 'But look at it as altruistic blackmail. The airline wouldn't tolerate Tim being married to a convicted felon.'

# Chapter Sixteen

Jennifer called Pamela Jensen on her mobile after she had driven past Tiananmen Square and asked if she could go round and stay the night. Pamela was a friend and a fellow American and right now she was just what Jennifer needed.

Jennifer first met the Jensens on the day the Asia currency crisis began, with the devaluation of the Thai Baht. Jennifer was tall and striking with gallons of long blonde hair and unlimited confidence. Pamela was small and mousy, self-effacing like Jensen, a university sweetheart, with her focus far away from the upheavals of the global currency markets.

But Pamela was intrigued by Jennifer's work and she was envious of Pamela's family life. They hit it off straight away, with Jennifer often dropping in to play with Davey and Amanda.

'Thank God you called, Jen,' said Pamela. It was well after midnight, but she could hear the children playing in the background. 'Jack's vanished across to the States; he called five minutes ago and woke the children.'

Davey was ten with curly black hair and a love for models: trains, planes, ships, cars. Glue and kits cluttered his desk and shelves. Two years younger, Amanda was at the stage of wondering why she wasn't as fascinated by models as her brother, and as soon as Jennifer stepped through the door, Amanda marched up to her, presenting her with a doll, whose plaits needed sorting out.

'Make her look like a train guard,' she demanded, 'so she can play with Davey's train set.'

Jennifer abandoned her briefcase, took off her suit coat and sank to the floor to help.

'Dolls don't work the signals,' objected Davey.

'Well, I could if I wanted to,' insisted Jennifer.

'And you would be the prettiest signalwoman in the world,' said Amanda.

Jennifer looked up as the phone rang and watched as Pamela conducted a short, angry conversation with Jack.

'Now, he wants us to fly back and join him in the States,' she said when the call ended. 'And I'll be damned if I'm turning their schooling upside down to do that.'

## *London, England*

Tim was in the deepest sleep, but his dreams were violent and disjointed, as if he was aware that he was in bed alone with no one to hear his secrets. The tape played itself backwards and forwards in a kaleidoscope of visions until he was unsure whether it was himself or Ablimet Nor who was being tortured.

Jennifer's call woke him suddenly. 'I miss you,' she said straight away. Her voice was soft, not speaking as if she had another agenda.

'Hello,' he said drowsily.

'Did I wake you?'

'It doesn't matter.'

'It's just that I'm really missing you, I . . .'

'I miss you, too,' said Tim, automatically. 'I want you here.'

There was a silence. Jennifer had always been good at silences. 'I want to talk to you properly so much, but I can't,' she said eventually.

'Me too,' said Tim. 'I thought about it a lot on the plane. I love you and I want to be with you.'

The call settled him. Who knew if he and Jennifer would last? But right now she was his soulmate and she cared enough to call him on a dreary London morning. He was glad Walmsley had frightened her and shown her a glimpse of his real life. He hoped she had guessed.

Tim got dressed, walked out into grey, cold drizzle and caught a cab to the corner of Tottenham Street and Charlotte Street in the West End. The video tape entrusted to him by Walmsley was in his coat pocket and, in a queue outside a coffee shop, he spotted Ian Holden, a large man in his late forties, with enormous talents for separating and identifying sound.

'If you give me the tape,' said Holden, 'I'll go down the basement and get started.' He poured loose change into Tim's hand as he took the cassette. 'A cappuccino and tomato and mozzarella roll,' he said. 'When you get through the main door, go straight down the stairs and I'll be in the first studio on the left.'

Tim, balancing two polystyrene coffee cups in one hand and carrying the rolls with the other, walked to Holden's offices. They were set back from the road, through large, dark blue double doors which led into a courtyard.

The reception of the company was through another set of glass doors, with pictures of old black and white films on the walls and stainless steel boxes for reel-to-reel film stacked up to create the reception desk and stools for clients to sit on. On the ground and first floor Holden ran a successful video company. It was only downstairs and then round a corner out of sight from the washroom that the secure world began.

Tim buzzed the door from where Holden could see him, X-ray him and let him through two security doors, one after the other, so that he was caught momentarily in an air-lock between them, like in an embassy.

'You've got a bum of a product here,' said Holden as Tim walked in. He uncapped the coffee and stirred it with a plastic stick lying on the desk. 'Take a pew.'

'I've seen it about five times already.'

'Yeah, well I've seen a bit of it once, and Holden doesn't like what he sees.' He pressed a button to fast-forward the tape. 'I'll look at the end to see if there's any difference. But my guess right now is that video enhancement would be a waste of time. We only need to concentrate on the audio, right, and hear what he says. We don't need to see what's in the room?'

'That's right,' said Tim.

'Well, you've got two males speaking, so it's going to be difficult to separate the frequencies. And visually, the interrogator is leaning over the prisoner, so if we do any lip-sync predicting we may well get it wrong.' He pushed his chair back on its wheels and looked up at Tim who was drawing a panatella out of its box. 'And getting it wrong isn't what we want, is it?'

'We have to get it right,' said Tim, putting the cigar into his mouth.

'No smoking in here.'

Tim put the panatella back in its box. Holden stopped the tape and set the machine to play. He turned knobs on a piece of equipment about an inch high, set in a rack to the left of the television screen.

'The tape is about a schoolkid, about sixteen or seventeen, getting tortured to death in a Tibetan jail,' said Tim.

'I don't need to know the plot. Because what I'm going to do is reduce the frequency spectrum, divide it up into

158

bass, middle and treble. Take out all the bass shit, that's the rumbles and background noise, everything below 900 Hz, take out the treble shit, everything above six kilohertz, and concentrate on what I've got left.'

Holden finished adjusting the knobs. 'Just tell me if there's anything specific you're looking for and where it is.'

'Yasin Omer,' said Tim, 'is the key. If you get anything like that, we can work around it.'

'Yasin Omer. All right then,' said Holden, pushing his chair back towards the equipment and putting on a pair of headphones. 'Why don't you bugger off for a couple of hours, while I get this sorted? But come back before I go mad and start imagining things.'

Tim's mobile rang in the middle of Border's bookshop in Oxford Street and he thought it might be Jennifer or Walmsley calling, but he heard the familiar, hesitant tone of Jack Jensen. He stepped out in Oxford Street and found a quiet spot in a nearby shop front.

'When you kept asking me about fifty kilograms of anthrax, you knew something didn't you?'

'What's this about, Jack?'

'That's what's missing from Bachu. Fifty kilograms taken by professional people who killed my man.'

'That about sums up what I know.'

'But you didn't tell me about the tape.'

'I don't have the authority,' said Tim. 'Your people should . . .'

'I've just checked. We only know of its existence. We haven't seen it. Have you?'

'I'm working on it now.'

'All right, Tim, I don't want to compromise your integrity or anything, but if you find anything about a Nor on that tape call me, day or night. A trucking company called Nor.'

The line broke up and Tim wasn't sure if he heard right. 'Spell it.'

'N-O-R,' shouted Jensen.

'That's the name of the kid on the tape.'

Holden paced up and down his courtyard carrying a half-drunk cup of coffee carelessly in his right hand. Drops of cold coffee fell onto the concrete.

'Jesus, Pack,' he said, as Tim pushed open the double doors. 'No wonder you didn't want to sit through that again.'

'Not nice, eh?'

'What happened? Did the kid die?'

'Yes. He did,' said Tim.

'I may have separated a couple of things of interest. Difficult to tell with the different languages. But to your first question. No, sir. There ain't no Yasin Omer on that tape.'

When Jack Jensen flew into Washington, he was told to report straight to the director of the Federal Emergency Management Agency, FEMA, which would handle the impact of any biological weapons attack on the United States.

John Frazier, professional bureaucrat, manager, civil servant and dapper dresser, saw him straight away, skimming through a report, marking sections with a green highlight pen. Without taking his eyes off the document, he drank from a cup of black coffee, and let Jensen sit in front of his desk watching him.

Right now his focus was on Libya, Iraq and the Arab world, and as far as Frazier was concerned China was a reliable ally with as much relevance to his work as a threat from outer space.

Frazier had ended up in FEMA after the Marine Corps,

the Gulf War, Somalia and a dozen other skirmishes against Islamic extremists. He didn't welcome the distraction from Jensen, but any man who had been held hostage by fanatics in the Sudan would get five minutes of Frazier's time even if he had nothing to talk about.

It turned out to be a lot longer than that.

Frazier turned over the last sheet. 'I'm not sure I know what the hell this is about, Jack,' he said, putting down his pen and pulling out the cuffs of his shirt to make sure the links were showing.

He flipped open another file: 'The guy shot by the Brit in Beijing was former Soviet military, attached to a special unit which guarded the Institute of Microbiology at Sverdlovsk. It says here he left as a corporal after twenty years' service.'

'He couldn't have been much good,' said Jensen.

'That's why he's dead and you're alive, Jack,' replied Frazier, with the bemused tone of a man who respected the brilliance of scientists, but had never been able to categorise them as being of this planet.

Frazier discarded the report and read through another. 'The British have confirmed a guy called Ablimet Nor in a military video.' He wrote something in the margin of the paper. 'How come we didn't get this video?'

Jensen shrugged. 'Not my area.'

Frazier picked up his coffee mug and drank. '*Nor* was the name of the trucking company carrying anthrax through the Karakoram, right?'

'It's a common name in Xinjiang.'

'Point taken.' Frazier marked the paper again. More silence. More reading. 'Have we, I mean us, the Americans, corroborated the British line that fifty kilograms of this shit is missing?'

'No,' said Jensen. 'That comes from the SIS station chief, Stephen Walmsley, who got it from the Chinese. The only corroboration of something happening up there is that Sergei Nalyotov didn't turn up.'

'Nalyotov?'

'I was hoping to run him as an agent at Bachu to get details on the weapons programme there. He was shot dead by the men who stole the anthrax.'

'Got it,' said Frazier, going back to Jensen's report, running the highlighter to the bottom of a page.

'But you believe them?'

'Who?'

'The Brits.'

'Yes.'

'Never trust anyone outside of the department myself.' Frazier gave Jensen a big, full-on smile. 'There's always someone around who wants to screw you.' Frazier pushed the papers away from him. 'Do you know the strength of the workforce at Sverdlovsk?'

'It was four thousand in the eighties, then it dropped fast because of lack of funds.'

'Less than two thousand are there now. Scientists worth their salt have got jobs somewhere else: Iran, Iraq, Syria, China, North Korea. As, it seems, have the security goons. Do you know how much crap from weapons of mass destruction is floating around the world?'

'No one does, I guess.'

'There's nuclear shit, biological shit, chemical shit and there's people like you, Jack, the scientists, who need to earn a living, feed their families and are going out doing what they were trained to do for whoever pays the highest salaries. You're as lucky as hell to be an American scientist so you don't have to be a whore like them. They are the serial killers of mass destruction. We know *who* they are. We don't know *where* the hell they are.'

Frazier filled up Jensen's coffee cup. He turned his chair

to look out the window, then swung back round again. 'The guy who died in Islamabad sniffed the stuff in a Nor truck coming in from China?'

'That's what he said before he died. The embassy in Pakistan say that Nor is a wealthy businessman from Kashgar. The driver of the truck died together with several others up at the customs post. So we know the Chinese anthrax has gone through Pakistan.'

'Could be anywhere,' said Frazier. 'The chances of those customs officers finding that bag was like winning the lottery. The only way we'll know where this stuff has been is if someone dies again. And I'm saying "has been", Jack, because by the time the first symptoms appear they would have been gone for two or three days.'

'So we wait?' asked Jensen.

Frazier closed the files. 'And prepare. I want you to brief our people here. The whole story and the impact.'

# Chapter Seventeen

*Jolo, Southern Philippines*

S torms battered the southern Philippine coastline. The tracks through the Jolo jungle turned yellow with filth and water. Cattle, peasants and guerrilla fighters churned them up, unearthing teeming colonies of red ants which invaded everything and at night mosquitoes fed off moisture and spread malaria.

Camouflage positions on the hilltops hid men with handheld anti-aircraft weapons, together with heavy machine guns which would bring down helicopters. The camp was ringed with an outer and inner perimeter of guards. Landmines had been planted on the hillsides and the only glimpse of abnormality from the air was the clearing for the satellite dish.

The hut outside Musa's quarters led to a series of rooms hewn out of a cave running deep into the hillside.

Air-conditioning units were installed, brought in on smuggling boats from Malaysia, together with laptop computers and satellite phones, all powered by portable generators. At the front of the cave, Musa created his meeting room, sparsely equipped with twelve hard-back chairs and two collapsible card tables.

Yasin, an African and not a Filipino, remained an outsider.

Musa banned him from all but basic military training, small arms, light machine gun, unarmed combat and mine-clearing.

Yasin didn't carry a weapon, unlike the teenagers who strapped bullets around themselves and weighed their belts down with hand-grenades. He wore civilian clothes and, using his privilege as Musa's adopted son, he spent most of his time on a laptop or reading books. For a time, Musa became an international folk hero, with e-mail messages coming in from guerrilla fighters around the world, many of whom had formed alliances with him during the seventies.

The African National Congress might be in power, and the Provisional Irish Republican Army might have sworn non-violence, but Musa had met and trained with their members, creating friendships and respect which lived on.

Yasin whittled a piece of wood with a knife while he watched the computer log on and pick up the latest messages.

'Anything interesting?' said Musa, appearing suddenly behind him.

'Nothing,' he said, turning round.

'Nothing. Always nothing.' Musa sat down, heavily. He used his stick all the time now and Yasin thought of him as an old man. 'I have arranged for you to go back to school. You are wasting away here.'

'I wouldn't be if you let me help you, plan with you.'

'No.' Musa shook his head. He passed him an envelope, the flap open: 'Here are the details of an account with the Bank Austria AC in Vienna, together with the security passwords. When you turn twenty-one, you and Samira can have access to it. If I die before then, you have immediate access, and that's why I'm giving it to you now.'

Yasin held it, not looking, not even putting it in his pocket.

He appeared more crestfallen than anything else, as if he was no longer wanted at the camp. 'Why?' he muttered after a while.

'I'm not having you wasting away here in a silly war.'

Yasin picked up his knife and began cutting the wood again. 'Then train me to really fight, to fight the right people. The sergeant who was arresting me was following orders. He was drafted into the army and stayed to feed his family. Killing men like him serves no purpose. Killing his officer is a waste of time.'

'You are wise for your age,' said Musa. 'Go and finish your school. Get a good degree. If you still want to fight after that, we'll discuss it.'

A figure moved into the doorway, casting a shadow across the small room. 'Listen to him, Abu.' Hatimil Hassan, dressed in full camouflage fatigues, stepped inside and put his AK-47 assault rifle on the table next to the laptop. Outside Yasin saw men gather around the door.

'I'm glad I killed that sergeant,' said Jesse, pushing through into the room.

'Then fight the people who actually caused this,' said Yasin harshly.

'What's the good of that?'

'We won't be killing poor Filipinos, Jesse. Don't you see?'

'You are dreaming dreams,' said Hatimil Hassan. 'Are you suggesting that we blow up American embassies like they did in Africa?'

Yasin shook his head. 'They killed innocent Africans, the poor, the people they are meant to be protecting.' He turned to Musa. 'If you start another war with the Philippine government now, it will go on for twenty or thirty years. How many will be dead?'

Musa shrugged and looked towards Hassan. 'Fifty, a hundred thousand or more?'

'Right,' said Yasin. 'Well, if I'm going to be involved in the deaths of a hundred thousand people, I would like them not to be Filipinos. I would like them to be the people responsible for creating our problems and I would like to win at the end of it.'

Musa laughed. It was a chuckle like before, when he smoked cigars and argued with Yasin about the world: 'Who will you blow up, then?'

'The banks. The people who destroyed your businesses.'

'Well, I'll support that. I'll send you off to blow up the G7 summit.'

Yasin was about to answer, quickly and angrily, but he stopped himself and pointed at Musa: 'You are right. The world's economic leaders. That's exactly it.'

'Even then, we can't win,' said Jesse.

Yasin spun round to face him, his sharp brown eyes flashing with enthusiasm. 'Yes we can.'

Jesse laughed nervously. 'We should stick to what we know . . .'

Yasin cut him short. 'And achieve what?'

'To show them . . .'

'To show them what? That you're as bloody as they are?'

'Seriously, though,' said Musa, 'what *are* you proposing?'

'I don't know yet. All I know is that America became a superpower by dropping an atomic bomb on Hiroshima. It was an absolute measure taken to win and end war, and so far, for them, it has worked.'

'You mean we have to find our own absolute measure?'

'Yes,' said Yasin. 'And it's not killing marine sergeants.'

Musa got up, unsteadily, and Yasin moved to help him, finding him the stick and making sure he was balanced on it. 'Until then, you should continue your studies,' he said lightly. 'And that's what I came to talk to you about.

You leave tonight with Jesse. Take the two best helmsmen. Anyone else you need. And, Jesse, don't come back until you make sure he's on the plane to Delhi.'

## Washington DC, USA

Jack Jensen counted eleven people around the table, some straight from the labs in their white coats, some in the khaki uniform of the Public Health Service, others in civilian clothes with clipboards and briefcases. It was a sunny room, a bright day outside with smells of pine trees and winter flowers wafting through the slightly opened windows. Posters on the walls of the conference room showed the grim side of their trade: a man mutilated by smallpox; the fang of a malaria mosquito on a black arm; dead sheep on Gruinard Island in Scotland, closed by the British for forty years after an anthrax experiment; the Kurdish victims of an Iraqi chemical weapons attack; aerial photographs of the eight-storey Institute for Applied Microbiology at Obolensk, forty miles south of Moscow.

Frazier put his coffee cup noisily down on the table, a sign that the meeting was under way. 'Jack Jensen, whom most of you know, or know of, may or may not have stumbled upon something about which we should all be aware,' he began. 'Keep it within your departments.' Frazier made a dramatic pause, while he eyed the liaison officers from the agencies in Washington, CIA, FBI, Customs and the Pentagon, those whose line of command was outside the Agency. 'We don't want this leaked. At this stage, we don't want anyone at the White House, Congress, the Senate and especially the media knowing about it. That's the way we work here; let's stick to it.'

As Jensen got up to speak, they clapped him as they

had when he first walked in from the Sudan. Jensen stood, embarrassed, adjusting his spectacles, rearranging his papers and trying not to smile. At the Agency he was the quiet local hero who went to places most of them only read about in files.

Jensen told them about the missing anthrax, the dead Pakistani customs official, and the Russian killed by an allied agent without mentioning Tim Pack by name or nationality. Frazier added that the Russian came from the Institute of Molecular Biology at Sverdlovsk. Jensen told the story of Sergei Nalyotov, who was going to deliver a phial of anthrax, but had been shot.

'We've got detailed reports of Sverdlovsk and Koltsovo scientists going to China along with the mid-nineties weapons deal of Kilo class submarines and SU-27 attack aircraft,' said Tom Carey from the CIA.

'If this stuff is now making its way over here, it'll be easier to get in than heroin, cocaine or pornography,' said Sam Burnett who was the permanent liaison officer from US Customs. 'Dogs can't find it. Each biosensor unit would have to be adjusted to detect the particular strain of anthrax and even if that was done they couldn't be handed out to every customs post in the world.'

'In short,' said Frazier, 'we could have an incurable strain of anthrax bacteria, freeze-dried and possibly micro-encapsulated, making looking for a needle in a haystack sound like the dream job.'

'And you want to keep this in-house?' said Burnett.

'Unless you can tell me what anyone would do if we didn't.'

'Except panic,' said Carey.

'Now, since Jack brought us all here and since some of you might not have been through this before, I'm going to ask him to outline the scenario if this stuff finds its way onto American soil. Many of you might be familiar with the details, but bear with us.' He finished his coffee in a big gulp.

The slide projector threw blank light onto a screen and Jensen asked people sitting near the windows to draw down the blinds. 'Khan, the Pakistani driver, was treated with ciprofloxacin, doxycycline, together with the human anthrax vaccine,' he said. 'We think he was treated on the fourth day after symptoms appeared. We don't know precisely because it took him two days to get to the hospital and two more for a diagnosis. So the timing for treatment was well delayed.

'Even so, ciprofloxacin and doxycycline are meant to be ninety per cent effective. The vaccine should be ninety-five per cent effective. But Khan died of anthrax poisoning as if he had not been treated. None of the medication worked.'

'Are you saying there is no cure for this disease?' said Carey.

'Even the best vaccines will not protect against newly engineered micro-organisms. In one test, we tried our vaccine against twenty-seven different strains of anthrax in guinea pigs. It worked against eighteen. Nine were vaccine-resistant. A new strain can be created within a week and we must assume that to possess an effective deterrent bio-weapon, the Chinese would have manufactured vaccine-resistant strains. The truth is, there is no reliable medical defence against biological warfare, even using the most advanced and expensive technologies.'

In the silence which followed, Jensen pressed the remote and put up the first image. It was a sketched cityscape, with a handful of tall buildings in the middle, spreading out to single- and double-storey houses in the suburbs.

'This is a typical American community with a population of 100,000. If there's an attack on Washington, New York, Chicago, think ten times that: communities of one million. The meteorological conditions, thermal stability, relative humidity, are optimum for an attack. The prevailing wind is from the south-west. The quantity is fifty kilograms. The terrorists could either fly past the city in a light plane, send up a pilotless drone, stand on the top of this building.' Jensen pointed to a tall building at the edge of the city centre. 'Or disperse the weapon from the back of a truck.'

'Not like planting a nuclear bomb,' said Sam Burnett dryly.

'Exactly,' said Frazier.

Jensen continued. 'An infectious inhalation would be 8,000 to 20,000 spores, and 8,000 spores are invisible to the naked eye. The rate of biological decay in the spores in the first two hours after release would be negligible, and a medium to strong prevailing wind would be enough to blow through the whole city. The micro-encapsulation means it wouldn't be threatened by ultra-violet rays from the sun, like most bacteria or viruses. Tularemia, for example, only lasts for a few minutes in sunlight.

'Nalyotov told us that the coated particles of anthrax measure three microns, meaning they have been made big enough to settle in the lungs without being exhaled and small enough not to be trapped in the phlegm and passages of the upper respiratory tract, nose hairs and all that. 8–20 micron particles lodge in the pharynx. Smaller than that, say 7–12 micron spores, and they'll get down to the trachea. Once they're in the 3–6 micron size, they're into the lungs and three microns and below they're down the alveolar duct, the most serious part of the body for infection.'

Jensen flicked the projector control and a graphic was superimposed on the urban sketch. 'It's estimated that a clear twenty-four hours after the attack, five per cent of the population or five thousand people, would show symptoms. Before that, no one would be aware that an attack had taken place. The terrorists could be in another country.

'On the third day, twenty per cent would be ill. On day four it would be thirty-five per cent. In this city, that's thirty-five thousand people. In New York, it would be three hundred and fifty thousand or more. Ninety-five per cent of those people would need hospitalization. They wouldn't get it. But that's beside the point.

'Eighty-five per cent of those diagnosed on day one would die. The scales slide to fifty per cent of those showing symptoms on the fourth day. There could be people coming up with the disease a week after the attack because of undiagnosed symptoms. Because of late treatment, only thirty per cent of those would survive.'

Jensen paused, then continued in a softer voice: 'In the pulmonary form which this would be it is a horrible death. You begin with flu. Then high fever and retching. Your body comes up in welts and finally you suffocate to death as the bacteria devours your lungs.

'We estimate that half of the community of 100,000 would inhale and become infected by the anthrax. Of those 33,000 would die. Most of them would not be able to get medical treatment. To talk about hospitalization and civil defence is well beyond my remit. But the financial cost for this one community of 100,000 would be twenty-six billion dollars. I don't need to multiply that into just one major city for you to understand the economic impact.

'There are two other things to remember. Khan's death in Pakistan indicated that we might not have medication for this strain of anthrax. If it is the same strain as was developed by the Russians at Stepnagorsk, it could be three or four times more lethal than the situation I have just described. We don't really know what the effect would be.'

# Chapter Eighteen

*London, England*

March

They climbed up to the door of the flat in silence. The house was paint-peeled with water stains from broken gutters running down the walls. They walked past uncollected letters in the hall with footprints on them. The lightbulb was broken outside the door of the flat and Tim had to fiddle with the key before the door opened.

The flat was chilly, with a smell of polish and clean linen. Fresh towels were folded over the handrail in the bathroom and empty coat hangers dangled from the wardrobe in the bedroom. Tim put on coffee while Walmsley showered and changed his clothes.

'Is this the best they had for me?' said Walmsley, coming out and looking round him in disgust. 'I love the way they call these things safe houses in the films. Your house still let out?'

'Moved back in three weeks ago,' said Tim. He poured coffee for them both and opened the long windows which led out onto a terrace above the front door porch.

'More settling, I expect,' said Walmsley, pausing to pour milk into his coffee, then getting to the point. 'I need you to find Yasin Omer, that boy who saved your life.'

'Why are you so sure he's the same one?'

'Parents killed five years ago. Ran a tea shop in a town called al-Karadou, next to where Jack Jensen was being held. Adopted by Abu Musa, Philippine industrialist, together with his twin sister, Samira. Sounds like the same one.'

Tim stood up, the cigar half-smoked, hanging in his fingers, and walked through the French windows onto the balcony. 'I agreed to see you for old time's sake,' he said calmly. 'My line manager is in Customs House on Lower Thames Street.'

'It's been more than two months now, Tim, and we have nothing. Absolutely nothing.' said Walmsley. 'You ever studied the mind of a terrorist? Most of them fail in everything they try to achieve except killing. They get obsessed with operations and bomb-making and never get anywhere.'

'Stephen, I'm not interested. You called me. I met you at the airport. But I don't work for you any more.'

'Terrorism is intellectual violence,' continued Walmsley, ignoring Tim's objections. 'The people who do it are thoughtful and intelligent, but they don't care about killing people. They make excuses to justify doing what they enjoy. By all accounts your friend Yasin Omer is a very bright and violent boy.'

'I don't even know why he's a suspect.'

'He was a friend of Ablimet Nor, whose father ran the trucking business which brought the anthrax from China to Pakistan. His father is a millionaire who opened fire on the Philippine police when they tried to repossess his house because of faulty loans. Omer, himself, shot dead a soldier guarding the house, then fled to Jolo, the head-quarters of the Muslim separatists. Now, are you still telling me he's not a suspect?' Walmsley seemed to fall into a pensive silence, sipping his coffee. Then he said: 'Find your new job interesting, do you? Chasing cigarette smugglers.'

'Yes, as a matter of fact.'

'I had a drink with Jennifer in Beijing. Never really talked to her before.'

'She mentioned it,' said Tim.

'She understands now.'

'What? That you have no right to interfere.'

Walmsley stared at him, using his bright blue eyes to the full: 'Clarify one thing for me. Are you digging in at Customs because of Jennifer?'

Tim drew on the cigar: 'Yes, if you really want to know.'

'Supposing I tell you we'll clear her?' Walmsley smiled. 'As a favour.'

'Clear her for what?' said Tim cuttingly. 'To be the mother of my children?'

'If that's what you want. Yes.'

'I work for you again. You give me Jennifer?'

Walmsley nodded: 'That's the deal. You're a man of violence, Tim, and in Customs you don't even carry a gun.'

Tim walked back inside. 'What is it you want me to do?'

'We've found the twin sister. She was blinded in a terrorist bomb attack in the Philippines. She needs a special operation to restore her sight. Apparently it's simple, but it can't be done in the Philippines. We'll do it at Moorfields. You'll fly back with her. Hold her hand. HMG pays. I want you to get close to her. Use Samira to get to him. You and he have a useful bond.'

Tim stayed quiet. 'Yasin didn't save me. He simply didn't give me away.'

'He made a choice to lie,' countered Walmsley. 'He risked his life in doing it. He knew you tried to save his family. He understood that.'

'There's no evidence he has anything to do with it.'

'You keep saying that like a bloody parrot. What is it? You don't want to revisit your past from the Sudan? Tell me, if you want. You've never really talked about it.'

A breeze blew papers across the kitchen sideboards. Tim closed the window.

'Mills got you out, didn't he? Saw you onto the flight,' said Walmsley.

'What about the taxi driver?' asked Tim. 'Why wasn't he brought in?'

'We played bloody hard ball with them. But Uttman was told to execute you, you know. A little Islamic shit in the President's office gave him twenty-four hours to do it, to show Britain it couldn't carry out an act of war on Sudanese soil. You know Uttman was the guy who told us where Jensen was being held.'

'You never told me and I never asked,' said Tim.

'Uttman found Abu Musa, too. Got Yasin and Samira well away from the Sudan. He didn't like his government. Thought they were dragging the Sudan into an abyss and asked me to guess whether his own body would end up in an unmarked grave on some Khartoum wasteland or dropped into the Nile from a helicopter.'

'Which one was it?'

'Firing squad. Thirteen months ago.' The words were barely audible, as a gust of wind smashed against the French windows.

In the silence that followed, Walmsley rang his club and began booking a table for two for supper. 'I won't be coming,' said Tim, overhearing the phone call. 'I need an early night alone.'

Walmsley looked more disappointed than surprised, his face revealing that this city was no longer his, where old friends were no longer friends and the safest refuge was a club table in Pall Mall. 'Oh,' he said, picking up his coat.

Walmsley pulled on his gloves and arranged his scarf. Then he brought out an envelope and let the contents slide out onto the kitchen table: air tickets and two plastic bags of currency, US dollars and Philippine pesos. 'Just supposing he does have something to do with it?' he said. 'Supposing he's got his finger on the detonator of an anthrax bomb and you're the only person on our side who's ever met him? What are you going to do, Tim, drink champagne with Jennifer while a city vomits itself to death?'

Tim lay on the bed with the curtain open and the lights off. A yellow streetlamp shone straight into his room, illuminating odd things: the open wardrobe door, the shiny cover of his unfinished paperback, the sword decorated with Red Sea pearls which Mills had handed to him before he boarded the plane, which Yasin had promised he would get before he left.

There was an irritating darkness in his bedroom, shapes he couldn't quite make out because the street light didn't reach them. He turned on his bedside lamp, rolled over, picked up the telephone and dialled Jennifer's apartment in Beijing.

He looked at his watch. It would be four thirty in the morning and he was breaking his own rule: never phone when she's meant to be in. It rang and rang. She hadn't even put on the answer machine. Tim cut the line, tried again, fixed himself a malt whisky and fell asleep with it half drunk by the bedside.

A persistent car horn at the traffic lights outside woke him close to midnight. He finished the drink, lukewarm now the ice had melted, and dialled Jennifer again. This time she answered before the second ring. 'Hi ya,' she said, without asking who it was. She sounded out of breath as if she had run for the phone.

'It's me,' said Tim.

'Oh, hi.' She had expected it to be someone else. But Tim didn't have the nerve to ask. Only to say: 'I was trying to get you last night.'

He sounded pathetic, even to himself.

'Oh, I . . . hold on a second, will you?' She was gone, while he listened to the call waiting tone and she was speaking to the person she had been expecting. He swung his legs off the bed and sat up, the receiver to his ear, listening to an intermittent beep. Then he rang off.

Jennifer first called back while he was in the shower and he didn't answer it. She called ten minutes later, when he was dressed and about to go out. 'Sorry about that. Something sensational has come up at work.'

He hesitated, angry with himself for not being more in control. 'Oh it was nothing,' he said smartly. 'I've got to go to the Philippines.'

'Back to Asia so soon?'

'There's a problem with one of the local managers and I'm free to handle it.'

'I'll fly down and see you, then.'

'No,' replied Tim, too quickly. 'I'll only be there about twenty-four hours, then they want me back in London.'

Tim put down the phone, feeling deflated, and wondering why they kept up the pretence of Jennifer thinking he worked for an airline, or even that they had a workable relationship.

# Chapter Nineteen

*Zamboanga, Southern Philippines*

The sea was flat like an airport runway and the helmsman let the boat drift on the current for the last few hundred yards, steering it between the stilts of the water village.

Jesse tied up the boat and they climbed to the huts where Musa had taken him the day after Samira was blinded.

'I am going to see Samira,' said Yasin.

'My orders are to take you to Manila.'

'My orders to you are that I go to the hospital,' said Yasin, smiling at Jesse. 'I am not going to Manila without seeing my sister.' As they walked towards land, Yasin saw that some of the men had come back, armed, not bothering to conceal their weapons.

Out of Yasin's earshot Jesse talked to the driver of a battered Toyota taxi, then beckoned him over. 'I'm doing this because you tried to bury my family,' said Jesse. 'He will take you to the hospital. Then come back.'

Yasin got the driver to pull up at the Spanish colonial Fort Pilar, just past the Zamboanga State College.

It had been turned into a museum now, with dugout canoes and fabrics of the impoverished sea-gypsies hanging in air-conditioned glass cases as if they were an extinct species, and not the beggars who clung around the Zamboanga port, riddled with disease and scavenging for a living.

'Built by the Spanish in 1635,' the sign outside the fort said. 'Attacked by the Dutch in 1646; threatened by Chinese pirates in 1663; reconstructed by missionaries in 1666; cannonaded by the British in 1798; abandoned by the Spanish in 1898; occupied by the United States in 1899; seized by the Japanese in 1942; taken over by the Republic of the Philippines in 1946.'

It reminded him of the Khalifa's House and the Omdurman Fort in the Sudan, where he and Samira had pick-pocketed tourists. Africa was lucky: it hadn't been attacked for as long as Asia. But the attackers were the same.

He got the driver to take him past the Lantaka Hotel where he had planned to go with Samira for a drink on the day of the bomb. He didn't go in, but through the open double doors he could see across the bar, over the heads of tourists and far out to sea, a shimmering, flat blue which had brought him all the way from Jolo.

They drove up along Rizal Street. Yasin got out at the Rizal monument and looked around the little square where he had drunk coffee with Samira before they went to the mall. Nothing had changed. It could have been the same day. The pawn shop, the China Bank, the Asiatic Trading Company, the Giordano clothes store, the Rizal Café store ran down one side of the square next to each other and Yasin recognised the same boy on his knees scrubbing the steps of the bank.

They drove on past the burnt-out Metro Plaza. No building work had yet begun. A grubby yellow tape stretched across the entrance. The paving stones were cracked and broken. Shop windows across the road were mended, but taped over in case another bomb was planted in the shell of the building. Office girls walked past with a movement of the eyes, a tip of the head, to acknowledge that something terrible had happened there.

They edged their way through the narrow streets of old Zamboanga, wedged in between jeepneys and motorcycles, past the throbbing public market out onto Justice R. T. Lim Boulevard, heading west towards the hospital. Yasin got the driver to go past and turn up by the athletic field and drive east again down San Jose Road so he could observe the hospital grounds from the north.

'The Philippine marine units have left,' said the driver.

'Is Samira still under guard?'

'Yes.'

The suit made Yasin look respectable. His hair was close cropped and his skin was slightly darker than theirs, but he had let it get sunburned, so the blotches and patches of red didn't make him look out of place.

He kept his head lowered. He shuffled with the crowds and never pushed. In the lift, passengers pressed buttons for every floor. He waited until it stopped at the tenth floor and he tumbled out with everyone else.

He stood alone in the corridor. He recognised little things such as the fire extinguisher between the two lift doors. But when he turned right, he noticed that a new counter had been put up, half blocking the corridor, like a reception desk. A notice said: 'All visitors must show ID.' A ward sister was there writing on a register of patients. She asked Yasin if she could help him.

'No,' said Yasin. 'I'm on the wrong floor.'

He turned away from her and pressed the lift call button. The sister continued her work. A nurse came with a boy in wheelchair, his neck in plaster, and waited behind Yasin. Two surgeons in green short-sleeved smocks stood behind him. When the lift doors opened, Yasin stood aside to let the wheelchair in first.

A European stepped out, smiling and nodding at each of them as if they were all friends. He saw the sister and went straight to her. 'I'm from London for Samira Omer.' Yasin heard the voice, confident and clear. The European leant over the counter, reading the register upside down until he found his own name there and pointed at it. 'She should be expecting me.'

'I'll show you to her room,' said the sister smiling. She turned, walking down the corridor with the European at her side.

Doctors held the lift door open, and Yasin smiled apologetically, telling them to go. He watched the two figures turn left and go out of sight. Yasin moved quickly along the corridor trying the doors of the private rooms, opening each a fraction and closing it when he saw a person or heard a television set. The sixth room along, just before the end, was empty and clean. He slipped inside and closed the door.

Samira sat in a chair, a bright cotton shawl around her shoulders, her head turned towards the open window, the sun on her face. A Philippine love song was playing on the radio and a breeze made the curtains swirl around above her. She turned and smiled when she heard footsteps, a knock, the sister opening the door.

'He's here,' said Rudy Osmeña, who was by the bed reading a newspaper. He got up and took his silver name-card holder out of his pocket.

'Mr Pack is here,' said the ward sister. 'This is Samira Omer . . .' She waited while Tim took Samira's hand, '. . . and Mr Osmeña, who is Samira's guardian.'

She was older of course and more vulnerable than when he had seen her in the shop. Her eyes still found his, like they had then, drawing him into her world, but they flared and blazed even more wildly, perhaps because they were empty of vision.

Osmeña spoke first. 'So your government is willing to pay for her operation?' he said offering Tim a chair next to his, facing Samira.

Tim took Osmeña's card. He didn't take the chair or shake hands. 'As far as I am aware . . . er . . . Mr Osmeña, this is a private arrangement between Miss Omer and Her Majesty's Government.'

'We have a very special patient here. We have to take precautions.'

'Who's we?'

Osmeña flashed Tim a smile. 'I'll help you as much as I can, Mr Pack. Abu Musa was one of my closest friends.' Osmeña was not his own man. Tim could tell that by his hallmarks of status, the embossed name-card, the Rolex watch, the Italian shoes, the Charles Jourdan briefcase. Men right at the top rarely bothered with such things.

Samira shifted her weight to face Tim directly: 'Why exactly do you want to help me, Mr Pack?'

'We read about the plight of you and your brother in the papers in England. We know you're not British citizens, but you are at school in Dorset so we would like to help in whatever way we can.'

'I've almost finished school,' she said, pushing herself to her feet, fumbling for her stick as she got up. She felt her way over to Tim. 'Take my hand,' she instructed. Tim took it and she pulled herself towards him with it, like bringing a boat to shore along a rope. Then she put her hands on his face. Tim's clothes were fresh from having changed quickly in his room at the Lantaka. But his face was damp with sweat.

She ran her hand down the front of his chest and up and down through his hair on top of his head, then sat down again. 'Thank you,' she said. 'I have to know who I'm talking to.'

'I'm sorry about . . .' Tim felt inadequate and stumbled over the end of the sentence. But Samira was ready for him. 'Whether you're sorry or not, Mr Pack, you are only interested in me because I was blinded in a bomb attack. Perhaps it is good publicity for your doctors.'

The roar of an airliner arriving from Manila saved Tim from making an immediate response. 'I think we had better take this step by step, Mr Pack,' said Rudy Osmeña. 'I did fax your office when I heard you were coming.'

'You had no right to do that,' snapped Samira.

'Don't forget whose money you're living on,' retorted Osmeña.

'You've already faxed it, you say,' said Tim more calmly. 'I would have left by then.'

'Unfortunately, we have to go through some procedures before we can trust Samira in your care.'

'We are trying to help . . .' began Tim.

'And we are trying to protect a Philippine citizen. You play by our rules or not at all.'

'Clearly you know very little about how government operates,' said Tim sharply.

Osmeña smarted. 'Nor am I interested in learning about it, any more than you want to learn about banking.'

'Then perhaps you will let me do my job. My appointment was to arrange for Samira to travel with me to Britain.' Tim used her first name as if they were old friends.

Osmeña's mobile phone rang. He answered it, turning towards the window to get a better signal. 'Fucking liar,' whispered Samira so that Tim could hear. She stretched out her hand towards him, and when he took it she gripped him so he would notice. Although, they couldn't see, her eyes seemed to correspond with her handshake, alive with defiance and boring into Tim to tell him to come back and see her when Osmeña wasn't there. 'Come back,' she mouthed to him so blatantly that no lip reading was needed to understand her.

'Mr Pack,' she said loudly for Osmeña to hear. 'Why don't you listen to his proposals?'

Osmeña finished the call and looked at his watch. 'I have a meeting at the bank in fifteen minutes. Why don't you come with me? I'd like you to talk to our family lawyers.'

'As I said,' Tim flipped over Osmeña's card to look at the name. 'As I said, Mr Osmeña, I came to talk to Samira . . .'

'Go with him, Mr Pack,' said Samira, affecting her English school accent and injecting it with sarcasm: 'As you can see, I cannot talk to you without my guardian's blessing.'

They sat in the back seat of his Mercedes, cooling off with the air-conditioning. An armed bodyguard was in the front with the driver and as he got in Tim's feet knocked two pistols which had just been left on the floor in the back.

'You're staying at the Lantaka?' said Osmeña as they headed out of the hospital grounds. A Pajero jeep flashed its lights behind them and pulled out of its parking space to follow.


Yasin recognised Osmeña's voice in the corridor. He heard them walk past his own room, talking, then he opened his door and found the hospital corridor quiet and empty. Within seconds he was in Samira's room. She was in the bathroom, door open, splashing water on her face to cool herself down. He locked the door and she jumped, gasping in surprise: 'Who is it?' she said, grabbing hold of a towel.

'Me,' he whispered. She dropped the towel at the sound of his voice and reached out with both hands. Her hands searched urgently for him and Yasin took them.

'You're crazy,' she whispered. Samira's hands were all

over her brother's face, feeling every crevice and curve to make sure it was him. It was too sudden. Too strange. Too rushed to know what to say.

'I might be going to London,' she blurted out. 'There's an operation and the British government says it will pay.' She swallowed heavily and her eyes welled up with tears. 'They cancelled my visa after you ran away. Can you believe why they did that? Because of you and Dad. They say you're both terrorists now.'

'So why do they suddenly want to give you money?'

'I don't know,' said Samira, still softly, still knowing Yasin shouldn't be there. 'He said we're victims of a bomb attack.'

'He? The European man here just now?'

'He had a row with Osmeña.'

Yasin was silent for a moment. Then he said: 'I don't understand all this. Why's Osmeña with you?'

'He's paying for all this. He's made himself my guardian which is crap. I'm over eighteen. But because of Dad, we don't have money any more. I hate it.'

He stood close to her so she could smell him and hear the rustle of his clothes. 'It's all crap,' he said. They were quiet again, getting used to being together. 'Tell me what it's like. Where you and Dad live.'

'Did you see my letters?' he said.

'A friend of Musa's brought them and read them to me.'

'It's horrible. People are dying of malaria. I think Musa will die there, too. He keeps saying they can't fight and win. But if they don't they'll die anyway.'

'The newspapers said you shot the soldiers in cold blood.'

'Do you think that?' he said angrily. 'I didn't even have a gun.'

She squeezed his hand, then left it, saying she supported him like she always would, but not knowing if she believed him.

'They killed Jesse's family, all together in their house,' said Yasin. 'All I wanted to do was bury them. It would have been all right. But Jesse came back and killed the soldiers.' He paused. 'Musa wants me to go back to school. But it won't work, because everywhere we go gets destroyed.'

'Why? You've done nothing wrong,' she said. 'Why can't you give yourself up?' She spoke in a hopeless whisper as if she didn't even believe her own question.

'They'll jail me. Don't you see?' He thumped his hand on the windowsill. Meetings like this were no good. Too quick. She touched his shoulder and felt her way down to take his hand again. 'Be more trusting. Not everyone is out to get you.'

He pushed himself away from the window, lay on the bed and looked at the pictures she had propped up next to it, each with a tear so she knew which was which. 'Everyone has a family except us and now we can't be together.'

'That man, the Englishman,' said Samira. 'I thought I recognised his voice. I'm getting good at voices now,' she added proudly.

'You haven't been with him, have you?' said Yasin, sulkily. 'Like the boy on the motorbike?'

That made Samira laugh out loud. 'Absolutely not,' she said, dropping her voice, remembering the danger. 'But you should get a girl. It's good fun.'

'You've actually done it?' Curious now, propping his head up on his hands. 'What's it like?'

Samira giggled. 'It's fun, like I said. You probably don't get much of a chance in stuffy old India.'

'I don't even think about it much.' Yasin moved away a pink teddy bear to give himself more space on the bed. Osmeña must have bought it for her because it was nothing like the toy animals she had collected in Musa's house. 'What about the English guy, then? You said you . . .'

'You'll never believe this, but he sounded just like the man who bought the swords from us the day Mother and Father were killed, the one you say tried to get us to move away.'

'You're sure?'

'No, of course not. But . . .' Samira didn't finish as if she thought she was sure, but he didn't want to hear it.

'They're using you to get to me and Musa,' he muttered, almost to himself. 'That's how it works.'

Samira shook her head. 'I don't think so.'

'Don't be so innocent,' said Yasin abruptly. 'I've been reading so much about all this. The English, the Americans, the Philippines: they're all on the same side against people like us. The government has asked the British to help find me because I killed . . .'

'Stop it. Stop it,' broke in Samira. 'Don't poison yourself like that. What happened to your dream to become a millionaire?'

'Is he coming back?'

'I've asked him to.'

'I should go,' he said, not moving, not wanting to leave, only reminding himself of the danger of staying.


Guards at the hotel made Osmeña take the gun out of his briefcase and leave it at the door. His bodyguard was let in with his weapon. The Pajero jeep stayed parked outside, engine running for the air-conditioning with three men inside.

'I wanted to discuss my proposal with you away from Samira,' said Osmeña, pulling out a chair in the empty coffee shop. In early afternoon, the hotel was deathly quiet. With the heat there was a huge stillness, as if everyone was asleep or getting drunk at the bar outside.

Tourists sat on stools there, loud Australians and Americans, shy Hong Kong Chinese with golf bags and scruffy Russians down from Vladivostock to pick up cheap deals from bankrupt Asian businesses.

'They say Zamboanga is on the edge of the world,' said Osmeña, as Tim looked around, his eyes both curious and cautious.

Tim drank the iced water straight down, leaving the cubes clinking noisily in the bottom of the glass. 'It is a place people invade and flee from,' continued Osmeña, smiling broadly as if that one clever statement told Tim all he needed to know. He opened a silver cigarette case which matched his name-card case, offered one to Tim, who shook his head, and took one himself.

'You know your government revoked Samira Omer's visa,' said Osmeña, enjoying the surprise on Tim's face. 'It appears contradictory that they are now paying for her to go there.'

'That must have been the Home Office. I am from a different department and I wasn't aware of that,' said Tim. 'But I am sure we can get . . .'

Osmeña opened his briefcase and gave Tim a letter on British Embassy paper. 'See, there was not even an apology or a reason.'

They were both quiet as Tim read it and then looked out of the window across the sea, where the fishing boats of the sea gypsies, their colourful cumbersome sails patched like quilts, splashed in and out of the water, heading for the mainland. He felt like a shit. A shit for his country.

'You know why they did this? said Tim.

'Her father and twin brother are both suspected terrorists. I gave guarantees. Put up money.' He shrugged. 'I am just a Filipino.'

'We can get this changed, I'm sure,' said Tim.

'That's no longer the point. I need to know exactly who you work for before I entrust her to your care.'

A call to Walmsley. A message to the embassy, copied SINGER. Another letter to Osmeña saying there'd been a mistake. Circumstances had changed. Just a visa. One bloody phone call and it would be fixed. Walmsley would handle the embassy and they would fly her back and fix the operation. In the evening he would spend a long time with Samira. *Come back*, she had mouthed to him. So she wanted him there. To say what? That her brother had fifty kilograms of anthrax for sale?

'A consultant at Moorfields Eye Hospital in London has developed a new technique for dealing with the sort of traumatic eye injuries which Samira has,' Tim said. 'When he read about them, he contacted the government to ask that we arrange her passage. He will waive his fees. As far as I know, there is no other place in the world this work can be done and it is not in anyone's interest that you stand in Samira's way.'

Tim arrogantly took Osmeña's gold-plated Dunhill lighter from the table. He paused while he lit a cigar: 'Besides, Samira is over eighteen. If she wants to go, she can.'

Tim let down the blinds of his room to stop the sun burning right through it. A smell of aromatherapy oils and cheap scent hung there from the masseuse who must have been in with the last occupant. The air-conditioner, rust caked into its vents, rumbled like an old motorbike. He stood in front of the cold air, cooling his body of its sweat and heat.

When he arrived from London, he had just dumped his bag on the bed, showered and put on a clean shirt. He unzipped the bag now and rummaged through to satisfy himself that Osmeña's men hadn't been there before him. He checked the socket and the mobile was still there charging, keypad locked.

He unclipped the phone from its charger, activated the keypad and dialled Walmsley's home number. Walmsley was awake and Tim told him.

'What time are you there?'

'Two in the afternoon,' said Tim.

'I'll tell the embassy now. It'll have to go through the appeals directorate at the Home Office in Croydon and they won't be in for three hours. If you get her to Manila tomorrow she can pick it up.'

Tim read off the fax numbers for Osmeña and the Lantaka and rang off. He was just about to put the phone back on charge, when it flared into life again. It was Jennifer.

'Your office in Manila says it doesn't know anything about you,' she began. The line sounded strange with her voice fading and strengthening just in that one sentence.

'Say again,' he said loudly. She repeated herself word for word. Tim bent down to turn the air-conditioner off and it died with a last obstinate burst of noise.

'Why should they know?' he said angrily.

Walmsley was right. Either the job or Jennifer would have to go. He couldn't work like this, when his own girlfriend could blow his cover. Airline manager, spy. Bloody mess. 'If I've been sent down to sort out a management problem, they're not going to tell head office, are they?'

He heard her gasp, a reminder to herself of how stupid intelligent, impetuous people could often be. 'You mean . . .'

'I mean I don't want to talk about it right now,' said Tim. And he wasn't faking it. The humidity was back immediately. Stickiness on his neck.

'It's just that I found out something really incredible and wanted to talk to you.'

'I'll be back in London the day after tomorrow.' He really

wanted her gone. Not that he thought Osmeña's men were tapped into his mobile. But he wanted to have a swim, a drink at the bar, a panatella, the air-conditioning on, a cruise through CNN and BBC World, maybe a massage and a sleep. He didn't want a girlfriend (and he noticed how his thought pattern threw up *a* and not *the* girlfriend) accusing him of being a liar, or a girlfriend having seen a gun through a garden window, testing him, pushing him for the truth when she knew he couldn't tell it.

He turned the air-conditioner back on just as she said: 'It's about Walmsley.'

The fresh clatter of obsolete machinery blurred the words, but he was almost sure that was what she said. In a split second, the image of Jennifer in his Beijing garden, seeing Walmsley with the gun, flashed in front of him as clear as day, like a warning signal on a motorway. Danger. Accident. Fog. Diversion.

Bad images. Trauma. Ablimet Nor in his cell, Jennifer on the grubby snow outside his house, Walmsley in the empty living room smelling of packing cases. The images were young, milling around with the bad old ones, the hooded sack, the vomit, the beatings, the ones which refused to go away, which insisted on staying fresh.

'In London. I'll call you,' he said abruptly and cut the line.

He set up the CD player and speakers and put on a gala of French Opera. It was soothing, like he imagined heroin would be if he ever took it. He thought of having a swim, but fell asleep to the rattle of the air-conditioner, the distant blast of foghorns in the Sulu Sea and the cries of the sea gypsies selling woven cloth and seashells on the beach below the bar.

# Chapter Twenty

W hen he woke, a single-page fax had been slid underneath his door. It was dark outside. Lamps swung from the masts of fishing boats and a weak, bluish haze hung over the sea.

Tim slipped on a pair of shorts and a T-shirt and went, barefoot, to the reception desk to get copies of the letter. It was fine, written directly to Samira Omer at the hospital on British Embassy letterhead, and giving the name of the consular official she should contact when she got to Manila.

The receptionist, whose badge named him as Edgar, disappeared into the back room with the fax, studying it as if it was his homework. A loud guitar riff sprang up from near the sea wall and Tim walked across to get a better look. A band was setting up, testing the amplifiers and, amazingly, a strobe light to work outside, competing with the lights from the sea and the moon.

Keeping an eye on the reception desk, he perched himself on a bar stool. The barman slid a bowl of peanuts towards him, wiped crumbs and puddles of drink off the surface of the bar and asked Tim what he wanted to drink. Tim shook his head.

The Australians and Americans had gone. The Hong Kong Chinese were onto XO brandy with piles of name-cards in front of them, pinned under weights so the wind wouldn't blow them away.

A lone drinker sat in the middle and Tim recognised the accent of an Englishman, about his own age, locking the barman in conversation and spinning back and forth on his stool searching for more interesting companions. Tim slid away.

A Russian was at the reception desk, stinking of booze and cheap perfume. Tim drummed his fingers and looked at his watch. Edgar stayed with the photocopy machine, gathering up the sheets with agonizing slowness.

The Russian stopped drumming and picked up a brochure with which he fanned himself. 'Hot,' he said.

Tim hoped that was all he could say in English. He smiled, agreeing, to which the Russian replied, 'I love the Philippines.' He dropped the brochure and sprawled a vast cupped left hand over the tensed biceps on his right arm to indicate the sexual pleasures of Filipina prostitutes.

'Me too,' laughed Tim, just as Edgar emerged with the copies held by a paper clip. He was about to begin writing a receipt when the Russian interrupted, demanding to be given his room key first. Edgar turned to get it. Tim stared silently at a tourist poster ahead of him.

It was then that he caught the flash of intent in the man's eyes. It was nothing tangible, more like recognising when a woman wants you to make a move; when a driver is going to cut in in front of you; or when a man intends to attack you, mess up your hotel room or kill you.

Tim knew he was right when the Russian walked away. It was the same walk, the same pot-belly that he had seen in Beijing, the same type of man he had beaten up in the China World Hotel. As if they came from the same unit of thugs for hire.

Back in his room, he unplugged the CD player, speakers,

mobile-phone charger and tossed them into his bag, together with the laundry which was on the floor in a plastic bag and four shirts on hangers in the wardrobe. He checked the room, the bathroom and outside on the balcony.

He asked Edgar to put his bag in the hotel safe.

'It is very big for the safe,' said Edgar. Tim peeled off a twenty-dollar note whose value had soared during the currency crisis.

'I met this crazy woman in Manila,' he whispered. 'You know how it happens.' He pressed the money into Edgar's hand.

'All women are crazy,' muttered the receptionist, slipping it into his trouser pocket.

'She's chasing me down here.'

'Give me a different room, don't tell her I'm here if she turns up.'

'Mr Pack, right?' Edgar took the bag and put it on the floor beside him. He looked at the rack of keys behind him. 'You'll be in room 126, OK?'

'Hey, I'm Joe,' shouted the tricycle driver outside of the Lantaka. 'You're the man from London come to help the blind girl, right?' This before Tim had even said where he wanted to go. Joe kicked the motorcycle starter while Tim climbed into the back seat. For such a contraption, it was surprisingly comfortable, until a gust of smoke from the exhaust blew right across his face. Joe looked over his shoulder.

'How do you know?' yelled Tim.

'Everyone knows.' He revved the engine. 'You going to the hospital?' He set off as Tim shouted that he was. They bumped their way out. 'Have you met her? I hear she's real pretty.' Unlike most drivers, Joe didn't use a rear-view mirror for eye contact. His head turned right round, ghastly, nicotine-stained teeth, pockmarked and scarred face, eyes crazed with enthusiasm and a baseball cap from the Barcelona Olympics.

'She is pretty,' agreed Tim.

He had worked out that he would go in the morning in one smooth movement: check out of the hotel, hospital, airport, Manila, airport, London. The Russian worried him and he would slip Osmeña money and get him to send a couple of his goons as far as Manila. If necessary, he would get a guy from the embassy to keep an eye on them on the leg to London. In a couple of hours he would call Walmsley and tell him about the Russian. But not now. It was too early.

'Wait here,' said Tim at the hospital.

Samira was alone, listening to a novel on a cassette, and Tim knocked on the door to get her attention.

'Who is it?' she said loudly, because of the headphones, and hesitant, knowing her vulnerability, fumbling to get the earpieces out and turning towards the door, towards the sound, the only sense to which she could react.

'Tim Pack,' said Tim softly. 'I just came to say, I think the trip's fixed. We should be able to leave tomorrow.'

She stretched out her hand and Tim took it. 'Will Osmeña let you?'

'He has no choice.'

Samira shook her head. Streaks of blood running through the whites of her eyes from her injuries, but the expression was there. 'In Zamboanga, he can do anything he wants. Did he ask for a bribe?'

'Not as such.'

'Give him one. Anything. Money. Whisky. Anything to let him know you respect him. If he asks, I'll tell him you're doing that. It'll be safer.' She paused, turning her head away, as if there was somewhere else to look, something else on her mind. 'Do you like sex?' she said. It was sudden, a non sequitur, and she didn't wait for an answer. 'Because if you do, go to the Mermaid. I'm told that's the best place in Zamboanga.'

She let go of his hand, unclasped it as a signal that their short, disjointed conversation was at an end. 'I like sex, but my brother disapproves. I'm trying to get him to find a girlfriend.'

Tim thought he was good at his job, credited himself with being observant, having an accurate memory, nerve and judgment. In the lift, he laughed out loud to himself at Samira's farewell.

'The Mermaid,' Tim yelled at Joe, as the tricycle engine spluttered into life with a black belch of exhaust.

'You want dancing?' He pushed it into gear and they pulled away.

'Dancing's fine.'

'Did you fuck her?' Joe was saying. 'She's African or something isn't she?'

'Something like that.'

Joe left his tricycle in a mêlée of others outside the club. Letters on the neon sign were broken, so Tim couldn't make out its name. They went up concrete steps, Joe sticking with him to get his commission, and when Tim's white face appeared at the door, there was a flurry of activity: tables being cleaned and pushed together, tablecloths unfurled and laid on them, chairs with cigarette-burnt seats replaced, ash-trays emptied, torn menus taped up, and a bottle of beer with flakes of ice peeling off it put on the table with a chilled glass and bowl of peanuts.

There were six other customers, two tables of three, Philippine men, four of them in uniform whose features were obscured by flashing lights from the ceiling. On stage a lone, bored girl, as delicate as porcelain, danced stark naked, apart from her high-heeled shoes. She chewed gum, partnering her own image in a mirror.

The song switched to Gloria Gaynor's version of 'I Will Survive' and he found himself tapping the table and drinking the beer more quickly than he had planned. The girl was getting into it as well, touching her reflection on the mirror.

He didn't have a bad job. Maybe it had just been London, the drizzle, the inefficiency, the vile coffee shops, the rudeness. Walmsley in his wisdom had seen that and sent him away again.

The girl bucked her head like a horse, climbed up a steel pole and hung upside down. *Did you think I would crumble? Did you think I would lay down and die?* went the words. Walmsley knew about flashbacks. God, the man probably had a hit-parade of them himself. He wondered why killing the Russian hadn't worried him. He had hardly given it a thought, certainly not a cinematic re-run like he did with the Sudan. Probably because he had won, like in Bosnia. There was no pain. He had done the right thing and won.

Another girl skipped out, deftly slipping off her panties as she appeared. The men at the other tables clapped. They lifted their glasses to Tim and ordered a beer for him. He was the British official, the only man in Zamboanga with any hard currency. When you've got the Russians coming in and the Americans running away, you know things are bad.

After that they put on 'Lady in Red' and the owner came over and sat with him. She tried to talk but everything was too loud and the bar was filling up. She asked if he wanted to sit with a girl, but Tim said he didn't. He ordered a hamburger with fries and ketchup. The first dancer smiled at him. She had a butterfly tattoo on her left buttock.

For some reason, when 'The Power of Love' came on, and

the girls were rolling together on the floor, he remembered his conversation with Jennifer. *It's about Walmsley*, she had managed before he cut her off. Stupid. One day perhaps he would balance impatience and control with curiosity. *I don't want to know*, he had told her. But it was a lie: he did.

His shoulder was being tapped, and Tim turned round to find Joe, standing next to him, unusually solemn. Someone slid into the seat beside him, the face hidden by a sea-gypsy scarf, head covered with a baseball hat pulled down over his eyes.

'If you make any move to let anyone know I am here, I will kill you.' He spoke as quietly as he could with the music. 'You say you want to help my sister. My name is Yasin Omer.'

Joe stayed with them, bumping along behind, while they were in the taxi. Yasin was in the back seat. He had told Tim to get in the front. It wasn't as if he was being abducted. He was the British official everyone in town knew about and he needed to talk to Yasin. They rode in a difficult silence heading east out of the city centre. Tim recognised the grounds of the hospital. They went past a cemetery on the left, a television tower, a church and a Caltex fuel station at a crossroads. On the other side was a school and after that the street lights became more intermittent, with big pools of blackness in between, and then they stopped altogether and it was like the road to Meroe, with dark signs and landmarks, flitting past, but meaning nothing.

After five minutes, they turned left towards the sea, onto a track with big smooth pot-holes, hewn out by rain and cars, and filled with water. There were bushes and clusters of palm trees on both sides. The headlights lit up people, mostly children, hitting along their cattle with sticks, and waving as the big car went past.

Tim turned back, but Yasin wasn't responding. He looked straight ahead, and Tim wasn't even sure that it was him. The driver changed down to negotiate a deep rut. Two rifle shots echoed across the emptiness from nowhere, going nowhere, shooting at the moon or at birds in the dark. Maybe Tim had set himself up for a killing.

When the road forked they took a left turn and drove over the brow of a hill. The air smelt different, of fishing boats and seagulls, and a few hundred yards away there were huts. Tim could make out the outline from the lamps shining around them and other lights sparkling out at sea.

'It reminds me of the banks of the Nile,' said Yasin suddenly. He told the driver to stop. Joe pulled up behind them.

'Yes, it does,' said Tim.

Yasin spoke in Tagalog to the driver, who got out of the car and walked round to Joe's tricycle. 'Do they know each other?' asked Tim, meaning: is Joe on your payroll? Was it a set-up for him to pick him up outside the Lantaka?

'Not that I know of,' said Yasin. He took off the baseball hat and removed the scarf. 'Recognise me?'

Tim did. The high forehead, the dark confident eyes, in control and curious.

'Thanks for saving my life.' Tim was turned in his front seat, his arm resting on the back.

Yasin shrugged. 'You tried to save us.'

'It didn't work though,' Tim softened his voice. 'I'm sorry.'

They were both quiet for a bit. Tim still wasn't sure how to handle him. Yasin was a kid, no more than nineteen, wrapped up in the old cliché of living through the crises of a ninety-year-old. It didn't show on his face. There was no twitch. No dull eyes. No flitting back and forth. No nervous scratching, like his agent who got shot. Probably

202

no flashes of trauma, undigested by the brain. Maybe he should tackle it head-on. *Just tell me, Yasin, that you haven't got fifty kilograms of anthrax in the boot and we can all go home.* He had the mobile phone clipped to his belt. They could ring Walmsley and Yasin could tell him directly.

There was the flare of a cigarette light from behind them as Joe and the driver lit up cigarettes. Tim took a panatella and offered it to Yasin.

'What's this?'

'What I gave you in al-Kadarou that evening. A small cigar. It's what gentlemen smoke when they don't like cigarettes.'

'You gave me three.' Yasin took it. 'What gentlemen smoke when they don't like cigarettes,' he repeated. 'You gave me Macanudos made in Jamaica.'

Tim chuckled. 'You have a good memory.'

Yasin put it in his mouth, then took it out, ran it under his nose and dropped it into the top pocket of his shirt. 'If you hurt my sister, I'll kill you,' he said.

'I won't,' said Tim. The flame of the cigarette lighter lit up the inside of the car. He did it to see what was around, whether Yasin had a weapon in his hand. He let the light flicker over the back seat as he rolled the cigar around in the flame. The back seat was clear. Yasin's hands were out on his lap and resting on the inside of the door.

Tim drew on the panatella. 'I'm taking your sister to England for an operation which might make her see again.'

'I know. That's why I found you.'

The conversation with Uttman came back to him. *I am an archaeologist*, Tim had claimed. *Then I don't value your chances*, said Uttman.

'I work for the British government,' said Tim.

'I know. That's why you could get my sister a visa so fast.'

'How do you know about the visa?'

Yasin didn't answer. Headlights from behind lit up the inside of the car and the bushes around them. A truck crawled past at walking pace, the driver had his head out of the cab window, shouting and taking a cigarette off Joe. The village by the water was illuminated and there were brief, static shapes of cattle grazing.

'Why are you interested in my sister and me?'

'Your friend Ablimet Nor is dead.'

Yasin looked up and stared straight at Tim warily. Something passed across his face like a cloud, showing not grief, not surprise but a glimmer of interest. He made a curving motion with his forefinger of a knife slicing a throat.

'Yes. I'm sorry,' said Tim. 'I saw him die on video.'

'How?'

Tim was certain he swallowed hard and tried to hide it. But it was difficult to be sure.

'He was tortured to death by the Chinese police.'

Yasin opened the car door to get out and then seemed to change his mind. He left it ajar, which turned on the inside light so Tim could see his face more clearly and maybe that was what Yasin wanted.

'There was a raid on your school. They took a Tibetan away as well.'

'Thondup.'

'I don't know his name.'

'Is he dead too?'

'I don't know. I watched a Chinese video tape of Ablimet. It wasn't very nice.'

'You're telling the truth.'

They could hear the murmurs of Joe and the driver talking. Footsteps as they paced around outside. A lighthouse flashed on a peninsula miles away, showing how clear the night was.

'The Chinese accused Ablimet of being a terrorist. His father too.'

'He was a drawer,' said Yasin, fumbling with his choice of words.

'A what?'

'A cartoonist. An artist. He wanted to paint.'

'Jesus.' Tim let the smoke drift out of his mouth. He looked away from Yasin. There was silence outside, a vast night-time of cattle, fields, jungle, beach and fishing boats. 'And his father?'

'A businessman. That's all I know.'

Tim threw the cigar out of the window. It didn't go out straight away and he watched the glow on the grass and mud by the car. Yasin shut the car door and it was dark inside again.

'You haven't come here to tell me that my friend is dead.' There was a cadence of anger in his voice.

'I've come to ask you if he was a terrorist. If you . . .'

'I didn't kill those soldiers,' Yasin said, too quickly. 'I was going to bury Jesse's family and go back to Samira.'

'I know. But is there anything else?'

'Like what?'

He was right. Like what? Tim thought, anticipating Walmsley's debrief. Did you actually ask him about the anthrax? Are you saying he denied it outright? How do you know he was playing straight, Tim? He had the control. He took you out of the night club. You were in his taxi. The absurdity would not translate to supper at Walmsley's club. The kid's lost his parents, twice if you count the downfall of Abu Musa. His sister has been blinded in a bomb attack. He's branded as a terrorist in a hick guerrilla war no one knows or cares about. You tell him his best friend has been tortured to death. You're sitting on a dirt track between a road and a beach and you ask him – what?

'Are you planning an attack with biological weapons?' said Tim. 'Was Ablimet Nor planning an attack with biological weapons?'

'That's what you came here to ask me?'

'Yes.'

'And if I tell you, your job is over?'

'This part of it, yes.'

'If I tell you, will you still take Samira to England for the operation?'

'We're on the flight tomorrow. I can fix for you to come too.'

'Ablimet wanted to be an artist. I want to be a millionaire.'

'Like Musa.'

'The reason I'm here is that Musa is sending me back to school.'

'Will they let you back?'

'Musa says they will.' Yasin looked at him suspiciously. 'If you give me away, I'll kill you.'

'I won't,' said Tim.

Yasin opened his door and got out. Tim opened the front door and they both stood resting against the tops of their open doors.

'What do biological weapons do?' asked Yasin. 'I've read a bit about them.'

'This one is a powder, a dust, you can't even see it,' said Tim. 'And a tiny amount can kill thousands.'

Yasin stood silently, deep in thought, then said: 'Like a nuclear bomb?'

'Easier to use.'

'You tell your government that I'm not a bloody terrorist,' said Yasin, his voice louder. 'Tell them I'm a schoolboy. Tell them I'm a spin bowler for the school. Tell them Abu Musa is my new father, that he's an old man who hasn't killed anybody.'

'I think he has.'

Yasin shrugged: 'It doesn't matter.' Then he grinned. 'You know, if I was going to be a terrorist, I would find a place where all the bankers, presidents, prime ministers, finance ministers were all together and blow them to smithereens. That would teach everyone a lesson.'

'Where are you going now?' said Tim, more softly.

'To school to try to become a millionaire. I told you what you wanted to know. Now you take my sister and make her better.'

'Come to London. I can protect you there, too,' Tim tried again.

'Like you protected my parents.' Yasin got into the front seat, and Tim saw the glint of a gun, resting on the driver's lap. 'All these people are Musa's people. So don't follow me. Don't give me away or they'll kill you.'

'You threaten to kill a lot of people,' said Tim as Yasin shut the door.

The engine flared into life, lights brightening, the car moving forward, bumping through pot-holes and heading off towards the beach.


Joe and Tim watched a fight on the steps up to the bar. Friends pulled two drunks, guns drawn, away from each other. Judging by the line-up of military cars outside, serious Zamboanga power brokers were in there. It was steamy hot, with smells of men's body odour and cheap perfume.

The night had peaked and the girls danced listlessly on the stage, more interested in the mirrors and the poles than their customers. The tables were cluttered with bottles of beer and whisky. The men smoked, red-eyed and cutting deals which would be broken in the morning.

Tim's table was waiting for him and his hard cash. Joe sat

with him and ordered a beer. The owner whispered in Joe's ear and Tim said: 'I don't want girls.'

'She said there were two Europeans looking for you.'

'Men? Women? What type of Europeans?'

'Poor. Russian, she thinks.'

'What did they want?' shouted Tim across the table.

'They were drunk and didn't have any money.' The owner melted away and Tim gave Joe a panatella. The band played 'A Whiter Shade of Pale', which seemed to perk everyone up. The girl with the tattoo on her buttock was on the stage, this time with a pair of red panties and a fake fox fur round her neck. 'She likes you,' said Joe.

'I'm married,' said Tim.

'That's a stupid answer,' said Joe, bursting into laughter. He liked the cigar. Its class. 'Those Russians were asking about you at the hotel as well.'

'Jesus,' whispered Tim.

Joe played the smoke around his mouth, showing a haphazard set of black teeth. 'If you want to rest easy tonight, you should go back with two. Not one. Take two, don't sleep with them. No one will touch you. No one will blackmail you.'

Room 126 was far down the corridor. The girls walked around the room fixing the curtains and the air-conditioner, knowing the room better than Tim did. He had taken the one with the tattoo and a friend of her choice, because Joe said they worked better like that. It had taken them an age to change, plenty of time for Tim to get himself another beer, one for Joe too, and one for the mamasan for goodwill.

They rode on the back of Joe's tricycle, exchanging names, and Tattoo unbuttoning Tim's shirt to feel his chest hairs. Lots of giggling, then serious talk with Joe, more money to get past the night porter at the Lantaka, then more again to get Tim's bag from the locked office.

Tattoo plugged her phone onto recharge and after finding MTV on the television, she channel-surfed, while her friend massaged her shoulders for her. When they got bored of it, they undressed and had a shower.

Tim's phone battery was on low, so he plugged it in next to Tattoo's. Joe was right – he felt safer with the girls around. Their line of protection ran through Joe to the mamasan to the military thugs who ran Zamboanga. Even the Russians couldn't be that stupid.

He took off his shirt, threw it in the corner of the room and lay on the bed with his hands behind his head. He probably dozed because the girls startled him when they came out, wrapped in towels.

It was when Tim was in the shower, sharp and cold to wake him up and cleanse the sweat from his pores, that he heard a frantic rattling of the door, which he had locked. He shut off the water, and he heard Tattoo's urgent summons. 'Mr Tim, Mr Tim, come quick.'

Tim opened the door dripping and naked because the girls had taken both towels from the bathroom. She was sorry. He could see it in a face which had been dealt too many of life's lousy hands and, by picking up the wrong phone, she might have just dealt herself another one. Tattoo thrust his mobile phone into his hand and gave him a damp towel. Tim held the phone away from his ear so as not to get it wet.

'I've just e-mailed you the stuff about Walmsley.' It was Jennifer. She knew it was one in the morning. Her voice was flat. 'But it was sent back. Have you changed your number?'

'Jen . . .' He was about to say 'I can explain', which is one of the more ludicrous things a man ever says to a woman.

'Any other way I can get it to you?'

'My laptop's in London. I'll check it out when I get back.' There was no clever remark about another woman picking up the phone at one in the morning. Jennifer was ice cool. 'Please. This is important,' she said and rang off.

# Chapter Twenty-one

## Chinatown, Manila

The forger looked at Yasin, then at the photographs laid out in front of him. He was about sixty, wiry, with squinting, bloodshot eyes. He wore a cloth around his neck and dabbed his forehead constantly with it to stop sweat getting on his work. Passports were arranged in front of him, according to nationality, and the forger then separated them into further piles according to their uses: stolen, and reported to the authorities; sold; and manufactured by the forger himself.

Jesse and Yasin sat on hard chairs on the other side of the forger's large table. Although it was mid-morning, the slatted window let in hardly any light because the wall of another building was only inches away. The passports were lit up by a desk lamp and a fluorescent light flickered overhead.

Jesse had directed the driver straight from Manila domestic airport, along Roxas Boulevard to the squalid riverside slums of Binondo. They had walked for the last half-mile, through meandering lanes between huts, damp with a stench of rotting food and open sewers, hot, but with no sun because everything was darkened by rain clouds.

Yasin felt a sense of something sinister about the whole area.

He had walked through squalor in Khartoum, Zamboanga and India, but never had he been subjected to so much foulness, such choking smells, footpaths of human waste and garbage and slime spilling out into ditches and then into the river where children played and washed.

The forger coughed and spat into a bowl on the edge of the table. 'For India, you should take this.' He picked up a dark blue passport and tapped it with the end of a ball-point pen. 'Australian. You don't need a visa,' said the forger. 'How many times will you use it?' He put the pen into his mouth, sucking on it and peering at Yasin.

'He has to come back,' said Jesse.

The forger put the Australian passport to one side, like a shopkeeper noting purchased goods. Then he half stood up and leaned over to get a maroon passport. 'Return here on a British passport, then. Again, no visa needed. Visas cause problems.' He flicked through the pages. 'This was stolen in Europe. So there will be no record here.'

He placed it on top of the Australian passport. 'Do you shave yet, boy?' he said bluntly.

Yasin ran his hand around his chin. 'Sometimes,' he said. The forger looked hard at him, then opened a book of passport photographs, inspecting them one by one with a magnifying glass, like a police album of convicted men, glancing up after each one at Yasin. Then he stopped and pulled one out from under the plastic cover. 'I will do two more things for you.' He turned to Jesse. 'You say money is not an object?' Jesse nodded; the forger went on: 'I will make you two passports, one British, one Singaporean, and give you two more which are real, a Philippine and a Malaysian. The British and Singaporean will have you without a beard, like now. The other two will be with a small beard, and it is better that you wait and grow one before you use them.'

He wrote down the order on a piece of paper and put it

on top of the other two passports. 'So that will be six in all.' He looked at his watch. 'The first two I can give you in one hour. The others you can pick up when you come back, or I can courier them to you in India.'

'But I have to hand my real passport in at school when I get there,' said Yasin.

The forger smiled and dabbed his neck. 'I will give you an Indian entry stamp for tomorrow's date. Your flight should arrive at 01:15.' Then to Jesse: 'There will be no charge for that.'

## Delhi, India

Yasin arrived in Delhi in the early hours, when international flights at the gloomy airport land and take off, tempers were frayed and life appeared to be at its lowest ebb, but the immigration official stamped Yasin's Australian passport without a second thought.

He had a new Citibank Visa card and had committed to memory the trust numbers of the bank in Austria.

The hotel driver sat hunched over the wheel wrapped in a blanket smelling of stale sleep, swaying along the expressway which took them to the city. He didn't speak. Yasin was a boy and black, of no caste or stature, so there was nothing to say. Yasin watched fires burning by roadside construction sites, bundles of itinerant workers, sleeping, warming themselves, oblivious to the swirling roar of traffic.

India was worse than the Philippines, thought Yasin, but better than the Sudan. The same reflections always came to him during this dreadful journey in from the airport and as he got older he wondered why India, the Philippines, the Sudan – any of his homes – could never make themselves as good as Europe or America.

The hotel was a bustle of people, as if it was the middle of the day, and when he got to his room, Yasin was wide awake, restless and impatient to find out if what Tim Pack had told him was correct.

He watched television until six o'clock when he called the school and asked to talk to Ablimet Nor. 'He has left,' said the boy who answered. He imagined him answering the ringing phone by the main door of the house, hit by the cold morning wind from the mountains and now regretting it. Yasin didn't recognise the voice. 'Left? Why?' he asked.

'I don't know.' He sounded hesitant. 'All those who were part of the Ablimet Nor clique have been expelled,' said the boy. 'Who are you?'

'I am a friend,' said Yasin, trying to sound American, anything but himself. 'Is Venkataraman there?'

'As I said, all those . . .'

Yasin put down the phone. Something told him to do it, something instinctive which seemed to protect him more and more since the fighting at Musa's house. He called the home number of Gurjit Singh, his finger on the phone to cut it off, if he felt the same again. As soon as he got through, Gurjit said, 'Where are you?'

'The Imperial Hotel.'

'I am coming, now,' said Gurjit and cut the line.

Gurjit refused to go to the coffee shop and insisted on meeting in Yasin's room. He told Yasin about the raid on the school. He, Venkat and three others had been expelled. Thondup and Ablimet had been taken away by the Chinese army. Gurjit had seen the trucks and the green-peaked military caps.

'You are booked here under your real name?' he asked when he had finished.

'Why?'

'They will find you. You have to get out of this hotel. Get out of this country. Go back to the Philippines.'

'I can't,' Yasin muttered. Then he told Gurjit what had happened; that he was wanted for murdering a marine sergeant; that he was a guerrilla fighter; that he had no home to go back to.

'What a bloody joke,' said Gurjit. 'Here we are, the next generation, trying to move on from war and these bloody people keep dragging us back into it. You know Venkat is in town?'

'Why should I know?' answered Yasin impatiently.

'His father has disowned him. He's joined the Tigers.'


## Vanni, Sri Lanka

Yasin lay shivering, half awake, half asleep. He felt as if he was being thrown around in a fast-flowing river. He heard faint jungle sounds like voices from another world and splashes of rain falling from a tarpaulin stretched over the back of the trailer.

The drops hit arid, gritty soil, turning it from yellow to black. Soon the ground steamed with water and heat. Rotting branches became waterlogged and hard ruts in the track softened into mud, the water trickled away into the undergrowth. The journey from the coast had been monotonous, endless, sad, and now with the bad weather it was irritating as well.

The heat, thirst, hunger, sun and rain, had each taken turns with him. He understood nothing of what the fighters were saying, but the noises of the fighters were like in Jolo, gun metal, boots in mud, chatter, wheels churning up soil, still, hot air and great clumps of slow-moving cloud, sometimes letting through the brilliant stars of the

Sri Lankan night, sometimes bringing more rain, mosquitoes and fireflies.

Yasin woke up properly when the trailer bumped to a stop and the tractor's engine quietened. As he stretched out, he touched cold flesh and remembered that the two boys lying either side of him were dead, killed in a helicopter attack that afternoon. The Russian Mi-24 gunship had flown in at treetop height just as they were trying to run from a jungle clearing.

It was so low that Yasin saw the gunner firing short bursts at individual targets, the white hands of the pilot on the control. He was from Ukraine, they told him, hired along with the helicopter.

By the time they had reached cover, the helicopter was back. With no identifiable human target, the gunner swept the jungle with fire, until they set up their machine guns and made it too dangerous for the pilot to come back again.

'Yasin, Yasin.'

He heard Venkat's voice before he saw the figure running awkwardly in military fatigues, encumbered by belts of ammunition criss-crossed over his chest. Yasin slid down from the back of the trailer, his clothes damp and his skin scarred with insect bites. Others lifted the bodies out and laid them on canvas sheets on the ground.

The arrival of the tractor was a big event for the camp because it brought supplies from the ship from Thailand: medicine, cloth, building materials, everything except weapons; they had plenty of those because of their raids on army camps.

'You made it. You bloody well made it,' said Venkat. 'What an experience you have had from being hunted down in the Philippines to becoming a guerrilla fighter with us. And just to think your actual home is in the Sudan. For me, it is a mind-boggling thing to imagine.' He greeted Yasin, out of breath, the buttons of his camouflage fatigues carelessly left undone like a rebellious schoolboy who wouldn't do up his tie.

'You're the first foreigner to be allowed to join us. I had to persuade them.' They embraced as they never would have done at school, two people seeking common ground outside of the environment they were in.

Venkat told Yasin that, after the raid on the school, he had been interrogated at the Indian army camp in Dehra Doon for two days. They beat him then threw him out onto the street, literally, pushed him so hard that he fell over, grazing his hands on the road. That was when he decided to join the Tigers. He had run away from home and the school and he hadn't even told his father yet where he was.

Yasin told him his own story. He wasn't sure whether Venkat sympathised or welcomed Yasin's experience as confirmation of his own ideals, part of a wider war, evidence that they were doing the right thing by fighting.

Everyone around knew Yasin was a foreigner. They skirted round the two of them talking and looked away when Venkat pointed to things in the camp.

At the far corner of the jungle clearing were rows of graves, each with a marker or headstone inscribed with a victim's name. In the middle was a Hindu shrine, ringed by trestle tables, each covered with a bright red flag fiercely emblazoned with the face of a tiger.

The mothers of the boys killed in the helicopter raid arrived, distraught. They set up incense sticks, lit them and brought out framed portrait photographs of young fighters to line up with those of others killed in the war: rows and rows of them, decorated by rings of yellow flowers, displayed side by side in their dozens. This was a real war, where mothers cried and children fought. New fighters in fresh uniforms gathered in a corner like schoolchildren preparing for a parents' day.

'You are so privileged to have been brought to Vanni as soon as you arrive,' continued Venkat. 'I had to go to Kutti to convince him that you should be with us. He wants to meet you. It's a big thing for us to have a foreigner with us. Do you know about our leader, Kutti? Have you read what a great man he is?'

'I've heard of him,' said Yasin.

Venkat pointed to a huge picture of Kutti near the shrine, looking relaxed, clean shaven with a moustache and open-neck shirt. Flanking him were pictures of the great commanders of the movement who had lost their lives: Kittu, Pranavan, Gena, Raja, and it went on.

'We'll fight until the whole of Tamil Eelam is liberated,' Venkat enthused. His eyes shone madly as if his main ambition was to have his portrait garlanded with flowers at his own funeral. 'They wanted to send you to Batticoloa, under the Eastern command, but I said you were too special, that you should be with me.'

Yasin wondered if Musa ever inspired the same fanatacism as Kutti.

'Special because you're educated, like me,' continued Venkat. 'Kutti takes a special interest in education. You know what he said? "My ambition is to mould a new generation of youth who will be the architects of our country's future".'

Venkat must have thought that he had summed up the whole campaign with that one quotation. He stopped talking and they watched the ritual for bringing in the dead. The bodies were adorned. Relatives swished flies and washed away blood. There was a smell of flowers and rotting human flesh. A lone voice from within the trees broke into song. A wounded boy screamed out in pain.

Venkat took Yasin to his quarters under a tarpaulin hut, strung out from a cluster of trees. He showed him the water supply and stayed while Yasin threw a bucket over him to wash himself. He ate with him and took him to the quartermaster to collect a uniform, webbing, weapons and a cyanide capsule attached to a chain, like a dog tag.

'All Tigers wear this around their neck,' said Venkat. 'If you're about to be captured, you bite it and swallow. All of us have one, even Kutti.'

'I don't carry weapons,' said Yasin. 'In the Philippines I didn't wear fatigues.'

'But this is the Tigers,' insisted Venkat, escaping into more slogans, like he had at school. 'The Sri Lankan armed forces are carrying out genocide against our people. They are bombing our civilian population centres. We must fight against the rape of our women, the murder of our children and the blockade of food and medicine to the liberated territories.'

So Yasin carried an automatic weapon, pouches of ammunition, and a cyanide capsule around his neck.

Yasin was ordered to go on an operation against the army. Venkat was enthusiastic and handed him over to the patrol commander, who was the same age as them but a generation and a world apart. He had lost an eye in a battle in the east. His surviving eye was calculating, steady and faded of colour.

'What can you do?' he asked in English.

'I've been trained on the light machine gun,' said Yasin.

'In action?'

Yasin shook his head. 'Only practice.'

It was dark and raining when they set off. At the main road, Yasin was told to stay in the jungle and watch while the commander laid explosives. It was a straight road heading north-south, but torn apart by the treads of armoured vehicles and water which swilled around in pot-holes and never drained away.

The commander found a culvert and sent two boys down to pack the explosives and run the wires out to the detonator. He looked up at the first signs of dawn. Soon it would be light.

The boys came out pushing the wires into the mud and hiding them in the water, then they went to the trees and Yasin set up the machine gun.

'He will stay and help you,' said the commander, pointing to one of the boys, who was wiping mud off his face with a rag.

As they waited, Yasin felt both lonely and tranquil. He wondered if the Sri Lankan soldiers would all be killed immediately, or would be wounded by the bomb and bleed to death in the road, which was when he was meant to shoot them. He thought he saw shadows on the other side of the road and felt himself go tense, but it was just the sun coming up and birds flying over. He looked at the boy next him and saw that he was laughing at his inexperience; he didn't like it.

By the time they heard the convoy, the sun had risen but it was the cool part of the morning, not yet hot. The first vehicle was an armoured personnel carrier which the commander let go past. The second was a truck filled with soldiers, teenagers mostly, who reminded Yasin of the young soldiers in Zamboanga. They were all the same, these government soldiers.

The driver of the truck stopped when he saw the water. Four soldiers jumped down to look for signs of explosives, two giving cover, two treading, peering in the mud, squatting to pull a twig, a stone, a leaf from a spot and declare it safe before moving on inch by inch to another suspect place.

The soldier at the front shouted, head raised towards the driver, pointing to a wire, stepping back. The other soldiers tightened their hands around their weapons, confused and inexperienced.

One stumbled, looking around for the enemy, for someone to fire at, but saw only jungle. And it was then, at the height of their dithering, that the commander detonated the bomb. Nails, shrapnel and the blast hurled the nearest soldier into the air as if he had wings, ripping away his right arm, severing his head and stripping him of his clothes.

The armoured personnel carrier exploded, hit by an anti-tank shell. Another was destroyed behind it and then the commander set off the second bomb. A soldier fell yards away from Yasin, bleeding all over and his leg blown off. He was alive and awake, looking straight at Yasin, moaning loudly, the rain pouring down his face, blood mixing with water and tears. His hand grasped at his stomach, his intestines spilling out and steaming.

Automatically, Yasin searched for a bag of emergency medical equipment, but the boy stopped him, jerking his reactions back into place, then the soldier shouted at him. 'Shoot me, Tiger!' In English. The voice was strong, a scream, a cry for the relief of pain, a command. 'Please . . .'

It seemed an age before Yasin pulled the trigger, his thoughts turbulent and distracted as if it was he who was about to die. Limbs lay in the road quite separate from any body. There was even a head, with an almost natural expression of surprise, caught in that moment between realisation and death. The body was somewhere around, but no one cared where. He remembered reading about Sri Lanka, that people massacred each other here like no other place in the world.

But Yasin had seen a bomb like this before; people ripped naked, their limbs torn off, all around him, and him protecting his sister, trampled upon, bleeding, crying for help. Now, thousands of miles away, soldiers' clothes hung in the trees, reminding him of Zamboanga. The sleeve of a khaki T-shirt. The leg of a pair of shorts. A sandal, hooked on a branch. Blood splattered high against a tree-trunk.

Then he opened fire without thinking. First the dying soldier, then others who were writhing and moaning in the mud. He opened fire as if, after a diversion, it was a natural sequence of events: the explosion, the quiet, the uncertainty, the firing, then death.

He put down a line of fire around the truck which killed soldiers stumbling out. He fired until no one was left standing, then put short bursts into bodies which showed signs of life. He held fire as the commander walked out into the road with six Tiger fighters, and gave cover as they checked each surviving Sri Lankan soldier and executed those in the throes of death. And only when the commander gave the all clear did he realise that the boy with him was dead, shot in the head by a Sri Lankan soldier whose instinct was to kill while he was being killed. The boy had died without a sound.

Two soldiers who were slightly wounded became prisoners of war and were bandaged while they lay on the road.

They walked back in single file through the jungle. Yasin followed one of the prisoners whose right forearm was roughly bandaged up. Blood was just beginning to seep through. He turned round and looked straight at Yasin who was carrying the machine gun on his shoulder, the weapon which had killed his friends. He had a face of hopeless tragedy.

Yasin smiled at him because he knew how he felt. They were both at different stages on the same path. The next time the soldier would handle it better, be more mature, less unpredictable and sad, like Yasin had been when he watched Jesse kill the sergeant in Zamboanga.

Soon death would be academic, whether it was you or someone else. Death was something that just happened, like the rain.

'What's your name?' said Yasin in English.

The soldier turned away with an expression of utter misery and shock.

## London, England

'We have a rule – never to operate on both eyes at the same time.'

James Stephens was alone with Tim in a private consulting room in the Cumberlege Wing on the fourth floor of Moorfields Eye Hospital in London. They sat either side of eye-testing equipment. A mirror hung in a corner reflecting different sizes of letters for eye tests.

Samira was sleeping in her room, the only one they had left at such short notice. If the operation was successful her first view out of a London window would be towards another grubby white wall of the building with black drainpipes and dirty maroon fire escapes.

'You'll have to break it,' said Tim.

'I hear you, Mr Pack.' Dr Stephens opened Samira's file, with a note from Walmsley on the top, stamped with a C2 graded confidentiality coding from the SIS. He tapped the sheet of paper. 'What we can do is keep her in the operating theatre under anaesthetic and work on them using separate sterile instrument sets.'

'I thought you were thinking of months apart.'

'We may be. We just never know.' He flipped over

Walmsley's memo and read down the medical notes from Zamboanga. 'A splinter of glass is lodged in the lens of her right eye. Five specks are in her left. The left is far more vulnerable.'

'How long before she sees again?'

'Using the latest small-incision surgery and an injectable lens implant – thirty-six, forty-eight hours from when we operate. But we don't know when it will be safe to do that yet. The astigmatism from the damage to the cornea can be repaired as well. It's a fairly new procedure. Only been around since the early nineties. I won't bore you with the details, but it means she would be able to see quicker, but it carries more risks.'

'What sort of risks?'

'Given her injuries. Ten per cent, I would say, that it won't work.'

'And if we go for the safer methods?'

'We won't know anything for at least a week. Basically, they are cataract injuries which should be fairly simple to fix. But there is always a chance that something else is there, another problem we would have to explore.'

'Then what?'

Dr Stephens looked at the file again to make sure he had her name right: 'Samira Omer would continue to be blind.'


'They said you did very well,' enthused Venkat. He was more nervous, his uniform buttoned up scrappily over a thin, gangly body. 'The commander needs to speak to you.'

The commander sat down next to Yasin and shook his hand, an acknowledgment of the part Yasin had played in the battle. It was the first time anyone except Venkat had talked to him outside the training ground. The commander didn't look Yasin in the eye, instead he played with a brittle twig, breaking it like a toothpick into tiny pieces.

'We are so lucky that our struggle has a leader who is the king of the Tamil people,' said Venkat.

'We have a problem,' said the commander abruptly in English, ignoring Venkat's adulation. Although intelligent, the commander's intellect was narrow. He was a disciple of Kutti and a killer of men.

'We have a problem,' repeated Venkat.

'*Another* problem,' mumbled Yasin.

Yasin felt tired and hot. After the ambush he had written to Samira, then he had torn the letter up because he couldn't express his feelings, even to his sister. He tried to ask Samira whether he should enjoy what he was doing. He hadn't felt nervous when he fired the machine gun, nor when he killed the men, although he had never done it before. All he felt now was an emptiness which could be filled either by going into battle again or by ending it all.

His feelings frightened him: he was getting to be like Jesse, where the only purpose was to fight, the only motive was loyalty and revenge, and every other higher ideal was forgotten.

The commander let Venkat do the talking, a stumbling, parroting Venkat, who began by saying that Kutti was the light of their civilisation. The commander drew circles in the sand with an unbroken twig.

'Kutti says no one must know a foreigner is fighting with us,' Venkat said. 'He wants to send you on a special mission to get something from Pakistan, but you must . . .'

Venkat looked towards the commander whose concentration on his sand picture remained unchanged. He ignored what Venkat was saying and talked to Yasin in English.

'Normally it is our policy to release Sri Lankan soldiers. Our fight is not against them.'

'What am I to do in Pakistan?' asked Yasin.

The commander glanced up at him. It was very quick, the flicker across his face. For Venkat, the question was a reprieve from the terrible task he had been assigned to see through. 'Kutti will tell you himself. He heard how cool you were at the ambush.'

'Then let's go and see him,' challenged Yasin.

'Later,' said the commander. He had done nothing to the socket where his eye had been. No patch, no eye glass, just a scarred cavern of nothingness.

'Our fight is with the government of Sri Lanka. We will live side by side with our Sinhalese brothers . . .'

'Tell him,' snapped the commander in English. Just for a second, the hazy, nonchalant good eye lit up with anger.

Venkat didn't. Or couldn't. His face was pale with moral choices so distant from the school study where Yasin had first heard them.

Yasin said. 'The two prisoners have to be executed because they've seen me.'

'Yes,' said the commander bluntly.

'Can't you keep them until the war has finished?'

Venkat recovered. 'Even then they can tell people, you see, Yasin,' said Venkat. 'You are here as a favour. Ours is an internal struggle of liberation. We do not need foreign help.'

As if the next stage had been choreographed, a Tamil guerrilla led the two Sri Lankan soldiers out of the undergrowth. The first was the one Yasin had talked to. He wiped grains of rice off the sling which held his arm. He kept his head lowered. The second prisoner had his hands tied behind his back. Yasin noticed he was an officer, walking with a slight limp, like Musa, with shrapnel in his leg from the explosion. He must have been in his early twenties and his skin was smooth and unmarked.

The commander produced a pistol, not his own which stayed in his holster, but one which he had brought with him for the execution, wrapped in a brown cloth. He held it out but Yasin didn't take it and the commander had to put it on the ground at their feet so it belonged to no one.

When he saw the pistol, the soldier Yasin had talked to let out a little cry. The officer spoke sharply in Sinhala and the soldier went quiet.

'Can we have some water?' said the officer in English. It was good English, like Venkat's, the English of the educated classes of the subcontinent.

'Water,' said Venkat in English, then repeating it in Tamil. He was on his feet, the courteous host, as if the two Sri Lankans were guests at his father's house. Water was found and poured into plastic cups for them.

The commander got up, scraped his shoe over the sand pattern, destroying it, and walked away without a word. The pistol stayed where he had left it.

Venkat dithered, beginning to hand the water bottle to Yasin, who didn't take it, then putting it on the ground next to the pistol. Spilt drops dampened the sand. Venkat followed the commander.

'Are you going to execute us?' said the officer.

The younger soldier started to speak, his eyes darting everywhere. The sun broke through the cloud cover which had hung over the jungle all day, its sudden harsh light taking them all by surprise.

'He is talking about his family,' said the officer. 'He wants me to make sure they know he died a brave Sinhala soldier.' He shifted weight to ease the pressure on his wounded leg. 'You don't know what nationalistic rubbish they try to instil in us before sending us up here.'

'Yes,' said Yasin.

'What you are about to do is against international law.'

'I know.'

He knelt down and unwrapped the pistol from the cloth. He unclipped the magazine – the commander had filled it – and snapped it back up again, like Musa had shown him how to. He slid back the safety catch, held the pistol in both hands and indicated to the Tamil guerrilla guarding the soldiers that he should now leave. The boy melted away.

Yasin thought of asking the officer if he wanted any message passed on. But it would be a useless, patronising thing to do, a veiled request for forgiveness, when Yasin deserved none and wanted none.

'Move back into the trees,' said Yasin softly to the officer.

'As I am about to die, I am entitled to refuse.' The officer didn't move. But the soldier, recognising Yasin's command, began to go back. He took a half step, that extra second to cling to life, until the officer barked at him to stay where he was. The soldier stopped, his eyes muddy and static, as if his fear was gone and sanctuary had come in the form of the last order from his officer.

'His name's Nimal,' said the officer. 'You asked him, didn't you? After the ambush.'

'Yes.' Yasin didn't want to speak, but he did.

'My name's Kingsley. Kingsley Dissanayake. My grandfather was a British planter, who impregnated my grandmother and then ran off.' He spoke in such a way that he might be recounting a story over the supper table. 'Remember us after you're tired of fighting.'

'Into the trees,' Yasin said.

Dissanayake shook his head. 'I prefer to die seeing the sky.'

Yasin meant it to be just two, but he fired three shots into Dissanayake's heart, allowing for the buck of the pistol, remembering the training in Jolo as if it had just been yesterday. He shifted weight, no pause between executions. The first killing had given him confidence to make it just two rounds this time, one in the throat, the second in the heart.

He breathed in heavily, taking in the smell of cordite. Nimal had knocked the bottle as he fell and water was draining out onto the sand. There was silence, a restful and accomplished quiet.

Yasin moved into the shade because the sun was irritating him.

'Dear *Ghazal*.' Gazelle. Her childhood nickname like his was *Hirba*, Chameleon. 'I killed two men today,' he eventually managed to write to Samira . . .

I am trying not to feel bad about it. How are you? But what a silly question to ask because you can't write back to me. You may have heard that my school was raided and I have had to come here to Sri Lanka to learn how fight. They're fighting a real war here, not like what we were doing on Jolo. That was a big joke. Musa is a broken man. He walks with a stoop and no one listens to what he says. He doesn't even smoke cigars any more. I wish you were with me. You would make a good fighter, Gazelle, because you're so brave and clever and I'm missing you a lot. I have no one to talk to except my school friend, Venkat, and he's really quite stupid. They have a leader called Kutti. I've never met him, but they have pictures of him everywhere and all Venkat does is parrot what he says. It's really annoying.

I think of you all the time. Did you go to England? And with that boy on the motorbike? Did you really go with him? When I think about it, I even feel a bit jealous, although you are my twin sister. If you married him, I would have no family at all, but I would have no family at all, but I would get over it. I suppose we will both get married one day. Have you been with any more boys?

Yesterday, we went on an ambush and blew up a convoy. I had to do the machine gun which means that once they have set off the land-mines, I shoot the people who come out of the armoured cars. I think I did quite well. I shot about six soldiers. It was very muddy because it's the rainy season. Next time I'm going to ask to do the detonator. I think that's a better job.

I feel very strange about doing it, though, because it was a bomb which blinded you and I've thought about it a lot. I killed soldiers, not shoppers and that's the difference. But I don't want to be like Jesse, who is an empty man. He can't talk about anything except killing, although Musa won't let him do it. You know I never wanted to do this, but now I can't see any other way because if I gave myself up they would put me in prison and I haven't done anything wrong at all. I don't suppose anyone else has told you what they did to Jesse's family. Has that been in the newspapers? It made me really angry that soldiers can kill people like that and no one does anything to punish them.

When I leave here, I will try and come and see you. I can't promise, but Venkat says they want me to go to Pakistan for them. At least, I'll get out of the camp. I feel better for writing to you. I wonder if you're still in hospital. It's nearly three months since the bomb went off. Killing people here seems all right, but I hope I don't have to do it when I leave Sri Lanka. You know what I think? We should find a way to really punish the people who cause all these problems and let people kill Jesse's family like that. Something like the Americans did to Japan with the atom bomb, because after that Japan hasn't done anything wrong at all.

I love you, Gazelle. Please, please, please look after yourself. I feel bad not being with you and don't marry the boy on the motorbike until I get back.'

He wrote by the moonlight, sitting on two boxes of ammunition, dabbing his face with a cloth to stop sweat dropping onto the paper. He hardly looked up, and let his imagination take him into his world with Samira. What he had meant to say to her was that he had found the reason for war. Men enjoyed killing and Yasin hated himself for it. But he couldn't think of the words, couldn't think how to explain it.

He folded the paper quickly, hearing footsteps behind him, then Venkat slapped him on the back as if Yasin had just won a school prize. 'Tell me,' he whispered as if others might be listening. 'How could you do something like that? It was wonderful.'

'What?' said Yasin, looking up.

'Carry out Kutti's orders just like that. How could you do that?'

'I knew what I wanted to achieve.' He pushed the letter into his pocket, annoyed by Venkat's mindless smile, then he remembered how useless it had been to write to Samira because there wasn't even a post box in the liberated areas of Tamil Eelam.

'What is that, Yasin?' enthused Venkat. 'What wonderful vision do you have now?'

Yasin shook his head: 'Ask Kutti if he will let me become a Black Tiger, to make the bombs.'

'But he wants us to go to Pakistan to meet the ship in Karachi. There is something for us to bring down.'

'Of course,' said Yasin. 'But first let me train.'

# Chapter Twenty-two

## Karachi, Pakistan

April

T he Pakistan sun beat down as harshly as it did in the Sudan, the Philippines and Sri Lanka. Yasin was getting to know these places and their people. It was the sun of the developing world, where heat helped created disease, poverty and rebellion.

The three of them, Yasin, Venkat and Igor Gromov, a Russian, climbed into the back of the truck, one of dozens stretching across a warehouse yard near the port, where, line by line and row by row, vehicles parked to unload goods for shipment out of Karachi. The Russian got them the passes and, once in there, people wandered wherever they liked, like looking through the massive sorting hall of a post office, the drop-off and pick-up point for the shipping lanes of the Indian Ocean.

'There are two vehicles,' said Gromov. He was fit, blond-haired, with a relaxed, colourful open-neck shirt, showing them around as if he was in charge of a removal company. 'The weapons are up here.' He slapped the back of truck. 'Do you want to take a look?'

'You go,' said Venkat, his face glistening with sweat.

Yasin climbed up, clambering over household furniture, until he saw wooden crates piled on top of each other. The Russian was beside him, his aftershave mixing with the musty smell of wood. He handed over a jemmy and Yasin carefully pulled up the lid, preserving the nails. Gromov picked up the AK-47 assault rifle on top and handed it to Yasin. 'Brand new, never been fired. The original,' he said.

As he put it back, Gromov asked. 'You want to see the rest.'

'No,' Yasin said. 'But, if you have cheated us, we will have to kill you.'

The Russian laughed and the cramped space in the truck made it seem louder. 'You think the little Tigers could take us on.'

'Let's not test it,' said Yasin. As they climbed out a breeze blew in from the sea, cooling them. They walked along, Venkat leading, trying to show he was in charge. But the Russian pointed out the second truck. Venkat stayed back from it, didn't even want to touch it, while Gromov and Yasin climbed up again. This time there were grey office filing cabinets packed against each side, a narrow, uncluttered corridor left in between. The Russian pulled away a thick green canvas cover from bags stacked up against the back of the cab, heavy duty white plastic, sealed at the top and the seams reinforced with green tape.

'Each one is 2.5 kilograms,' said Gromov, pointing, but going no further. 'There are three layers of protection; what you see there, hard plastic underneath protective against sharp objects, and transparent plastic. I will be down to supervise their loading onto the boat. After that, it is up to you.'

Yasin picked one up, weighing it in his hand. 'How do you open it?' he said.

'You don't.' The Russian took the bag from him and put it back on the pile. 'You don't,' he repeated, watching Yasin's perplexity with surprise. Yasin turned to look for Venkat, but couldn't see him, just the flap and the scorching sun outside, making them sweat horribly.

'You don't know what this is, do you?' said Gromov.

'No,' admitted Yasin.

'It is finely milled anthrax.'

Yasin didn't say anything. Gromov moved to go, and Yasin stayed exactly where he was, counting the bags, counting all twenty of them, fifty kilograms, thinking that this was exactly what Tim Pack had asked him about. He wondered if Ablimet Nor, his shy and talented friend, had died because of it; if that was why the school had been raided. If Yasin had convinced himself he didn't believe in God, he at least wondered why this weapon of mass destruction had been delivered so neatly into his hands when he wasn't even looking for it, didn't want it, didn't even know what it was.

As soon as they got back to the hotel, Yasin ordered his television to be Internet connected and the bell boy delivered a keyboard to the room. He found the Alta Vista search engine, used the words *anthrax* and *terrorism* and waited while the list came up.

He skipped the unreliable private pages and went straight to the Pentagon website on biological warfare:

anthrax (an thraks) n. *an infectious bacterial disease spread by contact with infected animals, handling infected products, eating infected meat, or breathing weapon-dispersed spores.*

As he moved through the different sites, he understood why Venkat was so naïvely excited and why Tim Pack had been sent to Zamboanga to find him. *Anthrax is extremely deadly and relatively easy to weaponise. Inhaled anthrax is 99 per cent lethal*, said the British Ministry of Defence.

Characteristics

- produces highly resistant spores that may persist in the environment for decades
- can readily be produced in large quantities
- aerosol dispersion is possible
- virulent antibiotic-resistant strains have been produced

Biological Weapons Effects
*Based on release of 50 kg of an agent along a 2km line upwind of population centre of 500,000*

| Agent | Deaths | Incapacitated |
|---|---|---|
| Rift Valley Fever | 400 | 35,000 |
| Tick-borne encephalitis | 9,500 | 35,000 |
| Typhus | 19,000 | 85,000 |
| Brucellosis | 500 | 125,000 |
| Q fever | 150 | 125,000 |
| Tularemia | 30,000 | 125,000 |
| Anthrax | 95,000 | 125,000 |

No bio-weapon was more lethal than anthrax. Yasin noted down the impact of fifty kilograms, which was what Tim Pack had said was missing and what the Russian had shown him in the back of the truck, ready to board the ship. It would be a hundred thousand dead, figures comparable to the nuclear attacks on the two Japanese cities, with the bombing of Dresden. Even if it was only ten per cent, it could kill millions. He opened another site: BW: The future weapon of choice

- short incubation period between infection and onset of symptoms
- no widespread immunity

- insusceptibility to common medical treatments
- ease of transport, storage and dissemination
- ability to infect in reliably small doses
- ability to penetrate unprotected ships, tanks or buildings

Yasin wrote rapidly: *Encapsulated spores would not be susceptible to sunlight . . . the main problem facing a bio-weapons producer is freeze-drying and milling the spores to the optimum size . . . this weapon is odourless and colourless with no technology or sniffer dogs available to detect it at border posts . . . anthrax is the poor man's nuclear weapon.* He switched from site to site as the information became repetitious, feeling sickened, excited and filled with questions, missing the classroom forum where he could ask, missing Musa, knowing he was on his own, that fate had dealt him a hand. Not that he believed in a god, but in coincidence, yes. If it was so easy to use, why hadn't anyone done it before? Was this the anthrax which Tim Pack had asked him about? What about the ultra-violet light which might destroy it? How could they get a plane to disperse it from Vanni? Did Kutti really plan to kill that many Sri Lankans? The poor people. The marine sergeant. The boy soldiers on the convoy. The people who did not cause the problems.

Although a 'Do Not Disturb' sign was hanging on the door, Venkat knocked, tried the handle and knocked again. Yasin put on the screen saver, got up and let him in.

'Do you trust Gromov?' said Venkat, walking in and sitting on the bed. 'I'm worried about him.'

'I didn't make the arrangements with him.'

'He won't double cross us?'

'If he does, we can kill him,' responded Yasin nonchalantly.

Venkat squeezed his hands on his knees, nervous and impatient. 'Why do we have to wait two days then?'

'It's the turn-around time at the port.' Yasin sat in the desk chair, facing Venkat. 'If Kutti was willing to pay higher bribes, I am sure we could load the ship earlier.'

'Kutti's judgment is right,' said Venkat, suddenly getting up. 'I'm going to shower,' he said. 'Let's have lunch in half an hour.'

This time, Yasin bolted the door and turned on the television so that it could be heard from outside. He picked up the telephone and dialled the direct line number in Vienna which he had committed to memory. He used the American Sprint calling card service so that the telephone system at the bank would not show up his number in Karachi.

'Hans Jancke, please,' he said in English.

'Hans Jancke speaking. This is my direct line.'

'I would like to inquire about a numbered account and have the password "L-2-7-L-N-Q-N."' Musa had told him that if you moved each letter on one and subtracted one from each number it came out as "M-1-6-M-O-R-O", simple but symbolic, the name of the weapon and the movement.

There was no passing him to another banker, nor telling him to ring back. Austria was vying to win the secret banking trade from Switzerland and knew that its clients appreciated speed, security and efficiency. Yasin heard Jancke calling up the password on his computer, then he asked, 'Date of birth?'

'Four, twenty-one, thirty-nine,' said Yasin.

'Address?'

Yasin gave the address of Musa's compound.

'I now have to ask a series of random questions in order to clear the first level of security,' said Jancke. 'The name of the wife.'

'Eva.'

'Is she alive?'

'No.'

'When did she die?'

'1975.'

'Mobile phone number?'

'911 685 4328'.

'The second password, please.'

'CBOKBV & hash', said Yasin. This time Musa had paid tribute to the Banjau sea gypsies.

Jancke went quiet for a while. Yasin couldn't even hear him using the computer. 'I am afraid the holder of this account has passed away,' he said, quietly. 'Please accept our condolences.'

'Passed away?'

'Yes. He died more than a month ago.'

Musa dead. Something inside Yasin screamed, but Jancke's professionalism, his calmness, his demand for an unemotional response, let him suppress all that: 'I am the new holder of the account,' he said.

'Password?'

Yasin told him the one agreed with Musa, then Jancke went through questions about him as Musa had said he would. 'Yes,' Jancke paused. 'The account has been divided into three. You have access to one third of the original balance.'

'One third?' Yasin slipped, showed emotion. 'What about the rest?'

'I am not at liberty to say.'

'Then how much?

More tapping. 'We can of course get you a detailed statement, but the balance of your account is broadly at two hundred and thirty million US dollars. There is also fifty million Swiss francs and thirteen million Euros.'

Yasin kept his voice steady. 'I would like to transfer some money later.'

'Our office hours are from 10:00 to 16:00, Vienna time,'

said Jancke. 'There is another number for out-of-hour transactions, but only for amounts over one million dollars.'

Yasin noted down the number and stared at the silent telephone set when the call had finished, then at the mindless
television news for a full fifteen minutes, before picking up
the phone again and dialling the satellite number on Jolo.
Nothing. Then came the twittering of the satellite line and a
continuous tone. He shouldn't have done it, not even using
Sprint. He was starting to act without thinking and he had
never done that before.

Yasin returned to the Internet, called up Alta Vista and
typed in the search words 'Abu Musa' and 'Jolo'. A list
appeared straight away, and Yasin picked an article from
the *Philippine Inquirer*:

*Zamboanga industrialist and Muslim terrorist, Abu Musa,*
*was killed last night in a shoot-out with a marine unit on*
*the island of Jolo. Musa, 62, died when his small band of*
*renegades tried to ambush a convoy of trucks delivering food*
*and medical supplies to villages in the south of the island.*
*No marines were hurt in the incident . . .*

'Crap,' said Yasin out loud. Musa wouldn't do that. Wouldn't
stop food going to the people. The article was dated just
after he had gone to Sri Lanka. Musa must have started
fighting again, like Yasin wanted him to. Knowing he
would die, he had let himself be killed in battle like the
warrior he was. A great man. Yasin's teacher. His guide.
Yasin's moral force. The man who took them in and tried
to give them a decent life. Yet Yasin had never thanked
him. He hadn't understood, like Samira, who had been
strong enough to show love for Musa. Yasin had treated
him badly. Musa, who had left nearly a billion dollars in
trust, who had taken on the Christian-Jewish institutions

and beaten them at their own game, until they decided to crush him. Then they had destroyed him, as if he was a fly, a bit-part player who they got bored with so they swatted him. That's what he had tried to tell Yasin all the time, on Jolo, each term before he sent him off to school. Musa had been the kindest man, who had given them a home. He had tried to teach them how to laugh. To give life. He had let Yasin challenge. He had let him argue. Let him brood. He had given Yasin more understanding of life than anybody else. He had treated Yasin as a son, yet Yasin had refused to let him be his father.

Yasin paced the room, clenching his fist around a pen, slapping the bed and the walls. He had treated Musa badly, shown no affection, but he didn't know then. Now he was missing him terribly, Musa was distant, his voice out there, his knowledge . . . Yasin tried to hold back the tears which were welling up in his eyes, until he couldn't any more, Musa was gone – Jancke had said so – and he let himself cry, sitting on the bed, the screen turning from the website to the hotel logo screen saver in front of him, Yasin's head bent, letting the grief pour out of him, until Venkat banged on the door and Yasin told him he would be another ten minutes, and Yasin cried until he felt strength return to him so that he could continue with the day.

He didn't tell Venkat about Musa, because Venkat would have said he wasn't as great a man as Kutti and Yasin would have had to hit him. So, they took the buffet lunch. For a while he listened to Venkat's drivel, then he asked, 'Do you really plan to use this weapon?'

'We have too, don't you see? It will end the war. Stop people being killed.'

'You will be killing your own people, poor people, peasants, the victims. The people who should die are in Europe and America, the bankers and politicians.'

Venkat didn't seem to know what Yasin was talking about. 'Kutti says it is a sacrifice for the greater good of Eelam.' Venkat stared at Yasin, his brow creased with worry. 'You must be with us? Kutti has trusted us. If you are not it will not be possible . . .' His voice trailed off.

'Don't worry,' Yasin said, smiling. 'I support you a hundred per cent. If Kutti wants it, we'll deliver it.'

After lunch, Yasin suggested they go to Venkat's room to have some Johnny Walker Red Label, just like when they were at school. They drank out of bathroom tumblers. Yasin led the conversation, lingering on the old times, talking about Thondup, Gurjit and Ablimet at length and laughing about the last night, when Yasin broke up the fight and hit Venkat, making his nose bleed.

'It was only after I told Kutti that story,' said Venkat, 'that he said you could come. He said you must have the right stuff.' Yasin kept the bottle and he splashed whisky into Venkat's glass while pouring only a drop into his own. 'No one else could have done this job except us because we're outside the movement. The commander is on the ship. And the captain has been with the ship for more than ten years. But to deal with the Russian, to be entrusted with such a job, by Kutti, is a real honour.'

In the early evening, when Venkat was in the bathroom, Yasin broke a capsule of cyanide and mixed it with about an inch of whisky, stirring it with a pencil from the writing desk. It was a thick liquid and turned the whisky darker, but not enough for Venkat to notice. Yasin was standing, holding both glasses, when Venkat reappeared, swaying and smiling. 'I'm off for a sleep,' said Yasin, handing him his drink for them to both finish in one. 'Bottoms up.'

'We have to meet the Russian tonight,' said Venkat. His words slurred and he didn't manage to swallow all the whisky in one. The cyanide took effect before he had a second chance, the glass falling out his hand and his body convulsing in a fit, gasping for breath. His eyes fixed, for a moment, on Yasin, long enough to be stripped of innocence, before his eyeballs rolled up into his head, retching, with vomit dribbling from his mouth, before his body quivered from inside and he died.

It was the first time Yasin had made his own decision to kill. He felt a thrill surge through him.

He washed out the glasses and put them back in the bathroom with Venkat's toothbrush in one. He cleaned the vomit and spittle from the face and lifted the body into the bed, fully clothed, covering most of Venkat's head with the sheet. He searched Venkat's pockets and took the money – wads of it in US dollars – all except a few hundred, and the room key which he slipped into his top shirt pocket. He left the credit card, airline tickets, Singaporean passport and fake name-cards and switched on the television to BBC World, just loud enough to be heard from outside. There was a faint smell of bitter almonds from the cyanide. When he stepped outside, he hung the 'Do Not Disturb' sign on the door and looked at his watch. It was just past 5 p.m.

# Chapter Twenty-three

Yasin showered with hot water, enjoying its sting, before turning it to cold, letting the exhilaration sweep through him, waking him up: he was feeling good after the killing. Wrapped in a towel and the hotel bathrobe, he logged back onto the Internet and set up a search. In fifteen minutes, after scrolling through the websites, he knew exactly what he wanted to do. He had argued about it with Musa and lost his temper with Jesse: kill those who created war and poverty, not the soldiers and peasants who have to live in them.

Once a year for more than twenty-five years, beginning in Versailles in 1975, the leaders of the richest nations had gathered in one place. It was called the G7 summit. But in May, less than a month away, they were holding an emergency meeting because of the Asian currency crisis. It was in London. The countries were the United Kingdom, the United States, France, Germany, Japan, Italy, Canada, and in the past few years Russia had joined. Yasin could think of no better way of carrying out his ambition.

An hour later, he sat in the hotel lobby with Igor Gromov. 'Venkat is not well,' said Yasin, when Gromov asked. 'We were drinking whisky this afternoon.'

Gromov said nothing. With Venkat gone, he was a harder man and there was a coldness about him which Yasin hadn't noticed before. He examined Gromov now as someone he had to deal with. The Russian was fit and kept his hair cut short, so he looked like a soldier or an athlete, probably fifteen years older than Yasin, old enough to be taken seriously.

'I have been instructed to change our plans for delivery,' Yasin continued.

The Russian raised his eyebrow, but stayed silent. 'I have been told to pay you five thousand dollars just to listen to our new proposal,' said Yasin, 'whether you agree to help or not.' He gave a laminated folder to Gromov which looked like a sales kit from an international conference. Gromov opened it, saw the bank notes, and closed the folder again. He glanced at Yasin, an instruction to continue.

'The bags I saw today need to go to Europe.'

It was some time before either of them spoke. Gromov used long silences as a technique and Yasin understood that to earn his respect he would have to keep his nerve and not say anything pointless. Until the Russian answered, there was no reason to speak. If he refused, one of them would have to die.

'When?' said the Russian, breaking the silence.

'By plane.' Yasin paused, because getting an aircraft was expensive. More money for everyone. 'As soon as possible.'

The Russian got up. 'Wait here,' he said and began to walk off towards the lifts when he stopped and came back to Yasin. 'No. If this can be arranged you will have to prepare payment. Let us both confirm our obligations and meet back here in an hour.' He gave Yasin a piece of paper torn from a lined notebook: 'This is an account number. You must confirm that funds can be transferred.'

In his own room, Yasin telephoned Jancke, who was at home with the sounds of children screaming in the background. Yasin read out Gromov's account number.

'It's in Dubai,' said Jancke. 'May I ask what sort of sums you will be transferring?'

'Substantial,' said Yasin, trying to sound professional.

'Of course. If you need half a million to one account and half a million to another, that is all right, Mr Omer,' Jancke explained, like a teacher. 'As long as everything is over a million. If you are considering larger transfers, of five million or above, we offer very competitive rates on our charges.'

Gromov sat in the lobby at the same table, when Yasin came back down. 'It can be done,' he said. 'A Tupolev-154 can fly down from Moscow in two days' time. It is really too big for what you need, but it is available and reliable. Do you just want the bags transported or the weapons as well?'

'Some weapons,' said Yasin. 'But not all.'

'You haven't told me where you want to go.'

'Western Europe.'

'We could fly there, but the risk with customs and documents is very high. What I suggest is Belgrade, where we can make guaranteed arrangements to take the bags to Western Europe on a Danube river barge. The journey to Rotterdam or Hamburg would take five to six days. I know it is a long time, but it is safer. The river is very badly policed. Once you are inside the European Union, you can load the stuff onto a truck and go through border posts more easily. If there is a search of the barge, the bags would be more difficult to find. And if you are challenged, you have more room to fight and escape than in a truck.'

'Yes,' said Yasin. 'Hamburg or Rotterdam.'

'Do you need passports, documents?'

'For the cargo and the boat, yes. For the people, no.'

'Will your associates be on the plane?'

'There will be some.'

Gromov stopped speaking again and they sat like that for

a full three minutes. Yasin found it easier now to challenge the silences. Gromov was a man of quick decisions and actions, and probably a killer. But he wanted money and that was his weakness. When he eventually spoke, Gromov's voice exposed his humiliation at having to ask, recognition that control was shifting away from him. 'How much will you pay?' he said eventually. But Yasin did not answer and it was Gromov who quickly broke the pause by adding. 'On top of what we have already received from Sri Lanka.'

'How much do you want?' said Yasin. 'For the plane, Belgrade and the barge, complete guaranteed safe delivery to northern Europe?'

'One million to me. Ten million to my superiors.'

'I will pay five million tonight. One million on arrival of the plane. One million in Belgrade and the balance once we get to Western Europe. One month after that, I will pay another five million if I am happy with the operation.'

Gromov nodded. 'And my money?'

'Two hundred thousand tonight. Three hundred thousand in Belgrade. The balance in Hamburg.'

The Russian unfolded another piece of lined note paper, spread it out flat on the table and wrote the sums which Yasin had told him against a list of bank account numbers – just numbers, no names or countries. He folded the paper again, slipped it across the table to Yasin, then got up and left without saying another word.

Yasin used Venkat's room to try to call the satellite telephone on Jolo. Venkat's body was a bundle in the bed and the air-conditioning was cold enough to keep the room fresh of decay for several days. While he looked around, checking, Yasin heard the dysfunctional signals on the line, meaning that the phone must be permanently disconnected. Instead, he dialled the number of the forger in Manila's Chinatown. The forger answered the phone himself. Of course, he said, when Yasin asked him to find Jesse and get him to go to Manila straight away. There would be a fee, and Yasin took down yet another bank account number. He gave the forger the names of the others he wanted Jesse to bring with him. Before he left, he telephoned the hospital in Zamboanga where he last saw Samira. But it was the middle of the night and Samira had been gone for more than a month. The nurse knew she had gone abroad for a special operation. Maybe America. Maybe England: He would have to ring back in the morning.

He locked Venkat's door and went along to his own room to telephone Jancke.

Tim and a junior doctor looked through the glass ceiling of the operating theatre. Samira lay under a blue cloth with a yellow blanket over her legs. Her eyes were held open with sticky plastic and she was unconscious.

'How long?' asked Tim.

'He's just finishing the left eye and the intra-ocular lens has been successfully injected. The lens inplant will now unfold within the eye,' said the doctor. 'The specks of glass have been removed. But there is a problem and we will have to wait several days until work can begin on the right eye. There is a risk of trauma.'

'How long?' he asked again.

'Difficult to say. Dr Stephens hopes it will be within a week.'

The following evening Jesse arrived with the helmsman who had taken them to the mainland, and an engineer they called the welder. They travelled on the forged passports and took a hotel car from the airport. Yasin talked alone with Jesse right through the first night about Musa, Samira, and Jesse's family.

249

'The camp was over-run,' said Jesse. 'They squashed us like flies and wrecked everything.'

'Where were you?' said Yasin.

'We weren't back yet from the mainland. The newspapers said Musa just stood there like a madman, shooting at them. He had no cover. He knew he would die. They put all the bodies in a mass grave. They weren't facing Mecca. That's what the papers said. But the army says they were.'

Jesse talked to Yasin as if he were now the leader and when Yasin told him they were going to Europe to avenge the death of his family, Jesse nodded.

'Don't you see now that the men who killed your family are just as much victims as us?' Yasin said. 'They kill us. We kill them and the people who start the violence never get hurt.'

Jesse's eyes were dark vacuous caverns still, but somewhere in there a spark burned. Yasin had given him purpose and Jesse was grateful. For the first time, Yasin told Jesse about the killing of his own parents, so the old gardener and the young guerrilla fighter understood the bond between them and the motive they shared.

The next afternoon, Gromov sent a car to the hotel and met them at the gates of Karachi's military airport in his own vehicle. The airport, with fighter and transport planes parked around its perimeter, was a short drive from the area where the trucks were parked with the anthrax and weapons.

The TU-154 taxied to its own area, away from the military aircraft. Gromov used papers to get them through the gate. There were no searches of the vehicles, no request to see their travel documents.

'You will not get an exit stamp from Pakistan,' Gromov explained as they crossed the tarmac to the aircraft. 'But you will get a visa and entry stamp to Yugoslavia. That has all been arranged.'

'Who do we deal with in Belgrade?' said Yasin.

'Milan Isakovic. He is a colonel in the Yugoslav army and will meet the aircraft.'

'If he doesn't?'

'He will.'

The sun and hot air thrown out from the engines of the airliner made the tarmac shimmer. Yasin stared straight ahead, squinting against the strong light. 'If Isakovic is not there, what should I do?'

'Don't push,' said Gromov quietly. 'We won't be careless. But there is something else. My superiors are only willing to release twenty-five kilograms.'

'At the same cost?' said Yasin.

'Yes. The quantity is ample. If you want to achieve your plan, I suggest you agree. This is something out of my control.'

'I told you if you cheated me, I would kill you.'

Gromov laughed. 'I am not cheating you. I am telling you.'

'I agree.'

A flash of surprise passed across Gromov's face: 'I like you, Yasin,' he said, then dropped his voice, looking away, trying to be nonchalant in his next remark. 'I told my superiors that killing Venkat was an example to us all of your skills and determination.'

Gromov knew. Gromov might have found the body, but Yasin remained expressionless. At the entrance to the lorry park, Gromov was recognised and the car was let in. Yasin waited in the air-conditioned car while Jesse chose the weapons. He watched customs agents and freight forwarders climb in and out of vehicles and saw their own truck shaking as the weapons were packed, moved to the back and Gromov handed them down to the driver who put them in the boot.

Then, when Jesse and Gromov climbed into the second truck with the anthrax, Yasin got out of the car. Jesse glanced towards him, enough to tell him he understood what he had to do. But Yasin was there, the flap down and the doors open so he had a view down the gap between the filing cabinets in case anything went wrong.

Gromov was right at the back, handing the bags individually to Jesse, then onto Yasin who passed them to the driver, who put them into the car. When it was finished, Gromov pulled the protective sheet back over the remaining ten bags and Jesse went at him with a knife.

Jesse knew knives. He had killed so many times with one that they had decided he should kill Gromov, because Yasin had never done it before, not close up and sudden like this.

Gromov must have known knives as well, because even with his back turned, he sensed it was coming and stepped quickly to one side, turning so that Jesse would have less of a target. Jesse wanted the neck, but instead the knive plunged right through the protective cover over the bags. Jesse pulled it out, its tip covered with anthrax dust, just as the Russian's elbow came up and caught him on the jaw, knocking him back so he caught his head on the edge of a filing cabinet.

By the time Gromov's second blow came, Jesse was ready, weaving the blade, slicing the Russian's forearm, up, over, down, up again in a confusing twisting pattern until he thrust it up into Gromov's chest. Not quite the heart. He could tell that by the way it went in, too soft, the scrape on a rib. Gromov lashed out, but Jesse didn't let it interfere with the knife.

He had taught Yasin how to lunge and be punched at

the same time. 'Keep the forearm taut, blade parallel to the ground, wrist flexible, feet apart if you can, knees bent, bounce with the punch, but don't stop your attack.' Jesse drew out the knife and came back on the neck, one slice. Gromov jerked back, escaped it, and Jesse hit him in the stomach with his free hand, just to bring him back, then took him in the throat. The artery jetted blood and Jesse felt the satisfaction of knowing that, after all these years, he could still fight and win against a man half his age.

Yasin telephoned Jancke. He instructed that the next payment into Gromov's account be cancelled, but transferred another million dollars to the account of Gromov's paymaster. The account holder was to be notified by the receiving bank that these extra funds had arrived.

Yasin paid for the rooms by credit card, except for Venkat's which he left running. Gromov, it seemed, had kept quiet about the killing. The TU-154 took off just after dark and turned west towards Europe.

Milan Isakovic was at the top of the aircraft steps when the cabin door was opened and a chilly wind blew in from across the Batajnica military airfield near Belgrade. He saluted Yasin like an officer, arranged for their visas and passport stamps, then drove them to the port where the bags were separated and stored in different cargo holds on a river barge. Isakovic acknowledged receipt of the extra money. Igor Gromov was not even mentioned.

'In Hungary, our network is strong. But once you enter Austria we cannot help you with formalities,' said Isakovic, almost apologetically, as if his mafia's crusade to corrupt the world had not yet spread far enough. 'If there is anything you need, you contact this number.'

Yasin was given his own cabin on the barge and they left

port as soon as the documents were ready. The next morning Jesse developed a fever.

Unusually, the skies over London were a deep spring blue with wisps of cloud and clear sunlight coming down onto the roof of the hospital across from Samira's room. The advantage of her poor view was that the room was quiet, without the traffic of City Road, and Tim had succeeded in wrestling open the Victorian window to allow a breeze to circulate around and blow across her face.

Stephens had removed the bandages while she was sleeping and the ward sister had alerted Tim that Samira was waking up. She stirred slowly as the anaesthetic wore off and woke without opening her eyes to begin with.

'How are you feeling, Samira?' said Stephens.

Samira blinked and was automatically bringing her hands up to rub her eyes when Stephens grabbed her wrists. 'Don't rub them,' he said. 'Let them work naturally. Mr Pack is here with me.'

He turned on the television, keeping the sound muted. 'Tell us if you can see anything.'

'Is Musa here?' she said drowsily.

'Just me . . . Tim.'

She smiled politely, her eyelids trembling. The daylight showed up the wounds from the bomb explosion, little slices still healing all over her face.

'Yasin?' she asked.

'We're trying to get him here.'

'Samira,' said Stephens. 'The intra-ocular lenses have been successfully implanted. The specks of glass have been removed. Open your eyes and tell us what you can see.'

She blinked, grimaced with the pain, then her expression suddenly changed to surprise. She lifted her hands, touched her fingertips together, moved them apart, then together again. She reached for three pictures which Tim had put by the side of her bed. 'This is my brother and my father in our shop in Omdurman.' She looked at it for a moment, then held it up so Stephens could look at it.

'Is it clear?' he said. 'Is your sight clear?'

'Not clear, but I can see.'

'Put your hand over your right eye and tell me what you see on television.'

'No.' Her voice was sad. 'It's blurred.'

'You can see the colours?'

'Better than before, but it's blurred.'

'Now cover your left eye.'

Her face lit up. 'It's the morning breakfast programme. I can see the clock in the corner of the screen.'

'It's worked,' said Stephens, more to Tim than Samira. 'The left eye was far more traumatised and will take longer to heal. Give it two or three days and she should be fine.'

The nurse knocked on the door and peered round. 'Mr Pack? A Mr Walmsley to see you.'

Walmsley was studying the crest of Moorfields Eye Hospital on the wall. 'The peacocks symbolise the two eyes, and the two shades of the moon must be the divide between light and dark, sight and blindness,' he said as Tim walked up to him.

'She's fine,' said Tim. 'It's worked.'

Walmsley turned to face him. 'An Asian man has collapsed in the street in Budapest with some ghastly disease. Died an hour ago. Could be anthrax. A friend of mine there has agreed to hold the corpse.'

'You want me to go?'

'He's Asian, not African. Could be a Filipino working with Yasin Omer. Take Samira. She might know him. She might be the bait which gets us to Omer.'

# Chapter Twenty-four

*Beijing, China*

'You wouldn't know where Pamela is?' said Jack Jensen to Jennifer, calling her in her office at four in the morning Washington time, sounding edgy as if he hadn't slept. Jennifer had shared a bit of the family tug-of-war which had been going on since Jack was called back to the States. He wanted the family to join him, but Pamela was refusing to mess around with their schooling.

'Not offhand, Jack,' Jennifer replied. She checked her watch. 'But I'm going there in about an hour or so.'

'Will you call me?'

'Even better,' said Jennifer. 'The kids should be back from school then. I'll get them to call you.'

Pamela Jensen squeezed the Peugeot estate between a Beijing Jeep and a Mercedes saloon in the car park outside the International School in Beijing. She waved at other mothers as she got out of the car and fell in with them on the way to the school gates. She would drop the children off at home, make sure the lasagna was ready to microwave, wait for Jennifer and then take off to a warehouse just outside Beijing, where she was negotiating to buy two Ming-style cabinets.

Amanda's nose was dripping. She clutched a handkerchief with her mittens which she didn't want to take off because of the biting cold. Davey was running round and round her with a model Stealth bomber, with big American markings on the wings.

'If you keep making that racket, everyone will know you're bombing them,' said Pamela. She crouched down, pulling a tissue from her pocket to wipe her daughter's nose. Amanda wasn't her usual perky self and her eyes looked dull. Automatically, Pamela touched her daughter's forehead with the back of her hand, thinking Amanda might have a slight temperature.

'Are you feeling all right?' she whispered gently. Amanda nodded and smiled. 'You feel a bit hot,' said Pamela.

Amanda suddenly changed her expression and shook her head. 'My head feels heavy and I'm sleepy, but my nose is blocked, so maybe that's why.'

'Brave girl.' Pamela lifted her up in her arms, making sure that Mary, the blonde doll and signalwoman, was firmly in Amanda's grasp.

'Davey. No!' she shouted as her son, in an over-ambitious turn, slipped on the ice and fell flat on his back. He lay there with a huge smile on his face, then scrambled to his feet. The Stealth bomber had not survived so well. A wing hung from the fuselage and the tiny cockpit window was cracked.

'The wing's broken,' he announced. 'I'll get some glue.'

'No,' said Pamela for the second time, as Davey was about to take off back into the school building. 'You've got glue at home and your sister has a fever.'

Davey led the way to the car and Pamela put them both in the back seat, making sure they did up their belts.

'Are you sick?' he said to Amanda, who shook her head and pointed at their mother. 'She says I am.'

'If you're sick you can't go swimming with Jennifer,' said

Davey. He lapsed into silence to study the damage to his aircraft. Amanda sniffed and Pamela leant over the seat to give her the box of tissues she kept on the dashboard.

'Don't spread your germs,' Davey told Amanda as Pamela started the car and pulled out of the car park.

'I think Mary's got a cold, as well,' said Amanda, imitating Pamela by feeling the doll's forehead.

'Then don't let her spread it to me,' said Davey, grabbing the doll. As Pamela concentrated on easing the Peugeot out into the Beijing traffic, there was a tug-of-war for possession of Mary.

'Let go,' Amanda squealed. Pamela's eyes flickered from a horse and cart piled high with coal on the road to her children squabbling in the back seat.

'That's enough!' she shouted.

'He's trying to steal Mary!' cried Amanda.

'Davey, knock it off,' said Pamela. She slowed the car right down and reached over to help Amanda retrieve the doll. As soon as it was back in her hands, and seeing that she had the support of her mother, Amanda lashed out at the wounded Stealth bomber, breaking off a bomb from under the surviving wing.

'Amanda's breaking my plane,' yelled Davey, by which time Pamela was back in the traffic again and could only witness events with snatched glances in the rear-view mirror.

'If you two don't stop fighting right now, there'll be no swimming, no playing, no nothing with Jennifer.'

The children fell into a submissive silence. Pamela was able to get into the outer lane, clear of lumbering trucks and carts.

'Sor-ree,' mumbled Amanda. Silence.

'Yeah. Sorry, Mommy,' said Davey with more assertiveness. They stayed like that, guarding their respective toys, until Pamela turned into the gates of Greenland Garden

Villas. Then, her cold forgotten, Amanda scrambled forward to get a better look at the swimming pool and Davey cried out in disappointment that Jennifer's car wasn't outside the house yet.

When Pamela pulled into the driveway they unlocked their seatbelts, hurled themselves out of the car and into the house. Davey leapt upstairs to his room, his mind once again fixed on aircraft glue.

The scream he let out made Amanda stop dead in the living room and drop Mary onto the floor. Pamela heard it from outside and ran in. The scream stopped as quickly as it had begun and from upstairs there wasn't a sound.

If there was one thing which was keeping Jennifer Chandler going throughout the morning, it was the prospect of having an exhausting swim with Davey and Amanda. She had kept her cool when another woman answered the phone in Tim's hotel room, reasoning that it was better he had a one-night whore than began a relationship with another woman.

She didn't ring again, although every emotional and female instinct was craving to do so. Instead she went into the office early to finish her report to London, some of which she had e-mailed to Tim.

When Henry Beaton arrived, she invited him into her office for coffee. 'Do you know anything about Stephen Walmsley?' she asked casually, as she tore open a packet and poured brown sugar into Beaton's cup.

'What do you mean?'

'He's a diplomat, right? Not a businessman?' She put the cup on the table and sat down next to him on the sofa.

'Amy not in today?'

'She's copying papers for me. Why? Don't you think I can make my own coffee?'

'Never seen you do it before. That's all.' He sipped his

coffee. 'Walmsley, you say. He's a career diplomat. May have come from the private sector years ago. Why do you ask?'

'He spent a lot of time with Tim. I just wondered if they had a scheme to set up together or something.'

Beaton sat back on the sofa. 'It's a thought. Walmsley must be on his last posting and looking for something else, something to top up his pension. But I don't advise it.'

'Why's that, Henry?'

'It's tough on your own in this town.' Beaton pulled a tobacco pouch out of his jacket pocket, opened it, appeared to have second thoughts and laid the pipe and pouch on the table. 'Your transfer might be happening.'

Jennifer was about to light a cigarette and stopped. 'You fixed it?'

'Not quite. It seems they want you, not in London, but over in New York.' He looked at her with a mix of congratulations and envy, and suddenly Jennifer felt so sorry for him. While she was being shuttled between Asia, Europe and America, he was in his mid-forties and going nowhere except China.

'Why New York?'

'Don't know, Jen,' said Beaton getting up heavily and scooping up his pipe and tobacco pouch. 'Maybe it's something to do with your skills at tracking dirty money. But don't shoot me, I'm just the messenger.'

Jennifer must have got to the Jensens' house minutes after the attackers fled. The front door was open. The Peugeot driver's door was open. The hall chair was tipped over with coats hanging from it, and the framed portrait which faced her when she stepped in was torn off its hooks and had dropped to the ground. Papers were strewn around

Pamela's writing desk in an alcove near the bay window. CDs and video tapes had been pulled out of shelves onto the floor. The cases had been opened. Some were smashed.

Jennifer walked in very slowly. Rocks, weeds, food, water, goldfish, from the smashed fish tank were strewn over the sofa and the electric piano which Jack had bought for Amanda for her sixth birthday. A desk lamp flickered on a broken electric socket. Carpets were torn up and left in heaps.

Jennifer stayed absolutely quiet when she saw Pamela, lying awkwardly underneath an upturned sofa. She righted the sofa, felt her neck and found no pulse. There was blood underneath her torso. Jennifer turned the body of her friend to see how the high-velocity bullet had made such a tiny entrance hole in her front, but had come out tearing her back and vital organs apart.

Jennifer felt sick, her stomach churning, and her whole body shaking. Trembling, she picked up the phone, but the line was dead.

'Davey,' she called out softly, looking up, her hand still on Pamela's shoulder. No answer. 'Amanda,' she tried. Nothing.

It felt as if she was walking through the debris of a fire. Her feet crunched on things, breaking some, stumbling on others, so she tried another way like crossing a stream on stepping stones. She went up the stairs which were littered with bits of paper, broken models and trains from Davey's room. By mistake, she kicked Amanda's latest doll, Mary. She had an arm torn off.

'Amanda,' she said again, louder, more boldly. She stooped down to pick up the doll.

At the top of the stairs, the mess continued. Towels and sheets had been pulled out of the airing cupboard. In Jack and Pamela's room, the mattress had been ripped open and then been upturned. Clothes had been wrenched out of the wardrobe. Underwear was strewn everywhere.

She found Davey curled up by the windows which led out onto the roof terrace. He was like a bundle and as soon as Jennifer saw the position of his limbs, she knew he was dead as well. She touched him. He was still warm, but colder than the living. His eyes were askew in their sockets and the glass around him was cracked but holding together like a shattered car windscreen. It seemed he had been smashed against it.

She glanced out of the window. Children were running around the slide on the playground and swinging in a huge rubber tyre hanging on ropes. There was no activity in the guard house. Whoever had done this must have left minutes ago.

'Jen,' said a faint voice. It came from outside the bedroom, round past the bathroom in Amanda's room. She only said it once. Amanda was too weak to speak again. Her face was drained and pale. She was slumped at the end of her bed, shivering and sweating at the same time. Her clothes were red with her own blood. Her hands were clasped over her stomach, blood seeping through her dress and spilling onto the floor.

# Chapter Twenty-five

*Beijing, China*

Jennifer had never seen anything so miserable as Davey's little coffin. For some reason it had been made white while Pamela's was dark wood, draped with the American flag, and somehow looking normal, because coffins like that were shown so often on television.

They did not seem to have a flag for a child's coffin, so a smaller paper flag had been put on with transparent tape and there was a little brass plaque with his name. Late the night before, an American consular official had called to ask if he should put Davey's aeroplane in with the body.

'That would be nice,' said Jennifer, wondering why they hadn't asked Jack, until the official said, 'Jack's completely devastated about this, and we wanted to do the right thing without . . .'

'That's fine. I understand.'

'But he did ask if you would see the bodies off from Beijing as a special friend of the family.'

'And Amanda?' she asked.

'We're sending a Boeing 727 hospital plane over. We think she's stable enough to make the journey.'

And there, in an isolated, windswept corner of Beijing

International Airport, was the 727. It was parked near a Tupolev-154 from North Korea, a Chinese-made MD11 from Laos and an ageing Boeing from Mongolia. The ambassador came with his wife. CNN was allowed the pool camera for all networks, although they weren't carrying the story live.

A lone marine bugler from the embassy played 'The Star Spangled Banner' as pall bearers marched with Pamela's coffin and placed it onto the cargo ramp. It was more awkward with Davey's coffin because it was too small to have the marines carry it shoulder to shoulder. So two of them took it underarm and they fell out of step, and no one minded because a child, killed with the gun of a madman, would not have wanted marching and the paraphernalia of warfare around him.

Jennifer felt very alone. When she had rung to tell Tim, he was driving in from the airport. He went quiet, then said he would try to call her from a better line, somewhere they could talk. But he hadn't and she felt she was losing him, had lost him, the same knot in her stomach when the shock had passed and she realised that Pamela and Davey were dead, and Amanda was hanging on to life with every difficult breath she took.

She cried, but didn't want to, especially when she realised the television camera was on her face. She wanted to howl alone and then talk to Tim. But instead the consular official stood next to her, hands ritualistically clasped in front of him, the man whose job it was to find coffins and planes to send dead Americans home from whichever country he was posted to.

He glanced towards Jennifer and she saw his sympathetic but professional expression.

The coffins were in and the cargo doors locked, when the ambulance drew up. It was an embassy vehicle with

American paramedics. Two specialists who had flown in on the plane were inside with Amanda.

Jennifer ran over as they wheeled her out. She was in a large incubator, breathing tubes to her mouth and nose, intravenous drip into her left arm, four tubes into her right arm with a cocktail of drugs. Jennifer noticed one was marked as 'morphine'. Her stomach was completely covered in bandages with patches of blood on them.

But her eyes moved. As they had her out on the tarmac, stopping for a few seconds to carry her up to the fuselage, Jennifer was next to her, her hand splayed over the top of the incubator and looking straight at her:

'Amanda. Amanda.' Her eyes flickered. She was conscious. 'Daddy will be there,' Jennifer said.

Amanda might have smiled. She might have nodded. But both movements would have been too slight to tell.

There was nowhere to go but to the office, nowhere to go in the office but to the computer terminal, nothing to do except work and wait. It was a Saturday and Jennifer went straight from the airport to the China World Tower, riding up the empty lift and walking out into corridors with no air-conditioning because they turned it off at weekends.

She let herself in, looking for solitude but hoping also to see Henry Beaton bumbling around with his pipe or Amy catching up with paperwork. For those who lived alone, the office was a substitute family. She turned on the back-up air-conditioning unit and as the computer booted itself, she watched the Saturday crowd twenty-five storeys below, going to Pizza Hut and the German beer house; she was glad she was not among them, wishing she was not even in the city.

She did not expect an e-mail from Tim, although she

checked. While she waited, she brought up the file on the money transfers and read through to remind herself how far she had got.

Ten million US dollars had been sent by telegraphic transfer to account RefTT/53701/840800/ for account number 610000078 at the Mediterranean International Bank in Cyprus. The sender, who had an account at Jennifer's bank, was CA Energy Ltd. CA, she had discovered, stood for Central Asia, a subsidiary of the huge UGO (United Oil and Gas) conglomerate with its headquarters in Docklands.

There was one e-mail waiting for her: 'Jen, this never came from me, but here goes.' Encrypted from David Antoniades in Cyprus. He had replied to her first one, remembering her, flattering her, warning her to wait and not contact him again until he had the information.

She read his message: 'Of the US$10 million transferred to the account, US$3 million has gone to the account of the Carlson Navigation Company in our bank. Check with your people in Singapore and you'll find US$2.5 million went from there to your branch by telegraphic transfer on November 9th last year RefTT/79521/580701/ for account number 800/017528/002. We received instructions to prepare a bank draft for US$6 million and advised it would be collected by a Singaporean national. It is more than my life's worth to give you more.'

Jennifer sipped her coffee, the hotness numbing her tongue. Bank draft. There was no way he would give her the name of the person who drew it. He could already be in trouble for telling another bank so many client details. But he must have been thinking about it, because he had sent a follow-up message half an hour later.

'Check northern Cyprus,' he wrote. 'Locals are banned from going across because of the partition. But a foreign passport holder can walk across the Green Line, deposit a draft in a Turkish bank there and we wouldn't know for months, if ever.'

She e-mailed him back: 'Thanks a million. Who uses Turkish banks in northern Cyprus?'

Then she decided to call Singapore. It was on the same time zone as Beijing and Jennifer thought her suspicion was worth a Saturday morning phone call to Jonathon Huckle, the country manager. The Singapore account had been used by Tamil groups before, but only for much smaller amounts of a few hundred thousand dollars.

'I was going to message you about it,' said Huckle, not trying to hide his irritation. Jennifer was used to the hostility of older but junior men having to account to her.

'But it arrived more than a month ago, Jonathon.'

'We have to be careful, Jennifer. The bank's reputation is at stake if we raise suspicions about our customers without real evidence.'

Jennifer flicked into split-screen and brought up the Tamil file: 'This is the same account which we tracked two years ago: 800/017528/002,' she said, knowing he could hear the tapping of the computer keys down the phone line. 'It contributed US$138,000 to the account of a South African arms dealer, also held at your Orchard Road Branch 800/026834/001. Total amount in from accounts linked to Tamil separatists was US$252,000.'

'Yes,' said Huckle abruptly. 'The same account.'

'Is the money still there?'

Huckle retaliated with his own tapping of the keys. 'It doesn't appear to have been moved on yet.'

'Two and a half million, Jonathon? It's a big jump from . . .'

'I'll get back to you as soon as I have something.' Huckle interrupted but didn't put the phone down first. You don't do that with compliance officers, however much you despise their interference.

'Thank you,' said Jennifer, making sure she exaggerated her East Coast accent. Not only was she younger and a woman, she was an American as well. If narrow-minded Brits like Huckle wanted war, she would give it to them.

The screen flashed with the message-waiting sign. It was David Antoniades replying already. He must be just like her, alone on a Saturday with nothing better to do except go to the office.

'My guess is Russian and Ukrainian organised crime. Why don't you fly over and discuss it over dinner?'

She had her hand on the telephone to ring him, but that would only put him more at risk. Common sense told her it was only a computer message from a randy Cypriot who had flirted with her for a few hours two years ago, and a wonderfully impossible suggestion. She smiled, the sort of smile which for a second erased the murders, the loneliness of the Beijing office, and the rockiness of her relationship with Tim, the voice of the Filipina in his hotel room. She sent the reply to Cyprus: 'Where and when?'

Then she logged onto the Companies House database in London and ran a search on Stephen Walmsley. While that was going on she rang Felicity Shaw at home in New York where it was just before eleven thirty at night.

Felicity and Jennifer had started with the bank on the same day. Jennifer portrayed herself as the all-achieving East Coaster and Felicity countered it with complete English reserve. Jennifer constantly threw back her head to get her hair out of her eyes. Felicity only did it when she actually needed to see.

When Jennifer had asked what people called her for short, Felicity gave her a withering look and said: 'Nothing.'

'Bit of a mouthful,' pressed Jennifer.

'I keep it at four syllables to ensure that men wanting to fuck me aren't too drunk to perform. You try saying Felicity when you're pissed.'

Felicity yawned when Jennifer tried to talk about careers. 'What you don't understand about the English upper class, Jen, is that all our achievement happened centuries ago. We're now relaxing on the laurels of our ancestors.'

It took some months for Jennifer to understand how much Felicity was hamming it up. 'A good smoke, a good deal and a good fuck in that order makes a good day,' Felicity would say to her. But her old money and family and class contacts in the City of London and Wall Street put her far ahead of Jennifer. She soon recognised Felicity as a natural international banker and a good friend. As Jennifer was listening to the phone ringing in Felicity's Upper West Side apartment, she didn't expect her to be in.

Felicity picked up the phone on the tenth ring.

'It's Jen.'

There was a pause. Softly but clearly in the background, Jennifer heard the overture to Wagner's *Tristan and Isolde*. 'Are you in New York or still in the dusty Middle Kingdom of China?'

'China.'

'Then you know what time it is here?'

'Of course. How are you, Felicity?' She listened to the flare of a gas lighter and the drawing on a cigarette.

'A French millionaire was meant to take me out to dinner then walk me home and fuck me. But he didn't turn up. Trouble with the modern millionaire is that he has to earn his money. Always going off to work like carpenters and plumbers.' She paused to take another drag of the cigarette. 'So I'm stuck at home listening to German love songs.'

'Poor thing.'

'China. You must be hating it. Come home, for Christ's sake.'

'Favour, please.'

'Anything to relieve the tedium of this evening.'

'How would I find a six-million-dollar bank draft drawn on the Bank of Cyprus in Nicosia, then deposited in a Turkish bank in northern Cyprus with money transferred to God knows where from there?'

'You wouldn't,' said Felicity straight away.

'Not even once it's drawn in the States?'

'A fortress of a bloody haystack to find anything in. But I said wouldn't. Not couldn't.'

'Go on.'

'Easier if you look for who's handling it.'

'Russians or Ukrainians.'

'The crooks?'

'Yes. And there's a link to United Oil and Gas in the UK and to the Tamil Tigers in Sri Lanka.'

'A truly tangled web.' Jennifer could tell that Felicity was taking notes. 'You mean those handsome young Sri Lankans who kill Prime Ministers all the time?'

Jennifer couldn't help but laugh: 'The very same.'

'They're banned in the States, you know. I doubt we'll find their trail. The Ukrainians are too common for the circles I mix in. But Russians know about class. Leave them with me.'

'Thanks.'

'You will have my undivided attention. But if the Frenchman comes back, you're on your own.' Jennifer was about to thank her again and ring off, when Felicity gasped: 'Oh my God, Jen.'

'What?'

'Have you seen the television from China. That little coffin? At the airport? And the little girl . . .'

'Yes,' said Jennifer quietly. 'I was there.' The phone line stayed open but neither woman spoke.

'Jen, Jen. Are you there?'

She didn't want to talk about Pamela, Davey and Amanda. 'It was a horrible murder of some American expats.'

'I know. I read about it.' Felicity exhaled cigarette smoke. 'They said she heard Russian voices in the house and she knew because she had a Russian schoolfriend.'

And that was when a knot tightened in Jennifer's stomach like she had never felt before. She heard herself repeat it. 'Russians,' she whispered. 'Russians.' Suddenly the strands were coming together. Amanda had recognised them speaking Russian as they killed her brother and mother. David had fingered Russian organised crime as the most likely recipients. A Russian had been gunned down in San Li Tun the night before Tim left.

'Are you OK, Jen?'

'Yes.'

'Are you alone in that office?'

'Yes.'

Felicity knew. Her instincts were sharp like that. She understood that Jennifer was alone and loveless on Saturday morning; that she had known Pamela and Davey. She sensed the sudden fear.

'Are you scared?'

'Yes.'

'Keep the line open. Get someone in there with you.'

She had to pull herself together. It was like a dream when you tumble through the air only to wake up and find everything all right. There was nothing to connect her to anything they wanted in the Jensen house. And David Antoniades was just guessing about northern Cyprus.

'It's OK, Felicity. It's just that I knew the family a bit. It's a strange feeling.'

'You sure?'

'Sure.' She laughed nervously. 'Call me when you've lured the right calibre Russian to your bed.'

Jennifer turned on the television. The report was ending with the correspondent saying no motive was known for the murders. Nor was it known who the killers were. CNN continued with a report that Beijing was no longer a safe city for foreigners to live in.

Jennifer muted the screen and turned her attention back to the computer terminal and the search from Companies House. She read through the results and what she saw filled her with increasing horror.

She pressed the automatic dial button on the telephone for Henry Beaton. When the maid answered she remembered that they were picnicking with the children at the Ming Tombs.

She wondered if there was anyone else, but her mind was numbed by what was on the screen in front of her. Three years in Beijing and the only person she could think of to trust was Henry Beaton.

Then her phone rang. It was her maid, talking hurriedly in Chinese and it took a moment to work out who she was referring to. A Mr Crabbe had called at her apartment. Wanted to go in, but the maid wouldn't let him. Halfway through Jennifer was startled by the ringing of a call on the other line. She put her hand to her mouth, taking the call on the speaker phone, quivering, saying nothing until she heard the cheerful European voice. 'Is that you, Jen?' It was David Antoniades.

'Hi. Yes. Hold on a sec.' She switched off the speaker phone and told her maid she would call back. Then she took a deep breath. 'Hi. Just getting something out the way.'

'I would have called you earlier but didn't want to get caught out on the telephone log from the bank.'

'Thanks for the stuff earlier.'

The breeziness continued. 'I imagined you on a bright Saturday morning sitting all alone in your big bank's office and thought you could do with some transcontinental human contact.'

'Well, I wondered about you doing the same thing.'

'I got in real early and I'm off sailing in half an hour. Want to come?'

Jennifer tried a laugh. 'Don't tempt me.'

'I'm not. I'm asking you. A beautiful woman like you shouldn't waste her youth sending e-mails from a high-rise office block.'

'You mean it would be more profitable drinking champagne on your yacht?'

'I always had faith in your high intelligence.' He sounded as if he was going to say more, but trailed off.

'And?' prompted Jennifer. 'What you're really calling about is . . .'

'What I couldn't say from the bank,' said Antoniades, switching his tone from that of seducer to serious banker. 'I don't know if this six million has gone to northern Cyprus. But let's say it has. Over the Green Line and deposited by a bag man.

'There is a system we know about which is controlled from Moscow. The Bank of Turkish Commerce appears to be a holding bank for Russian Mafia money involved in Central Asia. Oil and mining exploration and that sort of thing. Money is shifted out either to Dubai, Armenia or Kazakhstan. It's then moved on another stage, a paper screen to throw us off the trail, which sometimes brings in the Far East, such as Malaysia or Thailand. It might even go a third stage if they're worried about it being tracked.

'The money is used to get contracts, such as the Xinjiang pipeline, and I don't have to tell you how much the Chinese are involved in the whole of Central Asia. A lot of the money ends up right under your nose in Hong Kong or Beijing, where it's either packed into suitcases and handed over in cash to Chinese officials or put into numbered bank accounts belonging to the new Chinese aristocracy.'

'Where?'

'Used to be Switzerland. But after they opened up to help find the Marcos billions from the Philippines and the Bhutto billions from Pakistan, the Russians have tended to go to Austria.'

'But there's no chance of getting details?'

'Not quickly. But like I said, come over and have dinner.'

'I'm thinking about it,' said Jennifer, before saying good-bye.

When companies move large amounts of money, they often tag a one-line explanation onto the transfer to satisfy the curiosity of compliance officers. When Jennifer checked the transfer to Cyprus by CA Energy Ltd, she was told the US$10 million had been allocated to buy a ship in an auction taking place over the next week. The funds which went on to Singapore were earmarked as setting-up costs for oil and gas exploration in Central Asia. The bank draft, of course, had no explanation with it, which was why it was drawn as it was.

The picture became clearer with the information from Companies House. CA Energy was a wholly owned subsidiary of United Oil and Gas. It appeared to do nothing and, apart from auditing fees, twenty million dollars had sat in its single account gaining interest for more than two years, until half of it was sent to Cyprus.

Two years earlier, Walmsley had resigned as a director of United Oil and Gas and moved to the post of Managing Director of the newly created subsidiary, CA Energy Ltd. She knew about Walmsley. Somehow she expected him there. Then he had left and the current Managing Director was Jim Crabbe, who gave his address as the bank's New York headquarters in the Citicorp Centre on Lexington Avenue. Jim Crabbe, who had threatened her in the China Club with photographs of her past, told her he would ruin her if she stepped out of line and had just been knocking on the door of her apartment.

But it was the name of the Financial Director which made her feel really scared. Alone as she had never been before. Stupid. And, now, as she looked at it again, she knew she would not be spending another night in Beijing.

**The Financial Director** *CA Energy Ltd*, **Timothy Pack, 3 Cromarty Villas, Queensborough Terrace, Bayswater, London W2.**

His signature authorised the US$10 million transfer to the Tamil Tigers.

# Chapter Twenty-six

## Budapest, Hungary

May

'Why have you brought me here?' There were still scars around her eyes, but Stephens' work appeared to be invisible. Samira had been lively, like a little girl, when the bandages were taken off, but the next day, when told they were going to Hungary, she went quiet. He spoke. She obeyed. All Tim's attempts at conversation were rebuffed and the journey had been in silence. They went straight from the airport to the hotel to check in and were now in a taxi heading across the Danube to the hospital.

'We need your help,' answered Tim gently.

She shifted suddenly in the seat. 'Am I your prisoner?'

Tim chuckled politely, shaking his head: 'No, of course not . . .'

'What if I had refused to come?'

'You're free to . . .'

She thrust out her hand, palm open: 'Give me my passport, then.'

'There's no need . . .'

'If you want me to help, give me my bloody passport – now, or I'm getting out at the next set of lights.' Tim tried to take her hand, but she lashed out. The driver caught Tim's eye in the mirror, shrugging in sympathy with a man competing with a yelling woman.

'Crap on you,' Samira said. 'You want me to help you, give me . . .' She stopped as he pulled her passport out of his jacket pocket. She snatched it from his hand and slipped it into the back pocket of her jeans.

She sat back in her seat and they drove in silence for a while. Halfway across the bridge, with the spire of St Matthias' Church ahead of them, she said, 'See just behind us, the parliament building might fall down. The building was surfaced with a porous limestone which doesn't stand up to pollution.' She spoke as if the argument just now had never happened. Tim looked at her with amazement and Samira laughed. 'If you really want to know, it has 700 rooms and eighteen courtyards. It was finished in 1902 at the end of the golden Age of Dualism, the Hungarian Kingdom and the Austrian Empire.'

'How come you know all this?'

'We're doing the Austro-Hungarian period for European history.' Then her expression changed again. 'I was meant to take my A levels in the summer. That won't happen now, will it?'

'I don't see why not.'

'Yasin and I are already a year behind, because we didn't have a very good school in the Sudan.'

Tim recognised her sadness. Her newly repaired eyes gazed at the city, the river, the architecture as if her sight might be taken from her again. The taxi slowed in a queue. River barges, unwieldy, two hooked together, plied along the Danube. Violin music came from the car radio.

Budapest was not like London, which had been bombed, rebuilt and modernised with no time to rest. Nor was it like Khartoum, which had been created by another culture and then allowed to rot. This city had been conquered, liberated, occupied, destroyed, rebuilt and just recently it had taken fifty years off before re-emerging in sorrow and splendour.

Halfway across the Chain Bridge to St Janos' Hospital, she said softly, 'Why are we going to a hospital?'

'Someone has died. We think you might know him.'

'Yasin?' Almost a whisper.

'No. I don't think so,' said Tim.

She moved away as if she didn't trust him, using the window and the sights outside as her escape. She was no longer a schoolgirl, but someone coming to look at a dead man in a hospital, an encounter which would haul her back to face her own unavoidable history.

'You look as if you are Mr Timothy Pack,' said a slim, dark Hungarian in good, but accented English. 'I'm Andreas Gero, International Department of Hungarian Customs. Pleased to be of service.' Hand outstretched, Gero walked towards them through the gates of St Janos' Hospital. His shake was like a vice, giving Tim no chance to grip back. As soon as he released Tim, he turned to Samira,

'Samira Omer,' said Tim. Gero bowed slightly. 'And why do we have the pleasure of Miss Omer's company?' Ignoring his own question, Gero turned and spoke in Hungarian to the guard at the entrance, who picked up the telephone and punched in a number. 'I am asking the mortuary to be ready for us. Those places are so unpleasant.'

'There's a chance Miss Omer might be able to identify the deceased,' explained Tim.

'That one so beautiful could be associated with one so unfortunate,' said Gero, ushering them through the gates with a sweep of the arm.

A gust of wind blew down from the Buda Hills, messing

up Tim's hair, but somehow leaving Gero untouched. The Hungarian's maroon-striped white shirt, yellow tie, gold tiepin and carefully pressed suit showed Pack up as a scruffy Englishman. He self-consciously brushed his hand through his hair.

'Technically, Mr Pack, the police should be showing him to you, but your boss is a friend of my boss from the Cold War, so I was told to help you.'

The hospital reminded Tim of the grounds of a run-down stately home, with tall red-brick buildings and patients sitting out in the grounds enjoying a burst of warm weather.

Gero pushed open a pair of paint-peeled green doors, then turned round with a bemused look on his face. 'Perhaps you can tell me why a customs officer is involved in such a horrible death.'

'The wheels of the British government turn in mysterious ways,' said Tim, keeping the door open so that Samira could go through.

The hospital foyer was empty. Three collapsed wheelchairs and a trolley were pushed under a stairwell. An empty noticeboard pocked with rusted drawing pins faced them. The reception desk was deserted. A telephone rang somewhere along a corridor, but it stayed unanswered.

Gero led the way down chipped concrete stairs, taking them in leaps of two at a time, running his hand down the rail to keep balance. By the time Tim and Samira reached the bottom, he was working the combination lock. Double doors swung open inwards and a smell of chemicals and fresh paint wafted out to meet them.

Suddenly the hospital, or the mortuary part of it, was a living, modern workplace. Staff with clipboards brushed past them. They showed them passports and signed a visitors' book at a pinewood reception desk. Gero took them through another set of doors into a waiting room with red plastic chairs and a soft drinks machine.

'The deceased is in quarantine so we will carry out the identification through the video monitor,' said Gero, picking up a remote and switching on a television set on a coffee table by the wall. He looked sympathetically at Samira. 'Is he a relative?'

Samira shook her head.

'We hope not,' said Tim, suddenly regretting he had spoken. Samira scratched an irritation by her right eye and swallowed hard.

Without the monitor, Tim thought, he would have vomited. The television made it strangely surreal, as if he was watching a gruesome amateur video contest. The camera automatically went through its manoeuvres: wide shot, pan up the body, close-up on the face and settle for the identification. The face was a mess.

'You see, Mr Pack, he could still be contagious, so it is safer this way,' said Gero quietly. 'The blood is frozen, not clotted, you see. That is how he died – his skin and arteries would no longer hold his blood.'

The corpse was a skinny Asian man, fifty or sixty years old, with a moustache congealed with pus, bile and blood. There were bruises and welts over his face and an old scar which ran from his right eye socket to the bottom of his ear. His hair was swept back and frozen as if it had been gelled. Blood had frozen on his skin like sweat.

Samira stepped back to the other side of the room, her hand up to her mouth as if she was stopping herself from screaming. Her eyes flashed around like an animal which wanted to get away. 'It's Jesse,' she whispered, so softly that Tim hardly heard.

'Who?' said Tim.

'Jesse. Dad's gardener.' She sat down, staring at the

television while the camera automatically jerked through a second routine and stopped with a close-up of the wiry torso. It was covered in welts. Even the tag hanging from Jesse's wrist had a fingerprint of blood on it.

'His family was killed when the soldiers attacked Musa's house,' said Samira. 'Yasin was with him in the jungle. It's Jesse,' she repeated.

Gero drove them the few hundred yards down the hill to the Hotel Budapest. It was an ugly round high-rise with tourist coaches in the forecourt. 'He booked in here, but didn't last the night.'

He led them through the depressing lobby of dark brown wood and tubular gold light shades to a cramped bar just off the lobby and ordered coffees. 'The taxi driver picked him up in Moscow Square near here. He saw him get off a number 156 bus which comes down Kutvolgy from District Twelve.'

'What's up there?' said Tim.

Gero shrugged. 'Expensive houses. Barking guard dogs and forests.'

'So you wouldn't know . . .'

'Not the slightest idea.'

Samira spoke, trying to help, a delicate but confident voice which appeared to come from another level altogether. 'I knew Jesse. He would go to the jungle if he knew he was going to die.'

'But he came back,' said Tim.

'He hadn't got a ticket,' continued Gero. 'We have the old system in which you have to buy your ticket from a grocery or newspaper store before getting on any public transport. How would he know to do that?' He shrugged. 'So he had nothing and there was a row with the bus driver which didn't last long because of language. Then he got off and went to a phone booth. It was number 212 3389.'

Gero read from a notepad, proud of his thoroughness. 'He fumbled around for money and didn't have the right change. Our public phone boxes are not the best example of a modern city.'

'Did he make a call?' asked Tim.

'He failed. The taxi driver says he tried looking in the telephone directory but it was all torn. He stumbled and that was when the driver saw he was sick or drunk. Come,' he said, pointing at the three tiny cups of coffee sitting on a tray on the table. He offered sugar. 'He approached the cab looking like death and didn't seem to know where he wanted to go. He said Hotel Budapest, but he could have meant any hotel in Budapest. The driver was from City Cab, one of the more honest of our taxi firms. He followed his instructions to the letter and dropped him here.'

'It's terrible,' said Samira. Tim wasn't sure what to say. Gero leant across and squeezed her arm in support.

'It's sad, yes,' he whispered gently and allowed a few seconds before going on. 'His bag was still packed, the zip done up,' said Gero. 'He must have dumped it on the bed and come straight down again.' He checked his watch. 'It was almost exactly twenty-four hours ago, about five o'clock yesterday afternoon.

'He was walking down this ramp here,' he said, pointing to a curving walkway with a garish carpet and brass banister. 'He went past this bar and he fell opposite the kiosk, pulling down the rack of postcards. Although it was quite warm, he had on an overcoat and a scarf, probably to hide the wounds on his face. He got to his feet, brushed off offers to help and headed for the door. He collapsed just inside the gates of the hospital and died less than an hour later.' Gero smiled grimly: 'End of story.'

'And the bag?' said Tim.

'That is where there'll be a slight delay. Jesse was carrying a French passport under the name of Ernesto Ramos.'

'Can I get to the bag?'

'Not tonight. In fact, if you had arrived any later I couldn't have got you anywhere. Our old communist bureaucracy is creeping up on us. The police are involved. The French are involved. How do you say? We got in there by the skin of our teeth.'

Gero was quiet for a moment and Samira broke the silence: 'Jesse had never left the Philippines in his life. Will one of you tell me what he was doing in Hungary?'

Tim put down his coffee cup: 'We don't know. But we think he's with Yasin. That's why we need your help.'

'That's crap. How can you say that?'

'Jesse. Musa. Yasin. Wake up, for God's sake. We can't get a stronger link that that.'

Samira looked away towards the lobby. 'You've made my brother guilty before he's got a chance to prove his innocence.'

Gero coughed politely. 'I found traces of sunflower grain on the outside of his bag. In customs we see a lot of this in the river barges coming to and from Slovakia and Serbia along the Danube.'

'A river barge?' repeated Tim.

'I guess that what you're looking for is on a river barge heading for Hamburg or Rotterdam. Budapest to Rotterdam is five days' sailing. But we don't know when your man got off. I'm checking as fast as I can.'

They sat in the hotel coffee shop, showered, but drained. She wore a light blouse with bright yellow teddy bears embroidered on the front, laughing nursery characters so out of place with her mood and age. Her hair was pinned back, not like Jennifer's which fell all over her face so that her sentences were punctuated by her flicking it out of her eyes. Samira was much neater.

Samira kept picking up the corners of the pink tablecloth and running her fingernail down the creases. She looked straight up at the cream corrugated-iron ceiling, stared at the strange old aeroplane hung in the atrium, and her gaze moved jerkily up towards the tropical creepers hanging down from the roof. Her eyes were still bloodshot and she complained of the fluorescent light hurting, so Tim took her out onto the river front. They found a café in the square, with violins and a trumpet, and ordered cappuccino.

'Musa, your dad, has also been killed,' said Tim. Samira looked straight at him at last, her eyes filled with angry tears. 'The Philippine military raided his camp on Jolo. He died fighting. I'm sorry.'

She stared out over the river completely still and in silence, her hands gripped together. 'We have to talk about Yasin,' prompted Tim gently. She didn't react at all. Wind swirled litter into the air and towards them, but she didn't move.

'When you saw him that day in the hospital, where was he going?'

Nothing. Her face was tired, ravaged, but steady, as if she had made up her mind about something. 'Did he go back to school?'

Then she spoke. 'Yes.' It was a confident voice. 'Like he told you.'

'How do you know he told me? Has he contacted you?'

Nothing.

'Samira.' He leant forward and touched her hand. 'We think he has a horrible weapon which could kill millions of people. Not just unknown people. Not statistics like you see in the newspaper. My parents could die. My sister who works in London. The doctor who restored your sight. The nurse who looked after you. The other patients who were in the operating theatre after you. Innocent people.'

A man with thick grey hair stood up at the end of a long table of diners and began singing. He moved around, his voice strong and reaching out across the square, his hand resting on each woman's shoulder as he walked around the table. His song gave them a break and Tim closed his eyes for a moment, seeing Jesse's face, mutilated by bacteria, his own prison cell in the Sudan and the wretched figure of young Ablimet Nor dying on a Chinese torture bed.

'Samira,' said Tim, just loud enough to draw her attention from the music. 'If you tell me what you can now, everything will be all right.'

'No, it won't.' An expression of resignation, not happiness and a fixed smile.

'When we get back to London, they will take you away and make you tell them. They will use drugs, Samira. They'll lock you up. They'll be cruel. They'll tell you it isn't a game. We're in a world not many people know about. You might have been at school in England. But this would be different

Eyes wandering blandly. 'I'll run away,' she said.

Tim took hold of her arm and pulled her round so that she was facing him again. 'Look at me, Samira.' He pressed her hand onto the tablecloth. Coffee spilt from the cups.

'Why are you . . . ?' she protested.

'Yasin, Samira. Where is Yasin?'

'You can't . . .'

'Shut up and listen. You *can't* run away. The Hungarian police are watching us. You move from here, they'll arrest you. You try to leave this country, they'll arrest you.' He gripped her wrist harder.

She struggled to free herself. Tim held on for a few

seconds, but the singer noticed them arguing. He stopped his aria and cat-called them, teasing them as if they were lovers having a tiff in public.

Tim let her go and Samira pushed her chair back noisily, metal scraping on concrete. She was free, away from the table, but she didn't move. Perhaps because everyone was watching her. Perhaps she believed Tim about the police. Perhaps she had nowhere to go.

Instead, she offered her hand again, voluntarily and it hung there, for a moment, like an empty flagpole, until Tim took it.

'I'll show you,' she said.

They went back to the hotel, weaving past groups of prostitutes and gamblers outside the casino, up in the glass lift which took them above the palm trees and the coffee shop, down the corridor to her room. Samira confident again. In charge.

The room was immaculately neat. A brown leather sponge bag, zipped up, in sight through the bathroom door. The bed turned down, the white corner of the sheet and a chocolate left by the chambermaid on top. The curtains drawn back with the river lights glittering through.

A book by the African writer, Ben Okri, on her bedside table and next to it photographs of her family, all standing up in a row, the same pictures which had comforted her in hospital, the corners torn to distinguish them.

She moved a laundry basket from the front of the wardrobe, opened the safe, and turned to Tim. 'This is the last I have heard from my brother,' she said, handing him an envelope.

It was crumpled and stained with drops of water which had dried. The paper was poor quality, lightweight, absorbing the ballpoint ink and smudging. Yasin had written hard, tearing the paper sometimes, hard and quickly, page after page, in big sweeping handwriting. There was no stamp or postmark and no address on the envelope.

'When did you get this?' asked Tim.

'When I was in hospital, waiting for the operation. A Filipina nurse gave it to me.' She walked over to the window and talked with her back to Tim, resting her hand on the back of the armchair in the alcove. 'It's in Arabic. You won't be able to understand it. He went to Sri Lanka. He starts "Dear Gazelle". That's me.'

Tim turned the pages. He would get it to London and they would go over it with experts, machines, chemicals and translators.

'He became a Black Tiger,' she continued, talking loudly like a commentator on a Danube river cruise. Tim didn't ask what a Black Tiger was. She was talking now, clawing herself out of her shell. She would tell him in her own time.

'The letter is written in bits. He starts off saying that the Tigers are fighting for their own homeland in the north and east of Sri Lanka. They want to create a new country called Eelam. There was a friend from his school in India there, a boy called Venkat. He said Venkat had run away from the school just like him and had gone down to join the Tigers. As soon as Yasin got there, they made him go on a patrol and machine-gun soldiers after they let off a bomb. Then they made him kill two of them who had been taken prisoner.'

'And he did?'

'Yes.' She lowered her head. He couldn't see her eyes, read any expression. She was taking refuge in watching the river. 'He said it was a real war, not like the one in the Philippines where people died but nobody would win. He said the Tamil Tigers would win their war because they were ruthless.'

She turned her head quickly to look at Tim: 'That's how the word translates – "ruthless".'

Back again to the river, hair falling on her shoulders, the cream shirt coming untucked at the top of her jeans. 'A lot of people would die, but they would win,' she said, picking up her theme. 'After killing the two soldiers, he volunteered to become a Black Tiger.'

She repeated it in a lowered voice. 'Black Tiger.' Then she turned towards him, facing him, her back against the window, balancing on the sill, eyes challenging, confident, proud of her brother, as if through his daring Samira remembered her heritage.

'You would call him a suicide bomber.' Stressing the *you*. She was not an ally in this. She, Yasin and the Tamil Tigers were separate from Tim Pack. 'But he's not. A Black Tiger is a commando who takes on a dangerous mission. Often he is killed, but it is up to the commando to decide what risk to take.'

'You don't condemn,' Tim prodded gently. Silence. Stupid question. 'You, who were a victim of terrorism. I don't understand,' he pressed.

'He's my twin brother,' she replied. She took the letter from him and sat on the bed, thumbing through the pages she had read so many times before. 'Here. This is the name of the place that he attacked. He wrote it in English.' Her finger brushed the page. 'Here. Can you pronounce it?'

Tim sat next to her to read it. He felt old and cynical next to her. It had been a long time since he had been in any woman's room but Jennifer's. He was drawn by a faint unidentifiable perfume which she had put on before they went to the hospital, maybe even before they got on the plane. By the goose-pimples and the darkness of her bare arms. He remembered the same feelings with Jennifer, in the restaurant in Notting Hill Gate, in the taxi, the surge of first attraction.

'Kilinnochi,' said Tim. He knew it vaguely as a second-league disaster site for foreign correspondents, like Goma, Pristina, Aceh and the rest.

'They tested him in the ambush against the army convoy and the killing of two prisoners in cold blood. Then he wanted to become a Black Tiger. So he was trained more and in his first mission he drove a truck full of explosives into an army camp.' She watched Tim as if expecting congratulations. 'He was to set the fuse and drive it straight through the gate. If he could get out, he should, but the main purpose was to blow up the camp. He waited until dusk when the kiosks at the entrance of the camp were closed and the Tamil shopkeepers had gone, so the only people he would kill were the army. He waited back in the jungle where he set the fuse and then he drove along the road and was about to turn into the camp when he saw a boy trying to catch a cow which was running into the camp.'

'A Tamil boy?'

Samira nodded. 'The explosives were about to go off. So he accelerated the truck into the camp. He jumped out, picked up the boy in his arms, ran into the road and took cover in a culvert.'

What was she saying? Her eyes were shining with pride. She had told the story as a translator, running her finger down the lines of the letter as she spoke, moving closer, making sure that Tim could see. She stared at him for a reaction, for his agreement.

'Why?' asked Tim gently.

'He had to save the boy.'

'No. That's not what I mean. Why did he want to kill himself?'

'Because . . .' She faltered. 'I know it in Arabic. But I can't explain.'

'It wasn't even his war.'

'All wars are his wars.' It was a quotation. It must have been in the letter.

'Do you want him to die?'

'If he must.' In the letter again. Her grip slackened on the sheets of paper and she rested her hands on her lap.

'Why?' He kept it soft and repetitive, for the question was crucial.

'Because . . .' Hesitation again, drawing in the cultures from Africa to Asia to Eastern Europe. 'In Arabic, in our culture, it is to do with honour.'

She shook her head. She was quivering again. She let the sheets of the letter drop to the floor, where they blew slightly in the draught from the air-conditioning. She turned to Tim as if she was trying to stop herself from reaching out. She was nineteen. She was a schoolgirl. She needed to feel safe. Her watery, injured eyes pleaded for it and she couldn't help it, throwing her arms around him, burying her head in his chest and against his shoulder. He let her cry, let her be frightened, let her feel safe with him, squeeze his shoulders, cling to him for safety, use him as the father she kept losing.

He held her until her breathing slowed down and she wanted to wipe the tears from her face, so she let go and came back into the world, reaching for a handkerchief in the pocket of her jeans.

She dabbed her face and smiled, embarrassed at herself. She started picking up the sheets of paper and he stopped her, a gentle touch of the wrist, hands on her shoulders, then up to her cheeks, cupped around them, their faces inches apart, the breath, the smells, the confused attraction of age and race and the uncertainty between refuge and pleasure.

He held her head, his palms feeling the warmth of her cheeks, so that she would have to look at him.

'Would he?' whispered Tim. 'Would he really want to kill himself, and millions of others too?'

The movement of the head was the answer and he let her do it. He released her: 'Before. No,' she said.

'Before when?'

Silence.

'Sri Lanka?'

Nothing.

'Jolo. Jesse's family?'

'Yes. That. That definitely changed him.'

'Why, though? Why?'

'Don't you see?' She shook herself loose from him and stepped back, her hands out as if suddenly she needed to protect herself. 'He is my twin,' she shouted. 'I know how he feels and you know *nothing*.'

Tim stood up, stepping towards her, as he would with Jennifer when she yelled at him. But this was different and he hesitated.

'Get back and listen,' said Samira, her back to the window, as far away from the bed as possible. 'I'll tell you why he would kill himself and a million others. Because he believes there's nothing else he can do. He called me Gazelle in the letter. I translated it for you and you didn't even ask why. In Omdurman, we used to pick-pocket people. I would throw myself in front of them crying and pretending to be sick and he would cut off their money belts and snatch their cameras. I was Gazelle and he was Chameleon because he would vanish into the crowds like an invisible man.'

'Bian Shi Lung,' whispered Tim to himself. *The dragon which changes colour – a chameleon.* From the Ablimet Nor video. Samira ignored him. 'That was how poor we were. There were no tourists in the Sudan because you people said we were a terrorist state. So we had to become criminals. Then you killed our parents. When we went to the

Philippines, we really thought it would be all right. Then you attacked Musa and killed Jesse's family . . .'

'What do you mean *we* attacked?'

'You. You're all the same. What could Yasin do? Nothing. Don't you see? Don't you *see*?' She gripped the back of the chair, her whole body swaying from side to side. 'Look at you. All you know is to threaten. Take away my passport. Have me followed. Give me truth drugs. Threat, threat, threat, fucking *threat*! You make a human being feel like useless shit, and to be a human being again Yasin has to kill. Don't you understand? He has to kill or be killed to be alive.'

She sat on the chair, hunched forward, breathing hard, but not speaking for some time. 'There's a bit in the letter I didn't translate for you. It says: "The violence in Zamboanga began because of the economic crisis and it got worse when the banks closed down Musa's businesses. If that had not happened, Jesse's family would be alive now. You and I would be at school. We must find a way to really punish the people who cause all these problems. Something like the Americans did to Japan with the atom bomb."'

Suddenly, Tim was back in the Philippines, in the back of the car with Yasin, him grinning at the thought because then he still thought he was a schoolboy. *I would find a place where the bankers, presidents, prime ministers, finance ministers were all together and blow them to smithereens. That would teach everyone a lesson.* And suddenly, with dreadful clarity, he knew where Yasin was going.

'Would he do it?' he said, trying to be calm.

She looked at him, her eyes hard, proud of her brother. 'Oh yes. Yes, he would.'

# Chapter Twenty-seven

When Tim got back to his room, he called Stephen Walmsley. 'The target will be economic,' he began. 'He wants to punish the people who control the global economy.'

'Have you got an identification?'

'Let me finish,' insisted Tim. 'The G7 meeting in London next month is about the currency crisis which ruined Abu Musa. The dead man was Musa's gardener, a man called Jesse. He died twenty-four hours ago and the Hungarians think he was on a river barge heading towards Western Europe. Rotterdam or Hamburg is four or five days' sailing from here.'

Tim knew what Walmsley was going to say and he did. 'You had him and you let him go?'

'The barge, Stephen. We have to find the barge.'

'Don't go soft this time, Tim, or this stuff could be in the lungs of half London.'

A rap on the door interrupted and Tim opened it, still on the line to Walmsley. Gero stood there beaming. 'Your lucky evening, Mr Pack. There's an old man at the port who claims he saw a sick man get off a barge of sunflower grain. And we can go down.'

Tim told Walmsley they would talk later and picked up his jacket. 'I need someone to watch Samira's room.'

Gero grinned: 'Are you afraid she will run away or be unfaithful?'

'Someone who you trust completely,' continued Tim. 'She has just had major surgery on her eyes and suffers from bouts of post-operative depression brought about by the anaesthetic.'

'Follow me,' said Gero, suddenly serious. In the lobby he peeled off a wad of Forint notes, pressed them into the hand of the concierge and turned to Tim. 'He will personally sit outside the room until we get back.'

Tim moved a map and a copy of *Newsweek* from the front seat to get in Gero's Lada. Gero started before he had the door shut. 'You're lucky. I've been told to help you with everything, however crazy.'

Gero drove jerkily, flashing his lights, and weaving through jumbles of dirty yellow trams. 'He's off shift in twenty minutes, so we have to drive fast,' he said. They turned left outside the hotel and headed along the river. The brief dusk was finished and headlights swept along the big roads on both sides. Once out of the central district, the magnificence of the buildings faded. Budapest shed the public face of its history and replaced it with drab apartment blocks, with dismal concrete playgrounds and open spaces of rusting broken cars.

'I hate this place,' said Gero. 'I hate what the communists did.'

'I've seen worse,' said Tim

'Where's that?' Gero swung out to the left to overtake a tram.

'Khartoum.'

'Africa?'

'Where Samira comes from.'

'Africa. A big mess.' He brought the Lada back onto his side of the road. He was thoughtful for a moment. 'Big mess,' he repeated. 'Is that why you have to slap her around?'

Gero overtook a truck and a bus, just avoiding a face to face collision with a speeding Mercedes. Then he took a sharp turn right. 'Thank God you're here. I am in the middle of a divorce and my soon to be ex-wife is giving me hell. I got home and she started screaming at me. What had I done? Nothing. I tell you, I was born and I work. She wants a divorce. But she wants a big argument too. She is very young, only twenty-four, and still chasing dreams like we all used to.'

The street lights ended and the road became a single track in thick undergrowth. 'Is your wife beautiful, Tim? I can call you Tim, can't I?'

'Sure, but I'm not married.'

'Is she your girlfriend?'

'Who?'

'The black girl. She's very pretty, but who cut up her face? Her boyfriend?'

'An accident.'

He slowed the car on the corner. 'So you're not married?'

'That's right.'

A barrier was up ahead. 'I don't know if you're lucky or not. I love being married. My wife's beautiful, but crazy.'

He flashed his headlights at the guard. After a hurried conversation in raised voices, the Lada was allowed through. Warehouses stood out against the night sky like barren hill tops. The Lada bumped over pot-holes, through cobbled courtyards and across railway tracks. As they got closer to the loading bay they could see smashed windows and rusted metal on the buildings. Rail trucks stood neglected with grass growing around their wheels.

Gero hunched over the wheel, slowing when he thought

he saw movement in a dark patch away from his headlights, accelerating again when it turned out to be a changing pattern of moonlight caused by moving cloud.

They drove along the waterfront, passed worn boats and barges with lights in their cabins and figures clustered on the decks, examined and ignored by Gero in his search.

'Does he know we're coming?' said Tim.

Gero shook his head. 'If he did, he would run.'

'Then, if he sees us now . . .'

'Shhh,' insisted Gero. He took his foot off the accelerator and pointed across the railway tracks towards the river. A man was caught in the beam of Gero's headlights. He turned, shielding his eyes, leaning on a stick.

'Stay in the car,' Gero said. He left his door open.

The man's conversation began with a shake of the head, the headlights showing up a line of gold teeth and a trimmed grey beard. Gero pulled out his customs identity card, but the headshaking continued, more resolutely, the stance more confident, the hand pushing the card aside, as if he did not recognise the authority of modern Hungary.

The man opened his military greatcoat to show a red badge with stars and a sickle pinned to the lapel of his jacket. He tapped it angrily, then prodded the ground between them with his stick, marking out his territory as a frontier against all that Gero represented.

Gero pointed to the car. The man glanced up, reluctant but inquisitive, hands up in the light again to protect his eyes, a shrug, banging the stick on the ground in impatience, and then a distraction, the foghorn of a boat from the Danube, difficult to make out the vessel itself because a thin drizzle had begun to fall. A river barge appeared beyond the bend, its own lights showing up the different shades of rust on the hull. Piles of grain or sand spilled out from the holds and the flag hung limply in the rain. Gero slipped some money into the man's pocket.

The man's hand came up, a finger pointing to the sharp right-angle bend of the water-way. Perhaps the barge was too long to make the turn. Or perhaps he had seen a thousand barges come in before. The hand came down and felt inside the pocket, testing the texture of the note.

A nod and they walked towards the car. Tim scrambled into the back seat, but the man ignored him, climbing into the front, closing the door and filling the car with smells of old clothes and barge oil.

'His name is Kun and you owe me a hundred dollars,' said Gero in English.

Kun knew where he wanted to go. He guided Gero onto a railway line which ran between two warehouses. Advertising signs of multinational shipping companies – Evergreen, Hapag-Lloyd, Seaco, Matson – were nailed to the wall. The main double doors were padlocked and broken glass lay on the ground. Grappling hooks dangled overhead like birds of prey.

'Stop,' said Kun in Hungarian. They couldn't have gone much further because a rail truck blocked the way. Kun got out and walked around the front of the car, stepping over fallen power cables coiled like eels on the ground. He lifted up the stick, pointed at a darkened doorway on a small platform from where cargo was loaded. He talked to Gero.

'He says he found him here, asleep one night.' Gero and Tim got out of the car.

'When?' Tim said.

'I'm asking him.'

Tim stepped into a deep puddle with splintered wood floating on top. He felt the chill of cold water seeping into his shoes. They all climbed onto the platform.

'He wants to know if you've got any American ciga-rettes?'

'I don't smoke.'

Kun squatted, using his stick for balance and spat on the ground. He mumbled and Gero had to bend down to hear him. 'He wants to know if you think you'll live longer.' Kun was speaking again. 'He says even if you don't smoke you should know that an old caretaker at the docks would need cigarettes. We'll have to give him more money.'

'So give it to him.'

Kun spat again, noisily.

'Not so quickly.' Gero had his own cigarettes out, offering one to Kun, who began a new conversation.

'He wants you to know that he has worked here for twenty-seven years, since the days when Janos Kadar and Nikolai Khrushchev were making Hungary great. Did you know that Hungary was the most successful country in the whole of Eastern Europe?'

'Yes,' said Tim. 'Tell him I did.'

'Do you remember Janos Kadar, he asks?'

'Tell him I think Kadar was a brilliant leader.'

Kun pushed himself to his feet and answered. Gero translated. 'He says you're talking crap. You don't even know who Kadar was.'

Gero lit Kun's cigarette, showing their faces to each other, lighting up the doorway where Jesse had hidden among sodden litter with leaking water dripping noisily onto it. Gero snapped shut the flame, the light gone, their eyes adjusting again, the place even darker, except for two red glows of tobacco. Kun coughed and talked to Gero.

'He wants to know what is your most important question.'

'What does he mean?'

'I'm translating exactly.'

'But what does he want?'

'He wants what he's got. Our attention.'

'Jesus. Is it going to be like this . . . ?'

'Don't let him know he's getting you impatient.' Gero put on a smile. 'Should I say getting impatient or making impatient?'

'You should say "making". Making me impatient.'

'If we want to find out what happened.'

'The most important thing I need to know is when he found Jesse. If Jesse told him anything.'

More talking. More dampness inside Tim's shoes. His legs ached from the squatting, but to get up would be to show his irritation. No doubt Kun wanted that too.

Kun tapping his fingers on his stick, speaking in long unbroken sentences, while Gero nodded, handing over another cigarette, Kun pulling out papers, dog-eared, torn, the Party card and his army card, a picture of himself with a rifle.

Then suddenly a heated exchange. Was Gero play-acting? Did he care about the 1956 uprising? Did he hate Kun, the communists and all they stood for? Was Kun getting to Gero, like he had wanted to get to Tim, so that Jesse and the purpose of being here had become lost?

Gero standing up; Gero lighting his own cigarette but not Kun's; Gero raising his voice; Gero glancing up and swearing at water dripping around them; Gero losing his cool; Gero pulling out more money and showing it in such wads that Kun stared, mouth open, teeth glinting in the little bit of light around; Kun pushing it away, his trembling, brittle hand gripping the top of the stick, Kun showing off the communist badge again, better than money, didn't need money then, when the worker was a prince and the rich man a thief.

Gero moving back, peeling off a note, green, a hundred

US dollars. The second one. Both turning, distracted by shouting from the quay, the engines of the river barge coming alongside, trucks and cranes, the port alive again with the sounds of the past. Kun smiled in memory.

'What's happening?' said Tim.

'Don't say a word,' whispered Gero quickly.

Tim stood up and stepped back. His shoes squelched. Kun starting talking. The money seemed to be forgotten.

'He's telling us Jesse was sick,' said Gero.

'When?' pressed Tim.

'Let him talk.'

But Kun had stopped talking. He pushed his stick into the ground, leant on it and spat yet again. Then he shrugged and walked away, down onto the railway line, in front of the Lada, squeezing out by the disused rail trucks.

'We can't just let him go,' said Tim, jumping down onto the track. Gero jumped down next to him and grabbed his arm, holding him back.

'He wants to see the barge come in. Leave him.'

'Leave him and what?'

'Give him time.'

Tim shook Gero's hand off his arm and took him by the shoulders. 'Andreas, we don't have time.'

Tim's mobile rang, a piercing and modern shrill against the grinding mechanical sounds of the port. Gero watched with irritation as Tim answered it. Jack Jensen was on the line, calling from Amanda's hospital suite.

'I hear you're in Budapest with an anthrax case,' said Jensen.

Tim stepped away, talking softly so as not to disturb Gero and Kun any more. 'How did you find out?' he asked.

'I guess through Walmsley in London.' A monitor bleeped in the background. 'Sorry,' said Jensen. 'I'm at the hospital.'

'How is she, Jack?' He could imagine Jensen watching the green digital figures alternating between his daughter's pulse and the oxygen level of her blood.

'Fine. Well as fine as can be expected. The bullet's been removed from her stomach and her prognosis is good.'

'And you?'

Jensen sighed. He sounded exhausted. 'It'll be a long time. Even now I can't tell sometimes if she's drifted into unconsciousness or is just sleeping. These bloody alarms going off all the time.' He broke off, to talk to a nurse, then came back on the line again. 'Anyway, tell me about Budapest.'

'A Filipino travelling on a French passport has died, possibly of anthrax poisoning. They're testing it now. We think he was on a barge heading across towards Germany or Holland.'

'How long was he sick for?'

'We're trying to find out. I'm actually at the port now.'

'Do you know when he was found?'

'Hold on, Jack.' Tim saw Gero and Kun walking off, Gero squeezing out past the rail trucks following Kun, an unsteady, tottering figure propped up by a stick. Tim shouted at Gero, '*When* did he find him, Andreas? Find out.'

'One guy?' pressed Jensen.

'A port official. Not even that really. A night watchman. I'll call you back.'

There was shouting from the waterside, an argument between Kun and Gero. Tim jumped down from the platform, following them through puddles, weeds and grit, away from the warehouses into the open where it was cooler, the rain stinging his skin, the night unfurling along the docks as his eyes became accustomed to a different type of darkness, new shapes, trucks, bollards, ships.

Kun walked away from them along the quayside, close to the water as fast as he could with his gammy leg and stick, talking with a cigarette between his lips, the ash glowing in the darkness, bobbing up and down on his words.

Gero could have caught up with him easily. But he trailed Kun, within earshot, talking to him as well.

When Tim reached them, Gero waved him back. 'He says the boat was registered in Belgrade, built in Gdansk in 1953.'

'What's he doing?' said Tim, as Kun stomped further on.

'He's trying to remember. He's ashamed.'

'Of what?'

'Shut up. Stay back.'

Tim let them go. Gero, moving forward in pace with Kun, head upright, hair swept back, eyes straight ahead, cigarette packet in one hand. Marlboro. It had to be if someone wanted an American cigarette in a foreign country.

Kun slipped. He swore and tried to stop his fall with the stick, but the stick failed to grip on the wet cobble and flew out of his hand. He lost his balance. Gero dashed forward just in time to break the old man's fall, cupping his hand under the bare skull.

Kun twisted himself away from Gero and angrily tried to get up. Tim stood over them. 'Is he all right?'

'He's fine, I think,' said Gero. 'He's got some sort of memory loss, I don't know how you say in English. He cannot remember what has happened today or last week. Only far into the past.'

'But he remembers Jesse?'

Kun got to his feet, picking up the stick as he went. He brushed down the lapels of his coat and touched the communist badge on his shirt, checking it. He unclipped it, pinned it on the other side and talked to Gero.

'He wants to know why you're still here.'

'Tell him something – anything.'

'He's angry because he doesn't remember things. He says he can do ships and their numbers. Ships and numbers are his life, you see.' Gero paused, while Kun talked. Falling rain blurred the lights of the port; Tim felt it getting into his clothes. 'Yes, he remembers Jesse but it could be a face from thirty years ago.'

'You mean he might not be talking about Jesse at all.'

'It's barge number 1822, hyphen B.' Gero listened again to Kun. 'It was registered here by Mahart's, that's the old Hungarian shipping company which used to run the port. Mahart's knew the boat well.'

'You said it was registered in Belgrade.'

'It doesn't matter. It's a different sort of registration.'

'Can we check if it called . . . ?'

'It was going to Komarom,' Gero continued.

'Where's that?'

'The northern frontier control before the river turns west and runs along the Slovak border.' He spoke sharply to Kun. 'Any boat going to Western Europe would pass through it. It means nothing.'

'Can we check the boat? Whether it was here recently?'

'Sure. We'll wake up the Customs House.'

They walked through the rain to the office at the gate house, keeping Kun with them, not even trying to get him into the car in case he refused and became difficult again. The office was freshly painted, blazing with fluorescent lights and modern furniture.

A football match had just finished on satellite television. The duty officer was young and enthusiastic. He told them they had arrived just at the right time, at the end of the Hungary–Denmark friendly.

He brought down the file for the last month, a heavy

black hard-cover folder, with clips holding the papers in.
Denmark had lost 2–0, the first time since the end of
communism that Hungary had beaten them.

'You like Manchester United?' the duty officer asked Tim
in bad English as he opened the folder.

'They're my team,' lied Tim.

The customs officer looked up with a huge smile and
shook Tim's hand again. 'We are brothers, then,' he said.
He studied the documents. 'Ah, yes, here's barge 1822.
We've got copies of crew lists, bills of lading, letters of
credit. Whatever you want.'

'What was its cargo.'

'Sunflower grain. It was heading north and through
Komarom . . .

'The date,' pressed Tim. 'The date.'

The duty officer raised a nicotine-stained finger to his
calendar and Gero looked over his shoulder, shaking his
head.

'Eight days ago, Tim,' he said softly. He spoke in Hungarian
to the duty officer, who left the file open, walked to the desk
and dialled a telephone number. Gero talked to Kun, but the
old man was staring at the floor. The duty officer talked in
German to Hamburg. He reached over and pulled a notepad
towards him and wrote down a number. He dialled again.
This time he spoke in Dutch.

'He's talking to Rotterdam,' said Gero. 'The Danube dis-
appears south and the river and canal network to northern
Europe gets entwined and ends up with the Maas or the
Rhine.' Gero paused, writing something down. 'Entwined,
Tim. Is that the right word?'

'It'll do.'

The duty officer put down the phone and talked rapidly
to Gero, who whistled through his teeth. 'He says he's lucky
that a friend of his was on duty. The barge got to Rotterdam

three days ago. The cargo was cleared by customs and only afterwards did immigration discover that the number of crew members who arrived on the barge – well, there was one missing.'

'Jesse?' said Tim.

'Who?' Gero asked the duty officer, waiting for an answer, then translating it for Tim. 'Someone travelling on a French passport. Must have been your man. Either the immigration made a mistake, or someone was bribed. Given they were Dutch, I suspect the former. What is it, Tim? What is on that barge?'

'I can't say, Andreas,' said Tim. 'I'll tell you when I can.'

Gero shrugged. 'My guess is they would have brought it through Belgrade or Bucharest. The corruption there is so bad that if they can bribe an immigration officer in Holland, for the same price they can conquer the world from Serbia. The river is easy because we don't put resources into policing it. This barge, the customs people knew it.' He tilted his head towards the duty officer. 'He says they knew the captain.' Gero spoke as if he was apologising, covering up for not being up to standard. 'You know how long it takes to search a boat. Four days. You have to have a reason to do it, Tim. If you had let us know we could have helped. We have informers with the Mafia. The Ukrainians. The Russians. The Serbs.'

'We didn't know. It's OK.'

'We could have . . .'

'It's OK, Andreas,' repeated Tim. 'It's fine. But if the barge was in Rotterdam eight days ago, it means Jesse was here for three or four days with Kun before he died.'

The old communist, his eyes blank and watery, stood some yards away, grasping the top of his stick like high ground against flood waters. His mind was his own. It would tell them nothing more and, besides, Jesse was dead and the barge was days away. Kun had told them that at least.

Then Tim's phone rang again and it was Walmsley. 'The Hungarians have confirmed anthrax. The Americans have matched the strain to the stuff that killed the Pakistani driver who died in December.'

# Chapter Twenty-eight

## *Vlissingen, Netherlands*

On the long barge journey to Rotterdam, along the Danube and the Rhine, and the smaller rivers which Yasin had never heard of, they talked about how they would get the bags to England. Should they take them across in a truck, in a car or on a yacht? Yasin preferred a way where there would be no trace. No papers. No number plate. No passports. They studied the English coastline from maps on board the barge and looked at places to bring it in.

Jesse's sickness spurred them on more than anything else. They knew he was dying and, before he left the barge in Budapest to find a hospital, Jesse had contacted the Philippines and told four more people from Jolo to go to Rotterdam and meet Yasin there: a carpenter who spoke good English, two drivers who had worked in Malaysia and knew how to drive on the left, a navigator, a man whose night vision had guided boats across the unlit seas between Zamboanga and its islands.

'You must see it through,' Jesse had insisted to Yasin. 'For me. For my wife. For my family. For Musa. For yourself.'

Yasin had stayed with him as the barge turned sharply into the port and they looked at the lights and buildings of the strange country where Jesse would have to die. 'I understand now, what you meant,' he said. 'About not killing the poor people. Thank you for making me understand that.'

The drivers met them in Rotterdam with two vans rented on forged credit cards. The magnetic data had been copied from swipes at restaurants and hotels around South East Asia and sent to the forger in Manila. They were all corporate cards, belonging to international businessmen who were unlikely to even see the accounts before they were paid. The cards would be used just once and the car-hire companies would not put through the transaction until the vehicle was returned and the account settled. By then, everyone would be far away in other countries.

From his hotel, Yasin telephoned a property lawyer in Amsterdam whose number he had found in an international magazine. He said he wanted to take out a six-month lease on a house with a private garage in a secure location in central London. The property's owner must be domiciled outside of the United Kingdom. He faxed over copies of a British passport of a Richard Holden, a creation of the forger in Manila. He gave the lawyer Power of Attorney and rang Hans Jancke to transfer funds into the lawyer's account. None of Yasin's money ever entered British jurisdiction and neither his, nor Richard Holden's name, would appear on the lease.

Then Yasin and one of the drivers flew to England on Dutch passports. The car rental offices were busy with the early morning flights from the Far East. Queues stretched from the counters right out of the building, but Yasin was happy to wait, happy not to be noticed, grateful for the English inefficiency which Samira had told him about.

The drivers had decided on a five-cylinder Mercedes-Benz Sprinter. The welder wanted a high roof and a raised laminated sun-roof which could be used in the dissemination of the anthrax spores. The staff were so flustered they barely noticed the quiet, foreign-looking customers with a British driving licence. The driver hardly spoke a word, saying 'yes' to the extras, insurance, damage waiver, fuel, and handed over the American Express card specially created for the purpose.

They headed straight to the east coast and found the two landing sites the helmsman had wanted: Shingle Street in Suffolk or Horsey Corner in Norfolk, both isolated coastlines with shingle or sand to bring up a flat-bottomed boat. In the afternoon, they drove back to London and picked up keys to the house at a private compound called Tudor Court in West Kensington. They parked the van and went in by taxi to look. It was a modern compound, built like a Swiss chalet village, with a twenty-four-hour guard on the main gate, another gate operated by a fob key to an underground garage and then a secure roll-down door to a double garage. For Yasin's purpose it was perfect. Each level of security was a layer through which the police would have to pass to catch him.

The two drivers checked into the Olympia Hilton on Hammersmith Road and Yasin took the 21:50 KLM flight back to Rotterdam.

Two days later, Yasin stood on the beach at Vlissingen, the helmsman beside him. There were wisps of clouds but nothing that hinted at a storm, and while the North Sea was never flat like the Pacific, it was not turbulent as it had been in the past few days, nothing like the waters between the islands of the Sulu Archipelago.

'We will be ready tomorrow,' the helmsman said.

## London, England

Thirty minutes after Tim arrived home at Queensborough

Terrace with Samira, Stephen Walmsley called and gave him an address along Chiswick Mall. 'We've secured your house. Red-box surveillance. Leave her there and be here within the hour,' he said.

At the Chiswick house, a policeman outside knocked on the door when Tim approached. A female RAF staff sergeant showed him through the hall upstairs to a first-floor sitting room, sparsely and elegantly decorated with prints of the Thames on the wall, the floor stripped to polished boards and covered with carpets from the Middle East. The windows generously stretched from just above the floor to just below the ceiling, throwing in natural light.

The host was a large, animated man dressed in a charcoal-grey pinstriped suit, hand-cut to take in his barrel chest and ample girth. As soon as he spoke, in a courteous drawl from the American South, Tim recognised him as a former United States ambassador to the Court of St James.

'Mr Pack, I'm delighted you could make it,' he began. 'My name is Harold Parsons.' He paused while the question of his nationality, the house, his residence in Britain and the meeting hung in air. 'Yes,' said Parsons as if the explanation was a given. 'I couldn't face the prospect of moving again. Thirty-five years in the foreign service and I said no more packing boxes.' He tidied a flap in the curtain. 'So I stayed in London and I love it.'

'Why not leave some open, Harold, so we can catch the evening over the river?'

'Mr Pack, may I introduce Alexander Hogg, former chairman of the Joint Intelligence Committee?' said Parsons, pulling a cord to leave a gap of light through the windows. 'Mr Pack, as you know,' he was addressing the half dozen guests in the room now, 'has been on an odyssey through Asia, Europe and eventually to Chiswick, and we hope he's going to share some of his thoughts with us this afternoon.'

Tim looked around at the group of men, most of whom were at least a generation older than he. Walmsley was standing by a window at the end of the room. He acknowledged Tim, with the smallest nod. It was his way of telling Tim that he was on his own.

'I had not the faintest idea that anything at all like this existed,' Hogg was saying. 'Then it made so much sense that old war horses like us could be put to good use and not just out to grass in the rose gardens of Sussex.'

There was a murmur of response, but not laughter, because the mood was too subdued for that. 'I spoke to Bill Fallon, our former National Security Adviser,' said Parsons. 'We, that is America, appreciate your help so far. His view is that if we can contain it, all the better. By contain, he means handle it ourselves, within this group.'

'Hello, Tim,' a soft, embarrassed voice from a corner of the room. Tim hadn't noticed Jack Jensen sitting in an upright chair in the far corner. Jensen stood up and Tim walked over and shook his hand. 'What the hell are you doing here?' he said, glad to see a familiar face from the field.

Jensen smiled uncertainly. 'I wanted to finish the job.'

'But Amanda. How's Amanda?'

'She's just come out of intensive care. Her grandmother's with her.' Jensen's voice was lowered so the two of them appeared to be in a secret huddle, while the others stayed silent. 'They were Russians, Tim,' he went on. 'She had Russian friends at school and recognised the language.'

'Tim, take a seat.' Parsons, gently interrupting and shifting to first names, had his hand on a chair, and back to the window with the others in a semi-circle around him.

'Perhaps we should explain to Tim what we are all doing here.' A tall thin man, with wisps of grey hair, put down his teacup. 'My name is Dennis Cusk. I used to be a Mandarin in the Foreign Office. You will see how the meeting itself exposes the flaws in our democratic system, but don't let that put you off.'

'Matthew Bradley,' said another guest, short and muscular with signs that he still worked out in the gym, the sort of chest muscles which don't come from tending roses. 'I used to run the Porton Down biological warfare laboratory. I've been working with Jack Jensen and Felix Frazier over in the States.'

'The Prime Minister has the authority to delegate decision-making to this group without cabinet approval,' said a slightly younger man, late fifties probably but with a boyish face. 'I'm Adam Hodge. I am one of those civil servants who had a job which never existed,' he added with a smile. 'The PM telephoned me this morning giving us authority.'

Tim tried to catch Walmsley's eye but Walmsley was looking out of the window again.

'It seems that you might know Yasin Omer's motives better than any of us,' said Parsons.'

Hodge's voice was soft but it cut through the drawing room like a tannoy. 'You've also succeeded in winning the trust of Samira Omer, his twin sister, for which we all congratulate you.

'Nothing decided upon in this room is official,' said Hodge. 'We are not a government body or institution which has summoned you. We have no charter, no powers, no name. You, Stephen and Jack have been asked here to brief us. The rest of us, as you see, are retired. Our authority lies in our experience.'

'And our contacts,' said Cusk, touching his teacup with the back of his hand to confirm that the tea was cold and undrinkable. 'We are used by the government both here and in America for sensitive jobs which would threaten diplomacy. Our achievements might change the course of history, but our involvement would not even become a footnote in the history books.'

Parsons frowned. 'It's a scenario we have seen dozens of times, except this time it's real and it's got further than any of us feared.'

Hodge stood up, brushing down the creases of his jacket. 'We've had an anthrax death in Pakistan and now in Budapest. Both were infected from the milled spores stolen from China. If we don't stop it – or if the threat becomes known – we could have a global panic such as we have never seen before.'

He paced up and down by the window, his shoulder brushing the curtain. 'The President and Prime Minister have decided that it can only be handled by this group. Specialists like yourself will be brought in at each stage as necessary. There will be no leaks, no panic, no politics. If this weapon is released into the atmosphere, we do not have the resources to handle the deaths and illnesses of possibly millions of people. And since it can't be done, we're not going to tell anybody we're trying to stop it.'

Hodge sat down and there was silence in the room.

The helmsman watched the swell, imagining himself using the tiller of an outrigger against the pattern of the waves. They brought the rigid inflatable down to the beach with fishing tackle on the back.

It was lighter than an outrigger; it could be tossed about like a cork; and it would turn over more easily. But the forty-horsepower engine was more powerful and made up for lack of stabilisers. He could twist the inflatable into the troughs and coax it onto the waves. He tried it first at ten knots, then took it up bit by bit until he was doing eighteen knots in choppy waters, slowing right down in the big swells and taking it up again. He went out in darkness to check his night vision and found it was still good, and he was getting to know the waters, and sensing how to work with them at night.

The ten bags of anthrax were sealed, just as they had been in the back of the truck, and wrapped in strong black plastic sheeting, then put inside a water-tight plastic container.

They carried the container down to the shore like night fishermen and secured it in the back of the rigid inflatable. The helmsman took the wheel, strapping himself like a mountaineer to the boat in case it flipped over. The navigator sat next to him, checking the Global Positioning System which would get them to the right deserted spot on the Suffolk coast.

The navigator scanned an encrypted electronic code into radio sets stolen from the Philippine marines. The American military had moved on from the Leopard system of frequency-hopping transmission, but it was still good enough for their purposes. The call sign from the boat was Z35Quebec2. The answer from the shore would be 'one' for the pre-arranged first landing site. If that had to be aborted, it would be 'two', up to six different co-ordinates along the Shingle Street beach, enough to find a place where there were no fishermen, no lovers in cars, no midnight walkers.

The helmsman drove a straight course. He had no horizon and often no moon. He concentrated on the waves and his heart was back on the Sulu Straits, loving every roll and turn of the boat. For coastal radar operators he would be an indistinguishable speck amid a flurry of green snow which they knew to be waves. No one would suspect. No one would know.

'You're saying he wants to attack the emergency G7 summit?' said Parsons.

'There's nothing else happening in Europe which would

bring so many world leaders together,' said Tim. 'The Managing Director of the IMF and President of the World Bank are also going. These are precisely the people Yasin Omer blames for the tragedies in his life.'

'You're also telling us that Yasin Omer trained as a suicide bomber?'

'The Tamil Tigers draw a distinction,' said Tim. 'He's to survive if possible, but given that he may be wearing a waistcoat padded with explosives to disseminate anthrax, the option of survival is unlikely.'

'A waistcoat?' said Cusk. 'It sounds like a medieval horror show.'

'Unfortunately not,' said Hodge. 'They've been used in the Middle East by Hamas, but their pioneers were the Tamil separatists. A female bomber with a waistcoat of explosive killed Rajiv Gandhi in 1991.'

'I gather the head tends to be remarkably well preserved,' said Walmsley. 'Torn off and hurled far away from the explosion.'

'Is that sort of detail necessary to this discussion?' objected Hodge.

'Jack,' said Parsons. 'If a guy blows himself up wearing one of these things, would the anthrax spores survive?'

'Only one per cent of the spores might survive. But one per cent would be enough to kill thousands of people.'

'So why would he blow himself up then? I don't buy it,' said Parsons.

Hodge answered. 'The terrorist, and I use the term generically, wants to make a bang to prove his point. If he sets off a bomb but the anthrax spores only kill ten thousand people, the political impact might well be as great as having no bomb and killing a hundred thousand.'

Matthew Bradley banged a pencil on a pad of paper on which he had been taking notes and drawing diagrams.

'Do we know for sure whether this stuff has gone through a process of micro-encapsulation?'

'No,' said Jensen. 'It's one of the things we were hoping to find out.'

'What does it mean if it has?' Cusk enquired.

'The spores are coated with droplets of gelatin, sodium alginate, cellulose or some other protective material to a chosen size such as three, five or ten microns,' said Jensen. 'The coating can be custom-made, perhaps by adding ultraviolet-light blocking pigments or charging it electrostatically so that particles don't clump together during dissemination.'

'Then once the particles are in the lungs the polymer coating dissolves,' added Bradley. 'The bacteria are safe and in their ideal environment.'

'You're suggesting that if he blew himself up with coated spores, most of them would survive the blast?' asked Hodge.

'Possibly,' said Jensen. 'Probably.'

'My God,' said Hodge. 'Your scenario is of body parts being blown over an area of London in a dust of poison.'

'Yes,' said Bradley. 'Stephen's observation about the suicide bomber's head suddenly does not seem completely out of place.'

'Thank you,' said Walmsley quietly.

'He would do it.' Tim spoke more loudly than he had planned.

'Go on,' said Parsons. 'I really would like us to hear this.'

'Samira, his twin sister, thinks he would.'

'Isn't the objective of all Islamic fanatics to get the fast track to God through martyrdom?' said Parsons.

'He's not an Islamic fundamentalist,' said Tim. 'He doesn't believe in God, which makes him even more unpredictable.'

'I've never thought of God as having anything to do with religious wars,' said Walmsley.

'If it *is* Yasin Omer . . .' began Parsons.

'It is,' said Tim sharply. 'Right now, he's the only show in town.'

The cries of the rowers had long gone and the footsteps outside the house were less frequent. The fast walk of a single woman. The yobbish scream of a teenage drinker. The murmurs of lovers. Chiswick Mall and its river were settling down for the night and the men in the first-floor drawing room ate from a single plate of sandwiches put together from whatever the RAF sergeant had found in the kitchen fridge. The plate wobbled on the antique coffee table.

'It seems sensible to continue working through Customs,' suggested Hodge, whose whole career had consisted of arranging operative cells within the civil service network.

'Because no one would believe it,' said Cusk.

'That would be one bonus.'

'The Customs surveillance teams are second to none.' Tim found himself sounding defensive. But he always had.

'But still reporting to me,' said Walmsley.

'The one hitch with Customs is that they can't carry arms,' said Cusk. 'Have to go to the police for that.'

Tim glanced over towards Walmsley. 'We'll wing it,' said Walmsley.

'Wing it,' repeated Hodge quietly.

'If Yasin Omer succeeds, there's going to be a hell of a row, whatever happens,' said Walmsley.

'If any of us are still alive,' said Parsons.

Tim shook hands and was shown out while the rest of them stayed behind. They wished him luck. There was a pat on the back. The RAF sergeant saw him out. The rain hit him cold in the face.

# Chapter Twenty-nine

*Larnaca, Cyprus*

The sun struck Jennifer in the face. It streamed straight in through the open curtains which in the frenzy of the night before they had not bothered to close. She lay for a moment not knowing where she was or what time it was. Then she saw his imprint on the bed, the crumpled pillow and the emptiness on the sheets where he had been.

He had left while she was sleeping more soundly than she had in weeks, with a note propped up against the mirror on the desk by the window. She got out of bed, naked, enjoying the warmth of the sun on her body.

'I knew it would be worth asking you to dinner,' he had written in beautifully curved handwriting. 'You were wonderful and always will be. Love David.'

The simplicity of taking and using the pure masculinity of a near-stranger cleared her mind of everything clogged up there: Tim's leaving; Tim's treachery; Tim's evasiveness; Walmsley and Crabbe threatening her; the job transfer; and – the one thing she didn't want to think about – the image of Pamela and Davey murdered in their own house, an image which kept returning uninvited, more graphic than any other.

'Dear Mom,' she thought, composing the letter in her

head. 'I've just had a one-night stand with a Cypriot hunk and this morning I feel great about it.'

She slipped on a bathrobe, stepped onto the balcony and spent minutes lost in contemplation, bringing her thoughts back and forth with the swell of the shimmering sea in front of her.

David had not only given her good sex. He had also filled in the last strand of her web of bank transfers out of Cyprus. He had explained it to her in detail, even allowing her to note it all down, and telling her early in the evening so that he had finished before the champagne took grip and their interest in laundered money diminished.

He had satisfied her professionally and physically, stayed enough of the night so she would not feel rejected and left when she needed him no more. By Jennifer's definition, David Antoniades was a perfect colleague and a perfect gentleman.

She fixed herself some coffee and sat at the table on the balcony with her notebook.

As soon as she telephoned him to say she was coming, David had started work. He identified the person who drew the bank draft as P. Nagalingam, a Tamil travelling on a Singaporean passport. He didn't have a first name for him. He then checked the security video for the day. The bank kept tapes for three months, exactly for purposes like this. Nagalingam was filmed entering the bank with a Caucasian who sat in a waiting area while the draft was being written. The two men left together.

Antoniades called a friend who worked on the checkpoint of the Green Line. He confirmed that Nagalingam had crossed the line that day. A Russian passport holder was listed as crossing straight after him. The nationality of the person before him was Taiwanese, so he was ruled out.

The Russian's name was Igor Gromov, aged thirty-six, occupation businessman, born in Moscow.

The last call was the riskiest David had to make, to a satellite phone in northern Cyprus. Within two hours he had the answer he needed, faxed back to his own satellite phone set up on the roof of his yacht. Gromov had deposited the bank draft into the Central Bank of Turkey, firstly into an account under his name. Then he had transferred all but US$250,000 to a numbered account at the same branch.

'The US$250,000 was his fee, Jen,' David explained. 'It means he was more than a bagman. Or, to put it another way, they sent a very senior bagman for a very important job.'

Gromov had crossed back through the Green Line just before five in the afternoon when it closed. Nagalingam would almost certainly have flown out to Ankara and gone on from there. The six million dollars had been split three ways. Two million had gone to the National Bank of Dubai in Abu Dhabi; two million to the Nippon Credit International in Almaty, Kazakhstan, and two million straight to the Moscow Narodny Bank in Beijing.

'Why to China?' asked David, as much to himself as to Jennifer.

'Because they needed it there, and quickly?'

'That's what I reckon. Usually, they would bounce it through two or three banks before it reached the master account. Moscow Narodny is not a laundering bank and China is not a laundering country. Someone wanted that two million straight away, and for something that was going on in China.'

He ordered another bottle of champagne. 'That's all I have for you.' He shrugged, mixing his pride with an exaggerated apology that he hadn't got enough.

'You've been great.'

'You know, Jen,' he had said. 'Those movies where people hack into computers and get everything they want are so much crap. If you hadn't come here I couldn't be telling you this.'

'If you didn't have a friend on the Green Line you wouldn't know where the draft had gone.'

He took the almost empty bottle, little cubes of ice hanging from the napkin, topped up her glass, and gave her a huge smile. 'Human contact is everything, don't you agree? You can't seduce a computer into telling you anything.'

She burst out laughing. After China, his Mediterranean honesty was fantastic. 'Is this how you conduct your board meetings?' she said, clinking glasses with him.

'I like everything out in the open.' He drained his glass, looking at her all the time, and put it gently on the table. 'Now that we have finished our businesses, we will eat while you tell me all about your life in the Far East. Over coffee and liqueurs I will flirt wildly with you. Then, if it is your pleasure, I will seduce you and we will go to bed.'

'It is,' she whispered. 'It is my pleasure.'


With David gone, his note read, her money web untangled, her business in Cyprus was finished. It was ten in the evening on the East Coast and her flight was not for another eleven hours. She went back into the room and called the hospital suite where Jack Jensen was living with a laptop computer, a modem link in a suite adjoining Amanda's intensive care room. A woman's voice answered: 'Jack's not here,' she said. 'He's gone to England. I'm Jane, Amanda's grandmother.'

When Jennifer explained who she was, Jane said. 'Jack's talked about you a lot. Amanda's condition deteriorated last night.'

'How bad?' said Jennifer.

'Jack says her condition goes up and down all the time and she's still out of intensive care. The doctors are very good here.'

The contrast between the gleaming Mediterranean and the sad hospital room could not have been more ghastly. 'Is Jack on his mobile?'

'Absolutely,' said Jane. 'That's the only way to get him.'

Jensen answered straight away when she called, but his voice was dulled, not keen to talk. 'She got worse last night,' he said when Jennifer asked.

'Are you going back?'

'I don't know, Jen. She gets worse, better, worse, better and I'm going crazy sitting in the hospital all day.'

'Stay away,' she suggested. 'She's out of intensive care and I'm on my way to the States. I'll look in.'

He paused for a long time.

'Jack, are you there?'

'The doctors are honest. They say she has a fifty-fifty chance of pulling through.'

'You want to talk about it?'

'Thanks, Jen, but no. It's too technical and if I start telling you it'll get away from the fact that my daughter's really sick and I'm feeling guilty about being in London, but there's work to do here, really important work that might find out who set out to kill my family.'

'Do you have anyone to talk to?'

'Yes. Well. No. Pamela's mother's there. My sister's around, but these people have their own lives. My sister . . .' he repeated, then paused, changing his mind. 'Yes, Jen. It would be nice for Amanda to see a friendly face from China.'

'I'm on my way.'

'Please,' he continued, as if she hadn't answered yet, 'sing a song to Amanda. She can hear. I'm sure she can hear me.'

'Jack, I'm on my way.' He thanked her and he was about to hang up when she said: 'Can you do me a favour?' She felt like a bitch, but she had to ask it.

'Sure.' And he meant it.

'Are you in touch with Tim?'

He was every day, several times a day. But he couldn't mention it. 'I could be.'

'Just tell him to take my call if I ring. I really have to talk to him.'

She didn't tell Jack that she was actually going to London. Nor did she have any intention of telephoning Tim first. She shuddered at the thought of making love to him. Holding him. Loving him. Wanting him.

She called Henry Beaton, because she had only left him a one-line note saying she had to go to New York for personal reasons.

'Jim Crabbe has been looking for you,' said Henry Beaton. 'I told him you were on your way to New York.'

'Who's he?' Jennifer feigned ignorance.

'Says he's senior vice-president for special projects. Just walked in without notice and started using your office, because it was empty.'

'My desktop.' She had shut down the system. He would need to know her passwords to get in.

'Took over the whole bloody room. Bloody cheek.' Beaton had been ridden over roughshod by head office again, insulted but powerless. 'Told him we reported to London, not New York and he didn't take a blind bit of notice.'

'Henry, I'll check it in New York as soon as I can.' She had called him from her mobile, so he wouldn't know where she was. 'Meanwhile, why don't you ask Amy to get the itemised calls he made from my office? Do it discreetly.'

'Good idea, Jen.' She heard him stabbing at the tobacco

in his pipe. 'We'll get the bastard. He's probably here on a swan with his mistress.'

'Exactly.' She could never come to terms with Henry's naïveté.

'Your mother. Is she all right?'

She had almost forgotten that a sick mother had been the excuse she had used for her sudden absence.

'She's had a rough turn. It could be some days.'

The flight from Larnaca arrived at Heathrow at nine that evening. She would have her luggage transferred and checked straight through to Kennedy on the United Airlines flight at 07:55 the next day. She booked a room at the Heathrow Hilton and planned to be at Queensborough Terrace by ten. If he wasn't there, she would call. But only then.

A steady, cold fall of rain had sent home any fishermen who might have been out earlier. The helmsman cut the engine for the last half mile and they came in paddling, riding on the waves and the current onto the shingle at the first landing site. The moon threw enough light on the beach for them to see it was clear from one end to the other.

No one spoke, just as no one spoke when they brought the boats ashore in Zamboanga. There was nothing to say. Even in their wetsuits, they felt the howling wind. They heaved the huge outboard engine into the van first, covered it with canvas, collapsed the inflatable and put that on top of it. They wedged the container with the anthrax on the floor beside it.

They drove away from the coastline with only sidelights, until they were clear of the beach area. They crossed the Orwell Bridge outside Ipswich as the first light of dawn appeared. From the A12, the van went north onto the M25 and drove right round until turning east back into London along the M40, catching the first of the rush-hour traffic. In some parts of the motorway the street lights were going out. In others they glowed a fiery yellow on a dull morning.

They cut south from the M40 down to the Shepherds Bush roundabout, edging forward patiently with the traffic. The driver did not answer the road ragers, did not try to squeeze through gaps. At every orange light, he stopped and waited. The van was brand new, registered. Only the worst luck would cause the police to stop it. But the driver would not give bad luck its chance. The navigator and the helmsman slept deeply, curled up uncomfortably in the back.

Shortly after eight o'clock, the driver turned into the gated compound of Tudor Court. A security camera filmed the van going in and turning right between two blocks of luxury six-storey apartments. A camera midway into the compound picked up its journey into the underground car park and another followed it through the automatic gate and into the private double garage.

But the video was only kept for twenty-four hours and the driver had let himself into the compound gates with his own fob key when the security guard's attention was elsewhere with cars leaving, chauffeurs taking their employers to work. No written record was made of the number plate. Once inside, the van was alone, unseen. The garage led directly to a utility room, with stairs going up into the house.

# Chapter Thirty

The Tamil Centre for Human Rights was based in a shabby part of south London, a neighbourhood where litter blew about under railway arches and graffiti decorated low-cost Victorian housing. Mothers barely out of their teens struggled with pushchairs and pensioners hunched over sticks. This was where the state provided and the community gave nothing. It was a catchment area for England's disinherited, an apt home for the embassy of the most efficient guerrilla organisation in the world.

Tim took Samira there because she wanted to see what they looked like, wanted to see a picture of the Tamil leader, Kutti, whom Yasin wrote about. Walmsley had offered a full briefing from MI5 and SIS. He could have produced the head of the South Asia desk, but Tim turned them all down. He read the translation of Yasin's letter and researched the Tamil Tigers' record of bombing and assassination, of massacring villagers, hacking people to death with knives and axes. He read their homepages on the Internet.

The name was painted high up on the whitewashed walls. Eelam House was a free-standing building with its own double gate and black wire fencing. Tim drove past it, parked off the main road, two streets down. It was shortly after ten. As they came close to the building, they heard music, haunting, wailing, drumming sounds.

They walked past cars and vans parked in a narrow courtyard, Tim first, Samira following. They must have been watched because the door opened even before Tim pressed the bell. A boy stood there in silence with a thin expressionless smile.

'Is Jegan in?' asked Tim.

'A moment,' said the boy and slid off, barefoot, leaving the door ajar. Tim pushed it further open. On the wall in the hallway was a map of Sri Lanka with the area of the Tamil homeland coloured in red. Next to it was a big blow-up photograph of Kutti, a bulkier version of the boy at the door, the figure they all wanted to look like, strapped with an ammunition belt, wearing camouflage fatigues, his hand on the head of a child gazing up at him in admiration.

Jegan introduced himself halfway down the stairs. 'I'm Jegan, can I help you?' He came down quickly, two steps at a time. He looked in his early forties, wearing a dark suit and tie and with a trimmed beard and gold-rimmed spectacles.

'Tim Pack and Samira Omer,' said Tim. 'I called you earlier.'

Jegan was courteous, asking them in, reminding them to take off their shoes, ushering them upstairs into an open space which had been divided into cubicles for charity workers involved with Tamil refugees. People worked at computer terminals, their desks strewn with newspaper cuttings.

He apologised for the mess, for the books and videos piled up against a wall, for the scrappy carpet which he had bought cheap from a car-boot sale. He took them into a conference room, constantly attentive, able to be the civilised face of violence because he was so far removed from it. His world was press cuttings, video tapes and fund-raising pamphlets.

Jegan asked how they had got there and whether they had found a space for the car. Only when he closed the door did he ask: 'Are you from the police?'

'I'm looking for my brother,' replied Samira straight away.

He was relieved. He asked them to sit down. The coffee was ready, freshly made, and he poured three cups.

'Your brother is connected with us?' he said.

'He was in Vanni and involved in the bombing of an army camp.'

Jegan sipped his coffee. 'His name?'

'Yasin Omer.'

'That is not a Tamil name.'

'He went there from the Philippines.'

Jegan put the coffee cup on the table. 'And you say he fought with us as part of our struggle?'

'Yes.'

'That would not be.' He shook his head. 'Sorry. It just wouldn't happen.'

They had decided before going there to use the letter and Samira brought out a translation and a photocopy of the original. She put them on the table, flattening the paper with the palm of her hand. Jegan took it, his eyebrows rising with surprise. Samira passed the letter over to him and he looked at the Arabic silently, then read the English, going back sometimes and running his finger under the names Yasin had used.

'Was he an aid worker?' said Jegan thoughtfully when he had finished. 'With Save the Children or the Red Cross.'

'He was a fighter,' said Samira.

Jegan wanted to close the issue. He pushed the letter back across the table to Samira. 'I know nothing about this.'

Tim spoke for the first time, gently, allowing Jegan to

help them without being threatened. 'How long would it take you to find out?'

'I really don't want to waste your time. We are not like the Middle East or the old communist groups. Ours is a national, not an international cause so we don't take foreigners.'

'Send a message. Ask.'

'It's not like the old days, you know, the early days of the struggle. Then we could telephone Madras and wait on the line while they radioed across to our camps.' He took off his glasses and rubbed his eyes. 'I came to London in the 1974 diaspora when I was just nineteen. I still tremble when I see a policeman, even an English policeman. It's not that they killed us then. That came later. But the beatings, the harassment. You have to have grown up with it to know what it was like.'

'I don't care,' said Tim.

Jegan peered at him, his eyes reddened by the rubbing. 'I'm sorry. I don't understand.'

'I don't care about your struggle.' He pushed his finger down onto the table, pointing at the letters, his voice cutting and harsh. 'You will find out for us where Yasin Omer is.'

Jegan ignored him: 'What I was saying is that from the beginning of the struggle at independence until now we have not had a real leader for the Tamil people. Now we have Kutti.' He pointed up to a portrait hung at the end of the conference table like in an embassy. 'He is motivated only by his love for the Tamil people. He has become the light of our civilisation. He is the . . .'

'I need to know where my brother is,' said Samira, interrupting.

'What I am saying is that Kutti would not allow a foreigner to fight the war.' He shook his head and put his glasses back on. 'We are a self-sufficient army. It would just never happen.'

'My brother was with the Moros,' said Samira.

'In the Philippines?'

'Yes.'

'We know them. They are brothers. But ours is a national-ist movement. We fight with no one but ourselves. I would like to, but . . .'

'But you're not even trying,' said Tim standing up, mov-ing towards Jegan. 'Have you ever even been to your bloody little homeland?'

'Like I said,' stammered Jegan. 'I came to England in 1974. I was nineteen. And it has been difficult because our house is in Jaffna. We don't know what happened to it.'

'You haven't been back?' said Tim.

'It's difficult.'

'So you wouldn't know?'

'We keep in touch.'

'Your movement killed Rajiv Gandhi in 1991.'

'No. We have never said that.'

'President Premadasa in 1993.'

'No. We have not claimed that.'

'Neelan Tiruchelvam in 1999.'

'We do not target areas in which there are civilians.'

'I don't give a shit. But if you don't find Yasin Omer, I will make sure you are repatriated to Sri Lanka as a convicted terrorist by the end of next week . . .'

'You can't do that.'

'You want to test me?' Tim let it rest there. Jegan responded by getting up and making a fuss putting the cold coffee cups back on the tray like a tea lady clearing up around her customers. 'Rahim,' he said. The boy with the smile was at the door holding it open for them to leave. Jegan picked up pamphlets from a shelf behind him and put them on the table. 'These might help you understand why we do what we do.'

Jegan spread them out like merchandise and Tim looked at each of the covers. *Sri Lanka – 50 Years of Subjugation of Tamils*, with a photograph of an old woman being carried with blood streaming down her face; *Tamil Centre for Human Rights – An Appeal to the United Nations*; a plain light blue bound document with a dove of peace and the website address www.tchr.com; *Hot Spring – a fierce commitment to the cause*, with a teenage girl, carrying an AK47 and ammunition pouches; *Tamil Women and Children – Living and Dying under Sri Lankan Army Occupation*, with a bedraggled mother, a child either sleeping or dead in her arms, a rusting bicycle and a wall blown up behind her.

'Are these published here?' said Tim. He stayed in his chair, refusing to get up.

'We have our own publishing house.'

Jegan was by the door. Rahim held it open. Tamil music drifted up from downstairs and Tim didn't speak for a considerable amount of time. When he did, he fingered the brochures and stared at an empty spot on the table between them and the tray of dirty cups.

'This is what is going to happen,' he began. 'You are going to contact your people in Sri Lanka and ask them where Yasin Omer is and when he was last there. You are then going to call me and give me that information.'

Jegan started to object. 'On what authority . . .'

Tim ignored him: 'You will do all this within the next three hours.' He took out a card, one which had nothing on it except his name. He wrote his mobile and home number and pushed it across the table towards Jegan. 'You will also find out if your people are planning any unusual operations, either in Sri Lanka or overseas.'

'We carry out no overseas operations,' Jegan objected, but his voice was trembling.

'If you don't get back to me, this whole operation will be

closed down tonight. Weapons, explosives and drugs will be found on the premises. You will be arrested. The Tamil Centre for Human Rights will no longer function in London. You will be deported.'

'I'm a British citizen.'

'You don't seem to get the point,' whispered Tim. He unbuttoned his jacket and brought out a SIG-Sauer 9mm from his shoulder holster. He could tell Jegan wasn't used to being around guns. His eyes flickered around nervously, almost dancing to the rhythm of the music below.

But Rahim didn't move. His facial expression didn't change, except for his eyes which glanced for a second at the weapon, taking in the type and the position of the safety catch. Tim saw it and knew the boy was a fighter from the jungle.

'All right,' said Tim in a whisper. 'We won't deport you. I will kill you instead.' There was silence. 'After that, we will close down this operation and arrest everyone here as suspected terrorists. And after that we will kill Kutti.'

'You are a policeman,' Jegan managed.

'Worse than that.' Tim got up and for the benefit of the boy he slid back the safety catch and put a round in the breech. Still the boy didn't move. Jegan stiffened. Tim pushed back his chair, walked right up to him, then made an exhibition of pushing on the safety catch again and putting the pistol back in his holster.

'I'm the war itself, Jegan,' he said. 'The war you've only read about in your own pamphlets.'

They hired a second van, a Ford Transit, and one of the drivers and the English speaker bought materials in different parts of London on different stolen or forged credit cards. Before dawn, they took disused exhaust pipes from the rubbish skips outside KwikFit in Wood Lane, Shepherds

Bush, then shortly after 10 a.m., they paid cash for a Metal Inert Gas welding machine with two bottles of $CO_2$ and two coils of steel wire.

From there, they headed north up the Edgware Road to Kilburn where they hired a Plasma Cutter on a credit card stolen in London. After breakfast back at the house, they took the A3 south until they reached the yachting belt of southern England. There, from three separate shops, they hired air tanks for scuba divers, each on a different credit card, each transaction to sit in the till until the tanks were returned – which they never would be.

The Ford Transit van was taken to a separate secure garage in south-east London. The garage and the utility room in the Tudor Court compound were prepared for the work they had to carry out on the Mercedes Sprinter.

Tudor Court was mostly occupied by foreigners from the Middle East and Asia, who had bought into discretion, privacy and security in the heart of London. The rules of the compound said there should be no disturbances between the hours of eleven at night and eight in the morning. The busiest time was in the morning when the rubbish truck was there and contractors and delivery vans were arriving. That is when they would work and only then. For the rest of the time the house would be quiet. Only one of them would come and go, and always by vehicle, so the false number plate would become familiar, but not the face.

The curtains of the house stayed drawn, the window slightly open to let in air, the lights on. Their phone calls were on a mixture of overseas calling cards, Sprint, AT&T, Global and others, so telephone records would have to go through two or three stages before the numbers were discovered. Just like with the compound itself, the gate, the parking lot barrier, the garage door were each stages the police would have to go through to get to them.

In the third-floor bedroom, where a dormer window had been cut into the sloping roof like in an attic, Yasin put maps on the wall. Red pins indicated the known meeting places of the finance ministers and some heads of government before they went to Birmingham. The green pins showed their accommodation with blue pins for the accommodation of their staff, particularly the economists and financiers.

They listened to radio and television weather forecasts with particular interest. For the next week, the prevailing winds would be from the south-west. The skies would be overcast. It was perfect.

# Chapter Thirty-one

Jegan rang two and a half hours after they left Eelam House. 'I'm sorry,' he said. 'Yasin Omer was in Vanni, like you said.'

'When?' said Tim.

'It really is too dangerous to discuss this on the phone.'

'When?' repeated Tim.

'I will know more in two hours' time. I want to send Rahim with a picture they have faxed over on the sat phone.'

'OK.'

'It's a big risk using the sat phone. We are completely on your side. Kutti has ordered it.'

'Kutti has ordered it,' Tim repeated sarcastically. 'Tell Rahim to go to the Queensway entrance of Bayswater tube station.'

He cut the call and rang Walmsley. 'They've admitted it.'

'The Tigers?'

'Jegan said he had orders to help us.'

'Did he say where you were to meet?'

'No. Why is it important?'

'You didn't tell us you were going to see him, Tim. This isn't a James Bond film. We need to know where you are.'

Tim changed the subject. 'Anything from Rotterdam?'

'Seven on board. All except the crew passports were fake and there's no record of them being used a second time for hotels, car rental, getting out of Holland. The bloody Serbs say they're not going to talk unless they know why. But more importantly, twenty-five kilograms of anthrax has been found in the back of a truck near the port in Karachi. A Russian was also found with his throat cut. He's been identified as Igor Gromov, a gangster from Moscow.'

'Another Russian.'

'Your friend Yasin is leaving a trail, Tim, a trail of bodies behind him.'

Tim sent Samira to meet Rahim and let the surveillance teams follow her. She walked past the underground station, right up Queensway to the Oddbins wine shop, then back again, by which time Rahim was waiting, leaning against the wall next to the *Evening Standard* kiosk.

It had been she, not him, who suggested the cappuccino at Café Uno. Talking outside the tube station, she had pointed towards the coffee shop. They found a table by the window and he opened the envelope, pulling out the faxes which had been sent over. The red-box didn't have a camera on Café Uno. Nor was there any sound. The cyclist got inside, but his table was some way away. Samira put her hand to her mouth in surprise when she saw the picture. She talked excitedly to Rahim. He pointed at a different part of the picture, as if explaining things to her, then quickly wrote a note which he handed to her. They were in Café Uno for twenty-seven minutes. She saw him to the tube station and, rather than go back to Queensborough Terrace, Samira walked into a hairdressing salon and had a shampoo and cut.

'He asked me lots of questions about Yasin,' she said, when she returned to Tim, coming up the stairs with a denim jacket slung over her shoulders and a brown envelope in her right hand.

Pack was in the first-floor living room when Samira arrived, letting herself in with her own key. He was listening to Schumann's *Scenes from Childhood*. Calming music. Soft specific piano. He had opened a bottle of wine. She had had her hair layered and cut short almost above the ears.

Since Hungary, Samira seemed to trust him. Unlike Jennifer who asked constant questions, Samira seemed to either accept or reject all. Whether it was age, whether it was race – African harmony against American confrontation – he didn't know, and right now he didn't care. She had first hated him, then clung to him in Budapest, and hadn't said a word when he drew the gun on Jegan, but he thought it drew her closer to him. He was the one who would find Yasin, so she would stay with him, let him lead her.

She sat on the floor, legs curled under her, pulled the fax out of the envelope, handed it to him and touched him on the knee.

Tim looked at the faxed photograph of Yasin Omer, strapped in his suicide vest, climbing into a truck full of explosives to drive to the army camp in Kilinochi. 'So we have our proof,' he said.

'We already knew.' She had looked at the picture before, studied it with Rahim. The red-box team had told Tim. So that now it was just another photograph, not drawing out any new emotions, just a deepening sadness.

'What questions did Rahim ask?' asked Tim.

'His English is really good. Like you, he wanted to know whether Yasin would really kill himself. Like you did.'

'What did you tell him?'

'I said yes. Like I told you. And he asked about you.'

'Like what?'

'Who you worked for. Why you had a gun.'

'What did you say?'

She jumped up like a little girl, grinned and pointed at him.

'You owe me so much,' she said. 'Because I told him I knew nothing about you. Just that you were helping me find my brother.'

'That's true isn't it?'

'No. I saw you in Omdurman, didn't I? In the shop. You've got our sword here on the stairs. And I saw you that night outside our house, although I told the police I hadn't. Yasin told me not to.' She went quiet and they didn't speak for a while. Tim studied the picture of Yasin and in the quiet he heard the Schumann piano again and the screech of a car on the zebra crossing outside.

'What were you doing there? At our house?' It was the first time she had asked, as if in all the conversations they had had about Yasin, Musa and the Philippines, she hadn't wanted to stretch it back to Khartoum, to her real home and her real parents.

'I was helping rescue a friend from prison.'

She absorbed that, allowed time, then said, 'Did you succeed?'

'Yes. But I got arrested and Yasin helped me escape.'

'It was the day after my parents were killed.'

'I know.'

'Were you involved in it?'

'No.' He didn't say 'not really', or 'not directly'. Hers was a direct question and after he answered she asked no more, not because of lack of curiosity, but because none was needed. She understood it as a European and an American could not. His story, told in two or three sentences, was enough. A life of secret police, friends in prison, parents shot dead, tragic events and sudden upheavals was one where things happened without reason, so explanation was unnecessary, because there was none which would solve anything.

'Why did you get your hair cut?' he asked. It was thoughtless, asking that before saying he liked it.

She shrugged. 'Why does anyone do anything?'

'I think it's great,' he said quickly.

She smiled, the innocent smile of a girl reacting to a compliment. 'I hoped you would.'

'I really like it.'

She swallowed heavily and ran her fingers around the glass. 'Thanks.' It was a murmur, and she couldn't look at him, as if the haircut were more important than anything else they were doing. She went out to meet a terrorist and get a picture of her brother in a suicide vest, but the only thing that mattered was the haircut.

'It's really nice,' he said again.

'Thanks.'

He didn't want to say it, but he couldn't help himself: 'You've had one hell of a life.'

There must have been genuine compassion in his voice, because it hung there in the room with *Scenes from Childhood*, hung there needing her to say something, to match his signal.

She did it deliberately, by getting up and putting her wine glass on a coffee table. She walked over to him. She took the picture of Yasin away from him, sat on his lap and kissed him. Then she stopped and held his head in her hands, her palms on his cheeks, like he had done to her in Budapest, except she didn't ask him any questions.

'I need to be with you,' she said quietly. 'I can't keep being alone like this.'

She buried her head in his shoulders and he touched her, feeling the layered hair, different from before. She kept her head there, kneading his back with her hands, comforted by the closeness, the intimacy.

It wasn't like Jennifer. No clawing excitement. No craving for pleasure. Samira's motive was loneliness. He wondered if at nineteen she could distinguish between intimacy and sex. He wondered what it was like being nineteen. He lifted her head off his shoulders and her eyes were glistening with tears. Tim spotted joy there, too, as if she had been waiting for this, as if the haircut had been a catalyst, to turn her from a girl into a woman, from the blind girl in Zamboanga to a person to love.

She kissed him on the way upstairs, a deep, sad, wild, tearful action, pushing into and sucking out of him every incomprehensible emotion she had been hiding in the days which just passed. He carried her up to his bedroom, where she hadn't been before. That was important because it meant he would share it with her: the huge bed, the flowing green plants, the bathroom with the power shower and coloured towels and the window thrown open to the night.

He laid her on the bed and she pulled him down on top of her, her arms firmly around his neck. To be in his house, in his room, on his bed, each was a solution, each a separate guarantee. Samira sought refuge and if refuge led to pleasure, so be it. But it was not the aim.

Each movement of her tongue was sharp and frightened, touching and withdrawing, testing and possessing, and she gently slipped his jacket off, stripped down his shirt, hands spread, palms sensitive and gliding over his skin, but rushed, hurried, wanting to reach somewhere before everything was destroyed.

'Shhhhh,' he soothed. He put the tips of his fingers on her lips. The hand smelt of guns and Eelam House.

'It's safe here,' he whispered. 'Absolutely safe.'

She let Tim undress her, submissive, like the boy with the motorcycle had taught her. Tim did it slowly, kissing each part of her body as he made her naked. He folded her clothes and put them neatly one by one on the chest at the end of the bed, leaving her, returning to her, touching her with his fingers and his lips.

Goose pimples swelled on her shoulders and her thighs. When he unclipped her bra, she didn't let him fold it away, but left it, loose and crumpled by her, as she took his hand firmly and placed it over her breast. 'Leave it there,' she said. 'Warm me.'

He carried her to the shower, turning it on powerful and hot, so that steam filled the bathroom. She stood, barefoot, on the thick-piled carpet as he peeled down her panties. She stepped out of them, listening to the pounding of the water. In the swirl of steam, their reflections in the mirror faded like ghosts behind condensation on the glass.

She closed her eyes, but the image of Yasin flashed in front of her, Yasin as a soldier, a killer. She kissed Tim violently, eyes open. She took his hand off her breast, sliding it down with hers, entwining their fingers so they could explore together, his experience, her youth, both feeling her wetness at the same time.

He soaped her and she soaped him, just like Jennifer used to, except Samira's youth and Africanness made her more untamed. Sex was the only sanctuary she had and she seized it. They went to the bedroom, dripping, with warm towels around them. She shivered a bit with the open window and he lifted her into the bed, under the duvet, throwing away the towels.

Jennifer was behind his closed eyes. Walmsley with his red scarf and the prison in the Sudan, where his nakedness, amid his vomit and waste, had humiliated him.

His nakedness with Samira made him feel calm and strong. They began by holding each other naked and tight, feeling the warmth, the thrill, not speaking, not delving. Their chaotic thoughts were unfaithful, far away from each other, jumbled, uncontrollable, incompatible and ghastly. They let their minds work through until the memories and savage bouts of anger were gone, until their bodies craved each other and nothing else.

She moved her hands all over him, guided him, and when

347

it started there was no other feeling she desired, no other place she wanted to be anywhere else in the world.

Shortly after ten in the evening, he was woken by a shout, gruffer, sharper, different from the pimp's, the policeman's command to stop. Samira became tense beside him. Jennifer's voice below, American and unequivocal. 'Who the fuck are you?'

The policeman didn't know what to say. Didn't expect to be challenged. Tim went to the window.

'Who is it?' Samira asked.

'Someone I knew in China. Get dressed, but stay up here.'

'A woman?'

He kissed her on the forehead. The doorbell rang.

Jennifer didn't say hello. The policeman melted away. 'Who's that creep?' she said sarcastically. 'Your private fucking bodyguard?'

Tim stepped back and let her in. She recognised the hallway as if she had never been away, the hallway with the African embroidery above the telephone table, the Mahas sword against the wall by the bend in the stairs, the kitchen with the wooden wall cabinets, the table strewn with newspapers in the conservatory at the back.

She wanted to ask if he was alone, but instead she walked straight through to the conservatory and put her briefcase on the floor.

She needed a cigarette, but would wait. She didn't want to give her nervousness away by scrabbling in her handbag for a lighter. 'You ever heard of a company called CA Energy Ltd?' she said.

'Hi, Jen,' he ignored her question, closing the door, but not drawing across the bolt, not closing up for the night. 'Some rock star's taken the house next door. Put goons all over the place.'

Jennifer looked around for a woman's touch. She didn't plan to, but this was how her instincts were channelled. The kitchen was clean, the dishes washed, a faint smell of pine disinfectant, but not a crumb on the sideboard. The earth around the pot plants was damp with fresh watering. A fingerprint was lit up by the patio light, lingering on the clear, polished glass of the conservatory. She saw it all like the trace of an unknown woman.

Jennifer pulled out a chair, sat down, opened her briefcase and took out the folder with documents from Beijing. She had more copies inside, in her check-in luggage and with David Antoniades in Cyprus. Tim stood at the entrance of the kitchen, where the floor tiles changed to wooden parquet for the dining room.

'Coffee, tea, champagne?' he ventured.

'No thanks. I've just eaten,' she snapped back. She flipped open the folder and pulled out the search result from Companies House.

'If you're going to be such a bitch, you might as well . . .'

Jennifer looked straight up at him and he at her, their eyes duelling with each other. 'I'm here in my capacity as compliance and security officer for the bank. Not as your former girlfriend trying to patch things up over a cappuccino.' She looked at her watch. 'I want to get this sorted. I've got a flight in a few hours.'

Tim grinned: 'The airport closes at night.'

'I have a room at the Hilton.' She separated off the top sheet from the documents and pushed it across the table, waiting for him to move over and pick it up. 'I expect you know that under section 288 of the Companies Act 1985 it is an offence for the director of a company to change address without notifying Companies House within fourteen days.'

Tim stepped forward. 'What the hell are you talking about?'

'Under section 242(2) and Schedule 24, Companies Act

1985, directors are personally liable for prosecution, with a criminal record and a fine of up to five thousand pounds, for late delivery of accounts.'

Tim sat down opposite her. 'Jen, you're deliberately being a bitch. Why don't you tell me . . . ?'

She tapped the table and pointed to the piece of paper. 'Read it.'

She lit a cigarette, calmly, no searching for lighters, her nerves settled once she was inside the house. She got up and took the ash-tray from the hall table. Tim shook his head: 'I am not a director of this company. I've never heard of CA Energy.'

Jennifer slid another piece of paper across the table. 'Is this your signature authorising the payment of US$10 million to the Mediterranean International Bank in Cyprus?'

'Jesus,' said Tim.

'Is that your signature?' Jennifer repeated.

'No.'

'It bloody well is.'

'It's a forgery.'

'A forgery?'

'Yes.' Tim walked round the table with the document and slammed it down in front of her; his charm had gone. 'I am not a director of this company.'

'You are. The law says you are.'

'And I did not send this money.' He took a pen out of his trouser pocket and underlined Walmsley's name. 'He did.

'That's who you need to talk to.'

'Who is Walmsley, then?' she asked. He was reading over her shoulder, his smells, his familiarity around her. He didn't answer.

'You don't work for the airline, do you?' She said it calmly, as if she was making conversation. Tim put his hand over hers. She did not move it away. She liked him close. She needed to know that something was still there, that the past five years hadn't been a complete sham. He moved round and sat down next to her: 'I'm a customs officer,' he said.

She laughed. She didn't mean to, but it came out because of the way he said it: defensive, humiliated, admitting.

'A customs officer?'

He nodded. 'I was in the army, then I joined the customs.'

'Army?'

'Yes. Northern Ireland. Bosnia. A few other places.'

She didn't know what to say to that. She understood airline to customs. But airline to army was dangerous.

'Who's Walmsley?' He was still touching her hand. She didn't want him to stop.

'My boss.'

Tim didn't care any more. Walmsley had framed him. Or something. So he started telling her everything. The listeners would be across it and if they didn't like what he was saying they would make a call and tell him to shut up.

Jennifer made coffee while he talked and she didn't interrupt or prod. He started in Bosnia, in Zenica, shooting dead the Islamic mercenary who had just killed an aid worker.

'A friend?' she asked.

'No. Just an innocent.'

He told her about the Sudan, his first job under Walmsley's control. 'Just after we had made love for the first time,' he said.

'Right here,' she pointed upstairs. Her cheeks reddened. She was embarrassed, confused about her feelings, and it showed.

'Yes,' he said quickly, but with Samira upstairs, he couldn't afford the personal, so he surprised her by telling her about Jack's role in the Sudan, then the agent he had lost in Kashgar, the video of Ablimet Nor and how it had reminded him of his own imprisonment and torture there.

She squeezed his hand. 'Sorry,' she said under her breath. 'Sorry I didn't trust you,' without adding *Sorry, I still don't.*

He described meeting with Yasin in al-Kadarou and how their paths had crossed again in Zamboanga. He didn't mention the anthrax yet but talked about international terrorism. He mentioned without detail that Samira had been in London for the operation on her eyes, and that she had been with him to Budapest, looking for Yasin.

'Did you sleep with her?' said Jennifer automatically.

'No,' he said. She couldn't hide it. She didn't believe him, but she was glad he denied it.

They heard the first drops of rain at three in the morning and they went out onto the tiny patio, to feel it on their faces, Tim not caring that the house was under surveillance, Jennifer forgetting that her visit was just professional, Tim knowing that Samira was upstairs, sleeping perhaps, obedient, being quiet like he had asked her.

When they went back inside, he let Jennifer talk, not about her past because she had nothing to hide. She told him about the trail of money and brought in David Antoniades, saying what a great guy he was, that they had had dinner together, laughed a lot, enough to make Tim suspect, enough to make her veer from the professional.

She was being a bitch and she knew it until everything came together with blind simplicity. It was when she described Igor Gromov crossing the Green Line to northern Cyprus and keeping US$250,000.

'A quarter of a million,' said Tim. 'A big fee for a bagman.'

'A Moscow Mafioso.'

'There was a Russian in Zamboanga.' He said it as he remembered it. 'The hooker who picked up the phone. I had them there for protection. I was scared.'

'Oh yeah!' She grinned. She didn't care. The man she had loved was a different man. She had fallen for an airline manager and she found her love for him had been driven instinctively by her image of the future, the environment of her children and the work of their father. The man with her now was a soldier, and soldiers kill, betray, lie, leave and fuck differently from airline managers.

'My last night in Beijing, the night I met you in the Louisiana, I had just shot a man who was about to kill Jack.' He told her the story. 'He was a Russian.'

'The same people who killed Pamela and Davey?'

'Looks like it.'

'Paid for by the money from CA Energy?'

He tapped the Companies House printout with his forefinger. 'You say the money was sent by me to the Tigers' account in Cyprus. I had never heard of CA Energy. You can believe me or not. That leaves Crabbe or Walmsley, or both, who transferred the funds using my signature.'

'The Tigers sent most of it on to Gromov in Cyprus.'

'Who's now dead,' said Tim softly, stretching back in his chair, then leaning forward to take Jennifer's hand. 'The money was used to buy a weapon called anthrax.'

'Jesus, Tim,' said Jennifer withdrawing. 'I've heard of that. It's a fucking biological weapon.'

'CA Energy paid the Tigers to buy anthrax off a gang of Russian mercenaries who stole it from a plant in China. It was driven to Karachi. We know that because the driver who took it from China inhaled some along the way and died. Yasin was sent from his training in Sri Lanka to pick it up . . .'

'Why send him?' said Jennifer. 'When they hardly knew him?'

'I guess because he was a foreigner and wasn't known to the spooks in India and Pakistan. Yasin hijacked the whole operation and somehow got the stuff over to Budapest at least. That's as far as the trail goes. If you're right about CA Energy . . .'

'I'm right.'

'. . . then what I want to know is why Walmsley funded the whole operation.'

Jennifer drank some cold coffee. 'Your boy, Yasin, needs money. Barges, bribes, transport. He needs big bad money and bad money leaves a stinking trail.'

They both looked up, disturbed by a timid knock on the glass door to the conservatory. Samira stood there, silent, but with a presence, in her jeans and a white T-shirt, her new haircut and the denim jacket slung over her shoulder.

She could have been their teenage daughter. Tim got up and looked at his watch. It was four thirty in the morning. 'Jen, this is Samira Omer, who I've been telling you about.'

Jennifer smiled, a genuine smile, and held out her hand. There was no conflict because they were too different. Jennifer from the privileged East Coast. Samira from the Sudanese dispossessed. One could never match the other, so they could never compete. Jennifer's instincts were maternal. She insisted that Samira sit down and poured her some coffee.

'Tim says you've had a terrible time,' she said.

'I've been looking for my brother.' Her tone was flat, defeated, a child's voice in a bigger world.

'Do you think he's a terrorist?'

Samira looked sharply at Tim: 'You told her.'

'Jennifer has found out a lot which could help us.'

'I'd better be making tracks for the airport.' Jennifer looked at her watch. 'I promised Jack I would look in on Amanda when I got over there.' The flight wasn't for another three hours. Heathrow was less than half an hour away. But Tim kept quiet and rang for a cab. As Jennifer's taxi pulled up, Samira watched Tim's intimacy with her.

# Chapter Thirty-two

As soon as Jennifer had gone, Samira put her fingers to her lips and passed Tim the note written by Rahim in Café Uno. Tim was about to talk, but she touched his lips as well and said blandly: 'She seemed a very nice person.'

'Yes,' replied Tim, reading Rahim's writing. 'I've known her for years.'

Rahim had written down the address of a restaurant, Mannar House, in south London, asking Samira to bring Tim to it at five in the morning when they would have received another message from Sri Lanka. 'Pack's house is under surveillance,' scribbled Rahim. 'Tell him, he'll have to get rid of them before Jegan can talk.'

Tim checked the watchers through the sitting-room window. It was easier at this time, the streets empty and the surveillance team at a low ebb, waiting for the shift change at seven. He thought of calling Walmsley, but he could no longer be trusted. He had given Jegan's people ten million dollars in Tim's name, then got angry when Tim went to see Jegan without telling him. *This isn't a James Bond film. We need to know where you are*, Walmsley had said.

The watchers across the road were two black women muttering together on the steps of the hotel, ready to move quickly, and a motorcyclist was just in sight, pulled up at the kerb, smoking, to the north, towards Hyde Park. There would be more watchers, but Tim didn't know where.

He turned on Melody FM to keep sound in the house, led Samira up to the top floor and quietly lowered the collapsible ladder from the roof. He climbed up, unlocking the skylight which slid back, letting in the chilly night air. He got out first, helped Samira up with his hand, then slid the skylight back. He lay with her on the dark flat roof, keeping close to the chimney stack for cover. He spotted another watcher, lying in a shop front on the corner with Queensway. None moved, and Tim waited a full five minutes before setting off.

Keeping crouched, holding Samira's hand, he crossed onto the adjoining roof, waited by the chimney stack, crossed onto the next one, waited, crossed and waited on the roof of the last house in the terrace which was vacant and undergoing renovation. He jumped as noiselessly as he could onto the flat roof extension at the back, lowered Samira down, then climbed into the small garden.

Tim hoped that, less than fifty yards from the house, the watcher would be on the motorcycle, leaning back just away from the arc of a street lamp, the keys in the ignition, ready to go at any moment. They felt their way through the house. It smelt of fresh paint and plaster. Their feet crunched on debris on the floor, but Tim knew the layout, because it was like his. Right outside the front door was a skip, with traffic cones and markers to guide pedestrians around it. Through the spy-hole he saw that the street was empty. The builders had left a set of keys hanging on a board just inside the front door and Tim tested them. They worked, pulling back the locks, one at the top, at the bottom and the main catch in the centre, then testing the door, that it would open quickly and let them out.

'Just follow me,' he whispered to Samira. 'Stay right with me.'

Tim opened the door, swiftly and noiselessly and ran towards the motorcycle. The rider heard him, and turned, speaking into his radio. Tim caught the man in a neck-lock and hauled him off the bike, the watcher clinging on, bringing the machine down with him, but Tim not caring, and letting it fall on the man's leg. He cried out in pain through the crash helmet, the weight of a Kawasaki 750cc breaking his shin bone and foot.

Tim heaved the bike up, key in the ignition as he had predicted, turned it on and the engine roared into life. He didn't need to speak to Samira. She was on the back, holding his waist, and Tim roared off to Bayswater Road, turning left towards Marble Arch and jumping two sets of red lights around Lancaster Gate. He slowed down Park Lane, turning left into Piccadilly and then up into Half Moon Street and stopping in Berkeley Square where he found a motorcycle park for it.

He slipped the keys into his pocket and hailed a taxi, dropping off passengers outside of a casino. Before the driver could complain about the destination, Tim pressed a twenty-pound note into his hand. 'The fare will be on top of that,' he said, opening the door for Samira then getting in himself.

They drove through emptying streets, the windscreen wipers on slow for the steady drizzle and, once across the river, London became wet and depressing. Neither of them talked, except when Tim mentioned to Samira where they were: Elephant and Castle, due south through Clapham to Tooting High Street.

The further south they headed, the more dismal the city became, the gutters strewn with damp litter, restaurants with broken signs and people hanging around mini-cab offices. Then all life seemed to stop. They drove past closed underground stations with not a person on the streets. No movement at all except for the rhythm of the windscreen wipers.

'There it is,' said Samira, the cabbie catching her eyes in his rear-vision mirror. The restaurant was on the right, on a corner, a light showing through drawn curtains and a neon sign outside advertising Kingfisher Beer from India. Tim asked the driver to go past and turn into Broadway Road. The neighbourhood was empty. The rain was heavy now and making puddles on the road. Tim gave the driver another twenty pounds and said he didn't need a receipt.

They walked back, hunched against the rain, and Tim knocked on the side-door, as Rahim had instructed in the note.

A flicker of shade over the spy-hole, curtains and shapes moving across the frosted glass, the noise of locks and the door opening quickly, Jegan there beckoning them in, shutting it behind them with the same locks and the curtains back across the glass.

A Tamil song was playing softly on a speaker lost somewhere in swathes of thick velvet curtain. Drops of rain ran down the window. Street lights shone in, throwing an orange glow into the small unlit restaurant, only half a dozen tables, with smells of curry and tobacco lingering in the air.

'Sorry. Sorry. Sorry,' Jegan said. He fumbled around as if he was a waiter, clearing the sauces off a table near the little bar at the end of the room so they could sit down. 'Thank you for coming.'

He pulled out chairs for them. 'Kutti called me himself.' He seemed to become lost in his own thoughts, tugging at his beard. 'He used the sat phone. It's very dangerous because they know where he is then and he has to move camp. He's used the sat phone twice.'

Tim and Samira sat facing the bar. Jegan was at the end of the table, facing the window to the street, his back to the door. 'We own this restaurant, you see. We have hundreds of legitimate businesses all around the world to raise funds for Eelam.' He pulled out an unopened packet of cigarettes and put them on the table.

'Kutti told me to tell you everything,' he said. 'I have to tell you exactly what he told me.' He stopped talking and fiddled with the cigarette packet.

Tim put his hand on his shoulder. 'OK. Just tell us. OK.'

Jegan looked straight at Samira: 'Your brother betrayed us. After training as a Black Tiger, he was sent to Pakistan on a special mission. Instead he disappeared. He betrayed us.'

'What mission?' Samira asked.

'To get a new weapon for us. It had been driven down from China and was to be loaded onto a ship in Karachi. One of our ships.'

'Anthrax,' said Tim.

Jegan rubbed his cheek and nodded: 'I didn't know. We don't know here what they are doing.'

'It's the biological weapons that Iraq had,' said Samira, impatient, pushing him just like Tim.

'Kutti says we had paid a lot of money to arrange to get the weapon to Sri Lanka. But he says your brother paid more. He doesn't know where it is. Only that it's missing.'

'How much?'

'Fifty kilograms.'

'Where were you going to use it?'

'Kutti says we weren't. It was a deterrent to try to start peace talks, to end the war. We would just let them know we had it.'

'How?'

359

Jegan looked lost. 'Kutti didn't say.'

Outside, the roar of a street-cleaning truck slowly made its way along the street. A car horn sounded and the first footsteps were of people going to work. It was still dark. The drizzle was dirty and remorseless.

'Where did you get it from?'

'That's what Kutti wanted me to tell you. It was arranged through British officials. They paid for everything. We have a shipping company in Cyprus and he, the British official, transferred US$10 million down to us. Then Kutti paid . . .'

Jegan didn't get to finish his sentence.

Tim threw himself across Samira, wrenching her to the ground, reacting to the familiar plop of a suppressed pistol being fired. Jegan fell forward flattening the cigarette packet with his forehead. He jerked again as a second shot cut through the back of the chair into his spinal column in the small of his back.

'Get up.' The voice was English, southern counties, the sort that might make major and then leave the army. A man like Tim.

Tim stayed where he was, his right arm pushing Samira's head into his chest, covering as much of her body as he could, although he knew it would be useless, because he offered her no protection at all.

'Let her go.' He was a squat, barrel-chested man, his face colourless, ashen and flat. He wore a navy blue blazer over a maroon sports shirt and his eyes were killer's eyes, intelligent, watching, unemotional, a man doing his job.

'Let her go and move away from the window.'

'Paras?' said Tim, asking about his regiment.

'You have ten seconds to separate yourself from the girl.'

'Hereford?'

'You have my word I will not harm her. If you stay with her, I will have to kill you both.'

He went through the motions of checking that there was a round in the breech and that the safety catch was off, although it wasn't necessary. Tim knew that.

'Who sent you? Walmsley?'

'I'm counting.'

'Hodge?' A name. A flicker of the eyes. A clue against his anonymity.

'I'm up to four.' He had the pistol in both hands. A Browning Double Action 9mm.

'Kutti?'

Nothing.

'I've counted six.' He cocked the hammer manually.

Shouts from outside. The clatter of rubbish sacks thrown into a garbage truck, glass against metal, plastic against glass. The whine of the machine tipping the garbage back. The music had stopped. Tim couldn't remember when but it left a horrible vacuum in the room. Two separate pools of blood gathered underneath Jegan's body.

'You guarantee her safety?' said Tim.

'My orders were to let her live if I found her with you.'

'But to kill me?'

He stiffened. 'I'm on eight.'

'OK.' Tim's own weapon was in the holster and useless. The gunman saw it as Tim got up, a movement of the eye, down and back again. Samira's hands were round his waist, holding him tight.

'Let go,' he said. She clung to him even more tightly.

'Release yourself from him, Samira, and come over to me.'

'He won't shoot if I'm here. His orders were to . . .'

The gunman interrupted Samira. 'As I said, I will kill you both if necessary. I'm counting again. To five this time.'

Tim felt tired like in the Sudan when they said they were

going to kill him. His final seconds would be spent not in reflection as a dying man deserved, but on logistics. Against the backdrop of a Tooting garbage truck. Samira suddenly irritated him for hanging on to him. He had to get Samira away from him or he would die using her as a hostage. That would be how Walmsley would tell the story. The gunman knew it, and waited.

Tim unfolded Samira's fingers, which were tucked into his belt.

She resisted, digging them in. 'I will not let him . . .'

'He's going to do it anyway. He's a professional.'

The forgiveness of the executioner by the condemned. The truck's revolving hazard lights struck a mirror on the wall adorned with Sri Lankan embroidery. It threw fragmented yellow light around the room. Tim bent her fingers back, and forced her hands away from him. The gunman took her by the arm. Tim was alone in the middle of the room, his profile against the window.

'Move away from the window,' said the gunman. He didn't want to shoot him there because the high-velocity round would go through Tim, through the window, and could strike the workmen outside.

'No,' said Tim. Without Samira he was more confident.

'I'm counting. Five again. Then I'll do your legs and kill you on the floor.'

Tim stared straight at him and when he saw a shadow flit across the wall he didn't waver. He thought it was light from the mirror playing a trick.

Then it appeared again, quickly this time, behind the gunman, one movement, from shadow to man, from crouched to standing to uncoiling forward, with nothing it seemed, until Tim saw the glint of a knife, held with such ease it could have been part of his body, part of the fighting machine, which attacked the assassin from behind, knocking down the gun hand, and as he began a defence, running the knife across his throat, deep, purposeful, no hesitation, a smooth semi-circular movement which had been carried out many times before on many different enemies, the warmth of the first flow of blood on his hand, the signal of success, the bearing of a man's weight as he died, contorting, eye-balls haywire, between surprise and death, seeing him to the ground so that the killing would not make a noise, smash anything or disturb the routine of the environment.

Rahim laid the gunman between the tables. His head lolled round, falling into a pool of Jegan's blood. He knelt down and went through the pockets, pulling a wallet from the back trouser pocket and handing it to Tim. He grinned at Samira as if they had something going together, a Bayswater cappuccino before Samira's haircut.

The rubbish truck moved to the next block, the voices of the workmen fading, but more splashes of cars, more sounds of Tooting waking up.

Samira's hands were on Tim's arm again. No one spoke. There was a click and Rahim spun round, the assassin's gun in his hand. But it was the cassette player turning the tape. The music started up again, Tamil dinner music for the early morning.

Rahim squatted by Jegan's body and went through his pockets, just like with the assassin, keeping it propped up so it didn't fall off the chair. He found a wallet and a British passport. 'You knew him?' said Tim, pointing to Jegan, wanting to speak, to say anything to take his mind of almost being killed.

'Not really.' Rahim flicked through the pages to the back. He showed no emotion. 'He was a computer technician. He had never fought for the movement.' He looked at Jegan's photograph. 'I can use this to get to Europe.' He was talking to Samira. 'We have a bigger office in Paris.' Then he pointed to the gunman. 'He was hired by a Stephen Walmsley, who works for the British government.' His English was good, talking quickly, a nervous outburst almost, with a slight American accent.

'Stephen Walmsley ordered a hit on me?' Tim exclaimed to himself. Samira squeezed his arm.

'He works through a company called CA Energy,' continued Rahim. He slipped Jegan's passport into his back pocket. 'He flew to Canada to hire me. I used to be a Black Tiger, then I got pissed off with it and left the movement. Kutti is good like that. If you betray him, you're dead. But if you just want out, that's fine. He even fixed me up with a visa.'

'Slow down,' said Tim. 'Who are you?'

Rahim kept talking as he prepared to leave. He cleaned the knife on a bundle of pink paper napkins, uncocked the Browning, thumbed on the safety catch and wiped the weapon of his prints. 'Mr Walmsley found me in Vancouver and offered me a lot of money to be his spy in the Eelam office in London. I got a message to Kutti and he said go ahead.'

'A double agent?'

'Call it what you like.'

'But why? Why go back?'

'Canada's nice. But it can be really boring.'

He handed the pistol to Tim and continued wiping, the bar, the tops of the chairs, the door handle where Tim and Samira had come in. 'He was crazy to have thought that I would betray Kutti for his money.' He shook his head. 'Really crazy.'

'But you knew we were coming here. You told me,' said Samira. 'Why, why were you too late to save Jegan?'

'Jegan asked me to come here, but at five thirty. He must have wanted to talk to you alone first. I didn't know they wanted to kill him.' Rahim pointed behind the bar. 'We own the house next door and there's an adjoining cellar which is how I got in. I heard voices, but when I lifted the trap door, it was really quiet.' He pointed down to the gunman's body. 'I heard him counting to kill you. The rubbish truck was loud enough for me to climb up.'

He slipped the knife into his jacket pocket, stepped forward, looked at himself in the mirror and combed his hair. 'Should I take Samira?' he said, like a protective admirer. 'Will she be safer?'

Yes, she would, thought Tim. The further she was away from him, Walmsley and London, the safer she would be. But he shook his head. 'She stays here.'

'I stay here,' Samira repeated. 'My brother betrayed your movement, so with you I have no chance of finding him.'

Rahim took out a pen, wrote down a telephone number and address on one of the pink napkins. 'Did Jegan have time to tell you? Stephen Walmsley paid us to attack a Sri Lankan city with anthrax. Kutti took the money but he would never have done that. That is what Jegan wanted to tell you.' He gave the napkin to Tim. 'Stephen Walmsley is a dangerous, evil man. If you need to run from him, we will protect you.'

'Thanks,' said Tim, holding the napkin in his right hand, not sure where to put it.

'Give me ten minutes then?' said Rahim, heading for the door. 'Let me get away first.'

It was getting light outside and the blue flashing light appeared without the sirens, dancing off the mirror, like the yellow ones before, right outside and across the street. Silent. The opening of car doors, not closing them again, tyres on the damp road, no one talking, quick footsteps round the side of the building, shapes through the curtains, the unmistakable movement of men deployed.

Suddenly, the police hit the front and back door simultaneously with steel rammers, splintering wood, glass breaking, curtains torn from their hooks. Smash, quiet, then two men in each entrance, one on his knees with a pistol, the other standing, shoulders braced each with a Heckler and Koch MP5 submachine gun, one at the front aimed at Tim, the other at Rahim. Without speaking, Tim put the Browning on a table. He felt Samira's hand on him again.

'Easy boys.' It was Walmsley, unmistakable, wearing a dark Inverterre rain coat and a red cashmere scarf, pushing through the front door and past the two men as if reprimanding them for blocking the way.

'Good morning, Tim.' He undid the top button of his coat, looking around, eyes resting for a moment on each of the dead bodies. 'It appears I'm a bit late.' He turned back towards the door, where a plain-clothed policeman was standing, half inside, half in the street. 'Would you leave us alone for a moment, Superintendent?' said Walmsley.

'And the men, sir?'

'Outside, if you will. In their vehicles, in a back street. Keep a police car with two men at the door.' The men slipped away. Walmsley closed the door. As he turned back into the room, Tim picked up the Browning and pulled back the hammer.

Walmsley stopped, contemptuous and irritated. 'What are you going to do, Tim, shoot me?' He took off his scarf and unbuttoned the rest of his coat. 'You're bloody tedious at times.' He laid the scarf over the back of a chair, looked down at the gunman and back to Rahim. 'Is this your work?'

'Yes.' Rahim was defiant.

Walmsley's attention, ignoring the gun, moved to Samira. 'And you are Miss Omer?'

Samira said nothing. Her eyes were like Rahim's, mutinous, brave against everything Walmsley stood for. Tim kept the pistol levelled, holding it with both hands: 'Sit down.' he indicated towards a seat with the weapon. 'Push the chair right up against the wall and sit on it.'

Walmsley rolled his eyes, but obeyed. 'Do you really think . . . ?'

'Shut up, Stephen. I'm going to ask you questions. You're going to answer them. If you make me unhappy, Rahim here will start cutting you up.'

'Supposing I'm wired?'

'You're not.'

'Oh!'

'A wired man doesn't unbutton his coat.'

'Don't take your eye off the target, Tim. The anthrax, Tim, we've got to . . .'

The gun was suppressed. The silencer on the muzzle. Maybe he could just kill him, and get out with Rahim through the adjoining cellar, before the men outside knew what was happening. He felt the rush, like in Zenica, like in the San Li Tun market, the rush before the kill, an exhilaration like nothing else, something a killer couldn't describe to someone who had never done it.

Walmsley stopped mid-sentence, as if he knew Tim was about to kill him: 'All right. You want to know my role?'

Tim nodded. 'From the beginning.'

'I created CA Energy as a vehicle to carry out the experiment with anthrax which we so desparately needed to do. We called it Operation Dust Shadow. Through CA Energy I transferred funds to the Tigers. I used your name so that Jim Crabbe and I could distance ourselves from the transfer if it ever got out. God forbid. The thing is, Tim, that you had been expendable from the day you killed the Iranian mercenary in Zenica.' He nodded over towards Rahim.

'His lot were to use the money to get their hands on fifty kilograms of anthrax.' He paused, reflective.

'Why?' prompted Tim; the gun was steady on the area of Walmsley's heart.

'After the Gulf War, we, that's the British and the Americans, knew we had to set up a civil defence programme against a chemical and biological weapons attack. This wasn't like the nuclear superpower game with Mutually Assured Destruction. This was a war where any crackpot could go anywhere in the world with a suitcase of anthrax and kill thousands of people. It wasn't a matter of "if", like with a nuclear attack. It's a matter of when, and as far as all of us in this room are concerned, it's now.'

'Go on.'

'Rahim knows. He'll tell you if I start lying.' He was quiet, running his right hand down his face, creasing the skin, not wanting to say the rest. 'We needed a test ground, a civilian population to be hit. A city with infrastructure, hospitals, schools, churches. We needed to monitor the effects of an anthrax attack.'

'No?' Tim looked over towards Samira. She was utterly quiet, watching Walmsley with contempt but no surprise, as if she knew he was evil and was now only being told the details.

'Just think about it. We knew all we needed to about nuclear weapons. Piles of statistics from Hiroshima and Nagasaki, computer simulation, all the funding of the Cold War to protect us. But we knew nothing about the impact of these new weapons. In the late nineties, we picked up terrorist cells, sent here by Saddam Hussein to release anthrax if and when we bombed Iraq. They were arrested with the stuff. That's how close it got. And we had no idea exactly what the impact would be.'

'So you chose Sri Lanka as the guinea pig.'

'Yes. We had suggested Kandy, but the Tigers insisted there were too many Tamil workers in the tea plantations there. They decided on a place called Ratnapura about fifty miles inland from Colombo. A lot of gem mining there to make it an economic target and an historic Sinhala site. It is the sort of place they might have attacked anyway. We would send in a team of people, vaccinated of course, to monitor everything from the moment of the release.'

'We weren't going to use it,' said Rahim. 'Kutti said he wanted the deterrent. To get peace talks . . .'

'Let him finish,' snapped Tim.

'CA Energy sent money to their shipping company in Cyprus. The Tigers took their cut and sent the rest to . . . to . . .' he searched for the right word, 'to the Russian Mafia, I suppose. From then on, it really was out of our hands. Jensen's agent, Nalyotov, gave us details of the plant in Bachu which we passed on.'

He pointed towards Samira. 'And that's where Yasin comes in. The intelligence agencies in Pakistan and India are so good on the Tigers that Kutti needed a complete outsider to pick it up. So he recruited an idiot schoolfriend of Yasin's called Venkataraman and got him to bring Yasin down. But Yasin outwitted us all. The whole thing has boomeranged back on us.'

'Why did Kutti do it?' asked Rahim.

'Money, I suppose. And to get his hands on a new weapon.'

The blue flashing lights went off. Tim had stopped noticing them, but suddenly there was a dullness in the room like when a stroboscope stops abruptly at a discotheque. The police car and the ambulance were outside and red and white cones had been put up around them. A queue of traffic was building with the lights at the next junction, the steady drone of idling engines.

'How many people would have died?' said Tim.

'We don't know. That's why we needed the test. We would have vaccinated all but a handful . . .'

'Crap, Stephen,' shouted Tim. 'You are completely insane.' He felt the rush again. The need to kill such an ultimately evil man.

Walmsley knew. 'Let me finish the story.' His voice was raised too. 'You are naïve. How do you think we know the little we do about these weapons? Because of the Japanese experiments during World War Two. We freed their scientists in exchange for the information when they should have been hanged for war crimes. We condemned their science, but we used their results. This is a dirty little world, Tim, with dirty people like us running it. A series of terrible coincidences create men like Yasin and right now there's a chance he is right here in London with a terrible weapon and we have no idea at all of the ghastly effect it will have on the lives of innocent British citizens – the people whose taxes pay us to protect them, Tim. They pay so they can sleep peacefully at night, and we have let them down.' Walmsley paused, catching his breath. 'There hasn't been an anthrax Hiroshima and that's why we needed to create one. Can't you see that?'

'Who's we?'

'It's not people. It's governments.'

'Who's we?'

'The government.'

'Crap.'

'Christ, you're innocent. The government isn't people.'

Tim tilted his head down towards the body of the gun-man, then back again: 'Who's he?'

'A civil servant.'

'You ordered him to murder me.'

'He didn't expect you there. He didn't want loose ends.'

'You wanted Jegan dead before he told me.'

'Yes.'

'Jesus. How in the hell do you get away with it?' Tim whispered angrily.

'This isn't a game.'

'Tell that to Jack Jensen.'

'People die in this war, Tim.'

'It isn't a war.' Tim stepped forward, eye-balling Walmsley, the weapon digging into his neck. 'Tell me about Jensen, Stephen. Did you set the Russian onto Jensen because he knew too much. Did you send them into his house and have Pamela and Davey killed?'

'No,' Walmsley shouted. 'No.' He grabbed Tim's wrist and tried to push him away. But Pack stayed firm. Rahim took the knife out of his pocket, out of the sheath.

'The Russians found out that Nalyotov had been in touch with us.' Walmsley wriggled back, making more space between them, relaxing his grip. 'They thought he had given Jack something which would expose them and they wanted to find it. We lost control of them.'

Tim pushed the weapon harder against his neck: 'Your whole bloody game has gone out of control.'

'Not my game.'

'Your game.'

'I'm a civil servant.'

They had been in the claustrophobic restaurant with calendar pictures of Sri Lankan beaches and shrines for less than an hour. One body slumped at a table. Another on the floor, like a waiter who had fallen over and spilt the gravy.

If Tim was going to kill, he would have done it earlier. The rush had gone. He eased the weapon away, letting Walmsley straighten his collar. They were all quiet, like a family recovering from a horrible argument.

'Well done, Tim,' said Walmsley eventually. 'I suggest you put your personal feelings to one side while we solve the immediate problem.'

He pointed to Samira. 'You, my dear, are the key. Somewhere in London, your brother is planning an attack on the leaders of the eight most powerful governments in the world. As far as we know, you are the only person in the world he cares about.'

Samira broke her silence, speaking to Walmsley with contempt: 'You really think I will help you find him to kill him.'

'You have to.' Walmsley got up. Rahim moved to stop him but Tim indicated he should stay where he was. He unscrewed the silencer from the Browning, slipped it into his jacket pocket and pushed the pistol into his belt. 'How far up did it go, Stephen?' he said, much more calmly. 'You. Hodge. Then who? The Prime Minister?'

Walmsley picked up his scarf from the back of the chair: 'You can't indict a government,' he answered. 'Rahim, why don't you bugger off to your people in Paris? You got an EU passport?' Rahim nodded.

'The boys outside will clear all this up.' Walmsley glanced at the bodies. 'Poor old Jegan. He never knew he was fighting a real war.' Then at the gunman. 'As for Johnny-boy. Always thought he was the best in the business.'

They gave Rahim a few minutes to get out through the cellar, then walked through the broken front door into the damp Tooting morning, the rain holding off, but the clouds, low, grey and uncompromising in their bleakness.

A chauffeur opened the door to Walmsley's black Jaguar. 'You don't need a lift do you?' he said to Tim, as he got in the back seat. 'Have a shower, then give me a call.' A shout from the back window.

# Chapter Thirty-three

The rain started at three in the morning. Yasin saw the first drops splatter on the rail and on the wooden balcony boards. The forecast was for wet weather. There could be one day of rain. After that he had to attack. He closed the balcony door and went upstairs.

Yasin stood back from the map on the bedroom wall and examined his route. A plastic sheet covered the map so he could trace the journey of the van with a black felt-tip pen.

This would be the Hiroshima of international terrorism. It would be an attack absolute in devastation and human tragedy, forcing changes that millions of insignificant little deaths all over the world had failed to do. It would end the arrogance of leaders who didn't want to witness the impact of their policies. It would be the most generous act of warfare the modern world had ever suffered. Once it had happened, it would never happen again.

The people in the City of London were his enemies, although they didn't even know there was a war. Innocent people starved because of decisions taken by bankers to get big bonuses.

Throughout the City of London, the narrow pavements would be packed. They would all die and bankers would think again before pulling loans on the people of a poor country.

He noted the addresses of the embassies on a white board next to the map. **Italy**, 14 Three King's Yard, W1; **United States**, 24 Grosvenor Square, W1; **France**, 58 Knightsbridge SW1; **Germany**, 23 Belgrave Square, SW1; **Canada** (High Commission), Canada House, Trafalgar Square, SW1; **Japan**, 101–104 Piccadilly.

He missed out Russia because its embassy was at 6–7 Kensington Palace Gardens, the wide private road of diplomatic properties which ran between Kensington High Street and Notting Hill Gate. At each end there was a private security guard and vehicles needed a pass to get through. It wasn't worth the risk and besides the Russians weren't even proper members. They were as much victims as himself.

He gave **Great Britain** a separate box with an even more detailed map, showing the area of Downing Street with Whitehall to the east and Horse Guards Parade and the Mall to the north and west. The attack would begin there, then the City, and then he would take the van down across Westminster Bridge and east to Southwark where the van would be hidden away.

No one would be suspicious. No one would yet be ill. By the time the first symptoms appeared, they would all be gone. The van would be locked in a garage, not to be disturbed for at least a year when the lease ran out.

He bought *La Stampa*, *Le Figaro*, *The Globe & Mail*, *The Washington Post*, *Nikkei Shimbun* in English and *Handelsblatt* from different newsagents in Queensway in Bayswater and the Earls Court Road and from them he noted the detailed movements of each head of government. According to the newspapers, the government leaders would hold a late-afternoon meeting at Downing Street on the eve of the summit itself.

Between 15:00 and 15:30 the air around the diplomatic

buildings of the most powerful countries on earth and the government buildings of Great Britain would be so filled with anthrax spores that no one who stepped onto the streets there would survive.

Yasin closed the bedroom door and, deep in thought, went down the narrow stairs towards the basement. Inside the van, air tanks were encased by wood panelling. The welder and the carpenter had done a good job. Each tank had its own control for the valve. The tubes were hidden, running behind a sheet of plywood to the main duct. The funnels were big enough to take a 2.5-kilogram bag at a time, sealed at the top by perspex, to prevent spillage, with a clip to ensure it stayed in place.

Everything was painted white so the work would not stand out from the inside of the van. They had built a perspex glass partition between the driving seat and the back and installed an intercom for communication.

Yasin closed the doors of the van and sat at the work bench set up by the carpenter. He picked up a piece of clothing which looked like a Kevlar flak jacket, but it was lighter, a sleeveless vest made of Gortex, with pockets sewn inside.

He put on a respirator and plastic gloves and lifted a bag of anthrax onto the work bench. He took a strip of Semtex H plastic explosive and pressed it around the inside edges of a much smaller plastic bag. He pressed a tiny electric detonator into the explosives and ran a cord outside. Then he pierced the anthrax bag with a tiny metal tube. Once in, he sealed round the tear with tape. He poured the powder through the tube into the plastic bag, covering the explosives and filling it up.

After sealing the bag with tape, he sterilised the metal tube with the flame of a lighter and wrapped tape around its end. He spread the vest on the table and put the bag into an inside pocket on the left, attaching the cords to a nine-volt alkaline battery which he slipped into a higher inside pocket like a packet of cigarettes.

He repeated the whole process for a pocket on the right and, when he finished, he put the vest in a locked container. Before leaving and still wearing the respirator, he filled a bucket with water, mixed in ten per cent formaldehyde, and sluiced it over the concrete floor of the garage. He did it again, washing down the van and the work surfaces. If any anthrax spores had escaped, the formaldehyde solution would kill them. He showered and shampooed in the downstairs washroom and put his overalls in a sealed rubbish bag.

He wished he could isolate himself before the mission, like the real suicide bombers, cleanse himself of outside thought so he wouldn't change his mind. Yasin's training as a Black Tiger was to complete the mission, but to escape if possible. He would only use the suicide vest if he came down with symptoms of the disease or if he was about to be captured. He remembered the code of the Mahas river Arabs of the Nile: 'When you meet the enemy and there is no way to win, it is better to die than to run away.'

Stephen Walmsley and Harold Parsons were shown into the Prime Minister's office in Downing Street and they waited for the private secretary to leave, closing the door behind him. The Prime Minister offered to move to the comfortable coffee-table chairs, but they declined and took upright chairs on the other side of the Prime Minister's desk.

'We believe the G7 summit may be attacked by terrorists with biological weapons,' said Parsons. The Prime Minister, who was still signing papers, stopped and looked up: 'Do you know when, where and who?'

'It's anthrax, sir,' said Walmsley. 'What we call the weapon of choice for bio-terrorists. It is a random group, certainly not state-sponsored. We have an intelligence trail which, I believe, is going to end up here in London.'

The Prime Minister took off his spectacles and rubbed his eyes: 'I suspected as much when Hodge first contacted me. Who knows about this?'

'I am working through the National Security Adviser in Washington, sir,' said Parsons. 'I've spoken directly to the President. But no one outside that circle.'

'And what can be done to prevent the attack taking place?'

'If we don't find them, very little,' said Walmsley.

'I see. And do we have medicines, vaccinations?'

Walmsley shook his head. 'The vaccine takes at least a month to become effective and there is the question of whom we vaccinate. It is possible to treat people after the attack, but only before symptoms appear. Once they become ill, it's too late.'

'What do you do in the States?' the Prime Minister asked Parsons.

'The armed forces serving out in the Gulf are vaccinated. It's a shot every two weeks for six weeks. Then three more, one every six months. The total course is eighteen months. The President, as commander-in-chief, has had the full course and he's reaffirmed that he is coming to the summit.'

'Then I can't see the point of notifying other heads of government. I certainly won't cancel the meeting on the strength of a terrorist threat.'

'I agree,' said Walmsley. 'If the attack does not happen, but if the threat gets into the media, the impact on public confidence will be enormous. We have little ability to trace anthrax and very little civil defence ability to handle an attack. The less the public know that, the better.'

'What would happen to London?'

'It depends who you talk to,' continued Walmsley. 'We would have to evacuate and wash down the affected area with a formaldehyde solution – ten per cent formaldehyde with river water, fifty litres of water per square metre. I'm told that would do the job.'

'The symbolism is that it's your sovereign capital,' said Parsons. 'In our scenarios for New York and Washington we have contingency plans to move the seat of government and the financial services sectors.'

'What is the Scottish island which was contaminated for fifty years?'

'Gruinard, sir,' said Walmsley. 'The decontamination formula was used there.'

'But the only victims were sheep and the place is an uninhabited island on the west coast of Scotland?'

'It's the only real-life situation we have, Prime Minister,' said Walmsley. 'With anthrax there is no luxury of research as was given by the atomic bombs dropped on Hiroshima and Nagasaki.'

The Prime Minister stood up, stretched his back and put his glasses back on: 'Thank you, gentlemen. Harold, you will continue to liaise directly with the White House and Stephen, Hodge tells me he has already set up the control centre in New Cavendish Street. Let us just hope your intelligence is wrong.' As they were leaving, the Prime Minister called Walmsley back. 'Stephen, there is another matter, if you have a minute.'

With Parsons gone, the Prime Minister said, 'I had thought that by now we should have the statistics we need for something like this.'

Walmsley was quiet, seemingly lost for an answer. The Prime Minister pressed him, 'What's happened to Operation Dust Shadow, Stephen?'

'It is taking much longer to arrange than we thought.

Getting the right sort of community and minimising casualties yet getting the maximum research from it. We've been looking at Sri Lanka.'

'Is it still going ahead?'

Walmsley hesitated, then said, 'As far as I'm aware, sir. But I'll check.'

'Because if you don't, we might have to take the research from our own bloody citizens.' He pulled a notepad in front of him and uncapped a pen. 'What sort of casualties are we talking about?'

'In London, with the overcast weather and south-west winds as they are, it could be anything from a thousand dead to a million.'

'Precisely, my point. We don't know, do we?' he replied, angry and sarcastic. 'Why don't you tell me exactly what we don't know.'

'The survival rate of the spores through an explosive dispersion,' said Walmsley. He was standing in front of the Prime Minister's desk. 'It could be one per cent. It could be none. Dust Shadow would ascertain that for us. The effect of sunlight on micro-encapsulation. Again that is an element of Dust Shadow. The strains of anthrax resistant to existing antibiotics. We suspect the attack on London would be with a powerful weapons-grade anthrax made during the 1980s at the Stepnagorsk facility in what's now Kazakhstan. It has a horrifying level of toxicity and no known defence. The Dust Shadow victims would allow us to develop a preventative vaccine and antidote. There are other elements such as confirming the penetration of spore sizes into the lower lungs.' The Prime Minister wrote in neat columns, drawing a line under each, as Walmsley spoke: 'In the area of civil defence we would look into the capacity of hospitals . . .'

'But the Sri Lankan hospitals are far worse than ours.'

'That would be factored into the findings. The knock-on diseases both contagious and non-contagious which would result from overcrowded hospitals, such as cholera, typhoid, that sort of thing. A breakdown in civil order . . .'

'But a different society.'

'We would examine the timing, from the release of the weapon to the disintegration of government institutions, and factor in elements such as corruption, loyalty, professionalism. Local doctors and police would also be affected. The results of Dust Shadow would be adjusted to give us impact estimates from New York to Timbuctoo. There are wider elements, such as whether we find a signature left by the terrorist group, the global panic caused by the release of such a weapon; the impact on financial markets . . .'

'Point made,' interrupted the Prime Minister, holding up his hand. But Walmsley concluded: 'It would be conducted like a nuclear test with computer simulation for everything we need to know. It sounds horrific, but the end result would ensure that if a group of men were in London right now with this weapon we would know how to handle a worst-case scenario.'

'Do we know when they'll strike?'

'You are hosting a mid-afternoon meeting here the day after tomorrow for the heads of government. We think they might try to release the anthrax into the atmosphere at that time, simply because you will all be under one roof at the same time.'

'Your chances of stopping them?'

'A lottery, Prime Minister. This is not the IRA. Not Hamas. Not bin Laden. We have no history of the players. Anybody walking down the street could be strapped up with enough explosives to kill a million people in London.'

Stephen Walmsley waited patiently while an old lift carried

him to the basement of the building in 86 New Cavendish Street, which bore the name-plaque of a fictitious bank registered in the Channel Islands. Armed anti-terrorist police were deployed just inside the entrance.

The basement had been turned into a crisis control centre, one which could never become known to the public. The windows of the building were covered. The walls were reinforced to withstand the impact of high-velocity weapons fire, including anti-tank weapons and rocket-propelled grenades. The ventilation system would prevent the entry of the fall-out from chemical, biological and nuclear weapons.

The communications system was linked directly to Scotland Yard, the Government Communications Headquarters at Cheltenham and the Permanent Joint Operations Headquarters at Northwood, to where this operation would retreat if it could no longer function in New Cavendish Street.

As Walmsley walked into the room, images of London buildings were being shown on a screen at the end of the room. Arrows indicated where police snipers had been deployed. Most were equipped with the Accuracy International PM 7.62 mm or the SSG 3000 0.308, high-powered rifles, designed with a light bipod under the barrel and a monopod under the stock so it could be held towards the target for a long time without tiring the sniper. The effective range of the telescopic sight was a thousand metres. But this was urban warfare and each man was being told he would be expected to carry out a first-round hit on a head-sized target at a range of less than 300 metres, or 984 feet.

The target might be moving in a crowded street, in such a way that it would be impossible to get a clear shot. There were exceptional circumstances in which civilians could be sacrificed in order to neutralise the target and avoid a much higher death toll. The men were given the simple code, *Omega*, if they were to open fire under such conditions.

When the sniper heard that order, he was not to hesitate. Training – to avoid civilian casualties – which many of them had been given during the four-week course at the SAS killing house in Hereford did not apply. *Omega* meant it was all right to take out a mother and child with the target.

'We have every sniper in Britain on stand-by: Royal Marines, SAS, Paras. You name it, they're on our payroll.' A wheelchair came to a stop by Walmsley's side. 'My name's Norton. Jim Norton.' He held out his hand. 'I handle the disasters we don't want anyone to know about. Take a seat and I'll run through what we're doing.'

Norton rolled himself back and then came in again to get a better position at the desktop. He was in his late forties, and although bespectacled with a head of wild, unkempt hair and a thick beard, there was an immense calm about him. 'It's anthrax. Right. How much? Do you know?'

'Twenty-five kilograms,' said Walmsley.

'My God. I should be buying stock options in the undertaking business.' He looked up at Walmsley, smiling, but Walmsley didn't take the joke. Norton rested one hand on the wheel of his chair and used the other to work the computer mouse. 'So you're an expert on bio-terror weapons and I run the show on the ground which means I deal with disasters and I'll be your boss until it's over.'

Walmsley stepped back as if to show his disdain, but said nothing. Norton seemed to be used to the first reaction. 'I know it's weird that a cripple should do this job.' He smiled. 'But the Mayor of London reckoned he needed a disaster co-ordinator in the central control room and not running around the streets saving people like in the movies. So he picked a guy whose legs don't work.'

'Let's just agree to work together,' said Walmsley softly.

'Snipers. Two in each position, rotating four-hour shifts,' said Norton. He pointed as the pictures changed from one building to another. 'The environment around Whitehall is completely covered. If Yasin Omer is identified, he's dead. Two men in the clock tower in the Queen's Life Guard building, covering Whitehall. Horse Guards and St James's Park.

'Up here in the turret of the Old War Office covering Downing Street and King Charles Street. The Cabinet Office, Privy Council Office, Foreign Office, the Treasury and on the other side the Ministry of Defence. More men on the balustrade roof here of Banqueting House, and on the other side, we have them in the Cabinet Office and round here in Admiralty Arch, which gives them a clear shot down towards Buckingham Palace.'

'You've been thorough in protecting the heart of government,' said Walmsley.

'A civil servant protects his own,' replied Norton. 'Surveillance teams have been deployed throughout central London, brought in from all police forces, with direct communication to us here. They are recognisable to the sniper and to each other by a red three-digit number on their right shoulder.'

The screen showed a photograph of a girl, walking along a street with earphones and a Sony Discman. 'See. It looks like a designer logo, conspicuous enough to ensure no mistakes. Tim Pack and Samira Omer will be issued with the same.'

'Is the City covered?' asked Walmsley.

'Partly. But it doesn't have the geography of Whitehall.' Norton glanced across to Walmsley. 'Why? Do you think we should consider it's a target?'

Walmsley shrugged: 'He's after economic targets.'

'I'll move men across there.' He pressed a keyboard on the arm of his chair: 'Nick, Can you set up a unit for the City of London. Move it down there, then let me know what you've done.' He changed the image of the screen to a hazy aerial shot of central London: 'The Americans have swung an extra satellite over. Can't see it doing much good except taking historic pictures if he does blow himself up. We've got the whole of Britain covered with AWAC surveillance and we're banning all crop-spraying aircraft for the next two weeks.'

'The press are bound to get onto that.'

'A risk,' said Norton. 'But the most effective way to distribute anthrax is with a crop-spraying plane or even a drone. We've said it's to rearrange flight paths.'

Norton spun his wheelchair round and Walmsley followed him to another part of the room, where screens were built into the surface of a work bench. 'I'd like your view on issuing pictures.' He called up a picture of Yasin and raised the screen. 'The only two pictures we have of Yasin are of him playing cricket at school in India and dressed up in jungle fatigues like bloody Che Guevara.'

'If we release either of them, he could vanish with the anthrax.'

'Or release it early,' added Norton.

'Do you have photographs of Samira?' asked Walmsley.

'We have better ones of her. Are you thinking of drawing him out through her?'

Walmsley was silent for a while: 'It's a possibility,' he said. 'But also a danger.'

Norton's handset rang from the arm of his chair. He picked it up. 'It's for you,' he said, handing it to Walmsley. When Walmsley had finished speaking he turned to Norton: 'From GCHQ via Pine Gap in Australia. Yasin Omer called the hospital in Zamboanga on a Sprint card. The call originated in London.'

# Chapter Thirty-four

The ward sister in Zamboanga told Yasin that Samira had been sent to Moorfields Eye Hospital in London. They had not yet had a report back. They told him the telephone number, reminding him to use the prefix 44 to get to Britain. He moved to an adjoining booth in Kensington High Street underground station, but it was no good with the clatter of shoppers around him. He didn't understand the West and its culture and he needed a quieter place. He had learnt to be patient with the British and to ignore their rudeness. He had never been in a place where everyone seemed to be so unhappy. He crossed the road, walking east towards Kensington Gardens, remembering the television pictures of flowers left there for Princess Diana, and that was how he thought of London: The Royal Family and Irish bombs.

He paid cash for a booth in the business centre of the Royal Garden Hotel and, using an AT & T card, he called Moorfields.

'We do not give out any patient details.' It was a woman. Bored. Unhelpful.

'I am her closest relative and it is imperative . . .'

'Your name.'

'I am her brother.'

'Mr Omer, the only thing I can suggest is that you . . .'

'Don't you have a security system which would allow you to tell me?' said Yasin, remembering Hans Jancke in Vienna.

'I assure you, that if you write in . . .'

'Samira Omer is aged nineteen. Her birthday is February 14th. Her country of birth is the Sudan. She is an orphan from al-Kadarou in the Sudan. She was sent to you after being blinded in a bomb attack in Zamboanga. Her guardian in the Philippines is Rudy Osmeña from the Philippine National Bank. Her guardian here is Tim Pack . . .'

'. . . your letter with be dealt with immediately.'

Yasin paused, suddenly stopping himself from saying more. He put down the phone. Tim Pack. The address he had written years ago on the canvas bag. Queensborough Terrace, London, WC2. He remembered it as if it were yesterday. He would find Tim Pack and then Samira. Get Samira out of London, before the attack.

'He called Moorfields,' said Jim Norton. 'He was stupid enough to tell them who he was then rang off.'

'Location.'

'Coming through now.' Norton read from the printer on the desk: 'Royal Garden Hotel, Kensington High Street. AT & T card through New York.'

Tim was sleeping lightly when Samira slipped out of the door of the house and turned left towards Hyde Park. He was woken by the click of the door and his phone rang straight away. 'Let her go, Tim,' said Walmsley. 'We've got the full red-box on her without you beating up the watchers this time.'

The group of black women sat on the hotel steps across the street enjoying the spring sunshine. A cyclist with dark glasses and a yellow crash hat pedalled past her, then pulled up before the junction with Bayswater to pull on a pair of gloves. A couple on roller blades came out of Hyde Park at Porchester Terrace Gate, stopped at the pedestrian lights, but didn't even cross the road when they turned green. They chatted, seemingly oblivious to anything except themselves. A young man in a suit walked behind Samira, dropping back when she stopped, flicking open his map when she hesitated on Bayswater Road and decided not to cross into the park.

*Turning right into Bayswater.* Rollerblader to Norton. She walked slowly, almost dawdling, past the junction with Inverness Terrace and then right again into Queensway. She seemed happier there, where it was busier, less isolated than the deserted streets further along.

*Walking north towards Whiteley's.* Watcher in Café Verde to Norton. *Stopping. Gone into Queensway Arcade.*

'David, can you get in there?'

*I'm there.* Watcher moved out of Our Price Records to arcade. Samira, her attention-span used up, came out and brushed past him.

The red-box surveillance kept its pattern. Watchers lingered in the coffee shops and browsed the tourist stalls. Those who moved with her worked on signals as much as on radio messages – the brushing of a hand against a face, the removal of a hat, the flicking back of hair – signals which no one else would know except them and their controller; anything except direct eye contact.

*At Ehman newsagents.* David to Norton. Norton brought up the cyclist to go ahead. *Buying a copy of the* Manila Bulletin *from the foreign newspaper rack.*

'Hold back, there,' said Norton. 'Gary on the bicycle will take over and Richard's at the Tandy shop further up.'

Samira stood in the doorway of the shop, opening the pages, hungry for news about the Philippines, so absorbed that she had to be asked to move out of the way.

*Wandering. Doesn't seem she has an agenda.* Richard to Norton. *Unsure about Whiteley's.*

*Heading south-west-side pavement.* Gary to Norton.

The red-box team moved south with her again, notifying the teams in Hyde Park, Lancaster Gate and in Notting Hill, each section a square quarter mile, each covered on foot, bicycle, motorcycle, so she would move seamlessly from one to the other. They noted that she hadn't looked at the time, either on her watch or a clock on the street. She stayed on the western side of Queensway.

*She's looking at the Ann Summer's sex shop.* Man in suit to Norton.

'Go in. Go past her and in,' said Norton. 'Gary take over on foot.'

She had her foot on the doorstep, then seemed to change her mind.

*She's pensive and curious.* Man in suit to Norton.

*Heading into Boots.* Gary to Norton. Pause. No radio communication. Gary takes off his hat, the signal for the cyclist to dismount and watch outside the chemist shop. *She's buying a two-in-one bottle of L'Oréal shampoo.*

Samira kept heading south, no faster, no more purposeful than before, the cyclist scooting down the one-way street backwards, on the other side of the road. The man in the suit was behind her again. Gary moved up to Queensway Arcade, looking through the jackets hanging at the entrance.

*Reading the menu at the Royal China restaurant.* Man in suit to Norton.

*Heading for the park.* Rollerblader at Porchester Terrace Gate to Norton.

*Fuck . . .* Man in suit. Radio to static.

*He's shot.* Gary to Norton.

*She's at Queensway tube station.* Cyclist.

'Who's shot?'

*Brendan's down.* Gary.

Samira, newspaper folded, not rolled, looking to cross the road, jay-walking, not on the zebra crossing, opposite the CheckPoint bureau de change.

*She may have a weapon.* Cyclist, mounting, heading towards her.

*Doubling back.* Gary.

*Man running west. Yellow shirt. Asian.* Rollerblader to Norton.

'Brendan.' Norton into radio. Silence. 'Take her.' Norton to all.

*Five seconds.* Cyclist.

*She's running.* Gary. *She's seen something.*

A scream.

'What's that?' Norton.

*Richard's down.* Gary. *Shit.*

Second radio to static.


Yasin knew the red-box, recognised it as soon as the watchers moved when she left the house, because the Sri Lankan army, taught by the British, used it, and red-box was part of Black Tiger training. His team killed so quickly that no one could tell if they were black, white, young or old. The welder was the first trigger; Yasin, the second. The two drivers were decoys, so as the welder shot the man in the suit, the helmsman and a driver each ran in opposite directions, one in a primary-coloured red shirt, the other in bright yellow, and the welder in shabby beige and jeans, indistinct from a dozen other foreigners in the street.

Yasin saw the rollerbladers react, but they were too far away for a clean shot and by the time they were out of the park, too many people were crowding round and running.

As soon as the welder had fired, Yasin spotted the reaction of the cyclist, and killed him. He fired from under a newspaper, dropped it and kept walking, gun by his side, straight towards Samira. He looked like an Arab student, smartly dressed in slacks and blazer, taking her elbow and marching her down towards Bayswater. The street screamed, gaped and fled. Witnesses pointed towards the other men who had run away, the ones deployed to catch the public eye.

The evening rush hour was just beginning. Samira didn't struggle as he walked her across the road. She let him take her. As soon as his hand touched her arm and he spoke to her in Arabic, she relaxed and trusted him, as if God had sent her out that afternoon to wander and find her twin brother, as if the commotion around her was from another world. She hadn't seen the killing.

A maroon Volvo S40 estate pulled up and Yasin opened the back door, getting in first to cover the roadside and Samira automatically following him. The driver indicated, letting cars go past him, before gently pulling out. It was a new family car, a careful driver, completely unsuspicious. He took them up to the Shepherds Bush roundabout and north along the M41 to the M40, where he turned east again towards the West End.

'He's killed two of the watchers, taken her and gone either towards the park or into the tube system,' said Walmsley to Tim. 'Queensway, not Bayswater.'

'Can we stop the trains?'

Norton was on the conference line: 'And create a hundred thousand hostages? Turn the whole underground system into a gas chamber? No bloody way!'

'We've spent millions trying to prevent a bio-terror attack,' said Walmsley. 'Satellites, spies, long-range missile control, God knows what and in the end a bloody schoolboy walks into London with it in a suitcase.'

'Forget the tube station,' said Norton. 'The rollerbladers say they saw them get into a maroon Volvo estate, heading west.'

They didn't talk. They didn't need to. For Samira it was like before, the times of their childhood she had yearned for. He was Chameleon, she was Gazelle. London was no different from Omdurman because they were together again.

The driver dropped them at Baker Street underground station as the traffic became heavy. He walked her briskly down to the Bakerloo Line, slowed as the train approached, then quickly jumped on board as the doors were about to close. The watchers were gone. Soon the police would be there. But by then they would be safe. Only then, standing, squeezed together on the train, did he talk to her. 'You can see,' he said in Arabic. 'Your eyes are better.' He put his hand up to touch her face.

Samira nodded: 'What on earth are you doing here?'

Yasin smiled. 'Be patient,' he answered. He took her hand and led her out two stops later at Piccadilly Circus. As they came up, they melted into the rush-hour crowds, feeling completely protected by the mass of people. Above ground, they jumped onto a bus. It didn't matter where it was going; Yasin was certain they had broken out of the red-box, probably as soon as they got into the Volvo. The bus headed west along Piccadilly and Yasin waited until it had gone round Hyde Park Corner into Knightsbridge before getting off.

Doubling back on foot to Piccadilly, he criss-crossed the road, always on green lights, and moved into emptier streets. He looked round. But no one noticed him. He had escaped.

'Scotland Yard insist it's a straight murder hunt,' said Norton. 'They want pictures out on the main news broadcasts tonight.'

Walmsley shook his head. 'Do they know what's at stake?'

'No, they don't.' Norton tapped his fingers nervously. 'You know what I think, Stephen. Let's do it. Identikit, not a photo. Unless you've got any better ideas.'

'And Samira?'

Norton shook his head. 'Just Yasin. And no name.'

Yasin had already checked into the Park Lane Hotel and he took Samira straight to the lifts. The lobby was filled with Middle Eastern and Asian tourists, and the staff took no notice of the young well-dressed couple going to their room. Yasin had taken a suite, with a small sitting room overlooking Green Park. The television set greeted them: 'Welcome, Alexander Morton. There are no messages for you.'

Samira laughed out loud: 'You're not Mr Morton'. Yasin showed her the passport with the name Alexander Morton and his photograph laminated in. He wanted her to congratulate him on the suite, the beige sitting room, hunting prints on the wall, the elegant writing table, the thick floral curtains and the evening light across the park. He showed her the mini-bar, proud to be in a London hotel.

But Samira sat down, suddenly serious: 'Musa's dead,' she whispered. 'Did you know?'

'I found out,' said Yasin. 'We're rich. Did you know *that*?' He turned her face to the window and looked at her properly for the first time, more than three months since he had seen her in hospital.

'I can see,' she said.

'Good.' He smiled. 'That's really good.'

He touched her face again. 'Tim arranged it,' she said.

'I know. That's how I found you. I waited outside his house until you came out. I saved his life again,' he went on proudly. 'I could have killed him in the Philippines.'

She glanced up at him and his expression changed as if

he realised he was being arrogant, flushed with the success of breaking the red-box, awkward with his sister. He looked away, ashamed, almost, that his own eyes might look too hard for her now.

'He's nice,' said Samira. 'Tim, I mean.'

They had come from two worlds and were trying to make them the same too quickly. It was like when they talked in the hospital, before Sri Lanka, when it was too quick, nowhere for them to go together, a borrowed room with no memories. 'I got your letter,' she said. 'From Sri Lanka.'

'You were the only person I could write to.'

'You killed people?'

'Yes. I had to.'

Yasin sat down, pulled the gun out of his jacket pocket and put it on the desk. Samira didn't say anything. Yasin unfolded a piece of paper. 'I want you to leave London, straight away. Go to Vienna, where there is an account for you set up by Musa.' He smiled. 'We're both millionaires.'

Samira took the paper and read the name 'Hans Jancke', the address, telephone numbers and passwords, looking at them without taking them in.

'Musa set us up an account each before he was killed,' Yasin continued. 'We have enough money to do anything we want.'

Samira looked out of the window at the first leaves on the trees after winter and the silhouettes of birds above the park in the dusk. She shook her head. 'The gun. What are you doing with a gun?'

'It's necessary,' he said. 'I needed it to see you.' He hesitated. 'I wanted to see you before you went.'

'I'm not going anywhere,' she retorted. 'They're looking for you because they think you're a terrorist.'

'I am,' he whispered. 'And I'm going to do it.'

'Why?' Her voice cracked.

'*When you meet the enemy and there's no way to win,*' he recited. '*It is better to die than to run away.*'

Samira leapt at Yasin blindly, her arms flailing against him, hands open, forgetting everything except he was her twin and that she was mad at him. She clawed at his shoulder, pulling him off the chair and hitting him on the head, slap, slap, slap! The gun was swept from the desk and landed on the carpet. Yasin fell to the floor too. She kicked out at him frantically, trying to change him back to what he had been before, trying to kick them both out of the hotel to the sands of Omdurman, so that the birds of Green Park would become the river birds of the Nile and the fog and chill over London would turn into the dusk of North Africa.

She felt her wrists being held together, the bones pushed against each other and hurting. Yasin, stronger than her, as he got up, hurting her. She recognised anger in his eyes, like after the bomb in Zamboanga, like after the shooting in al-Kadarou when he had held her, protecting her, underneath the blue metal tables. 'Why don't we go, now?' she pleaded. Yasin was shaking his head. 'We could catch the Lufthansa flight tomorrow. We're still Sudanese citizens. If we're so rich, think of what we can do to help.'

Yasin let her go and she sat down, drained. 'Why?' she asked again. 'Why?'

'So it doesn't happen again.' His voice was flat. Unemotional.

'So *what* doesn't happen again, for God's sake?'

'Musa. Our parents. Us.' He picked up the gun. He opened it up, took out a handkerchief to clean it. Looked at it rather than at her. 'I want you to help me,' he said.

'Help you kill? You're mad.' She pointed to her eyes. 'Who do you think caused this? People like you, Yasin. People like *you* who've got no answers for anything except killing other people.'

'No,' shouted Yasin. 'You don't understand . . .'

'Yes I do.' She pointed out of the window, down towards the street. 'Look at all those people out there. Parents like ours who were killed. Children like us.'

'. . . that someone has to teach them a lesson.'

She grabbed hold of his shirt and dragged him towards her. 'Just look. What lesson? Don't tell me there won't be a Sudanese or a Filipino person there who you'll be killing. Just tell me, why? You're not a terrorist. You're not a religious fanatic. Why do you want to kill them?' She yelled at him, then she cried, and she had been holding it back for so long that she stood up, cried against his chest and kept trying to forget where they were.

'No, I'm not,' he said, holding her. 'But fate has given me this weapon and if I use it properly it means that they will stop killing us.'

She pushed herself away again: 'Who's "fate"? Who's "they"? You keep saying "they".'

'Rich countries bomb and kill the people of poor countries. If I bomb them, they'll stop because they know it hurts.'

'You really believe that?'

'Yes,' said Yasin. 'Yes, I do.'

The phone rang. 'Turn on the television,' a voice said in Tagalog. They watched in silence. A sketch of her twin brother. Wanted for murder in Queensway that afternoon. Where she had been. Pictures of the underground entrance. Pictures of the Volvo, abandoned. Things she hadn't noticed. Blood. Cordons across the road. Witnesses were speaking, but she couldn't take in what they said. Pointing. Crying. Policemen. Then Tim, just a figure walking across the screen. Tim was there. But no one took any notice of him. Tim was safer than Yasin, because her brother had gone mad.

'I want your help,' Yasin said. He was writing on the hotel notepaper, ignoring the television, not caring.

'They're going to arrest you,' she whispered.

'What I want you to do is fax this to Tim Pack, then get out of London. He has a fax, hasn't he?' Samira nodded. Yes. It was in an alcove past the stairs, before you got to the conservatory. 'These are my demands,' said Yasin, still writing, making neat bullet points with the pen. He finished the first sheet and handed it to Samira: 'It's less than twenty-four hours now. They might agree. Then I won't have to do it.'

Samira read out loud in English. 'All debts of developing countries with international banks should be renegotiated and in the cases where people are threatened with starvation and hardship the debt must be cancelled.'

'You want me to fax this to Tim?'

'What do you think?'

'They'll laugh at you.' Samira, her feet on the sofa, drew her knees up to her chin, and wrapped her arms around her legs, making herself as small as possible. She didn't say anything else. There was nothing to say.

Yasin stood up. 'Don't you understand what I'm doing? Tim Pack and all those other people don't care about you at all. You're just a black orphan girl who has a crazy brother and they're going to use you to get me. If they kill me and get the anthrax, they won't care about you any more and they'll go on and on organising wars in the Sudan, in the Philippines, wherever people are too poor to look after themselves. He'll get us all to kill each other.'

'Not Tim.' But it was a whimper.

'Yes Tim, Gazelle. Tim, too.' Yasin's voice was soft, but confident. 'Even if you slept with him, I don't care. I know you do that sort of thing. But I bet he has a proper girlfriend. A rich white woman with a big university degree, who he plans to marry. When this is over, he'll go to her.' Samira squeezed her hands together, gripped her knees harder. 'That's what they do with people like us. They pretend to like us, but they use us. My life might be worthless but I can do something tomorrow to make the world a better place. They kill my people and now I'm going to kill them, because they've never been killed before. They don't know what it's like.'

'But why kill, why not . . . ?' tried Samira.

'That's what Musa did. Don't you see? Musa tried to be part of their world. He gave up fighting. He played the game of the banks and the governments. And they crushed him like an ant. You think I'm crazy, but people like me change the world. Nelson Mandela used to be a bomber and he became an international hero.'

'How are you going to do it?' said Samira, changing the tone.

'It's a secret. It has to be a secret.'

'When?'

'Tomorrow. There is a summit in Downing Street. All the western leaders will be there.' Yasin held Samira's hands, drawing them away from her knees, towards him 'Why don't you do it with me? We were born together and we will die together.' His eyes gleamed at her. 'We will be famous throughout the world. They will build statues to us like they have for Nelson Mandela.'

She pushed him back, twisting her wrists to get away from him. 'You've gone crazy,' she said. 'Something has made you deranged.'

Yasin smiled. He was sitting on the floor looking up at her, shaking his head. 'If you won't do it with me, you must leave London. We are blood, twin-blood of the Mahas, my little Gazelle. I will never hurt you. I promise you that.'

Samira nodded. Her hand slipped down from her knee to touch Yasin's hand. 'Death is hurting me,' she said.

'Not if you want it. And you will never hurt me, will you? You know that, don't you?'

She squeezed his hand, as if they had reached a new understanding. They stopped talking, quiet together. Twins. Tolerant of each other. 'Let's go to the river,' said Samira. 'Let's go and pretend we're at home on the Nile.'

'Will you leave London?' Yasin said, getting up and putting the gun back in his pocket.

Samira nodded.

'Promise.'

She nodded again.

'And you'll fax Pack my demands?'

'Yes,' she said. 'I will.' Her eyes were warm, welcoming and she saw his eyes change from coldness to love. The eyes of her brother. He handed her his coat: 'You'd better put this on. It might be chilly outside.'

# Chapter Thirty-five

'Tim Pack, my name's Jim Norton. I run the disaster operations no one's meant to know about. There's been a positive sighting. Coloured couple down by Hammersmith. If it's Omer, we assume he's armed, but have no idea whether he's strapped up with an anthrax bomb. We're sending a car. Stephen will be calling you shortly.'

Tim had hoped the call was Samira. From the airport. With Yasin. From anywhere safe, to say life for her was back to normal. After he had walked around Queensway, adhering to the cordons, avoiding the television interviewers, he returned to the house and waited like a lover stood up for a date.

The phone rang again. 'Ah Tim, something's cropped up,' said Walmsley. They hadn't talked since the shooting at the Tamil restaurant. Walmsley spoke as if nothing had happened at all: an issue had come up and he had simply dealt with it. 'Not sure if it's them,' he went on. 'But we need you down there because he might have one of those bloody suicide vests on.'

'Where exactly?'

'Hammersmith. Down by the river. But my guess is they've gone inland by now.'

'They would stay on foot,' said Tim, not knowing why he thought that, but wanting to know more than Walmsley, tell him that Samira was his.

'I've sent a car round with a couple of respirators, but for God's sake don't put one on, until we're sure you need it. We're a cigarette paper away from the media getting hold of this.'

The evening was damp and cold, though showers came all the time. Tim looked up at the three helicopters overhead. He was used to helicopters in London, but these were louder and more lingering than usual. Their searchlights jigged around the streets as if there was a war.

'Where would you like to start, sir?' said the driver. They had driven along Shepherds Bush Road and were heading down Brook Green. They slowed by the EMI building for the red lights at Hammersmith Road.

'How about in there?' said Tim, half-joking, half-serious.

'Just rock stars and bikini girls in there, sir. Besides we would need a warrant for that one.'

He asked the driver to go slowly along the Hammersmith Road, getting out at a pub, then staying on foot and crossing the road to a wine bar. Cars came at him, racing for the traffic lights. Young people, ties loose and suits crumpled, drank on the pavement. First time since winter. They talked about the helicopters above Hammersmith.

A squall arrived, throwing wet mist at the cars' head-lights. Tim walked west, jogging some of the way, look-ing for a couple, a brother and sister, a man with a bomb round his waist. The driver kept the car crawling behind him. He kept on towards Hammersmith Broad-way. The streets went dark and dull; a boarded-up old hospital, side roads which vanished under the flyover, bleak Victorian buildings. Then the sound of the horn from his car. The driver waving him over, bringing the window down to talk: 'We have a second sighting, sir, Chiswick way.'

They were through the lights at the Hammersmith Broadway, following the signs to the M4 and Heathrow. 'A young dark fellow, sir, Middle East-looking. Seen with a black girl at the Blue Anchor by Hammersmith Bridge and they took off along the river. The barman just called the police, said he looked like the man on the television.'

They swept round, ignoring Hammersmith Bridge Road. 'Thought we'd go down Ravenscourt Road or Black Lion Lane to cut him off, as it were.' He slowed as a queue banked up because of another squall, and switched the wipers on. 'Which would you prefer, sir? Ravenscourt or Black Lion?'

'Which is further?'

'Black Lion, sir.'

'Go there.'

'The barman described them as both very tall, but we don't know whether that's what he actually saw or whether the police description egged him on, if you understand my meaning, sir.' He turned left and eased them between the tightly parked cars on both sides. 'I used to be with the Met, before I retired. Always had problems with witnesses, like this.'

The driver pulled up at the Black Lion pub. Tim told him to wait, while he got out and ran back, trying to cover quickly the ground they had missed by driving. He jumped over the low fence to a children's playground, then stood on the river path watching people, both those passing him and distant figures. The tide was high and water slapped against the river wall.

Tim leant on the wall, looking like a solitary man in thought, watching for movement in the houseboats rocking against each other, looking for clues along their walkways, the shadow of a tall man, or of a boy preparing a bomb from the cabin of a boat.

This was a place where Yasin would go. He was right to

look here. Yasin was a child of the river, as one with its flow, its tides and the old vessels moored in the cold, black water. Yasin would come here to feel at home.

Tim climbed onto the unsteady gangway, slippery with rain. Holding both rails, he made his way down towards the first boat, a heavy black vessel, with sad pot plants on the foredeck drooping from constant dampness.

A figure moved across a light below decks, a woman with blonde hair held in place with a headband, and she was up on deck before he was halfway to the boat, shining a torch in his eyes. 'Can't you read?' she snapped. 'This is private property.'

He could have flashed a pass, just to prove a point. That he was more powerful than her. 'Sorry,' he said and turned round to go back. *We would need a warrant for that one, sir,* the driver had said. They'd need a warrant for the whole of bloody London.

'You didn't have time to take this, sir,' the driver said as Tim climbed back in the car, turning in his seat and handing Tim a tiny radio with an earpiece. 'Your ID is . . . let me see,' he pulled down a sheet of card from his sunshade. 'It's Alpha-Two. Very cloak and dagger, if I might say so, what with the lady on the loose and everything. Is it that you know her, sir?'

'I think you'll find that's classified information.'

'Of course. Just I can't think of a reason they'd send you without back-up, unless you knew her, like. Had to negotiate with them alone.'

He turned right, driving slowly, the moon and street lights showing up everything they needed to see, passing the expensive houses of Chiswick Mall, the road almost empty because of the night and the rain, just a few people with dogs or each other, but none tall and black, none with the bulge of a suicide vest.

'I almost forgot. They wanted to know if you was carrying,' said the driver, reaching for the glove box. 'Because if you wasn't . . .'

'I am.'

The driver drew back his hand. 'The helicopter should be overhead soon to help you. They're busy with another sighting up near White City. Terribly understaffed we are for something like this. Resources, I reckon. That's the problem.' They came to a sharp right turn in the road opposite a church. 'If we go on from here, I have to go back onto the A4 to the Chiswick roundabout, down the A314 towards Richmond and come back down Coney Road to the river. So you'd miss some of the river front.' The driver pulled the car off the road onto a dirt track. The wheels splashed through water coming up from the river. He turned in his seat to face Tim. 'It's a modern housing estate there, sir. Which do you prefer I do, sir?'

'Drop me here.'

'I'll meet you down Coney Reach then.'

There was too much water on Tim's side, so the driver moved away and Tim got out. He let himself through a low black wrought-iron gate. The rain blew strong, then sank into a thin, biting drizzle, and he walked hunched and fast, looking into the houses where the curtains were open, where lives were being lived as governments intended.

He was alone on the promenade. It was modern and ordered with advertisements for house developers and allocated car parks. He heard the clatter of a helicopter and looked up to see the searchlight swinging above the rooftops, the water and woods on the other side, leading towards Barnes. The radio crackled and he fumbled with cold wet hands to slip in the earpiece.

'Alpha-Two. We're joining you now. Do you have a sighting?'

'Negative,' said Tim.

'We're staying with you.'

He reached the Pier restaurant, its glass riverfront doors closed against the weather, but the sound of a jazz saxophone making it through to the outside. He checked, but this wasn't for Yasin or Samira: there wasn't a coloured face amongst them.

Then he followed the sweep of the helicopter searchlight and he saw them, fifty yards away, darting around, running from the glare. 'West of the restaurant,' Tim said into the radio. They brought the spotlight round, just as they vanished from the arc of the street lights and ran into darkness and undergrowth. They were tall, like the driver said.

'What's along there?' Tim asked the helicopter crew.

'Playing fields. Woods. Rowing sheds. We'll seal off Barnes Bridge. Get back-up for you down there by road.'

As soon as he passed the last house, blackness came down on him. The lights were distorted. A low mist blurred everything. Tim stopped halfway between the promenade and the undergrowth. He tried to listen, but the noise of the helicopter made it useless.

The searchlight wrecked his night vision. 'Samira,' he shouted. Telling them he was there. A friend. He could hardly hear himself for the helicopter. He drew the 9mm. He was careful on the path, which was so muddy that there was no telling who had just been down it. He ran past the first clump of bushes, brambles and high stinging nettles, and came out into open fields, a gloomy expanse, but empty, a glow of flat parkland. The river was through bushes to the left and straight ahead he could make out the shape of a bandstand or a pavilion, where the ground seemed to dip.

'Pull back,' he told the helicopter. 'Give me some quiet.' The helicopter swooped straight up like a lift, assertive and pushy, the clatter becoming a throb, then just a silent light like any other aircraft.

He thought he saw a face, or the eyes in a face, but it could have been the reflection of a branch, a light from somewhere catching on the rain.

'Call out for them.' Walmsley on the radio.

He shouted, keeping to the path. A foghorn sounded on the river. He called out again and kept quiet, waiting for a reply, like a bird singing a mating call, except the other didn't sing back.

Yasin held her hard by the wrists, forcing her forward, pressing her arms into the mud and hurting her back. 'Come with me, Gazelle. I need you with me!'

She struggled. 'Let me go.'

'Did they know we were here? Did you tell them?' He gripped her more. In the other hand he had the gun, watching, for movements ahead of them.

'No. No. No,' she repeated.

'You suggested we go to the river. Are you one of them? Did you betray me?'

A searchlight flitted over the trees, but didn't stop. Samira bucked to free herself. She wanted to scream, but she didn't because it would give them away, and this was a fight between the twins and no one else. A scream was as good as killing her brother, when she could still get him back. They had argued before. He had been crazy before, and always he came back to her. Always. His hold was loosening, his concentration on new lights ahead of them – and somewhere out there was Tim, but she couldn't see him. Couldn't tell him where they were. Ask him to help.

Two cars came down fast from the main road, straight towards the river, high beam, one with a flashing blue light. The helicopter crew and police tactical firearms were planning across the radio, excluding Tim. The helicopter came back down, the spotlight unforgiving, trying to penetrate the undergrowth and the dark areas around the pavilion.

The first shot was a clear sound above all that, a muzzle flash from near the river, going anywhere, towards the helicopter, towards the police car. The police driver had seen it, too, and stopped, haphazardly halfway down the road.

'Yasin!' Tim yelled. 'Samira! Are you there?' Nothing. They would have heard it this time. The shot was barely a hundred yards away. Tim took the safety catch off the 9mm and waited. His eyes were better now. He noticed a clearing in the undergrowth and stone steps or a ramp leading down to the river. The pistol was in both hands, steady, elbow on the ground for support.

Someone on the radio: 'Alpha-Two, Alpha-Two.' Tim didn't answer. Yasin was good at river sounds. He would hear it, his ears working above the helicopter and the rain. A car door opened, then another, and men got out with flak jackets and weapons. They crouched and ran, heading for the sloping dead ground by the pavilion.

'Don't shoot, please don't shoot.' Samira's voice. High-pitched. Frightened.

'Samira. It's Tim.'

'Get a river boat down there.' Norton's orders coming across his radio in New Cavendish Street. 'Rig up a loud-speaker on it. Link it to here.'

'It's in place.' Another voice. Unknown.

'He wants to give himself up. Don't kill us.' Samira again. Her voice cracking.

'Alpha-Two.' Tim into the radio. 'I've made contact. He's giving himself up.'

'We're holding fire,' said Tim to Samira without authority. But they heard what he said. 'Get rid of that helicopter so

I can hear them,' he shouted. Then to Samira: 'Is Yasin with you?'

'Yes,' she said.

'Yasin. It's Tim Pack.'

Silence from the undergrowth. But movement. He could see activity. He had a feeling about the river, a place Yasin would claim as his own.

'He says you've got snipers who can see in the dark,' said Samira. 'If he speaks you'll pinpoint him.'

'We're not going to kill him. He's a kid.' Norton's voice from the river boat, booming from a boat. A second muzzle flash. Going nowhere. 'Did you do that, kid?' called Norton over the loudspeaker. The boat's spotlight picked out Samira, more steadily than from the helicopter. She was sitting, legs up to her chin, on the wet ground, moisture and dirt on her face. 'If that's you, Samira, stick up a hand and tell your brother to lay off the trigger.' She lifted her hand, just an inch or so off the ground.

'Good girl. Good girl. It's been a rough day and we're going to make it better as soon as we can. I'm not on the boat. You understand. I'm watching you through a monitor here, where I am. Now, raise your hand again if Yasin is with you and if he can hear me. We don't need to see him yet. We don't want anyone to die. I just want you to tell us if he's there.'

The hand came up again.

'So both you kids are there. That's good.' Norton stopped talking. A whine of feedback started up on the loudspeaker. 'I've been reading your file, Yasin,' continued Norton. 'You're pissed off because your parents got killed by mistake. I'm sorry. I really am sorry, kid. But we all have problems like that, and at the end of the day you have to learn to live with them.'

'He's got demands,' said Samira softly.

'What's that,' said Norton. 'I didn't hear that.'

Tim relaying: 'She says he's got demands.'

'Demands? Well, that's something new. We've all got basketsful of those. You know, kids, I'm a cripple. I got no legs worth talking about because some little shit like you shot me in the spine and I haven't walked since. You nearly had no eyes, isn't that right, Samira? You were nearly blinded because a kid like your brother planted a bomb in a shopping mall. I bet he had a list of demands as well. If every person who'd lost a parent or lost their legs went around blowing up the world, we'd all have been gone long ago.' Norton paused.

'What's she saying?' Norton into the radio.

'He's got demands. He'll negotiate,' said Tim. He didn't know if Samira could see him. She looked alone and cold. Yasin must have gone to ground near her. He would shoot it out if necessary. Give up his sister and fight to the end. Tim crawled, face down, through the mud, gun in his hand, just like in Bosnia. Each time Norton spoke, he managed to get closer to her. He asked Norton to keep talking.

'I've seen a hundred of you guys with some fancy ideal about saving the world,' said Norton. 'Christian, Muslim, nationalist, Armageddon. You hole yourself up with a bunch of hostages and a bomb, threaten this, threaten that, kill a few people and then get killed yourself – all for some cause no one gives a shit about. And you're doing it with your own sister.'

'I'm not a hostage,' she shouted. They all heard it. Samira angry. Getting defiant.

'That's good,' said Norton, straight back at her. 'Because that's one less law your brother's broken. So let me tell you kids something. The world is as the world is. I didn't make it. You didn't make it. And if it treats you badly, you pick yourself up and move on.'

No one was talking suddenly. The drone of the river boat. The helicopter. Searchlight skirting, teasing, never falling on Samira, but wrecking her night vision, letting Tim get closer. He didn't have to worry about making a noise. There was so much going on.

He was almost there. Samira was down a bank and he would have to get up, leap at her, expose himself to Yasin. But he couldn't see Yasin anywhere. No shape. No shadow. And Samira's expression was of someone alone. Rigid. The gun in her hands. The finger on the trigger. Pointing out. Arms wedged back against the knees. Head turning from the park to the river, not knowing which was more important. The safety catch was off. He could see it clearly. Yasin had taught her that.

'Tim? Tim?' Faint. Vulnerable. Tim didn't answer. Kept his head down in the mud.

Norton from the river: 'Yasin, why don't you start by throwing out your weapon? Then we'll all be a lot safer, kid . . .'

'We're not kids.' Samira, loud again. Shaking.

'You're whatever the hell I want to call you,' replied Norton. 'You want us to blow you both to hell? That's fine by me. I do this for a living, like some people sell cars. Win some. Lose some. Sometimes we save lives. Sometimes I just give the order to open fire and people like you die. Never lose any sleep over it.'

Tim sprang up, got a grip on the firm grass on the side of the path, and leapt towards Samira. She saw him, shadow caught in a searchlight, crushing down on her and she raised her hands, pistol as well, catching Tim on the head. She shouted at him, angrily, and he wrenched the gun from her, throwing it out into the park, turning her over, face down, face in the mud, screaming, wriggling against him, hands behind her back, feeling down her body for more weapons, treating her like a mercenary in Bosnia, satisfied she was beaten and rolling her back again so she was looking up, facing him. He yelled at her: 'Where's Yasin?'

Her face was wet and smeared. Her eyes, red, wild, swelling up with tears. She struggled, but Tim held her wrists: 'Where is your brother?' he said again, more quietly.

'He's gone,' she whispered, panting. 'He got away.'

# Chapter Thirty-six

The force of the current was incredible, sucking him down, then tumbling him over and over, and throwing him back up to the surface. A squall tore into him and the wake of a boat splashed over his head. He went under again, trying to get out of the turbulence and find a place where the water would take him. He knew he would be all right then, because he had swum the Nile and he understood the forces of a great river.

He banged against the hull of a boat, tearing his clothes and skin on the barnacles, and he realised how cold the water was, colder than the Nile and filthy. He came up again in the shadows and saw that the river was running against itself, the current going upstream, while the water flowed south. He swam with it, filling his lungs, and staying under, up again, watching the searchlights as they moved around where he had left Samira. He swam, moving to keep warm, losing sight of the spot, each time he surfaced. The commotion was more distant, quieter, as he spun in the water, looking for landfall.

He crossed the river, like he had the Blue Nile and the lagoons in Sri Lanka. Samira was delaying them, as she had promised. They didn't know he was gone. They would take her and she would be safe, whatever he did. She had done nothing wrong. There were street lights on his left and black emptiness on his right, a rough bank, but all right to scramble up.

He shivered as he hauled himself out, choking as water caught in his throat. His clothes hung off him and the wind cut through like ice. Ahead were football pitches and tennis courts, and a couple walking towards him with a black Labrador running back and forth around them.

Yasin took his knife from his sodden jacket pocket and drew it from the sheath. He only needed the man, but he would have to kill them both or they would talk. As they got closer, he was glad they were white; they looked rich, quite young, too. They could have been bankers. He lay in the grass, like a drunk, until they saw him and began to skirt around. He moved so quickly that it was the dog who sounded the alarm, but only as a welcoming bark. Yasin threw himself forward, knocking down the man, who didn't know how to fight, flailed around, threatening to get the police, until Yasin had him on his front, pushed the knife into his chest, feeling it slide neatly between the ribs to the heart.

The blood was warm on his cold hand, soothing, but there was not much of it, and he brought out his handkerchief to soak it up and save the clothes. The woman screamed and ran. She was a good runner and for a moment Yasin thought he might not catch her before she got to the road. The dog scampered with them too, yelping, jumping up at Yasin's knife hand in a game.

He threw himself at her, tackled her, like in a rugby match. She was face down and the dog tumbled onto them, licking them both. Yasin grabbed her hair and yanked her head up. She twisted round. She was strong. 'Please . . .' she was saying as he slid the knife into her throat, bringing it round, feeling her go limp and letting the blood go wherever it wanted because it didn't matter with the women. He didn't need her clothes.

He walked back to the man, undressed him and changed into his clothes. They were expensive, slightly too small. The playing field stayed empty. The dog lay mournfully by the woman, his game over. Yasin dragged the body of the man to the undergrowth. Then he returned for the woman, wondering if the drizzle would wash away the bloodstains on the grass.

He wondered about the dog, which followed him, whether he would have to kill it too. But when he left, the dog stayed behind, resting its head between its paws next to the woman's face. Yasin walked up onto the main road by the bridge and hailed a black cab. He got the driver to take him right into Tudor Court. His money was wet, but it had been raining. Umbrellas were out and the cab driver didn't seem to care.

The men were in the house, the two drivers, the helmsman and the welder. They had all escaped and they were proud of Yasin because he had escaped too and was now famous. He'd been on the news all evening.

Jennifer didn't even have time to call Jack Jensen in London. She was sitting by Amanda's bed, holding the little girl's hand. Amanda was weak, but there was colour in her face and they were playing at guessing the names of trees from a picture book.

Jennifer was turning the page and Amanda was laughing – Jennifer couldn't afterwards remember why – when the colour drained out of her and, then she went purple. Amanda convulsed, arching her back. The monitors screamed, whining and bleeping, and the nurses rushed in. Jennifer didn't know when Amanda lost consciousness. She held out her hand to her, but a nurse brushed her away. A doctor rushed in, and they wheeled Amanda out, with the machines and the drip, off to intensive care.

Amanda Jensen, aged eight years and seven months, died just before six in the evening of unexpected multiple complications from a bacterial infection to the stomach – brought about by a gunshot wound.

An hour later, Jennifer was on the phone to Jack: 'Everything just seemed to pack up,' she said, not caring that she was crying. 'And she was doing so well.'

'Or I wouldn't have been here,' said Jack. Guilt. Love. Justification. They talked for nearly two hours. Jack was quiet. Then he cried with her. They talked about Pamela as if she was still alive. They spoke as if they were still in China. They had long transatlantic silences, with neither of them caring about the time or expense. Jack just wanted to talk with the last friend who had seen his little child alive.

'Are you coming back?' Jennifer asked.

'Sure. I'll come back,' said Jack, his answer distant, not thinking about logistics.

When they finished talking, Jennifer did what she had done last time a Jensen died. She went to the office. The bank had given her a desk at the Citicorp Centre on Lexington Avenue and linked her up to her own database and e-mail in Beijing. She walked in a daze through the coffee stalls and shops of the atrium, noticing the smell of cinnamon which seemed to be everywhere, bumping into the evening crowd in a daze, saying sorry and walking on.

In the office, she flicked through her e-mail, automatically, not taking the messages in, until she saw one from David Antoniades in Cyprus. 'Call me. Whatever time.' After that she burst into tears and went back to her room at the Intercontinental Hotel, away from the open-plan office. Even at midnight there were people there, working on the Asian markets.

'Thanks for getting in touch,' said David. He was subdued, no flirtation in his voice. 'I'll tell you what's happened, and you tell me what you think.'

'Go on,' she said.

'Remember the Russian bag man who crossed into northern Cyprus?'

'Igor Gromov,' said Jennifer.

'He's dead . . .'

'I know. How do you know?'

Atoniades paused. 'Why don't we hold back on that for a moment and go over the information. My contact tells me he had his throat cut in the back of a truck in Karachi, near the port. I don't know why, but I do know there was something in that truck that everyone wanted. The army were around it like flies at a honey pot. The Yanks and the Brits are involved. And a day before he was killed US$200,000 landed in his personal bank account. Over the next two weeks, five million dollars went to the main account of the racket there, the mob in Moscow.'

'Where from?' said Jennifer, lighting a cigarette.

'Not CA Energy, as far as we know. But a numbered account in Austria. Anything you know, Jen, which sheds light on what's happening?'

'I think so,' she said. 'How come you're involved?'

'The Russians have closed both accounts. My contact in northern Cyprus called me to see if I knew why.'

'As soon as I know something, I'll get back to you. Can you give me details of the account in Austria?'

Antoniades recited the details and Jennifer read them back. 'It's a numbered account. No names. Just signatures and passwords. The guy in charge of overseas transactions is Hans Jancke,' said Antoniades. 'He's as hard as nails. Makes a Swiss bank look like a leaking boat.'

With the call finished, Jennifer thought of Amanda, the

last moment of happiness the child had had before she died. She lit another cigarette off the back of the first, and rang Tim who answered straight away as if he was waiting for a call, not sleeping. 'Amanda's dead,' Jennifer began.

'I know. Jack's round here. It's been a hell of a night.' The police were all over the house, front, back, patio, outside the spare room where Samira was resting, sleeping, maybe. Jensen had been round and they'd drunk a bottle of wine. But Tim had never had a child, or lost anyone who mattered so much and he could only help by drinking with Jack who had lost everything. He let him talk, so some of the horror would go away. Let him sleep upstairs, in a place more personal than a hotel room.

'Look after him, Tim. He needs a friend like you.' He recognised a soft edge in Jennifer's voice, heard the draw on the cigarette. 'You said Yasin hijacked the anthrax in Karachi.'

The red-box surveillance was still there. They would hear the call. Know he had talked out of line. He didn't answer and let Jennifer continue. 'The chances are he used a bank in Austria to transfer funds.' She read out the details. 'Austrian banks are notoriously tight. If I even showed interest, they would slam shut the doors. But if you can get to a man called Hans Jancke, the chances are you'll get a step closer to Yasin.'

'What do you mean – me?' Tim responded cautiously.

'You. The government. The people you work for. Jesus, Tim, burn Jancke with cigarette ends if you need to. Find Yasin and we'll find the fucking bastards who killed Amanda, Davey and Pam. Just . . . just do it.' Tim just heard the dreadful sobs of grief, the same as he'd heard from Jack, the ones which had made him cry as well for the death of a little girl. Jennifer cut the call.

As soon as Tim put down the phone, Walmsley called.

'We got that, Tim. We'll handle it. Get a couple of hours' sleep. I want you both in Whitehall by the time the Prime Minister's finished his breakfast.'

Less than an hour later, Hans Jancke answered the door bell at his house in Grinzing in the Vienna woods and was pushed straight back inside. He fell heavily to the floor, then felt himself being lifted up and put down on his hall chair. Three men stood in front of them. One flashed a identification card in front of his face, but it meant nothing to him.

'Yasin Omer,' said the man with the card.

'If this is bank business, I suggest you . . .' A hand smacked across his face, cutting his lower lip. He tasted the blood. Jancke raised his head.

'Mr Jancke, we do not have time for formalities.'

Five minutes later Hans Jancke was alone, shaken, and ashamed at having revealed the name of W. G. Hooft, the Dutch lawyer to whose account he had transferred Yasin's money for the lease on Tudor Court. Forty minutes after that, the Dutch police raided Hooft's offices in Amsterdam. His staff said Hooft was on a business trip in the States, and it took another thirty minutes to get a warrant to search his files. Then after only minutes of looking through the orderly filing system, they found the transaction which gave Yasin Omer access to Tudor Court in West Kensington. In Britain, it was just before nine thirty in the morning.

Keith Plant, head of security for Tudor Court, prided himself on the effortlessly smooth way in which the compound operated, the quiet opening and closing of the oiled red gates, the silent monitoring by the video cameras, the series of fob keys which gave residents the layer upon layer of security they paid for when they bought into the compound.

During the Gulf War, Plant had trained men to use

nuclear, biological and chemical warfare suits. He got them to put their respirators on within nine seconds, the time between the alert and certain death from a chemical agent. By the time they left Plant's course, troops could change the activated-charcoal filter in three seconds in a smoke-filled room with explosions going off all around them.

Though Plant missed army life, the Gulf had proved a good watershed. He took advantage of redundancy under Options for Change, and ran Tudor Court with the firm efficiency of a gentle military operation.

When the Mercedes Sprinter pulled up at the gate to leave the compound, Plant was outside, checking the number plate of a removal van. He stepped out from behind the truck and saw the driver of the Sprinter, a young man in his twenties, Asian or Middle Eastern, but there were plenty of those in Tudor Court. It was unusual, though, that he was in a workman's van. Most tenants had expensive saloons or coupés, the Mercedes S Class, BMW 3 series, Turbo Porsches, and sometimes a Ferrari or a Lamborghini.

The number plate corresponded with the secure underground garage of the tenant and the driver had his own fob key. But as Plant was waving through the van, he caught a glimpse of something he would recognise anywhere in the world, so beautifully designed that he could identify it in thick fog, darkness, under fire, in driving rain.

A passenger in the back of the van was holding an SF10 respirator. Plant could recite the specs in his sleep: *Polycarbonate eyepieces resistant to attacks by chemicals and solvents; flash-resistant protective lenses; right-hand screw on filter.* The passenger must have seen Plant's glance. He quickly retreated backwards and slid shut the compartment door between himself and the men in front.

Plant immediately called a friend who was still in the business, just to see if anything was going on. He was made to hold for two minutes, then another person came on the line and asked Plant to repeat every detail. Within five minutes the information was with Jim Norton in New Cavendish Street, just as he was reading the police messages from Amsterdam and Vienna.

While waiting at the traffic lights on Hammersmith Broadway, Yasin adjusted the vest so that it felt more comfortable. He could feel the two pouches of anthrax against his waist. The weight of the batteries pulled the jacket down at the top and he wished he had brought the stronger material from Sri Lanka. He checked the battery connections and clipped the detonator button onto his belt, with the tiny plastic safety catch on.

The deflated raiding craft and its motor had been taken up into the loft. Apart from them, the house in Tudor Court had been cleared of everything, ready to re-let. Nothing had been left behind, not even a grain of sand from a Suffolk beach. Everything was in the van, including the weapons which had come over from Holland.

The one nagging worry Yasin had about Tudor Court's security was the logging of number plates, but he had planned for it. He instructed the driver to turn right towards the Hammersmith Broadway, and then left down Fulham Palace Road.

It was a clear, dry morning with a swirl of wind which should keep the spores in the air for a long time. The day was ideal and if it became slightly overcast, all the better. The traffic edged down towards Putney Bridge, through a desolate and neutral part of London, not worthy of any attack: a hospital, a cemetery, rows of drab houses and litter blowing along the pavements.

The two drivers were in the front; the welder and the helmsman sat in the back with Yasin. He got the driver to double back, along New Kings Road, then south down Wandsworth Bridge Road. The helmsman and the welder had their instructions, ready with the blue tape and the new number plate. Just before the river, they turned left into Townmead Road.

Yasin had investigated this area a few days earlier, finding a place to change the number plate in the grubby streets around the gas works, where, even if anyone saw, no one would care. It took less than two minutes, one man on each plate, then the bright blue tape, a single strip down each side of the van. No longer all-white. No longer V896 PEW.

From there, they drove over the river, then along the main roads south of the Thames, past Chelsea Bridge, Vauxhall, Lambeth, Westminster, Waterloo and finally Blackfriars, where they turned right and found the railway arches of Great Suffolk Street.

They pulled up in a side road and the helmsman jumped out. The key was where he had been told it would be, under a loose brick behind a motorcycle repair shop. It opened a large set of roller doors which came down across a dank, Victorian arch. Inside was the Ford Transit van and a vast dark and empty space for the Sprinter to go when they had finished. The arch shook as a train went directly overhead.

The helmsman transferred their bags to the Ford Transit. There was a risk, in that the man who left the key was a Filipino working illegally in London, who had been given an instruction and needed the money. But a safe risk. They wouldn't meet and it was only for twenty-four hours. They all had new passports for the night, separate short-haul flights confirmed to Paris, Frankfurt and Brussels, and hotel rooms booked.

The helmsman locked the roller door and got back in. The three men in the back put on the respirators, helping each other adjust them, pulling out loose bits of hair like with a snorkelling mask. Yasin spoke through the microphone mounted inside the mask in front of his lips with a long trailing wire connecting him to the intercom.

The driver pulled out and eased himself into the traffic, turned left into Borough High Street and into the lunchtime traffic heading across London Bridge.

The helmsman turned on the first air tank, gently bringing up the pressure, checking that the ducts were working properly. When they stopped at the long traffic lights by St Paul's Cathedral, the welder held the funnel and the helmsman poured the first bag of anthrax into it and sealed the lid.

Samira said she couldn't go through with it again. Last night had been a mock execution of sorts and she couldn't help kill her brother twice.

'We're not going to kill him,' Tim soothed. He tried to pull her towards him, but she stiffened and turned her back to him.

'Yes you'll kill him.'

'No. Not if we can help it.'

She curled on herself as tight as she could. It was the image he saw of her by the river, the girl hunched, sad and alone in the undergrowth. Now the same, naked in his bed, after a tearful quick love-making, snatched in between disasters in case it could clarify the world around them. But it had failed. 'Yasin said you have a rich white girl with a big university degree. Is that right?' she asked. 'Is she Jennifer, the girl you stayed up with all night?' Tim didn't answer.

As they dressed, she said, 'He'll try to kill you. You'll have to kill him.' Her voice quivered.

'It won't happen,' he said. 'It won't . . .' He couldn't finish the sentence, because there was nothing truthful to say.

'Why are we going out there then?'

'To stop him.'

Walmsley came round unannounced, as if he knew about her doubts, knocking on the door, not ringing the bell, keeping his coat on, taking off his scarf like in the Tamil restaurant, sitting in the conservatory while Tim made coffee.

'They were holed up in a gated compound near Hammersmith,' he said. 'Your girl was spot on.' He glanced round to see Samira flinch at his reference to Jennifer. 'Your brother was living hardly a mile from here,' he said to her. 'Did you know that?'

'No,' Samira answered angrily. 'I told you, he took me to the Park Lane Hotel.'

'We found traces of formaldehyde. That's the decontamination solution for anthrax. He's out there, Samira, and he's going to attack today. We desperately need your help.'

'Don't you think I know that?'

'If he sees you on the streets of London, he's not going to release the anthrax,' he said gently. 'He's not going to kill you, is he? We need you to save the lives of innocent people.'

# Chapter Thirty-seven

'The French President is entering Whitehall now for Downing Street,' said Norton into the radio. 'The American President is due in ten minutes. The Prime Minister has again refused advice to close off Whitehall. Repeat. Whitehall is staying open to the public.'

Tim picked up the message in his earphone. He walked with Samira among the tourists from the quiet of the Mall under Admiralty Arch and into Trafalgar Square where the noise of the city hit them like a wall of heat.

As they stood at the red lights waiting to cross, Samira had forgotten all thoughts of running. She hated Tim Pack, Stephen Walmsley and their culture for changing Yasin into what he had become. She watched a party of schoolchildren across the road, waiting for the lights just like her, satchels on their back, the British flag in their hands, two teachers snapping commands. They would grow up into an evil system which had turned her brother into a murderer. But she could never allow them to be blown up, poisoned, destroyed. Her twin brother had gone mad.

Tim tried to talk nonsense, anything but the silence, anything to get away from talking about last night. 'Across there is the National Gallery,' he said pointing beyond Nelson's Column. His hand moved and he had to shout against a bus's air brakes. 'St Martin-in-the-Fields.

They have lunchtime concerts there. The South African Embassy.'

'You're showing me your civilisation,' she said curtly. 'We did it at school. Yours, not ours.'

'I'm showing you his targets,' said Tim.

The lights turned green. They walked over two traffic islands. She didn't take his hand. Walmsley had given them jackets with three-digit numbers on their shoulders. He told them that snipers were positioned to kill any pedestrian in central London.

He was explaining another building and she turned obediently towards it, but on the roof of the Old War Office the reflection of the sun on something caught her eye, like the flash from a torch in daylight, light on glass, and movement on the roof, then gone behind a turret wall.

'Snipers,' she said softly. Tim didn't hear because the lights had changed and traffic was roaring past them.

No, she didn't want his hand. He had been a false refuge, and if love wasn't to feel safe, what was it for? She didn't run away. She couldn't. She had seen Tim fire the pistol and the snipers would do the same at her.

*The police are watching us. You move from here, they'll arrest you.* Just like he had told her in Budapest. *They will use drugs, Samira. They'll lock you away. They'll be cruel. They'll tell you it isn't a game.*

Pack talked, pointing down towards the Houses of Parliament and Westminster Abbey. Two yellow cranes flanked Big Ben, jerking around like the legs of a cockroach turned on its back.

'We're here to save your civilisation, aren't we?' she said. 'You can bomb my country, but we can't bomb yours.'

He stopped and took her by the arms. They were standing by the Whitehall Theatre. A play he had never heard of was running. A white van pulled up next to them, hazard lights flashing. Samira jumped. Her nerves were strung out. The driver came round and pulled open the back door. He jumped up inside, where the van was lined with racks and looked at a clipboard, turning inside, checking stock, with his company logo *Mr Kipling Cakes* emblazoned on his overalls.

'Close call, Alpha-Two. It's a Ford Transit, similar design. All Alphas, we are looking for an all-white Mercedes Sprinter van registration number V896 PEW. The bomber may be using this for transport.'

Between the van and the theatre, a hand on each elbow. No smiles. Father lecturing daughter. 'You want to go? Go,' he said. 'But if Yasin is here today and you're not, I tell you now, Samira, your brother will die. The men on these buildings have instructions to aim for his eyes. The bullet will hit the ANS, the automatic nervous system based in the lower brain, the brain stem which controls heartbeat and breathing. Do you understand?'

He moved his hands up to her shoulders: 'They go for it because if he has his hand on a detonator, nothing will happen. The muscles will be gone. Your brother, the man who saved my life, will be a corpse on the pavement. Nothing, Samira. Nothing. Do you understand that? A corpse on the street.'

His hands were on her face, like in Budapest again, except the palms were chilly. She didn't reject him. She looked straight at him, her eyes pleading for an explanation, a motive to help kill her brother.

Pedestrians walked round them, groups of tourists splitting in half to get by. He stopped talking until they were gone. His voice was lowered. She could feel his breath on her face. 'If we find him without you, we will kill him. If you are there with me, if you can get to him and persuade him to stop, we have a chance of saving his life and thousands of others around us.'

She nodded.

'All Alpha. All Alpha.' The radio was rigged up through the jacket and into the earpiece. 'The Italian Prime Minister is now approaching Downing Street. We can assume he could attack any time from now.'

As they drove towards Whitehall, Yasin imagined the power of his weapon, so quiet, so invisible and so lethal. At the lights at the bottom of Ludgate Hill, he watched five businessmen cross the road, deftly moving to avoid a woman walking briskly in the opposite direction. A man drank a take-away cappuccino while waiting for the lights to change in his favour. Yasin looked at a motorcycle dispatch driver, revving his throttle next to him, covered in red and black leather, with visor and crash helmet, but still as unprotected as the pigeons which fluttered away when the lights changed. He felt nothing about his crime because he was used to killing now.

Walmsley walked between the desks in the basement of New Cavendish Street watching the monitors' pictures from Whitehall. It was a dreary spring day. A breeze sent ripples across the pond in St James's Park. Clusters of tourists hung around outside Downing Street, waiting to catch a glimpse of the world leaders. Civil servants came and went between government buildings. Long lunchers staggered out of the Red Lion opposite King Charles Street and turned left towards Trafalgar Square.

'The PM's not mentioning any terror threat at all,' said Walmsley to Norton. 'The snipers would be there anyway for this sort of summit.'

In the middle of Whitehall, Samira pulled out the sheet of Yasin's demands, which she had forgotten to show him last night, when she was so tired. He read them, on the original notepaper from the Park Lane Hotel. 'Can't you say you'll agree, announce it over the radio or something?'

'I'll try,' said Tim. 'If we get through the next couple of hours, I'll try. Then, when it's all over you can go to university or something.'

Her eyes lit up, surprised at his comment: 'I suppose I can. Musa said all my school fees were paid in advance. Yasin said we were rich now.'

Tim had been in these false oases before, when you were amid normality and forgot about the dangers around you. He let Samira talk for a few minutes, then he spoke to Norton: 'She's produced a list of demands. He gave them to her last night before the river.'

'Jesus!' said Norton. 'Congratulate her on her timing. Are they realistic?'

'Absolutely not,' he said softly, so Samira couldn't hear. 'They're about international debt and re-working national borders.'

Flanking motorcycle outriders, lights flashing, roared past them from Trafalgar Square. Three limousines flying the American flag were with them, soon gone, because the traffic had been cleared in advance.

'What did they say?' asked Samira.

'They're looking at them,' he lied. 'They'll get back to us.'

*A corpse on the street*, Tim had said. She thought of her white education, learning the words of the great white bard at her expensive white school to get a white-accepted exam called an A-level. That's what Yasin would have thought of it. She thought of a Sudanese poem: *'My bones become white. My brother has gone. Who will hold my life?'*

They walked on and looked along Downing Street, at the policemen, the high gates, the black and yellow ramp in the middle of the road. She thought of Musa, back in the compound in Zamboanga, of having Rudy Osmeña and his family round for lunch. She thought of diving into the pool in her bikini and doing laps.

The traffic going into Trafalgar Square was piled up because of the Japanese Prime Minister's convoy. Yasin saw the national flag of the limousines, happy that they were keeping to schedule. His newspapers had been right.

He told the helmsman to prepare two more bags of anthrax. They went round Trafalgar Square, because they were early. Yasin watched the traffic flow, checking his wing mirror to see if there might be a trail of dust. But the road was a swirl of exhaust fumes and it would be invisible. The weapon would be pure in its destructiveness.

'The Canadian delegation is leaving the High Commission in Trafalgar Square now,' said Norton. 'Once in Downing Street, the leaders of the seven most powerful nations will be there under one roof. We are on the highest alert for the attack. Repeat. Highest alert.'

They had a good run of lights into Whitehall, but the traffic was jammed further up and they edged their way along, stopping opposite the Ministry of Defence. Yasin wanted the first release to be the highest concentration of spores, in case they were intercepted immediately. Yasin wanted to be sure that the contamination of the government areas would last for many years to come, that the whole seat of government would have to be moved.

He planned to release 10 kilograms, or four bags, infecting

100,000 to 300,000 people. He would start outside Downing Street: with the wind coming in from the south-west, the spores would blow back towards Trafalgar Square. The helmsman would have the air tanks on the highest pressure to get all the spores out in time.

'Mercedes Sprinter entered Whitehall,' came the message over the radio. But there were Sprinters being seen all over central London. The message was getting repetitive. A few seconds later – 'Non-matching registration plate.'

Then: 'Blue stripe identified. Not all-white. Stand down alert. Whitehall Alphas resume concentration on pedestrians.'

Yasin spoke into the intercom. 'Ready to release the anthrax any time now?'

The welder had the funnels filled with anthrax, sealed up and clipped in, one after the other to change like magazines in a machine gun. The welder inserted the first funnel of spores into the main duct.

The helmsman prepared the pressure gauge so it would be higher than ever. His hand was on the nozzle, waiting for Yasin's instruction. They made it down to Horse Guards Parade, before coming to a halt in traffic.

Yasin could recite the names of the roads like a poem. Horse Guards, Whitehall Gardens, then Richmond Terrace, opposite Downing Street. He had stared at the map for hours, for nights, his thoughts wavering between the best place, between symbolism and practicality. His childhood which had ended with the death of parents, his youth which had ended over an unfinished grave in Musa's shot-up compound; now his wealth which had given him power, and his joy, the only real joy he had ever known, of being with his twin sister. He hoped she was all right. Things had gone wrong last night, because he hadn't planned. She had wanted to go to the river, not him.

They were moving slowly towards Downing Street. If they had just one chance at one funnel, it would go out there. Yasin looked out the back window, then through the perspex compartment at the wing mirror to check the road behind.

He thought he saw dust, thought the helmsman had started already, without his orders. He looked towards the helmsman, but the presure gauge was at zero. He was waiting for orders. Yasin checked out the window again: it was the exhaust of a lorry going towards Trafalgar Square.

He didn't take his eyes off the road behind him. In those few seconds between the traffic jam and the attack, he let his memories continue to pass by like fellow soldiers wishing him well before action. His life lit itself up before him, with all its horrors and brief joys, and through the window, mixed with the images of his imagination, he saw a woman on the street with a map asking a policeman the way. Dawdling tourists took up the whole pavements as they stared at buildings. A cyclist's brakes squeaked. He was right up against their wing mirror, foot on the road, squeezing past the van.

Then he saw her, not sure at first if it was another memory. Not certain like with the dust which turned out to be exhaust fumes, unsure, but recognising the new haircut, with a European man, Tim Pack – he knew him as well – not holding hands, but together, very alert, heads moving around from building to building, vehicle to vehicle, remembering her curiosity just like that, restless and probing, and, at last, being sure it was her by recognising the way his sister walked, like a soldier recognises familiar movement in the jungle.

'Stop,' he screamed, forgetting about the intercom, tearing

off his respirator. 'Open the door,' he ordered the welder. The welder pushed it open before the van stopped. He was in front of Yasin. In the way. Yasin turned inside, where the driver was looking round at him with astonishment on his face. It was too late. He had slipped up. Without thinking he had called out as if he had passed Samira by chance on a city street, one part of his mind thinking he could just give her a lift like in Omdurman, the other part knowing it was all over.

'It's the Sprinter Suspect spotted. Alpha-Two?'

'Yasin Omer,' said Tim, running to catch up with Samira.

'Sniper report on Sprinter.' It was Norton's voice. 'Life Guards?'

'Negative.'

'Banqueting House Sniper One.'

'Negative.'

'Cabinet Office. Any roof sniper?'

'Negative.'

'Big Ben. Sniper Three. Clear shot, sir.'

'Alpha-Two. We have a clear shot. Confirm suspect.'

The welder jumped out, jacket done up, but bulging.

'Tim,' Walmsley dispensed with codes. 'Is it Yasin?'

'Unclear,' said Tim. He was running towards the van, Samira behind him.

'Big Ben. Sniper Three. Report.'

'Affirmative, sir. Clear shot.'

Three schoolboys, standing on the pavement, walking up to the pedestrian lights, broke away from their teacher, thinking the van had stopped to let them cross. They were small, nine or ten, but the teacher was a tall redhead, running out to rescue them from the traffic which was roaring past the van. The red hair swept right into the cross hairs of the telescopic sights. Through it, through the swirling hair and bobbing head, the welder was a stationary target, a clear shot at the base of the neck.

'Negative, sir. Civilian obstructing.'

'Any of you got a clear shot.'

No answer.

'Big Ben. Sniper Three? Clear shot on Omega?'

'Affirmative, sir.' Shot one kills the obstruction. Shot two kills the target.

'Tim?'

The welder's left hand went towards his right pocket. Tim couldn't see a weapon, but it was where he would reach for his own gun. Samira was there. Too close.

'Big Ben. Sniper Three. Clear shot now, sir.'

'Tim?'

'Target confirmed,' said Tim, his hand pulling out his weapon.

The welder crumpled onto the pavement. Just fell, like Tim said he would.

'Second targets, sir.'

'Confirm.'

Blood splattered against the windscreen as the driver and passenger died, head dropping onto the steering wheel, head slumped against his chest.

'Clear shot. Rear doors. Any sniper?'

'Cabinet Office. Sniper Two. Angle shot, sir.'

'Life Guards. Sniper One. Clear shot, sir.'

'Target anyone who comes out.'

'Could be a hostage.' A new voice. Hodge perhaps.

Tim looking down at the corpse. Not Yasin.

'Omega,' said Walmsley. 'The spores . . .'

'Life Guards. Sniper One. Alpha-Two obstructing, sir.'

'Tim, get back.' Walmsley's voice was raised.

The van door was ajar. No clear view in. Tim had his left hand on the handle, his back to Trafalgar Square. One split second of recognition and Yasin might hesitate. If he saw Samira. If he knew, he would stop. Tim pulled on the handle.

The helmsman pushed open the van door and was out on the street, respirator still on, snapping the wire to the intercom. A sniper fired and missed.

The helmsman tore off his mask, rolling on the road, and the sniper missed again. The helmsman was quick, his instincts telling him where to go, how to move, but not telling him that whatever he did he only had seconds to live.

He crawled under the van door. Walmsley wanted sniper identification. He gave the order for Omega. But New Cavendish Street wasn't Whitehall right now. It was too fast. They knew their orders. None had the helmsman in his sights. He was down, in the gutter, hidden by the van door, staring straight into the barrel of Tim's 9mm.

Staring enough for Tim to see the flickering emotions of a man before death. A man stopped by a gun in his face. He kept his eyes on the target, both fixed on each other. He shot the helmsman between the eyes, destroying the brain stem, so the muscles were dead straight away, no power to detonate a bomb.

'Target neutralised,' he said.

Then Yasin jumped out of the van, straight past Tim, knocking him aside. Samira was running towards him, her arms outstretched just like they should be, a smile on her face, horror on her face, his sister not knowing what to feel except to greet the brother she thought would be dead.

'Get away,' yelled Yasin. He ran towards Richmond Terrace. Tim on his knees, a 9mm against a moving target. He screamed, '*Yasin!*'

Yasin fired first, the bullet hitting Tim's right forearm

and tearing the weapon out of his hand. Samira shouted in Arabic: '*Hirba!*'

Yasin turned, shaking his head, knowing that he was far enough away not to harm his sister with the explosion.

'The gun,' shouted Tim to Samira. 'Pass me the gun.'

Samira picked it up. But there wasn't enough time, and as she looked at Yasin again, he was turning to her, because she had the weapon. It was his instinct. Hers too. She understood it and he had a wild, animal look in his eyes of her killer and not her twin, to destroy the threat, not caring whose it was.

'Shoot,' yelled Tim from the pavement.

Samira's finger on the trigger, both hands, running awkwardly towards Yasin, screaming but not hearing her own voice. His pistol was on her and he raised his left arm, fist half clenched like he was holding a sword above his head, then he brought it down, reaching inside his jacket as if feeling for the detonator button.

But he didn't fire and his eyes changed back, no longer cold, filled instead with determination. And love. It was the face of the twin brother she had grown up with, who had stayed with her through the tragedies of their lives, her best friend, the face of a Mahas warrior from the Sudan.

'Shoot, for Christ's sake,' yelled Tim again.

Samira fired. Hit Yasin in the face. She fired again because she couldn't stop herself. She missed, but by then Yasin was already dead, although she kept stumbling forward like a riderless horse, only pulling up because her brother's body lay in the street, like a fence too difficult to jump.

Samira screamed, dropping the gun, hands reaching out, then clawing at her own face.

'Well done, Alpha-Two.' Walmsley again. Walmsley who had ordered Omega.

Footsteps around them. The helmsman's body searched, only in a shirt, no suicide vest.

'Well done, sir,' a policeman said. A hand on Tim's elbow, helping him up. 'Are you all right, sir?'

Tim nodded. Samira hunched over the body of her twin. He touched her shoulder and she looked up, eyes glistening. '*A corpse on the street,*' she whispered.

Before anyone could stop her, she reached into Yasin's pocket, where his hand had been going and she pulled out a photograph, stood up and gave it to Tim. He had seen it before, except this one had no tear. It was a copy of the one by her bed, in Zamboanga, in Hungary, in the little spare room in Queensborough Terrace, then by his own bed. Of Samira, Yasin and their father in his shop in Omdurman souk, where Tim had bought his swords, the first time he had seen her.

'I killed him . . .'

'He would have . . .' he started to say. But it didn't mean anything at all. As they drove away, the bio-terror response vans came down Whitehall with the police, the army and the scientists from Porton Down, looking like spacemen.

'Cordon off at Trafalgar Square, King Charles Street, Great George Street, Broad Sanctuary, St Margaret Street, Bridge Street and all routes leading in off Victoria Embankment. No one leaves their offices.'

A new voice. Not Walmsley's. For him, like Tim, the job was over.

# Chapter Thirty-eight

June

'Your champagne, sir.' The stewardess put the glass on the tray beside him, glancing at Tim's bandaged arm. Tim watched a bright clear London disappear below him as the plane climbed. He sipped the champagne. The arm hurt as he moved it, but the pain from the wound was getting less every day.

Samira had vanished hours after Yasin died. Walmsley came round to Tim's house the next day to say he had arranged for her to go. 'Better for all of us, don't you think?' he said. Tim showed him the sheet of paper with Yasin's demands and Walmsley chuckled. 'Give it a decent interval, then frame it and hang it in the bog,' he said.

A week later, Tim got a call from Rahim and they met for coffee at Heathrow airport. 'Samira's in the Sudan,' said Rahim. 'Mr Walmsley gave her a passport to come to us in Paris and we helped her from there.'

He gave Tim an envelope: 'She wanted you to have this, just so you know I'm telling the truth.' A single, creased, grubby photograph was inside, with the corner torn and a smear of Yasin's blood across the picture of the sword shop in Omdurman. 'Mr Walmsley wanted her out before she said anything about Dust Shadow. You remember the plan to bomb Ratnapura?'

Tim turned the picture over, hoping to see a message on the back. But there was only the dirt of a London pavement. When he asked, all Rahim knew was that she wanted to live with the river Arabs.

After Amanda's funeral, Jack Jensen called from New York and asked for Tim's help. He didn't need to explain further: Tim agreed straight away.

Walmsley invited Tim to supper at his club to talk about an official transfer from HM Customs: Get the pension moved and all that, he said. Afterwards, Tim insisted on going back to Walmsley's flat in Redcliffe Square for a nightcap.

Jack Jensen was inside waiting for them, and Tim brought out the 9mm Browning taken from the gunman in the Tamil restaurant.

Jensen stared through the French windows at the apartments across the street. He spoke without looking at Walmsley. 'Did you tell the Russians about Nalyotov?' he asked, Trying to keep his voice under control. 'My contact in Bachu, who was murdered?'

Walmsley didn't answer. He took a step forward, but Tim ordered him back, away from the window.

'Is that why they attacked my house?' Jensen's voice cracked. Walmsley was quiet.

'Is that why my family is dead?'

Walmsley lifted his hand to unwrap his scarf. 'Answer him, Stephen,' Tim whispered.

'Look,' said Walmsley. 'We're all a bit tired, I expect . . .'

Part of Tim had hoped Walmsley would say sorry and allow him to step back and lower the gun. As soon as he spoke, though, Tim knew he was wishing the impossible and he fired a single shot into the side of the head.

They were both quiet for a while after Walmsley fell. Then Jensen whispered: 'Thank you.'

'He had to be killed,' said Tim. 'Nothing else you can

do with men like that.' He wiped the gun and arranged it with Walmsley's body on the floor. It had been drawn from the armoury on Walmsley's authority. Either a convenient suicide, a murder by the Tamils. Whatever the explanation, Tim didn't care.

They shared a taxi to Heathrow. 'You don't mind about Jennifer, do you?' said Jensen, paying the fare. 'I find I'm relying on her more and more.'

Stinging sand whipped Tim's face as he stepped off the plane. Theo, the hotel manager, had said he would try to reach her through the tea house in al-Kadarou. A runway light flickered then went dead, and from the white robed figures huddled by the terminal, he saw Samira step out. She waved, fist half-clenched, above her head. She ran across the tarmac and threw her arms around him, not caring about the wind and the howling dogs. 'I didn't know if you would come,' she shouted above the noise, both laughing and crying, her breath on his ear. 'Welcome back to the Sudan.'

## If you enjoyed this book here is a selection of other bestselling titles from Headline